Bethany Clift is a graduate of the Northern Film School, the producer of low-budget British horror film *Heretic*, and the Director of her own production company, Saber Productions. *Last One at the Party* is her debut novel.

BETHANY CLIFT

LAST ONE AT THE PARTY

HODDER

First published in Great Britain in 2021 by Hodder & Stoughton
An Hachette UK company

This paperback edition published in 2022

1

A CIP catalogue record for this title is available from the British Library

Paperback ISBN 978 1 529 33216 2
eBook ISBN 978 1 529 33214 8

Typeset in Plantin Light by Palimpsest Book Production Ltd, Falkirk,
Stirlingshire

Printed and bound in Great Britain by Clays Ltd, Elcograf S.p.A.

Hodder & Stoughton policy is to use papers that are natural, renewable and
recyclable products and made from wood grown in sustainable forests. The
logging and manufacturing processes are expected to conform to the environ-
mental regulations of the country of origin.

Hodder & Stoughton Ltd
Carmelite House
50 Victoria Embankment
London EC4Y 0DZ

www.hodder.co.uk

For my mum, who gave me my imagination and taught me how to use it, my dad who gave me the book that changed my life and for Peter without whose love, support, guidance and childcare this book wouldn't exist. I love you all very much.

February 8th 2024

'Fuck You!'

Those are the very last words that I spoke to another living person.

If I had known that they would be my last, I would have chosen them a bit more carefully.

Something erudite, with a bit more wit.

'Fuck you' is coarse and rude and far from the sparkling repartee I have always hoped I was capable of.

But unfortunately there is no changing it.

The last person I ever physically spoke to thinks I am the sort of woman who phones them, yells abuse down the line, and then screams 'Fuck You!' before hanging up.

There were extreme circumstances that led to my outburst – their absolute refusal to bury my recently dead husband for a start – but that is probably still no excuse.

So, I am sorry Tom Forrest, Funeral Director at the Co-Op. That phone call was not indicative of who I am or, rather, who I was.

Not that it matters any more of course.

Because by now Tom Forrest is dead and what he thinks of me is of no consequence whatsoever.

I can't decide whether I am writing a diary or a journal.

I'm not really sure of the difference, or if there even is one, and I can't google it any more. The internet no longer exists.

Either way, I am writing this because there are things I think should be recorded somewhere, and I am, or was, a writer and journalist, so it feels like it is my duty to do it.

Plus, I am the only person here who can.

Because I am the only person here.
In this country.
Potentially, in the world.

I need to go back to the beginning.

October 23rd 2023

They named the virus 6DM and it began, not in China or some tiny African village, but almost exactly in the middle of the USA.

In Andover, Kansas: a small suburb of Wichita, population about 12,000.

Nobody I knew had ever heard of Andover in September 2023, but by the end of October I didn't know a single person who couldn't place it on a map and tell you about its rapidly decreasing population.

There is no record of the first infection, no official patient zero, because 6DM mutated and spread too fast for anyone to track it. But it is generally agreed that the first patients were recorded on October 23rd 2023 and by Halloween (that's irony for you my American friends) all of Andover's 12,000 citizens were either dead or dying – painfully but swiftly.

The virus having originated in such a white, suburban neighbourhood you'd have thought it would be impossible for the right-wing press to try to link it back to immigrants or a foreign country, but they did. They speculated that patient zero was likely a local high school student who'd volunteered in West Africa and returned to the town carrying 6DM with her.

Of course, by the time the article emerged the high school student was far too dead to either corroborate or deny the story, but they printed it nonetheless.

It didn't matter anyway – people were too busy being terrified to have the time to blame or hate each other any more.

To their credit the American government acted swiftly and decisively to stop the crisis.

No one wanted to make any of the mistakes that happened in 2020.

This time they were ready.

Andover was quarantined within five days of the first death, and scientists immediately began work to discover what the virus was and develop the inevitable cure or vaccination against it.

But they were already fighting a losing battle.

By the time Andover was quarantined, cases had been reported in New York and San Francisco, both over 1,300 miles away.

The scientific community never got the opportunity to study 6DM properly, so to this day I have no idea where it actually originated or how it is spread.

The US government instigated Martial Law, closed their airports and banned international travel in or out of the country on November 2nd – less than two weeks after the first reported case.

There was mass panic and hysteria. People across the United States completely disregarded the president's plea for calm, and rioted for food, water, transport and whatever drugs they could lay their hands on, not knowing whether they would help or not.

This was not the regulated response they had had to Covid-19, this was chaos and madness.

By November 14th, America was a wasteland in the making. The few remaining international journalists reported horrific images of cities deserted, whole towns on fire, and mass graves with hundreds of bodies thrown in.

Newspapers reported the death of the president on November 18th and the collapse of the federal government on the 23rd, exactly one month after the first reported case of 6DM.

The last report on November 24th said that, with few to no government officials left, citizens were now on their own.

There have been no verifiable reports from America since then.

November 3rd 2023

By the time America was burning itself to the ground the UK government was taking 6DM incredibly fucking seriously.

We may not have known much about the virus, but what we did know was terrifying.

No one knew what the incubation period was, but it started as a head cold, then fever, vomiting, diarrhoea. Within 72 hours your vital organs started to disintegrate. Not degrade or even fail: DISINTEGRATE. If you were lucky your heart or brain went first, and you died of a massive heart attack or a stroke. Unlucky, and it was your lungs – so you drowned. Really unlucky, and your stomach lining rotted and you were essentially eaten by your own stomach acid.

There was nothing gentle or noble about dying from 6DM; it was a juggernaut of pain and suffering. Most people died in agony, begging to be put out of their misery.

Six Days Maximum. That was the number of days you could expect to survive after the first signs of infection and where the nickname originated: 6DM.

The death toll was staggering.

The virus moved so fast and was so deadly that it was impossible to keep accurate figures, but there were no reports of any one surviving it so the mortality rate was reported to be one hundred per cent.

Entire populations were wiped out. In America there were approximately 200 million dead, Japan lost nearly 70 million in just three weeks, Russia's last toll was around 110 million.

For hugely populated countries such as China and India the figure was estimated at around one billion each, before the news bulletins stopped.

Densely populated areas fared worse. Delhi's 25 million population was reportedly wiped out in just nineteen days.

For the sparsely populated and more remote countries (New Zealand, Australia, parts of Canada) things seemed more positive. Reports came in that the virus had yet to reach them or was being successfully contained.

Of course, as soon as people read this, they found whatever means of transport they had and headed straight for the 'safe zones'.

And they took 6DM with them.

The safe zones tried to repel outsiders, but were mostly ill-equipped to fight off large mobs. Have you ever heard of Canada's army? Neither have the Canadians. Australia was worst hit. Such a massive country, so much shoreline, so many flat areas to illegally land a plane. Australia went from doing quite well to obliterated in little over a month.

For us, the UK, things were different. We were almost specifically designed to survive this thing. Small, containable, manageable population, good infrastructure, good history in manufacturing and food production, strong armed forces, good healthcare. And, since the debacle of Brexit, fewer 'friends' to have to care about.

Plus our government had learnt extremely valuable lessons from 2020's disaster.

Theoretically we could close our borders, repel refugees – who were now almost exclusively upper class, rich, and trying to land their superyachts on our shore – and survive on our own indefinitely.

On November 3rd 2023, anyone living within a 100-mile radius of Dover was awoken at 2 a.m. by a massive explosion. Without consulting anyone outside the cabinet office, the prime minister had taken the decision to collapse the UK end of the Channel Tunnel.

The PM made a statement on the steps of Number 10 at 9 a.m. and every television channel broadcast it live.

Our borders were closed, armed police would patrol with a shoot-to-kill order for anyone trying to enter or leave the country.

If you were abroad when it happened, then tough, you should have come back sooner.

Schools and all businesses closed immediately, and a 7 p.m. to 6 a.m. curfew was imposed. We were ordered to stay home. NHS staff would be taken to work by the police. The military would staff all food shops and ensure that food distribution was fair. Police would patrol to make sure ~~no one left their houses~~ everyone was safe.

They said there was no need to panic.

There was little to no protest or complaint. No one cared about freedom and foreign nationals when there was a very real chance they might have to watch their five-year-old die in agony.

And they needn't have bothered with the military or police. No one wanted to go out. No one wanted to leave the safety of their home.

People stayed in, hugged loved ones close, and watched horrific images on the TV while thanking God for our tiny little island.

The government was quick to take control of the new, restricted world that we found ourselves in.

They had announced that they would continue to control food distribution for the time being and were working on plans to increase production and provide citizens with the opportunity to be self-sufficient. They hadn't yet expanded on what that meant. All online shopping was closed – no Amazon, eBay or supermarket deliveries. There were rumours that armed soldiers guarded some of the bigger distribution warehouses.

All commercial TV channels had ceased to broadcast (understandably) and the government was now running BBC1 and BBC2, the only channels still broadcasting. Normal programming had been abandoned, and the channels now ran government-approved factual and news programming combined with endless nature programmes and sitcom repeats – nothing like the calming tones of David Attenborough or a few episodes of *The Vicar of Dibley* to help you forget your impending doom.

The internet was still working, albeit slowly. Twitter had stalled on the day the Channel Tunnel was destroyed. We were assured this was just coincidence. Those posting negative or 'controversial' opinions and stories on Facebook or even their own websites found that their profiles and pages disappeared without warning.

People feared it was just a taster of the restrictive world to come. Of course, that turned out to be the least of our worries.

Fourteen days after we were shut off from the world there was still no registered case of 6DM in the UK, and employers were getting restless about continuing to pay for employees who were sitting at home wondering when, and how, they could start stockpiling food.

The government had announced no interim payment process and, as money still held value, employers, employees and certain cabinet members were keen for everyone to get back to work.

Tentatively, a semblance of normality returned. Shops reopened (albeit with purchasing restrictions in place – no one would get to stockpile toilet roll this time), transport was up and running again, and most people went back to work.

People quickly returned to their pandemic routines – face masks and social distancing became the norm without any government instruction or guidelines.

It soon became pretty clear that we were going to see some major lifestyle changes now that we were literally cut off from the rest of the world.

For starters, we could only eat what we grew and manufactured. So, bread, milk, meats, root vegetables and eggs were easy to find, but sugar, fruits, salads and spices immediately rocketed in price.

There was a rumbling of major civil unrest when the public learnt there was currently only one tea plantation in the whole of the UK, but the government were quick to quell the riots by reassuring us there were enough stockpiles to last until we planted and harvested more.

For the record, even without the buying restrictions in place, I don't think there would have ever been any food, water, or even toilet roll shortages.

6DM kills your appetite immediately and then kills you pretty soon after, so there was no need for prolonged sustenance of the population by the beginning of December.

I went back to work on November 19th.

I knew during my first hour back in the office that I would be looking for another job within a couple of weeks, and that my new job would be blue collar, much harder work, and much lower paid.

The economy might not have been completely dead yet, but most of the industries that currently supported it soon would have been.

I worked in a re-insurance company in the New Business Team. Our company insured other insurance companies, specifically those that insured big ships: transportation ships, ferries, or cruise liners. All of which now sat in docks either empty or full of dead people.

I walked back into my office and was greeted by a room full of people staring at their computer screens with absolutely nothing to do.

I turned my computer on and accessed my emails to find . . . nothing. No out-of-office replies to messages sent two weeks ago, no one chasing late work, not even pleas for help or support. Not one of our international clients was answering the phone. Our UK clients were bluntly honest; no one is insuring anything when money might not even exist this time next week.

One of the company directors gave a consolatory speech to the Senior Management Team: 'Just a blip, we can ride it out, concentrate on our domestic clients, pharmaceutical industry will need us when the cure is launched, back to normal in a few weeks.'

Office-speak rubbish.

After three days of clearing my inbox, tidying my desk, and 'riding it out', I went for a (now very expensive) lunch with Ginny – one of my best friends.

Ginny was the strongest and most self-confident person I knew. She had started at my work on the same pay, at the same time as me, and was now chief of staff at a bigger and more prestigious firm; a position that she had achieved and maintained while having a child, creating her own networking group for black women in banking and running a successful mentoring programme.

She bowed down to no one and was scared of nothing.

Until now.

Normally my lunches with Ginny are full of laughter, bitching about mutual colleagues, and her showing me a thousand new photos of her six-month-old daughter, Radley.

Not that day.

Ginny was breastfeeding, so I hadn't seen her have a drink for over a year. That day, she ordered the two most expensive bottles of wine on the menu and downed four large glasses during our ninety-minute lunch.

Ginny was scared.

She didn't want to discuss work or jobs. She said I'd have my current job for another week, if I was lucky. I already knew that, so wasn't surprised. She said there would be no government bailout. She doubted there would be a government a few months from now – at least not one that we recognised.

But she didn't stop there.

She started asking me questions about my survival plans. Did I have any idea how unsuitable I was for how life would become? Could I grow my own food? Make my own bread? Did I own chickens? Could I milk a cow? Did I know how to make my own clothes? Did I have any transferrable skills?

Obviously, the answer to all of these was no.

My husband, James, and I lived in a flat in central London with a 'no pet' clause, so the chickens and cows were definitely out of the question. We had no garden, just a window ledge with a dying pot plant and a herb pot on it; so, unless this counted as growing food, we were also out of luck there. As for the rest I, like millions of others, was cash rich and time poor, so sourced my food, clothes and anything else I needed from those with far less money than me.

Ginny said that money would soon be worthless. That we would live in a world of survival of the fittest – provide what you could for you and yours and then beg, steal and borrow what you couldn't.

Ginny said I should get a gun. I laughed.

Ginny didn't.

She poured the leftover wine into a plastic water bottle and told me she had been stockpiling food, water and medicines since the day after the first case of 6DM had been discovered in Andover. Her husband, Alex, had family in the middle of nowhere up in Yorkshire and they were leaving to go there in three days.

They'd bought two guns to take with them.

When I told James about lunch that night he laughed and said Ginny would never survive that far from Selfridges. James promised that we would be fine, he would take care of us, like he always did.

But later, I saw him looking at our flat with fresh eyes, in the same way I had been doing since I got home, and when I looked at his phone later he had been googling *'easy vegetable growing'*.

In the end, of course, Ginny's dire prediction didn't have time to come true. There was no time for the economy to fail completely, no government collapse, no time to start growing our own food, and no need to buy a gun.

Ginny and her family are some of the hundreds of people about whose fate I know nothing.

I like to think that she made it to her Yorkshire wilderness. But I'm pretty certain that she didn't.

November 24th 2023

Britain had its first reported case of 6DM on November 24th.

We never knew whether someone with the virus had managed to sneak into the country or if the incubation period was longer than we thought and it had been here all the time.

Scotland and Wales immediately tried to separate themselves from Britain by whatever means possible. Wales blew up all the bridges of the River Severn – no one knew where they got such weapons of destruction from – and Scotland closed and patrolled all roads across their border.

But of course, it was too late.

I was at work when the first case was reported.

It was a Thursday and by then we had all been told that Friday would be our last day. Most people had stayed in order to earn as much money as possible, but about a quarter of the office had not bothered coming back to work once they'd received the news.

There were already signs that Ginny's tale of doom would become reality: food prices were rising steadily and most petrol stations had signs to say they were empty.

I hadn't stayed for the money (which I was pretty convinced would soon be worthless anyway), but because I was trying to delay the inevitable. Trying to delay the moment at which the comfortable little life that I had built for myself would become completely obsolete.

At about 3 p.m. on November 24th, the New Business Director opened the door to her office and stood in the doorway. I think only a couple of people noticed at first, but one by one the eighty-seven people in that massive room became aware of the increasingly oppressive silence around them and reluctantly looked up.

We saw her grey pallor, her slack-jawed, hopeless expression, and we all knew immediately.

A couple of people jumped up and left straight away, the rest of us waited for the inevitable.

'You should all go home.'

No one asked for clarification.

The office split in two. Those with families were out the door within seconds. Those of us without kids or, in some cases, without anyone, milled about, unsure of what to do.

This didn't feel the same as 2020. This already felt like an end of sorts. We knew that when everything shut down this time it wouldn't be opening again.

I think it was George who first suggested it, but I can't be sure.

In any case, someone said: 'Let's get drunk.'

I can't remember much about that night to be honest.

I know we started at a pub, then a bar, and then moved on to a club for some dancing, and that is when things begin to get hazy.

I know at some point I was ready to go home, but was pretty easily persuaded to stay and go to another club.

Then it all got increasingly blurry before I face-planted on to my bed at about 4.30 a.m.

Is it weird that the pubs and bars and clubs stayed open? Is it weird that we went out and got blasted rather than going home and sealing ourselves in?

Yes.

But the city was madness that night.

It didn't just *seem* like half of London was out to get pissed, shagged, and fucked-up; half of London *was* out to get pissed, shagged, and fucked-up.

There would be no coming out of lockdown this time.

People knew this was the last stand of humanity and our last night of freedom.

And in true Blitz fashion we were going to do our British best to mark the occasion with beer, vomit, and other bodily fluids.

I woke up at 11.30 on the morning of November 25th with 6DM.

All right, I didn't have 6DM, but I am sure what I had felt pretty close to it.

It turned out to be a three-day hangover.

I could barely leave the bed for the first forty-eight hours. I was expelling the contents of my stomach violently from both ends of my digestive tract, and my brains were slowly being pushed out of my eyes and ears by the regular *BOOM, BOOM, BOOM* of my head.

Death would have been sweet mercy.

But, by day three I could open my eyes again, and on day four I was suddenly better, starving, and desperate for chicken in any form.

I am ashamed when I look back on those three days now. Not because of my hangover, but because of what it meant for James. Maybe things would have worked out differently if I had been able to leave the bed.

Maybe not.

Either way, by the time I had showered, brushed my teeth, was pink, perky and dribbling chicken juice down my chin, the world as I knew it had changed.

Late November 2023

The last two weeks of civilisation can be best summed up by the following newspaper headlines:

22 November 2023 – *We Must Stand Strong: UK continues to repel refugees. Keep UK 6DM free.*

24 November 2023 – *FIRST 6DM CASE REPORTED. STAY IN YOUR HOMES. AVOID ALL CONTACT WITH OTHERS.*

27 November 2023 – *Government close to developing 6DM cure as number of reported cases rises to over 2.6 million.*

29 November 2023 – *Parents disgusted as Government admits there is no cure for 6DM and offers T600 'death pill' instead.*

1 December 2023 – *'Give us T600' cry distraught parents. 'Our children are dying in agony.'*

2 December 2023 – *Grieving families told bodies must be burnt in mass graves as death toll reaches 22 million.*

3 December 2023 – *God Save The Queen . . . and us all.*

That was the last time a newspaper was printed.

The government made T600 available without prescription on 1 December.

T600 was quick and painless. Two pills, then a deep sleep and death.

At first it was supposed to be rolled out on a need-by-need basis, but within two days the need outgrew the process, and pharmacists had other things to worry about, so boxes were left on counters and in doorways for people to take.

One of the only good things about that last week is that no one abused or tried to take advantage of the T600 situation. No one hoarded boxes or stole the pills and sold them on. When I went to get mine there were plenty left, and people were only taking one or two blister packs as needed. It may have been that everyone was just too sick to take advantage, but I hope not. It felt as though it was a choice, and one that would have made me think under any other circumstances that there was hope for the future of humanity after all.

If we had had a future of course.

It seems around a quarter of the population got the breakout news on the 24th, grabbed whatever they could, then sealed themselves in their homes and never reappeared. We think flat number 11 on our floor of the building did this. For a few days we heard them moving about as normal, radio on, TV, sounds of cooking, laughter even. A few days later we heard a long, sorrowful wail. Then silence for a couple of days, before the regular moaning began. We were on the top floor of our building so had no flats above us or to one side but as the volume and regularity of the moaning from Flat 11 increased, we became aware of similar noises in other flats below us, so we started to leave music or the TV on all the time.

Those who didn't confine themselves to their homes became like ghosts. People no longer walked the streets, they darted or flitted from spot to spot, heads down, avoiding physical or even visual contact with anyone else.

In 2020 we had been advised that two metres was a safe distance, but this had now organically increased to three or even four. If you got closer than this, people bristled, shouted, and moved quickly away. No one was taking any chances this time. Everyone wore a face mask of some description: some people had official masks, but others made do with gas masks, dust masks; even a bandana wrapped around your nose and mouth was better than nothing. Most now wore bio-terror suits, dust suits, or something homemade fashioned from plastic coveralls – even bin bags at a push.

It was ridiculous really; without knowing how the virus was transferred it was impossible to protect against it. It might have been carried by plastics or fabric for all we knew.

While I had been in bed/throwing up, James had been providing for our future.

We didn't have a car, so he took both our suitcases down from the top of the cupboard and went shopping.

Well, I say shopping, really he went polite looting.

On the morning after 6DM arrived James got up as I was going to bed and went to our local supermarket. It was 6 a.m. and the shop was due to open at 7 a.m. There were already about fifty people there, standing in silence, three metres apart, in the relentless drizzle that the British weather system does so well.

No one came to open the shop.

At about 8 a.m., the queue, which was now at least a hundred strong, started to get restless.

A bedraggled woman wrapped in black bin bags walked to the front of the queue, causing rumblings of dissent from those waiting. She looked at the closed doors and then calmly took a brick out of her shopping bag and threw it through the automatic door, shattering the glass. She picked her way delicately through the shards and took a shopping basket.

James said the queue paused for maybe five seconds and then all walked politely inside in turn. He said there was no pushing, no violence, everyone kept their distance, and there was even some polite chitchat.

It was all terribly British.

James went to five shops that morning. Two had been broken into, two had left their doors open, and one was yet to be looted, so James smashed the window himself.

He said he'd felt exhilarated and then terrified he was going to be arrested, so he came straight home after that one.

James emptied our freezer of ice cream, ice cubes and the frozen ginger I'd never got around to using, and replaced them with milk, bread, cheese, fresh fruit and veg. He got tins of beans, bags of rice and pasta, candles, matches, and huge plastic tubs to store water in.

And yes, he got toilet roll.

He had provided us with everything we needed to survive when society completely broke down.

He had provided for us.

While I lay in bed for three days, he had left the flat time and time again with only a fabric face mask for protection.

He had taken care of me, and, just like he always did, he had made things better.

Like he had been doing from the very beginning of our relationship.

————

I met James when I was still working as a journalist.

Well, I say journalist, I worked in a very junior position for one of the national music papers reviewing gigs and interviewing the bands that no one else was particularly interested in, so there wasn't too much research or undercover work involved.

I had blagged the job at the end of the noughties, at a time when the British print music press was just about hanging in there and there was still money to be made and jobs to be had. I was young, blonde(ish), pretty(ish), posh(ish), and had written a couple of reviews for my college newspaper, which happened to be read by someone's brother who worked for a national. That was enough.

They sent me on a trial run to review The Pain Beneath at a small venue in Windsor. I didn't have enough money to pay for my taxi and a ticket so had to pretend to be a roadie to get in. Hilarity ensued. I wrote a 500-word review with only 25 words being about the band ('They were good but should try looking up from the floor and at the audience some time. I especially liked the song about the hat.'). The paper loved it. I finished university and went straight into a job writing for them full-time.

And that was how I spent the next four years of my life.

I wasn't the best writer, never managed to delve that far below the surface of on-the-road antics and origin stories (hence the reason I was still a junior staff member after four years) but bands, and the people who looked after them, liked me. I was polite and friendly (but not so friendly that I shagged everyone or tried to stay past my welcome on tour), I drank (but not so much that I was a liability), I didn't take drugs (but wasn't judgmental of those who did), and my interviews could be spiky but I was never mean. I travelled the world, slept in hotels, villas, mansions, tour buses, and on a couple of floors in the beginning. I drank the best alcohol and ate the finest food.

I used any free time to work on my first novel, loosely based on my experiences: it was the tale of a young woman who falls in love with a rock star but soon learns a life of luxury in the spotlight is not all she thought it would be. It was funny, full of interesting details gleaned from my time spent with bands, and had a strong female lead. I was convinced I would soon be able to add novelist to my CV.

Those four years were free from commitment and worry. I couldn't drive, didn't own anything that wasn't small enough to put in a suitcase, and none of my relationships lasted more than a few weeks because I was always too busy travelling to my next assignment. I didn't care; I was perfectly happy in my own little carefree, commitment-free world.

But, as the decade came to a close, things started to change. Girl power was here to stay, and a new wave of female writers was emerging. Writers with ideas and unique voices. I was now in my mid-twenties, old enough to start having my own opinions, and my spiky irreverent style wasn't enough: people wanted to know what I thought about wider issues, rather than which major band was going to implode next.

I became increasingly aware of women writing powerful pieces about gender and sexism and what it meant to be a woman in the modern world. Of course, women had always been writing these pieces, but now it felt like I should be writing them too. What were my politics? Why did I wear make-up? Did I wear skirts because I wanted to, or because that was what was expected of me?

I didn't know the answer to any of it. I didn't know how to change a plug, let alone work out if I could wear lipstick and still be a feminist. I felt an increasing urgency to define who I was and commit that to paper. But I wasn't ready for that sort of commitment. I wasn't ready for any sort of commitment.

At about the same time that I was beginning to recognise the lack of any real substance in my articles, and maybe in me, my novel was being rejected for the exact same reason by literary agents across London. They 'loved the world', declared I wrote 'with vivid detail about the machinations of life on the road' but also (literally) thought 'the central character lacks substance' and that 'she just seems to drift through the novel with no emotional journey of her own'. One particularly memorable rejection note explained: 'she learns nothing about herself in the novel'.

They were polite but final – every single one declined to represent me.

Within a couple of months my easy, carefree world started to crumble. I had no coping mechanism for what was happening to me, for the changing emotions and newly developed doubts that were crowding my mind. I'd never had to think about the purpose of my life or my writing before. I don't think I really knew how to.

What I should have done is had a serious think about what I really wanted to say, what I really wanted to write about. I should have thought about my me, thought about my journey, written about not being ready to define myself, about feeling pressure to say who I was before I even knew. I should have realised that I wasn't the only one feeling like this, that I wasn't the only one who didn't feel like she had all the answers at the age of twenty-five. But I didn't.

Instead, I began to doubt myself and all of the choices I had made. Sure, I travelled the world and experienced things people only read about (in my articles) but I'd never properly paid rent or bought a TV licence. I'd gone directly from childhood home into university halls and then back to my parents' again. I should probably have moved out, but what was the point when I was hardly ever there?

I'd always thought I was strong and independent. I'd always been happy with who I was and hadn't required the approval of others. I didn't need a gaggle of girlfriends to discuss my latest purchases or conquests with. I wasn't prolific on Facebook or Instagram or Twitter, I didn't post for likes.

But now I wondered if this was all by choice. Was I alone and independent because I wanted to be, or because I had no other options?

I started poring over other people's Facebook accounts. People I'd known at school and university were settling down, getting married, having kids. They were being bridesmaids and organising baby showers. My best, and pretty much only, friend was gay and didn't believe in marriage or children, so I wasn't likely to be called upon to offer up these services anytime soon.

I began to sleep badly, drink more, and have a constant knot of fear in my stomach.

I knew I wanted to change my life, but was too paralysed by indecision to know what to do first.

It took about three months for the knot of fear to develop into low-key panic attacks, and another couple of months for those panic attacks to wear me down to the point where I thought I was going to have to admit to someone that I was having trouble leaving my room in the morning.

And just then, into my strange dark world, came James.

James was the new advertising manager for the music journal, and he became the office golden boy within a week. Good-looking but not unattainably so, funny in a sarcastic, throwaway way that was confident but also completely self-deprecating, good at his job but not so good that he made other people look bad, friendly with the management but not so friendly he couldn't take the piss out of them.

He was ten years older than me, embodied everything that I wasn't, and had everything that I didn't: a career, a house, a car, and a washing machine that kept breaking down. He talked of long-term life plans, career trajectories, of saving for a mortgage deposit, of two-week summer holidays to places that cost half my yearly salary. He also had a long-term girlfriend whom he lived with and who was angling for a proposal, but I chose to gloss over that part of his enviable lifestyle.

His grounded and adult world made mine seem even more transitory and baseless. What was I doing with my life? If anyone had the answer it was James.

Without even acknowledging it to myself James became my reason for leaving the house each day. At least during the working week.

He was the balance to my chaos, a calming centre of normality and routine.

We discovered we got the same train into work and so started to sit together.

Those train journeys were when I fell in love.

Squashed together for forty-five minutes we talked of everything – past, present and future. We compared childhoods, school, first time having our hearts broken, our jobs, dream homes. We talked about work and how he wanted to move into something more creative. I talked about having my novel rejected – something I hadn't even told my parents.

We had absolutely nothing in common. James had started work at sixteen, wanted to work his way up the career ladder and then invest in property; I, obviously, still lived with my parents, had fallen into my one and only job by accident and spent all my spare money on going out and travelling.

But, somehow, it worked – we worked.

I memorised every physical detail of him. The length of his eyelashes and the laughter lines that wrinkled the corners of his eyes when he smiled. The way the sun would catch the lighter ginger streaks in his hair and the smattering of grey in his sideburns. How on a Wednesday he would have a layer of stubble before he shaved again on Thursday. The tan that he returned with after a two-week holiday. The smell of him in the morning, fresh from the shower, aftershave sharp and citrus. The smell of him on the way home, a slight tang of sweat, the residue of the office still on his skin. The warmth that came from him as we sat close together.

I lived for our train journeys. James got the train three stops after me and I would save the seat next to mine, frantically apologising to people who tried to take advantage of the space. Sometimes people sat there despite my protests, sometimes he wouldn't get on my carriage, sometimes he would get another train. These were dark days. But, on the days he sat next to me, he made me feel better. He made the knot in my stomach loosen and the fog lift slightly. When I was with him I didn't have to think about me because I was too busy thinking about him. When I was with him, I felt okay. I felt normal. I felt safe.

As I said, from the very beginning, James made things feel better.

James made me feel better.

———

Why did James get 6DM and I didn't?

Was it because he went out in those three days? Did I miss some weird contraction window? Maybe we both had it, but my disgusting hangover symptoms had expelled it from my body? If doctors had induced extreme vomiting in the early stages of the virus could they have purged it from everyone?

Maybe I really am the ultimate anomaly, the only person with immunity in the whole world. Maybe I am actually the cure.

Whatever.

James sneezed at 4.36 a.m. on December 3rd and I knew he was going to die.

December 3rd 2023

I hate clocks.

I hate the flickering numbers and constant shine of digital clock faces; the scary omnipresence and constant tick, tick, tick of grandfather clocks; the shrill alarm that always interrupts your best moment of sleep; the ever-present reminder that all clocks observe your life slowly ebbing away second by second.

I hate having them anywhere in the house, but the bedroom is the worst. It's like having a prison warden at your bedside – go to bed now, get up now, finish doing your make-up now, don't spend too long in the bath, fall asleep in the next nine minutes or you'll not get the recommended eight hours' rest.

James was obsessed with being on time and liked to set all the clocks in the house ten minutes fast to give him extra leeway. So, on the morning of December 3rd the clock actually read 04.46, but I automatically subtracted the extra ten and there it was: 04:36.

The sneeze.

We both jumped, went rigid, and then made a big display of relaxing and pretending to sleep.

Never have I hated a clock as much as that neon devil, and the eternity it took to click through the next three hours that needed to pass before I could get up without raising suspicion.

Even 7.30 a.m. was early for me, but by then James had been up for nearly two hours and I couldn't wait any more.

I stood outside the living-room door and arranged my features into a normal, bland, early-morning expression.

Opening that door was the most frightening thing I have ever done.

He looked up and smiled brightly.

'I think I have a cold. Must be because I went out without my big coat.'

'I told you to wear a hat you idiot. Want tea?'

I wept in the bathroom. Quietly.

Then I made the tea.

We spent the day on the sofa watching movies and studiously ignoring James's cold, which was worsening by the hour.

By 3 p.m. he was radiating heat but shivering uncontrollably. We had *Die Hard* on, because he loves *Die Hard* and it always makes him feel better, when his first stomach cramp hit. He crunched up in pain and I squeezed his hand so hard he cried out.

'Sorry!'

We had been avoiding looking at each other for the last hour, focussing our attention on the Bruce Willis mission, rather than facing the reality of death in our own living room.

'Don't break my hand as well!'

I turned to look at him.

His eyes were huge and frightened. He looked like a sick, sweaty, twelve-year-old boy. He tried to smile and burst into tears.

I held my forty-six-year-old husband as he cried. The man I had loved and lived with for eleven years. The man I had thought, at one point, I'd have kids with, grow old with, be with for ever.

And, in the end, I was with him for ever.

It was just his for ever, not mine.

The next twenty-four hours were the worst.

James became delirious. But not out of it enough to be unaware of his pain and suffering. He rolled around our bed shivering and vomiting and shitting. I mopped his brow, held his sick bucket, dragged him to and from the toilet, changed the bed sheets after he soaked them through with sweat.

I crushed up every over-the-counter painkiller I could find, dissolved them in water and trickled them into the corner of his mouth. I worried that I was exceeding the recommended doses and then realised that probably didn't matter any more.

At 4 p.m. on December 4th he finally fell asleep, and I went out to find help.

It was the first time I'd left the house since the outbreak and I was petrified.

It wasn't even that I had purposely avoided it; there had been no reason to go out. James had fetched us everything we needed, and the advice had been to stay indoors.

I spent nearly twenty minutes fashioning a face mask out of an old bandana before I realised there was no point. I had flecks of James's sweat, vomit, and shit on my face, in my hair and up my nose. If I was going to get 6DM it wouldn't be from going outside.

Films and TV shows about the end of the world always show people taking to the street en masse; rioting, looting, fleeing, rallying against the fall of mankind – much like what had happened in America.

That is not what happened here.

There had been no mass exodus from London, no nose-to-tail traffic jam blocking the streets, no gridlocked car park on the M25. Nobody tried to flee – where would they have gone? They had tried that in America. It hadn't worked.

6DM was everywhere, you couldn't escape it.

For the first half hour I wandered the streets aimlessly, unable to comprehend the wasteland that London had become.

Even though I had experienced lockdown before, this immediately felt different, unreal, like the population of London had just moved somewhere else temporarily and would soon be back. The lights were still on, Christmas decorations still twinkled in shop windows, adverts for upcoming movies smiled glossily on billboards, tables and chairs sat expectantly outside cafés and bars. Everything was waiting for the people to return like they had last time.

There were few people, fewer cars, no buses or lorries – public transport and deliveries had stopped as soon as 6DM arrived.

The only people on the streets were the people like me, scurrying along, face masks on, heads down, intent on getting somewhere and back as soon as possible.

It was quiet but not yet silent. There was some residual noise from buildings where generators were still working, underground vents, street lighting, soft music being piped from the open doorways of shops left abandoned.

There had been images on the TV in previous days showing huge army trucks moving bodies to mass burial sites. The trucks were always accompanied by stricken relatives, sick themselves, but alive enough to mourn the passing of those they loved and the injustice of the impersonal transport taking them to their final resting places. There were no trucks now and, when I thought about it, I realised the news hadn't reported anything about the burials in the last twenty-four hours.

The shops were empty of people but most still had some goods in them. Some had windows shattered or doors smashed in but others simply had their doors open; an invitation to take whatever you wanted. Goods and money were worthless now.

I stopped outside the local church on the high street. In the entrance was a big wicker basket filled with small, cheap hand-made wooden crosses. The sign next to the basket read 'Remember your loved ones'.

I walked around to the back of the church. The lawn and graveyard was covered with the crosses. Some ornately decorated and lovingly inscribed, some with names scrawled on them in biro. Some had one name, others had three or four. One had sixteen names with ages ranging from seven months to eighty-two years old – an entire family of four generations. There were hundreds, maybe a thousand crosses. Each one placed there by someone who had watched their loved ones die and was now dying themselves.

I was horrified and transfixed by the makeshift graveyard until I heard a cough at my elbow. An old man, doubled in pain and clutching a cross in his hand, stared at me with sharp, watery eyes, his nose streaming with snot.

I made the mistake of reacting as I would have at any other point before 6DM.

I smiled.

'You're not sick?'

I backed away shrugging, unsure what answer he wanted from me.

'You're not sick?' he repeated, louder.

I turned and started to walk away from him.

'YOU'RE NOT SICK!'

He screamed his accusation this time, and I began to run, frightened of what he would do next or what others might do if they heard him.

I buried my face down into my scarf and kept to the shadows of the buildings.

I went to the chemist first and was hugely relieved that the door was open so I didn't have to attempt to break in. You could still get your fill of expensive perfumes and face creams, but the shelves were empty of cold, flu, and stomach medicine. All the children's meds were gone. No one had bothered taking the antibiotics – you can't fight a nuclear war with a water pistol.

The only painkillers left were morphine tablets that I found behind the counter in a cupboard that had already been broken open, so I took them all.

They still had boxes of T600 at the front of the shop. I didn't take any.

Our doctors' surgery was closed and a handwritten sign on the door said that they couldn't help anyone, and that T600 was available at the local pharmacy.

Pretty final.

I thought at first that the hospital was open.

The car park was rammed, and a queue of ambulances was lined up outside A&E. A paramedic was smoking on the back step of one of the ambulances. He looked up as I walked past but didn't say anything. Still, his very presence cheered me and gave me some hope.

The automatic doors to A&E were still working, but as soon

as they slid open I knew that small amount of hope was worthless.

I'd never smelt death, but I am willing to bet my entire fortune (which is pretty considerable, seeing as I may now be the ruler of the whole world) on it smelling like the blast of warm air that greeted me when the doors parted.

It smelt of vomit and faeces and disinfectant and hand sanitiser and – something that I had never smelt up until that point, but am becoming quite used to now – slowly putrefying flesh.

A brief glance told me that everyone in the room was dead or dying, there were no medical staff, and that, if I did want to try to catch 6DM, this was the place to do it.

As I turned to leave there was a low moan from somewhere in the room that haunts my nightmares to this day. It was something that had once been human, trying to communicate its pain and suffering. For a moment I almost believed that I had stepped into a world where the dead would soon come back to life and try to eat me. But then the moan turned into a cough and then into a retch and then into the more acceptable sound of someone dying. I clapped my hands over my ears and jumped back through the doors into the car park.

Outside, the paramedic was vomiting.

I know I should have rushed home to James, but I had never needed a drink so badly in my life, and, if I am honest, I didn't know if I could face going home to watch James die if I were sober, so instead, I went to a bar.

I went to my favourite bar.

I didn't expect it to be open, but it was, and a sign on the bar said, 'Help yourself'. If it hadn't been my favourite bar already, then that would have made it so.

The fact that it looked like nothing had been drunk or taken was as much an indication of the death of the nation as the state of A&E.

I had a whisky. I hate whisky, but I needed something that would get me drunk straight away. So, I had a whisky and then a bottle of beer. In fact, I had two whiskies and then a bottle of beer.

I sat at the back, away from the windows, so that no one would see me if they walked past. No one did walk past though.

I had another couple of whiskies and another beer, and then I made a phone call, and then, a while later, someone else came into the bar.

It was obvious that he was dying too.

Later , on my way home, I stopped at the pharmacy and picked up two packs of T600.

The next morning James said he felt better. He wasn't as hot, didn't feel sick any more, and was able to move to the sofa. He said he had a banging headache but otherwise felt okay. He drank a cup of tea and ate a banana.

He staggered to the shower and when he came out, I was changing the sheets on the bed. I was bent over and he came up behind me and rubbed his erection against my arse. I wasn't wearing knickers underneath my nightie, so he yanked it up and was in me in seconds. I normally enjoy being surprised like this, but this was the first time we had had sex in over six months, and the complete lack of foreplay and fact he might be infecting me with 6DM-ridden sperm pissed me off.

Until I realised he wasn't making love to me, he was fucking me to prove that he could, as though his life depended on it.

Which maybe it did.

So, I faked an orgasm and reached back to stroke his balls and help him come. It was all over in about ninety seconds. Still, he looked pretty pleased with himself.

I was showering when James called from the front room. I rushed in, naked and dripping, fearful of what I would find.

He was on the sofa, pointing at the TV screen.

Television by this point had been reduced to emergency broadcasts on all channels with a five-minute pre-recorded newscast repeated at the beginning of each hour on the BBC.

This was different.

Moira Stuart sat in the news seat, sweating and shaking. She had retired a few years ago, but had come back in as other presenters had fallen sick.

This wasn't a recording, she was live.

She was painfully blunt.

The Queen and all members of the royal family were now presumed dead or dying. The PM had died two days ago. There had been no overseas contact for four days. It could now be presumed that the entire world had succumbed to 6DM and that life as we knew it would cease to exist. There were no longer emergency services provision, or any sort of burial services, so people should take care of their dead in the best way they could. Government advice was still to burn the bodies. T600 was still freely available, but please remember to administer to children before yourself. She paused.

'No one is immune to this virus. So, if you are sick and have children who aren't . . . they will become sick at some point. There will be no one to take care of them once you are gone.'

Her meaning was painfully clear.

Her voice broke and she stared blankly at the monitor.

'This will be the last news broadcast from the BBC, but we are going to leave the cameras running for as long as possible. All doors to Broadcasting House will be open and signage will point to the studio. If you are alive you can come to the studio and broadcast to reach others. Good luck.'

She struggled to her feet and then, just as she was walking out from behind the desk she paused and looked back into the camera. She was crying.

'It turns out we really do end, not with a bang but with a whimper.'

James and I sat and watched the screen in silence for the next couple of hours.

No one else came.

Later, James's headache got worse, so I gave him the morphine. He was pretty spaced out, and we were attempting to watch *Die Hard* again (fucking *Die Hard*) when he started to spasm violently.

He jerked right off the sofa and then went fully rigid for a few seconds before foaming at the mouth and passing out.

I sat open-mouthed throughout the entire fit, which lasted less than a minute, but seemed to go on for ever.

When he finally lay still, I had no idea what to do. There was no one to call, no procedure to follow. I checked to see if he was breathing and his heart was beating and then I cradled his head in my lap and prayed to a God that I don't believe in to let him wake up.

And, as I held him and stroked his hair and whispered platitudes of hope that I knew were lies, I realised that I had never done that before; I had never cared for James when he was ill. I don't think James had ever *been* ill. James was one of the most vital and alive people I had ever met. He was strong and vigorous and dynamic and all the things that I once was, but now seemed to have forgotten how to be.

James had rescued me at a time when my life was falling apart, and had literally saved my life on the night when we first kissed.

And now he was going to die, and I was completely unable to save him.

———

Eleven years ago, at the same time as I was falling out of love with myself and in love with James, things at work were really falling apart.

I had completely lost my ability to write.

I was so worried about not having anything important or insightful to say that I couldn't think of anything to write full stop. I had the worst kind of writer's block, the kind where there is no block because there is nothing to block, your mind is just blank. I tried to give myself a talking to and get it together – it wasn't like I was writing for the *New Yorker* or *Huffington Post*, just write the bloody article. But it was no good, my mind was empty. I missed three deadlines and was called in to see my editor. Maybe I just needed a break? A polite way of saying 'take some time off or be fired'.

I tried to talk to James about it on the train the next morning, but he was distracted and distant.

Later that day he told me he wouldn't be getting the train any more; his mate was going to give him a lift.

The one constant star in my imploding universe was now rejecting me as well.

I felt like I couldn't breathe.

So, I did what any mature and level-headed person would have done in my situation. I panicked and ran away.

I persuaded my best friend Xav that we needed a break, and booked us flights to Thailand. For three months. I was leaving my job in two weeks.

I told James that same day. I don't know what I was expecting. Him to beg me to stay? He hardly even seemed to register what I had said.

The next fortnight was miserable. My editor had given me one last chance to write a gig review and it had ended in complete disaster, so he moved me onto reviewing albums for unknown bands on the paper's website. I didn't blame him. I was a mess, thrown into panic and uncertainty, desperate to leave and desperate to stay, unable to concentrate on anything and being forced to listen to some of the worst music I'd heard in years.

I hardly saw James. He came in late, rushed out early, and was short and snappy with everyone in the office.

I fell into a deep hole of despair, unable even to muster a smile, until most people couldn't wait to see the back of me.

Then, the day before I was due to leave, James stopped me in the corridor.

'Sorry I've been a bit of an arse the last couple of weeks.'

I shrugged. I barely heard him through the fog that surrounded me.

'Things have been a bit tough, I've had to find somewhere else to live. I've left Emily.'

My head shot up to look at him and then I jerked it back down to the floor again, petrified he'd have seen the desperation in my eyes.

I tried to think of something to say, but it seemed like my writer's block was affecting all areas of my life, and I opened my mouth but no words came out.

Then Rebecca stuck her head out of the office.

'James, Rob wants you.'

I could have wept.

'See you at your party tomorrow.'

My party. My leaving party. I was leaving.

Shit. I was leaving.

I ought to have got an acting award for the show that I put on during my leaving do. I was bubbly and happy and laughing and witty and absolutely dying inside.

I just wanted it to be over.

My senses were so heightened I could feel James wherever he was, like my entire body had turned into a James homing beacon, ready to zone in on him at any point. Standing at the bar in a group of people, he brushed the small of my back, and my entire body spasmed in response. The imprint of his hand burnt into my skin.

The evening dragged on and on until it was just James, me, and a drunken chap from accounts who just refused to leave.

James met me as I came out of the toilet. He was holding my coat.

'Let's go.'

'What about Dom?'

'Fuck him.'

Outside in the cold night air I was suddenly sober and shy.

'Do you have to rush home?'

I shook my head.

'Let's walk then.'

So, we walked. I thrust my hands into my coat pockets, not trusting them not to creep towards him if I let them hang at my sides.

We wandered through the back streets of London for over an hour and he made no move to kiss me. My jubilation turned to despair. I would leave for Thailand the next day and never have the opportunity to kiss this man, who I was deeply and ruinously in love with and whom I truly believed could be my future, and save me, and—

'WATCH OUT!'

I'd been so wrapped up in my own thoughts I hadn't noticed the huge rubbish lorry bowling down the narrow street towards us.

James grabbed me and shoved me against the wall, pressing against me with his body. The truck careened down the street, missing him by centimetres.

My heart was hammering with shock and my mind was filled with images of a stinking death, so it took me a moment to register James's body against mine. I could feel his body heat through our clothes, his breath warm on my cheek. He put a finger under my chin and lifted my face so that it was level with his.

Then he kissed me.

Is there anything better in life than a really good kisser? That moment when you first kiss someone whom you've wanted to kiss for ages and you discover that your mouths were made for each other. That their lips fit yours exactly, that their tongue is just the right length, and that they know how to use it. Not plunging it down your throat, but teasing and darting in and licking the inside of your mouth in a way that is just so erotic that your knees go slightly weak and your breath gets short and you gasp with pleasure. And every time you gasp you breathe in some of them, some of their breath, like you are consuming their very essence. And how they use their hands to complement the kiss, cupping your face, then in your hair, now in that sweet spot in the small of your back where all the nerve endings meet, and then roaming over your bottom until you feel like you're on fire and your whole world becomes that kiss and you are so completely wrapped up in it that nothing else registers.

It was a perfect first kiss. The most perfect first kiss of my life.

––––––––

James came round after about twenty minutes, disorientated and crying again. He was scared and clung to me when I tried to get him a blanket. In the end, I managed to drag him into the bedroom and onto the bed. He was moaning in pain because of his head. I didn't want him to have any more morphine in case that was what had caused his seizure, but in the end I couldn't stand to see him suffering, so I gave it to him and he fell straight to sleep.

I lay next to him and wept quietly.

I wept for James because he was in pain and he was dying. And I wept for me because I was scared and selfish and didn't want to be left alone in that frightening new world.

When James woke up he couldn't seem to move properly, so I propped him up on a couple of pillows. In a very small voice that I hadn't heard him use before he told me he couldn't feel his legs. I pulled back the duvet and he tried to wiggle his toes. Nothing. He tried to lift a leg. Nothing. I jabbed his shin with a sharp knife that I fetched from the kitchen drawer. Nothing. As we were concentrating on his legs, he whispered, 'Oh God, oh no.'

I looked up. A wet patch was forming and growing at his crotch.

He looked at me.

I smiled brightly.

'Don't worry. If we'd had kids I'd be used to this by now!'

It was a bad joke on many levels, but he attempted a smile anyway, and I loved him for it.

I dragged him out of his wet pyjamas, but couldn't find any clean ones so I dressed him in a T-shirt and pants. I changed the sheets and put a plastic tablecloth that we used for parties underneath him in case it happened again.

Afterwards I gave him more morphine and held him as he fell back to sleep.

'I'm sorry . . . about everything . . . I love you,' he mumbled before closing his eyes.

I knew then what I had to do.

I felt James stirring next to me at exactly 10.14 a.m. (damn you neon clock) on December 7th.

Before he fully woke I got quietly out of bed and went to the bathroom. I scraped my hair back and then washed my face in hand soap so that it was blotchy and pale. I spent the next ten minutes groaning and fake retching while dumping cups of water violently into the toilet and flushing it repeatedly. There was nothing I could do about not having a temperature, so I just had to hope he didn't notice.

When I came out of the bathroom James was fully awake.

'You as well?'

I nodded, eyes downcast, hugging my tummy.

The relief that washed across his face was so obvious it was almost funny. He flipped back the covers and I climbed in beside him. It was his turn to comfort me as I counted down the minutes to my next unnecessary bathroom visit.

With each fake vomit his concern grew, but so did his not-so-secret relief that he wasn't the only one dying. I didn't blame him; no one wants to die, and they definitely don't want to die alone.

I also felt some reprieve in the knowledge that he was just as selfish as I was.

By late afternoon I was staggering to the toilet every five minutes for increasing lengths of time (I had stashed a couple of magazines in there earlier). James was positively giddy that he wasn't alone in his misery, but then his headache returned with a vengeance and I groaned my way to the kitchen to grab him a fistful of morphine.

As soon as he was asleep, I rushed to the kitchen and drank two pints of water straight down. I was desperate for some toast, but didn't want James to smell the cooking; plus, I couldn't be certain how long he would sleep for. So, I had to settle for chunks of bread and cheese and ate them standing up at the counter. It still tasted bloody good.

At 2.46 a.m. on December 9th I heard James mumbling next to me, but it was a good five minutes before I realised the mumbling was incessant and increasing in urgency.

I reached over and turned on the light.

He'd had a stroke.

His face was collapsed on one side and he was dribbling and spluttering out of his sagging mouth. For a moment, I hardly noticed this because I was looking into his eyes; eyes like rabbits have in those anti-vivisection films. The ones where someone has the rabbit by the throat and you know that the rabbit knows what's coming because its eyes become huge and frantic and dart back and forth wildly even though its head is clamped still.

That is the look that James had.

I didn't know what to do, but I had to calm him. I cupped his face in my hands, put my forehead to his and, for want of a better description, I crooned to him. I whispered all the things that your mum says to you when you are scared and hurting. I shushed him, I petted him, I stroked him, I poured love into him in any way that I could. I enveloped him in all the love that I had once had for him, and every part of me willed him to feel it.

It worked. His breathing slowed and I sat on the edge of the bed and held his hand until he could hold my gaze steadily. I got a towel, wiped away the drool, and propped his head straight on the pillow.

Then I went to my side of the bed, got the neon clock, opened the window, and threw it out.

I can't be sure, but I think James smiled.

I went to the kitchen and got the two packs of T600.

I sat on the edge of the bed again and showed them to James.

'*Yeyth.*'

It was the last word he spoke.

I changed the bed sheets for the final time. I stripped James and carefully washed him down before dressing him in the Christmas pyjamas that we had already bought to wear on a Christmas morning that we would now never see.

I put on my own Christmas pyjamas, brushed my hair, and put on lipstick.

I dissolved the T600 into two glasses of water and put one glass on my bedside cabinet.

Neither James nor I ever mentioned my weird recovery from my fake illness. Maybe he didn't notice. Maybe he didn't care.

I sat beside James with his glass of T600.

I didn't want to cry, but I did. Endless silent tears that I didn't wipe away.

James's tears fell sideways off his slanting face.

I held the glass up. He tried to talk, but couldn't form words. His eyes were strong and clear though. I slowly spooned the liquid into his mouth, making sure he swallowed it all.

Then I kissed him on his sagging mouth that was so different to the one I had first kissed eleven years ago.

I wanted to tell him so many things before he died; how much I had once loved him, how much he had once meant to me, how sorry I was that things hadn't worked out how we had both hoped they would, how I should have given him more and taken less, how I should have trusted him and been trustworthy myself, how none of the bad things that had happened to us were his fault, how much I wanted his forgiveness for any way that I had hurt him. How none of what had previously happened mattered any more.

But I knew that I would only be saying these things to make myself feel better and that easing my guilty heart on his deathbed was not the right thing to do. I may not have been the best girlfriend or wife when he was alive, but now that he was dying I could make up for that with one final act of silence.

So, instead of pouring my guilt out onto him, I wrapped my arms tightly around him and sang love songs. Songs written by dead people that would never be played again. I sang until I couldn't think of any more to sing, then I just sat with him in my arms and rocked him.

By the time I finished singing James was sleeping deeply, his breath slow and short. Without realising it I began to match my breathing to his.

In puff . . . out puff . . . in puff . . . out puff . . . in puff . . . out puff . . .

December 10th 2023

I lay with James for a very long time after he died. I don't know exactly how long as I'd thrown the clock out, but long enough for the sun to come up and go down again.

To begin with I wept slowly and steadily and thought I would never stop crying, but, after a long, long time, the sobs turned to sniffles and tears slowed to a stop, and then I simply lay there, unmoving, unthinking for the next few hours.

I think I was too sad to be scared at this point. Being scared came later when the sadness eventually lessened.

I stared at the glass of T600 on my bedside table.

I didn't drink it.

I kidded myself that it was because I still had too many questions about what was happening, that I still believed there were others alive, that I still had people I needed to check on.

I didn't admit to myself that the real reason was because I was too scared to drink it.

Even once I knew that I wasn't going to take the T600 I still didn't get out of bed. How could I leave James alone? His body was still warm beside me. When I got out of bed his body would go cold and that would mean he was really dead. When I got out of bed I would be leaving him for the final time. I began to cry again.

In the end, simple physiology took over and demanded that I leave the bed before I wet myself.

When I came back from the bathroom and saw his prone body lying there, I finally understood that James was gone, it was just the shell that had contained him that was left.

I spent the rest of that long second night wrapped in our spare duvet on the sofa. I was still too numb to be scared or panicked. I stared at the wall, silent, unthinking, and motionless for hours.

I didn't throw the T600 away and twice I picked it up to drink it, but I finally got bored of my dramatics and told myself either to take it or chuck it.

As the sun started to rise I got up off the sofa, threw the T600 down the sink, and made myself a cup of tea.

At some point during that morning I made my fateful phone call to Tom Forrest, the undertaker.

To this day I don't know why I rang, and I don't know why he picked up.

I could tell he was sick as soon as he answered the phone.

In summary, I asked him to bury James, he acted like I was insane. Had I not seen the news? I tried to appeal to his basic human kindness, he said he was dying and had none left. I got angry, he got angry. I told him to fuck off and slammed the phone down.

I told a dying man to fuck off.

I really hope I'm not the last human alive.

I now had a problem. A six-foot one-inch, thirteen and a half stone problem.

I needed to bury James.

We lived in a fourth-floor flat with no lift. There was no garden to bury him in. It was winter, and had been dry and cold for days; the ground was like iron. I didn't even own a shovel.

I sat and thought and became aware for the first time of the deadly quiet that surrounded me. I couldn't remember when the moaning and sounds of pain had stopped reverberating about the building, but they had. I couldn't remember a time when the building had been quiet; even during the last period of isolation there was the background noise of a TV or radio in the distance, someone entering or leaving, a cough, a sneeze, muffled conversation. Now there was nothing. Just the quiet hum of the fridge and the gentle shush of the central heating.

I put on my coat, ran downstairs, and stood outside the front door.

Silence.

No people, no moving cars, no rumble of the underground, no planes passing overhead, no distant sirens.

Nothing.

I was on my own.

I felt the first tiny prickles of fear collect in the small of my back.

I crossed our road to the park in the middle of the square we lived on.

It was, predictably, empty.

There was a small patch of grass in the middle and I bent down and stuck a random plastic fork from my coat pocket into the frosted ground to test it. The fork broke. The ground stayed the same.

There was no way I could dig a grave.

I thought about lighting a fire on the ground to warm and soften the earth, but I didn't know if it would work or how far down the warmth would reach. Plus, I didn't know how to light a fire.

I thought about pouring water on the ground to soften it but, again, was that practical for grave digging?

I was beset with fear and hesitation.

I stood up and looked at the houses surrounding the square, hoping and praying for a light on, someone staring out, some sign of life – anything to show I wasn't alone. All the windows were dark and silent.

Ginny was right. I was completely unsuited to the new world, and this was only my first day in it.

I was cold so I went in to get a jumper.

I opened the door to our bedroom, forgetting for a moment that James was in there, and the smell was so horrific I gagged and retched. The heating was on full blast in the flat, the window was closed, and James had been dead in there for nearly forty-eight hours.

My first of many mistakes.

My instinct was to flee. *Under no circumstances should you enter that room* was what my brain was telling me. But I knew I couldn't just leave him.

James couldn't stay in the house, but I had nowhere to bury him and nowhere to take him. Damn you Tom Forrest.

I decided to take James outside and then find a way to bury him. I would dig with my hands if I had to.

I put Vicks VapoRub under my nose (it's what they do in *CSI*) and went into our bedroom.

Visually he wasn't as bad as I had expected. James had a distinct purple tinge to him and was ever so slightly puffy. But there was no sign of actual decay yet, and there didn't seem to be any bodily fluids leaking out of him. So that was good.

My definition of 'good' was rapidly shifting.

I left James in his Christmas pyjamas, but was worried about him being cold so manhandled him into his dressing gown and put a scarf and hat on him. Then I took the hat off and re-styled his hair because he always hated his hair being messed up.

I put my hands under his armpits and dragged him off the bed.

He was really, really heavy and surprisingly gassy. As his legs hit the floor, he let out a massive fart. My first instinct was to laugh, but then I remembered the six flights of stairs I still had to get him down, and my laugh disappeared.

I dragged him across the bedroom, down the hallway, and to our front door.

By this time, I was accustomed to the farts that accompanied each jolt of his body, but not to the lolling of his head and the way his arms flailed around each time I moved him.

It had taken forty-five minutes to drag him about twenty feet. I was hot, sweaty and knackered.

I sat for five minutes and then stood up and hauled him to the top of the stairs.

I dragged him to the edge, turned backwards to the stairs and hoisted him up under his armpits again. I went to take a step back, missed my footing, and the dead body of James and the living body of me tumbled down the stairs in a heap of arms, legs and slowly atrophying flesh.

The breath was knocked out of me and I lay under James, too stunned to move.

Then I remembered he was dead, screamed, and pushed his body off me. It took a moment of jumping up and down, dramatically brushing imaginary death particles off my body, to realise I was fine and hadn't hurt myself in the fall.

James hadn't fared so well. One of his arms was at a funny angle and his shin had broken and now poked through his purple skin and pyjamas. The blood that stained the material was dark brown.

I clearly couldn't carry him down the stairs, he was too heavy.

Before I had time to think about how wrong what I was about to do was, I pushed his body to the edge of the next set of stairs and shoved him down them. He fell sluggishly and haphazardly, landing in a sprawled heap across the bottom three steps.

I hurried down the steps and dragged him onto the hallway. His other arm was now broken, and one side of his face had sort of caved in.

I sat on the floor and cried again.

I couldn't do it.

There were four more flights of stairs, plus the steps outside down to street level, plus the thirty feet to the gardens, plus digging the grave, plus putting his body in and putting the earth back on him.

I couldn't do it.

This wasn't the sort of thing I did.

Moving anything heavy was the sort of thing James took care of.

I'd like to say I didn't even think of just leaving him there on the landing.

But I did.

I spent a good ten minutes planning how I could make him

comfortable using a duvet and pillows and how there must have been thousands of people in this situation who did the same thing.

But I didn't do it. I was too ashamed.

I am still ashamed that I didn't bury him. But at least I didn't leave him in the hallway.

I went back upstairs to get the spare key for Flat 9 on the third floor.

Greg and Michael lived in Flat 9. I liked them. We had bonded over a shared love of 90s American teen dramas and used to meet once a fortnight to binge on the escapades of teens far better looking and emotionally mature than us.

James thought Greg and Michael were 'too gay'; an expression that I should have, but never did, challenge.

I'd introduced them to my best friend, Xavier, once, as he too was a lover of men. Afterwards he said to me 'Remind me to introduce you to my friend Lorraine.'

'Why?' I asked.

'Because she's a woman,' he had deadpanned.

I actually knocked before I went into their flat. Yes, even in times of great stress and sadness one should never forget one's innate British manners. Of course, there was no answer.

I steeled myself for the sight and smell of them, and reapplied the Vicks.

I thought they'd be in the bedroom, but they were sitting on the sofa together, empty glasses by their sides. Their eyes were closed, but they had turned to face each other in the last moments before they had fallen asleep.

It was such a simple gesture of love in their dying moment that my heart ached for them. I felt bad to interrupt something so pure.

But my selfishness won out once more and I went to get James.

Through luck or judgement Greg and Michael's heating had gone off and their rate of decay was markedly different. They were purple-tinged and slightly puffy, but had almost no smell.

James, on the other hand, was now deteriorating rapidly, so I dragged him straight through to the bedroom and manhandled him up onto the bed.

And there he was. My dead husband. For ever condemned to spend eternity in the bed of two people he thought of as 'too gay'. There was a weird poetic justice in it that made me feel good and bad at the same time.

I lessened my bad feeling by making James as comfy as possible. I wrestled his dressing gown off, re-aligned his broken limbs, took his hat off and redid his hair again. I plumped the pillow, snuggled him into the duvet and put the bedside light on for him.

Then there was nothing else to do, so I wept.

I wept for him, for the horrible way he had died, and for the life he would now never live. But mainly, I wept for me. I wept because I could still remember so vividly the time when he was the love of my life and I would have taken T600 in a heartbeat to be with him in death. I wept because, now that he was gone, I already missed him – despite everything, he had always taken care of me and I didn't think I would be able to take care of myself. I wasn't sure I knew how. I wept because, for the first time in my life, I was now alone. Really and truly alone.

Before I left the room, I put the clock forward ten minutes.

After I left Flat 9, I climbed the stairs back to my own flat. I could already feel the familiar rising tension and tickling fingers of fear pianoing up my backbone, and by the time I reached the top of the stairs I was in full-on panic mode.

It was 2 a.m. and I was knackered, sweating, and filthy. But there would be no sleep for me that night. My heart was racing, my breathing was raspy, and adrenaline was pumping through my body as though it was trying to push its way out through my veins.

This level of panic was, unfortunately, an emotional state I was well acquainted with.

I had my first full-blown, heart-racing, vomit- and diarrhoea-inducing, unable to breathe or think panic attack when I was on my last ever assignment for the paper, just after I had booked the trip to Thailand and during the time that James was ignoring me.

It made the smaller panic attacks I had experienced previously feel like a gentle walk in a cool, dark forest.

There is nothing embarrassing about panic attacks or depression or discussing your mental health.

I know that now.

But my first panic attack was in 2012 and very few people were talking about mental health as openly and acceptingly as they now do. In 2012 I was still convinced that if anyone found out how mental I was I would be locked up. I was also, stupidly, incredibly embarrassed by my crumbling mental health. I was embarrassed that I was suddenly unable to commit to writing an article without feeling sick, or get into the lift at work without hyperventilating. I was embarrassed that I was only dragging myself out of bed in the morning to see James, and that most nights I went straight back to bed after getting in from work and just lay there. I was twenty-five, with an interesting and exciting job that I (previously) loved, loving parents, somewhere comfortable to live, food to eat and money to spend. I didn't feel I had the 'right' to be this unhappy or that I had anything 'worthy' of panicking about.

There wasn't some massive trigger that caused that first full-blown panic attack. I mean, something happened that caused it, but I can't say that one thing was the reason. It was the steady build-up of things not feeling right. Of me not feeling right.

I suppose my brain had just had enough.

I had been in Paris attending the last gig I would ever review. I was acting on autopilot; smiling, drinking, chatting to the band but, in reality, I was watching a happy fake me take part in my life while real me hid sadly at the back of my brain.

I was desperate to feel something, anything.

So, I broke my own cardinal rule and slept with the lead singer. It was rubbish.

After a perfunctory tweak of my nipples, he reluctantly pulled on a condom (I at least had the self-preservation to insist on that) and we were away. After a couple of minutes he started to rummage around between my labia promising, 'this will feel better'. I assumed he was looking for my clit. He didn't find it.

Afterwards we made five minutes of awkward small talk. Then he fell asleep and I stared at the ceiling until I crept out of the hotel room to get my flight home.

I was on the plane back to Heathrow, knackered, hungover and ashamed, when I felt a weird tugging 'down below'. I went to the toilet and thought my vagina was falling out. Reaching beneath, I almost passed out as I pulled something from within me.

The used condom from the night before.

He had pulled it off while we were having sex.

And then left it in me.

Stealthing wasn't yet a thing at this time, or at least I'd never heard of it. Maybe this was the man that invented it, or maybe it was a complete accident that he left it in me, who knows.

I think I was in shock at first.

I put it in the bin, cleaned myself up, washed my hands thoroughly and headed back to my seat.

Walking back from the toilet, I had a sudden urge to open the emergency exit. Not a fleeting thought. A full-on vision of leaning past the woman sitting next to it, pulling back the handle, and shoving the hatch out into the open air, sucking us all out with it. I actually stopped and leant forward before snapping back and no doubt matching the woman's look of horror with one of my own.

I rushed back to my seat, strapped myself in, and sat on my hands. Then I started to struggle to breathe. My heart was thumping out of my chest. I couldn't get enough oxygen into my lungs. My vision started to go black at the edges. I was going to pass out. No, actually, I was going to vomit. Which I did. All over me, and the seat in front. I hardly noticed. I was busy having a heart attack, trying to breathe, sit on my hands and not scream all at the same time.

I had no idea what was happening. I thought I must be going insane.

The stewardess rushed over, moved the people next to me to different seats, and started to mop me up.

I wanted to tell her. I wanted to tell her I was crazy. I mumbled something, stumbled past her, ran past the exit door and clattered into the toilet just before I shat myself. I sat on the toilet, leaking sperm and faeces, with my hands clapped over my mouth to stop myself from screaming.

I stayed like that until the announcement came to take seats for landing.

When I stood up I didn't recognise the wild-eyed, gasping woman with vomit in her hair who stared back at me from the mirror.

Which was appropriate because I had no idea who I had suddenly become.

I made it back to my sour-smelling seat, strapped in, and looked for something, anything, that might help me cope.

I focussed on the corner of the window next to me and whispered, 'Corner of power', and gently touched the corner with my fingertip. I counted to ten and then did it again. And again. And again. Until they opened the door to let us off the plane.

Christ knows where the corner of power came from, but it has saved me from tipping over the edge more times than I like to think about.

I was convinced I was going to be arrested as I left the plane; that they must think I was a drug mule. But – despite sweating profusely, shaking, hopping from foot to foot at passport control and practically sprinting past customs – no one came for me.

One of the unfair privileges of being white.

I needed to get the morning-after pill.

I sat in the A&E waiting room for about four hours. Well,

actually, I paced in the A&E waiting room for four hours because I couldn't keep still. I went to the toilet to throw up and expel copious amounts of watery diarrhoea again and again until there was nothing left in my body to get rid of.

Obviously, I didn't need to go to A&E, I could have just got the pill from a chemist, but I think I was hoping that by going to A&E someone would recognise my madness and help me.

They didn't.

When the triage nurse called me in, her look of disapproval for wasting valuable NHS time due to my inability to use a condom properly or visit a chemist was enough to make me burst into tears. She passed me a tissue and patted my hand reassuringly. I very nearly yelled, 'DON'T PAT MY HAND! I'M FUCKING INSANE. PATTING MY HAND ISN'T GOING TO HELP!' Instead I gulped my tears back and took the pill she proffered.

Then I left.

I knew I should stop, go back to the reception desk and tell them the truth. 'Please help me. I think I am going insane.'

But I couldn't.

If I told them, I was convinced they would send me to a mental institution and then that would be it. I would be labelled crazy for the rest of my life. I wasn't ready to have that label, yet.

I should have taken solace in the fact I was still capable of thinking about my future, but I was spiralling out of control, so instead I went to the car park and stood in the rain.

Once I was dripping wet and soaked to the skin I knew I had to make a choice. Go back into the hospital and be honest about how I was feeling, or go home and hope for the best.

I went home.

———

I hadn't had a full-on heart pounding, vomit inducing, brain scrambling panic attack in a few years but I still recognised the signs of one approaching. I stumbled up the stairs from Flat 9, slammed through my front door and took the hottest shower I could handle.

I tried to eat and drink, and promptly threw everything up again.

I grabbed a bottle of gin from the cupboard and drank straight from it.

Then I went into the bathroom and threw that up too.

James was everywhere. His toothbrush in the bathroom, his dirty pyjamas hanging out of the washing basket, his unwashed tea mug sitting by the sink, his smell permeated from everything he sat on, slept in, touched. I couldn't move without seeing or smelling him.

In the end I cleared everything that reminded me of him out of the living room – photos, his slippers, the half-read book he would now never finish – and spent the rest of the night pacing, touching my window corner of power and watching the BBC broadcast their empty news desk.

No one came.

As soon as I could see it was getting light outside I showered again, washed and dried my hair, got dressed, and did my make-up. I practised hiding my horror and smiling normally in the mirror.

Why?

I have no idea. Who did I think I was going to bump into who would worry about the state of my hair and face and whether I was panicking? The neighbours? My boss? Random people in the street? Did I really think that any other person currently still alive would run from me because my hair was wild and my face covered in a greasy sheen of fear?

The world had moved on. I hadn't.

I packed a small overnight bag with all the things I would need for a weekend away and tidied the flat so that it would be clean when I got back.

I didn't need to do any of this. It was needless instinct and routine, but it soothed me, and by the time I left the flat I was still panicking but no longer felt like I was having a heart attack.

I didn't think about the significance of leaving our flat for the last time. I couldn't cope with the finality of leaving my life and husband for ever. Instead, I allowed myself to believe that I was just visiting my parents for a couple of days and would be back soon.

I closed the front door on my way out.

As far as I know it has stayed closed ever since.

I didn't have the energy to cry again.

December 13th 2023

I needed a car. There was no longer any public transport, the place I had to get to was a good twenty miles away, and there was no other option of getting there.

James and I had never owned a car and most people we knew didn't own one either – there had never seemed much point in having one in central London. Luckily, I had learnt to drive a couple of years ago, otherwise I would have been completely buggered.

Greg and Michael from Flat 9 owned a car. A massive Range Rover, which was a bitch to park and was forever breaking down, which was unsurprising as it should have been used for long journeys and off-roading in the country rather than a three-mile drive to Selfridges at the weekend. It was their pride and joy. It was parked outside the house. They kept the keys in a dish on their window ledge.

As I closed their front door behind me, I glimpsed James in the bedroom, but I didn't go back in.

The roads were empty, which was good because I hate driving at the best of times, let alone when I am deep in panic mode and can't remember the last time I slept. I had to employ both my corner of power and repetitive singing of 'Merrily we roll along' to stay focussed on getting where I was going and not just pull over and spend the rest of my life hyperventilating at the side of the road.

I still drove very, very slowly, and the journey that James would do in forty minutes took me an hour and a half.

I was on the outskirts of London when I saw my first pyre. I spotted the smoke from a couple of miles away. I thought maybe a building had caught fire, but even from that far away, and with the little I know about fires, I could tell that it was nothing like the blanket of smoke that comes from a raging blaze; these were lazy, thick black plumes rising sluggishly into the sky in separate towers of darkness.

I was on an overpass above a large patch of wasteland and the smoke was coming from below. I instinctively knew what it was before I stopped to look. A voice at the back of my head repeated *'Don't. Don't. Don't. DON'T!'* as I grabbed something to cover my nose and mouth from the fumes, opened the car door and walked to the edge and looked over.

I don't know how many bodies there were. Some were already ash, some were blackened and twisted, and some lay on the surface, untouched by the flames and heat. The fires had been started but not maintained, so the top third of the pile (hill? mountain?) was simply decomposing bodies.

There must have been thousands.

The overpass was surely sixty or seventy feet high and, had I hung from it by my feet, my hands could have touched the bodies on top.

I had stopped the car by a series of abandoned dumper trucks close to a smashed hole in the side fencing of the overpass. I now understood why the fencing was broken. When the pile got too high to add to from the ground, they must have driven the dumper trucks up here and dumped the bodies over the edge.

I don't think it is possible for the human brain to comprehend this level of horror. At least I know it wasn't possible for mine to.

I took the cloth away from my face and vomited. Then I took a deep breath in, smelt the revulsion of hundreds of burnt, decomposing bodies, and vomited again.

I got back in the Range Rover and screamed.

The three minutes spent on that overpass take pride of place in my nightmares to this day and, I believe, will continue to do so until the day I die.

When I set off again, I was, once more, incredibly thankful for the empty and clear roads. I was now shaking so much the Range Rover was juddering from side to side as my hands jerked the wheel back and forth.

Every so often there would be a crashed car nosed into a hedgerow or lamp post, but other than that there were no clear signs that the end of the world was taking place.

I saw three other moving cars during my ninety-minute journey.

The first passed with exaggerated slowness; a man driving with a woman and two kids in the back. The woman and kids were slouched together, but the man wasn't sick, or at least wasn't yet. We stared at each other as we passed. It was only as I drew level with them that I saw the woman and children were already dead.

I drove past the next car at speed and didn't look at the car or driver.

The third car was weaving across the road in front of me. It came to an abrupt stop by mounting the kerb and driving into a wall. No one got out of the car and I didn't stop to investigate.

It was getting dark by the time I finally arrived home. Although I haven't lived with my parents for over ten years, it is still the first place I think about whenever anyone talks about home.

But, parked in the driveway, I suddenly didn't want to go into the house. I couldn't face the final horror of finding my parents dead after all the other horrific events of the past week.

I decided to go for a walk instead.

I walked the streets that I had previously strolled along with my parents at this time of year, admiring the Christmas lights and decorations in our neighbours' houses. I used to love peeking through windows to get snapshots of other people's lives – warm, cosy, filled with love and holiday cheer.

That evening it looked almost exactly the same. Solar-powered or timed outdoor fairy lights were on, driveways were packed with cars, 'Santa stop here' signs were placed in gardens; but there was no warm glow through the windows or bustle of activity in the houses. I walked for over an hour, but I didn't see movement in any of the buildings I passed.

After a while it began to feel like a creepy village of the damned, where occupants are forced to pretend to have a jolly Christmas. There was nothing behind those lights – no joy or love or laughter. Just dead people.

I went home.

My parents were upstairs in their bed.

I sat in the corner and cried.

––––––––––––––

My parents were both teachers, the good kind of teachers, the kind that think of it as a vocation and not just a job with good holidays.

They were excellent at teaching – clever, knowledgeable, creative, exciting, strict enough to keep control but not stiflingly so, and always interesting and interested. My parents were fascinated by everything: new ideas, new ways of teaching, new places and people. They were interested in the kids that they taught; they actually wanted to know about them and how best they could teach them. They were both offered senior leadership and head teacher jobs but they never took them – it was teaching they loved, not admin. They retired at the same time from the school they had taught at for twenty years and at their leaving event nearly seven hundred ex-pupils turned up to say goodbye. They had to hold the ceremony in the playground.

They had me very late in life (for the time) – my mum was thirty-seven when I was born. They kept her in hospital for the last month of her pregnancy even though she, and I, were perfectly healthy. She'd had six miscarriages before having me.

My mum and dad were brilliant teachers and brilliant parents. I was an only child and always felt like I was the complete centre of their world. I was safe, happy, loved and cared for. I wanted for nothing physically or emotionally. My parents were lovely and happy people who just wanted me to be as lovely and happy as they were.

My childhood was idyllic.

We didn't have much money, but Mum and Dad had time, unlimited curiosity, and endless creativity. We spent winters and wet days building dens under the dining table, rockets and space-ships out of cardboard boxes, kites out of sticks and old cloth, making wormeries or ant farms, assembling kit cars, exploring dusty old museums where security guards snoozed in corners. As soon as spring came, they would dig our leaky old tent out of the corner of the garage and, on a Friday afternoon once school had finished, they would stick a pin in the map of the UK; if it was within two hours' drive, off we would go. Camping trips to the seaside, down along the Thames, to the Malvern Hills, to the unsung joys of Daventry and Wendover, other dull commuter towns where they always discovered something worth-while and interesting to do.

My memories of these times are always tinged with a rosy glow. I don't remember the cold, dank darkness of winter days, but I do remember snow and sledging down hills on a tea tray, landing in a tumble of limbs at the bottom. I don't remember rain leaking through the roof of the tent but I do remember the joy of sausages sizzling on the camping stove when we had successfully survived another stormy night. I don't remember the name of the first boy who broke my heart, but I do remember how my mum held me and listened to my endless eleven-year-old diatribe about how I would never love again. I don't remember when I crashed my bike into the car, taking out the wing mirror, but I do remember my dad telling me that as long as I was fine it didn't matter about anything else – that was just stuff, and stuff could be fixed.

An entire childhood of small, wonderful memories combining to form years of contented happiness.

Growing up had been filled with joy and wonder and fun and love, I was safe and happy and cared for by people who loved me. So, is it any surprise that I expected the rest of my life to be equally easy and idyllic?

———————

When I finally stopped sobbing and climbed up off of the floor in my parent's room I realised they must have both been very ill before they took their T600 because the house was a complete mess.

The kitchen was a disaster zone of half-prepared, half-eaten rotting food, filthy dishes, and dirty surfaces. All three bathrooms had remnants of vomit and diarrhoea. There were clothes left all over the house, dirty bed sheets by the washing machine, and dust everywhere.

My mum must have literally been at death's door to allow things to get into this state.

I still couldn't face disposing of their bodies, not yet, so I did the only thing that I could think of that would make Mum happy and take my mind off the ever-growing panic inside of me.

I cleaned.

I scrubbed the house from top to bottom: kitchen, living room, bathrooms, bedrooms, the lot. I cleaned out cupboards and cutlery drawers, I did six loads of washing, I dusted on top of shelves and wardrobes, I changed sheets and bleached shower curtains, I even did the skirting boards. I cleaned for fourteen hours straight, stopping only for water and cups of tea.

I couldn't do much about my mum's beloved garden, not because she had neglected it, but because winter had rampaged through and killed or fatally wounded most of her plants. I tried to remember the gardening lessons she had given me about the things that need to be done during winter, but my mind was blank. So, instead, I tidied things away, raked leaves, and cut off anything dead or rotting.

I was removing Mum's gardening gloves to put them back in the shed when I stopped suddenly. They were her favourite pair, bought for her by me a couple of years ago, covered with mud and grass stains, physical proof of the hours she spent immersed in her garden, immersed in joy. I couldn't leave them here, to be forgotten. I put them upstairs in my overnight bag, still soaked through with mud.

I cleaned Mum and Dad's room last.

They must have been bed-bound for a couple of days. The sheets were filthy.

I carefully moved their bodies side to side, awkwardly stripped the bed, and put clean sheets on under them.

Then I washed and cared for them with all the love that I could, all the love that they had given to me time and time again for the last thirty-six years. From the first time that they had bathed me in the washing-up bowl when I came home from hospital, to the time the previous year when I had flu and came home so that Mum could nurse me back to health. A seventy-two-year-old woman still caring for her thirty-five-year-old daughter.

I wiped their hands and faces and brushed their hair. I dressed their pale and somehow shrunken bodies, bodies that had shielded and protected me until the day they died, now prone and vulnerable. I laid them gently back onto plumped fresh pillows.

They were lighter than I thought they would be. As though my mum and dad were no longer really there and these bodies were just the shells they had inhabited for a short time. Still, I was careful to do no damage to them, to show them the love, respect and care in death that I should have shown them more of in life.

Strangely I don't remember how decayed they were or if they had started to smell yet. I think I loved them too much to care or even recognise what state they were in. They were my parents, they would always just be my parents, not corpses, not dead people.

Before I left them for the final time I re-entwined their fingers so that they were holding hands again, just as they had been when I found them.

I loved them very much. I hope they knew.

As I shut the door to my parents' bedroom I was assailed by a wave of tiredness that sank me to my knees.

I hadn't slept in over two days. I literally crawled across the hallway to my childhood room and dragged myself onto the single bed. The last thing I saw before falling into a deep, dark dreamless sleep was a framed photo of my parents, my best friend Xav and me that Xav had given me for my nineteenth birthday.

We all looked stupidly happy and carefree.

————————

The photo beside my bed was taken on the first family holiday that Xav came on with us. We were both nineteen, had been friends for over two years, and Xav felt like one of the family.

Before I became friends with Xav I didn't really have many friends and definitely not a best one.

My parents were such a joyful, interesting and comforting presence in my life I didn't really need good friends. If I wanted to talk to anyone, I could talk to them.

I was perfectly friendly and chatty and well-liked at school. I went to parties and got invited to hang out at the youth club. I had people that I could text, go to the cinema with or to the pub when we got older. I had plenty of people to hang out with, but good friends? Friends that you can have serious conversations with, that you can message at 10 p.m. and ask to come over, friends that actually cared if you were sad or anxious or just needed a hug? I never really had that, and never really thought I needed it.

Until I met Xav.

I was sixteen and wanted to go to a gig on the other side of London but didn't want to go on my own so, when a girl in my year mentioned her cousin was going, sixteen-year-old, clueless me asked if I could tag along.

I didn't think it would be just me and him.

I didn't think he would view it like a date.

I definitely didn't think he would see this as his chance to go to a gig, get E'd up, and lose his virginity, all in one go.

At that time I had very little experience with the opposite sex. And no experience with sex.

I was leaning against the grubby wall of the grubby underground venue regretting my decision to schlep seventy minutes across London to see a bunch of Muse-like wannabes with the cousin of Claire Turner, who, far from being the music-lover I had hoped he would be, was actually only here to try to score drugs and accidentally touch my boob at every opportunity, when some random blond bloke sidled up and stood next to me.

'You realise he slipped an E in your beer?'

'What?'

'E. In your beer. That bloke you're with put one in.'

Claire Turner's cousin was 'having a slash'. I looked in my beer. At the bottom of the plastic glass a small white tablet was gently fizzing.

'Don't panic. I sold it to him and it's an aspirin so it's not going to do anything, unless you're having a heart attack. Also, E doesn't really melt well in beer so, even if it was real, it wouldn't have done anything anyway, so he wasted his money on both fronts. This band is shit. Shall we go somewhere else?'

And that is how I met Xavier Alexander William James-Stuart.

December 21st 2023

Five days after arriving at my parents' I was sitting in Greg and Michael's Range Rover outside Buckingham Palace, eating stale bread, and listening to the radio. The car had a Bluetooth sound system, but I had no idea how to work it. Every radio station was playing the same emergency broadcast, so I eventually switched it off and sat in silence.

I didn't know what to do.

I was struggling to keep my thoughts straight and everything was getting mixed up. I would burst into tears and then be unsure if I was crying for James, my parents, me or a combination of all three. My dreams were haunted by images of dead family members, hospital waiting rooms, and giant piles of burning bodies.

I hadn't been able to bear staying at my parents' and didn't want to go back to my flat.

I had other people that I cared about that I should have checked up on, but I didn't really want to spend my last days alive on a macabre tour of 'dead people I used to know and love'. Plus the idea of going to see James's sister and her two kids made me burst into tears all over again.

I knew I had to try to find other people who weren't yet sick, so I had driven the Range Rover (slowly) to the local police station, council offices, even the RAF barracks near to my parents'. They were all closed and empty.

I'd then driven back to London but hadn't wanted to go back to the flat, so I'd spent a miserable night parked on a random street, sleeping in the Range Rover. The back seat was surprisingly roomy and comfy but, despite my coat and the single duvet I had brought with me, I almost froze.

In a last-ditch attempt to find someone or raise some kind or reaction I drove through the deserted streets of London beeping my horn.

Every so often I would see more black plumes of smoke rising into the sky but, now that I knew what was causing those plumes, I gave them a very wide berth.

Finally, I stood outside the front gates of Buckingham Palace and yelled and screamed and waved my arms and beeped the car horn and played the radio as loud as it would go and generally made the biggest scene I could.

Nothing.

The blank face of the building stayed blank. There was no twitch of curtains, no movement of the security cameras, no face peering out from the shadows, no figure darting across the courtyard. It was still and silent.

Everywhere was still and silent.

I didn't see anything alive. Even the pigeons and birds were gone. London was deserted.

I say that I didn't see anyone, but that is a lie.

I did see people. I saw hundreds of people. People standing behind curtains, around corners, in shop windows. Hundreds of times I saw them, hundreds of times my heart would jump into my mouth, I would screech the Range Rover to a halt, throw myself out of the car and stumble towards my fellow man to find . . . no one. Shadows.

Every time it would be a trick of the eye, an awkwardly placed Christmas tree, a shop mannequin grinning at me inanely. One time I pressed my face hopefully to a living-room window to see three pairs of yellow eyes staring back at me. It wasn't until I spied the corpses in the corner and then the owners of the yellow eyes meowed pitifully that I finally accepted it was not a human I had seen through the curtain.

It was exhausting and depressing, and each time I was painfully reminded of my new solitary status.

Even now I still see people out of the corner of my eye.

It still makes me cry.

I don't know why I didn't kill myself at this point. I suppose I still thought that someone else must be out there, that maybe there was some secret bunker filled with scientists, or that the Queen had a deadly-disease panic room she was hidden in. It still seemed too unbelievable that I was the only one left. I hadn't properly accepted the fact that James and my parents were dead yet, so I definitely wasn't ready to accept the idea that everyone else on the planet might have died too.

I tried to think of a good plan to find other survivors, but everything that I came up with sounded ridiculous. Should I just drive endlessly around London beeping the Range Rover horn until I ran out of petrol? What would I do then? Swap the Range Rover for a handcart, get a hand bell, and roam the streets ringing and yelling 'Bring out your non-dead'?

I chewed on my stale bread and felt a tear roll down my cheek once more.

It was hopeless.

I was hopeless.

And then I stopped.

It wasn't just hopeless, it was also ridiculous.

If I was the last one left alive in a land of plenty, why was I sitting in the cold, eating stale bread?

I should at least have been sitting in the cold, eating stale bread while drunk on the finest champagne in the land.

And that was when I realised what I needed to do.

I needed to take a tip from one of the Hollywood movies my mum loved so much.

———

For her thirteenth birthday present my grandma took my mum to see her first 'adult' movie at the cinema. It was *Doctor Zhivago*.

At over three hours long and set in a world she had no knowledge of it should have bored my newly teenage mum.

It didn't.

My mum lost herself in the film. She was enthralled by the snowy, foreign world, the costumes and sets, the dancing and music, swept up in the epic romantic love story. She told me that it was a completely visceral experience and when she left the cinema she felt like the world around her was in shades of grey compared to what she had just witnessed. That one celluloid experience shaped the rest of my mum's life, defining her vision of romantic love and creating a lifelong adoration for romantic Hollywood movies, anything from *Casablanca* to *Sleepless in Seattle*. Movies that she felt echoed her own experience of finding true love and the happiness that would bring.

My mum never seemed to notice the sadness and pain that a lot of these movies put their female characters through.

My mum and dad had a Hollywood romance. A genuine fairy-tale love that lasted for fifty years.

They met on my mum's first day at her summer job, when she was seventeen and my dad was nineteen. They rode the same minibus to work and on that first morning one of the other girls told her to watch out for my dad because he was a charmer but only interested in stealing ciggies.

My mum took up smoking immediately.

My mum applied to and was accepted at the same university as my dad and took the same university degree as him. They married as soon as my mum turned eighteen, and had shared their lives, and every major decision in those lives, ever since. They decided to move away from Sheffield together, decided to become teachers together, decided to keep trying for a baby after my mum's sixth miscarriage together. If you looked up the words 'together', 'love' or 'happy marriage' in the illustrated dictionary it would, or should, have a picture of my mum and dad next to each of them. They were as in love on the day they died as they were on the day they married.

My mum wanted me to be happy more than anything else in

the world. She had experienced unconditional love and true happiness in her life and she wanted that for me. She wanted me to have the same ultimate love story that life had given her: my very own Hollywood movie storyline.

This was very loving and very sweet.

It was also a lot of fucking pressure.

By the age of seventeen I had never had a 'proper' boyfriend and never brought anyone home to meet my parents.

So when Xavier Alexander William James-Stuart pulled up to our house one Friday night in his vintage Jaguar I honestly thought my mum might faint.

Xavier Alexander William James-Stuart – Xav – was literally everything my mum could have wanted. He was rich, well-educated, good-looking, charming, funny, kind, generous, and loving.

Of course, he was also gay.

Actually, he hadn't officially defined himself as gay when he first met my parents. Xav experimented with both men and women until he was about nineteen, but then announced he was gay when we were eating breakfast one day. 'I don't like the unpredictability of the juice with women. At least with a man I know roughly when it is going to happen and can prepare for it. And, let's be honest, with women it's all quite hard work. Men are a lot easier all round and I am very lazy.'

He really was. Lazy.

Xav's dad (Rupert) was a distant relative of some minor member of the royal family. Rupert had failed to inherit the grand but crumbling country pile and had, instead, inherited a pile of money. Rupert had then added to this pile by being the top trader at one of the big city banks and working twenty-hour days to increase the fortune of a family line that did, and would always, end with Xav.

Xav had a trust fund and, after his father died, an even bigger trust fund.

Xav didn't work. Ever.

In the twenty years that I knew him, Xav never had a job, never had a lasting relationship, he didn't even commit to a contract for his mobile phone. The only people apart from me that he saw regularly were his personal trainer and the family accountant.

People and lovers came in and out of Xav's life, and he could never be bothered to care.

Except for me. He cared about, looked after, and loved me.

Within a year of meeting we were best friends and, for me, that was enough. I never needed another best friend, or even good friends. I had Xav.

Xav was like the brother that I never had, and we were the family he had always wanted. He came on holidays with us, spent birthdays, Christmas, and Easter at my house, came to Sunday lunch every weekend. My parents loved him.

I loved him.

But, unfortunately, not in the way that my mum thought I was destined to when she opened the door on that gloomy Friday evening to find Xav standing on the doorstep jiggling his car keys.

December 22nd 2023

I wanted to start my new Hollywood dream by getting myself an extremely expensive hotel suite but, like many other things in this new world, it wasn't as easy or straightforward as I had hoped it would be.

Some hotels had had the audacity to actually close as soon as 6DM reached us and I wasn't yet brave enough to smash my way into anywhere that was locked, so they were off my list. Some of the smaller hotels that had stayed open until the very end had a smell that I couldn't, and didn't want to, identify, so they too were out of contention. For the ones that were left I soon discovered that most hotels have a key card system for their doors these days, which are programmed by computers that I had no idea how to use, and therefore the wonders that lay inside these doors were destined never again to be viewed by human eyes.

I spent a fruitless, cold, depressing day driving around London unable to stay in any of the hotels I stopped at for one reason or another.

Then I tried the Langham.

My God, it is a beautiful hotel. The front doors were closed but not locked, no one was in reception, everything was spotless, if a little dusty. The lobby and reception area had huge high ceilings, marble floors, and giant bouquets of fresh flowers only just starting to wilt. The dining rooms with their massive windows, plush furnishings, and grand pianos were just waiting for humans to return and take afternoon tea in them. The sun chose this moment to come out and the glorious way it lit the entire ground floor with a dusky light made the beauty of the building soar.

My heart lifted for the first time since James had become ill, and I knew that I would stay here even if I couldn't get in the bedrooms. I would sleep in reception if I had to.

But I could get into the bedrooms. Through luck, human error, or system failure the doors to all the rooms were unlocked.

I had my pick.

I looked in at them all. Two-bedroom suites, four-bedroom suites, even one with six bedrooms. They had sitting rooms and dressing rooms and luggage rooms and cinema rooms and kitchens and pantries and TVs as big as cinema screens, bathrooms the size of our flat, beds the size of our bedroom. It was like nothing I had ever seen. I ran from room to room, marvelling at the beauty and extravagance, my dire situation and painful loneliness momentarily forgotten when presented with such opulent glory.

At one point I stopped to have a bath simply because it was the most humongous bath I had ever seen, and because the hot water was miraculously still working. I relived my childhood and mixed up the most extravagant concoction from all the lotions and potions I could find, producing four foot of bubbles when I poured it under the running water.

In the end I settled for staying in a one-bedroomed suite with a separate lounge and massive wrap-around terrace filled with flowering winter blooms, that overlooked Regent Street. I walked around the suite pretending that I was just on an expensive weekend away in an amazing hotel rather than alone in a city full of dead people.

For the first but definitely not last time I turned to exclaim to James about the beauty of the room, how lucky we were to stay there.

There was no James.

I needed a drink.

I went down to their bar, Artesian. It was exquisite, empty, and set as if waiting for my arrival. Sunshine flooded in through the windows and bounced off the ornate bar and row upon row of expensive bottles of booze. Massive vases of flowers adorned marble plinths and filled the place with the light perfume of a spring that was still months away. Small tables and chairs along with larger leather sofas and banquettes were ready and waiting for a clientele that would never visit again.

I looked at the bar menu, which told me that the Laurent-Perrier Grand Siècle was the most expensive champagne available, but I like rosé champagne, so I settled for the Dumangin Brut Rosé. The fridges were still working so it was icy cold. I popped the top in a way that would have made the sommelier wince, poured it with a complete lack of grace, and then downed the first glass in one. I had immediate brain freeze, but it was still delicious.

I drank the rest of the bottle.

I moved from the bar, to a sofa, to a window seat, and then sat at the back of the room and just admired the view. After one bottle of champagne I was feeling happy and light and the lack of anyone to enjoy the champagne with bothered me much less than it had before.

I spent the early evening hours on the outside terrace of my room wrapped in not one but two fluffy dressing gowns, swigging a second bottle of champagne straight from the neck and staring down at Regent Street.

It was deserted.

Not just deserted of people but of everything. No people, no cars, no buses, no tourists, no roadside kiosks selling overpriced fruit from silver bowls, not even a stray cat or dog.

I could no longer hear the distant rumble of the underground, the faint chime of piped music from shops, or the hum of a car from far away. The sky was devoid of planes and helicopters, and even the birds seemed to have taken the evening off.

I was completely and utterly alone in my fancy hotel room and in my street and, in all likelihood, the entirety of London.

I didn't want to think about that.

I downed the rest of the bottle, went back into my suite, and flung myself on to the bed.

I had just enough time to think that it was like sleeping on a soft, wonderful cloud before I passed out.

My head was banging the next morning and I scrabbled in my bag for some sort of painkiller. I lay in bed and reflexively checked my phone for Facebook or Instagram updates. There were none. The panicked post that I had written about still being alive on the night after James had died was top of both feeds.

I staggered up from the bed, clutched my pounding head, and waited for the paracetamol to kick in.

It is surprising how much luxury and opulence can soothe pain. I stood under the seven-jetted shower for an extraordinarily long time and then slathered myself in the expensive toiletries that were kindly provided, before drying my hair with a hairdryer that cost more than my TV (my hair had never looked so shiny). By the time I was dressed in clean clothes from my suitcase, spritzed with perfume, and had put a bit of mascara on I felt semi-normal.

And starving. Completely and utterly starving.

I couldn't remember the last time I had eaten properly and was not about to go and get the stale bread from the Range Rover. So down into the bowels of the hotel and into the kitchen I went.

The visit wasn't as productive as I hoped. What I wanted was to walk in, open a fridge or cupboard, and find shelf upon shelf of delicious pre-made delicacies and delights that would tantalise and tempt my taste buds. But, it turns out, posh hotel kitchens do not pre-make food in batches ready to then be microwaved as and when necessary. Instead, they have fridges and cupboards full of raw ingredients from which their incredibly talented chefs can create fresh masterpieces to order. James did most of the cooking in our house. I can tell an avocado from a passion fruit, but I probably couldn't use either of them in a recipe.

There wasn't even any pre-made bread.

I looked around the huge kitchen to see if there was anything I could use to cook the ingredients. I could recognise the toaster and microwave, but everything else looked like it was designed for someone with a culinary degree, not me. I couldn't even find a kettle.

Eventually I ate some fancy cheese with no crackers, some nuts that I got from Artesian, a huge chunk of black forest ham that was probably £40 a slice, and a selection of berries that I drowned in some cream that was just about in date. It was very tasty but not the cordon bleu creation I had been hoping for.

I knew I would have to go out and get some food from some-where, but I just didn't feel ready, or desperate enough. I wasn't as brave or well organised as James. I wouldn't know which shop was the best one to go to, definitely wouldn't be able to break into one if it was closed, and I wouldn't know what to get anyway.

No. I decided it was best to stay in the luxurious sanctuary of the Langham for now. I had plenty of bar snacks, cheese, ham, and berries – that was almost representative of the four food groups, so good enough for me.

I went back to my room and barely moved for the next three days.

I didn't leave the hotel, and only left my room to get food and more booze and magazines.

I discovered if I maintained a mild state of drunkenness – just barely tipsy, not head-swimming levels – I could mostly stop myself from dwelling on my lonely and frightening situation. As long as I kept busy.

So I kept busy.

The TV worked. All channels were tuned to the empty BBC studio, but the on-demand movies still played. I watched all of them.

I got drunk, got horny (yes, it's weird, but I am sure there are lots, or rather were lots, of studies about how death and sex are linked) and spent an afternoon watching nothing but porn. At least, I planned to spend an afternoon watching nothing but porn, but, after a couple of hours when I just couldn't face masturbating again, I got bored. When I found myself starting to analyse the plot holes rather than anatomical ones, I turned it off.

I read all the fancy magazines from the coffee table and then raided the other suites for different fancy magazines.

I ate all the bar snacks, cheese, ham, and berries and then moved on to anything else still edible in the hotel, including the olives and maraschino cherries from the bar and the boiled sweets from the lobby.

I sat on my balcony, wrapped in duvets, drinking strange and unusual cocktails that I invented myself from Artesian's collection of booze and mixers.

From my balcony, I watched the BBC building at the end of Regent Street to see if anyone went in or out or if there was any movement in the windows. There wasn't.

I strained my ears for a sound, any sound. I heard birds singing, the wind whistling up and down the empty streets, the rain bouncing on roofs, the hum of a streetlamp. My own breathing, my heartbeat drumming in my ears; loud and rhythmic.

I didn't hear anyone else.

By mid-morning of my fourth day at the Langham I had finished the food, finished the films and the porn, finished the magazines, and couldn't face another three-hour bath as my skin was starting to permanently wrinkle.

I wandered down to reception and stared up at the huge Christmas tree. The giant flower arrangements were now wilting, but the tree stood firm, an homage to the calendar humanity had once lived by.

Christmas.

Christmas!

I jumped up and ran back to my room, grabbing my phone.

I hadn't bothered checking the date or time for days – there didn't seem to be any need. But today might be special, today might be . . .

I was right.

It was Christmas Day.

Christmas Day. Over two weeks since James had died.

Shit.

James was dead.

Everyone was dead.

I sat down abruptly.

Two whole weeks since everyone had died and I had only made the most cursory attempts to find any other survivors.

I had watched porn instead.

I needed to find other people . . . or at least I needed to try.

I stood up and then sat down again.

But not today.

And not tomorrow.

The apocalypse could wait a couple of days while I celebrated the most wonderful time of the year.

The idea of celebration galvanised me into action. I couldn't spend Christmas Day without food or drink or happiness, my mum would never forgive me!

My mum loved Christmas. Christmas Eve was her favourite day of the year and even when I was very young I always knew the special day was approaching when dishes of nuts and Quality Street magically started to appear on the coffee table. My mum always . . .

No.

No.

Christmas Day was not a day to remember how good things had been, not a day to cry, not a day to spend silently staring out of the window with tears dripping off my face.

Christmas Day was a day of celebration.

Celebration and food and drink and fun.

Fuck it, I was going to go shopping.

Christmas Day

I went to Harrods.

I reasoned that it would have the widest selection of things under one roof and, given free rein of all the shops in London, I was hardly going to visit the local Sainsbury's.

God, I hoped it wasn't locked.

It wasn't. A window had already been broken and a mannequin knocked to the floor (ooh – anarchy). Once inside nothing seemed to have been touched. Counters of perfumes, bags, make-up, sunglasses, scarves, jewellery, and a hundred other items that no one would ever want again sat gathering dust.

It was weird and depressing.

It was also dark as Hades in there. No one had been in to switch the lights on, and the one thing you never think about in these massive stores is how little daylight actually gets in. Ten feet from the window I was struggling to see, and that, combined with the complete silence and looming mannequin displays, was freaking the hell out of me. There was no way I was getting through to the Food Halls.

So I left, found the nearest electrical store and got myself a couple of the biggest torches I could find plus one of those head torches for good measure.

Once back in Harrods, I'll be honest, the shadows cast by the miner's light and torches didn't make me feel any more at ease, but at least I could see where I was going.

At first, I just walked around occasionally touching items and tentatively picking things up, still half-convinced I was going to feel a hand on my shoulder telling me to put it down.

After fifteen minutes of dithering, I said 'Stop being stupid!' out loud, and pulled an LV holdall down from a display, waving it in the air in defiance.

The room stayed silent, the mannequins stayed still, no phantom hand grabbed my shoulder.

So I went wild.

I grabbed a couple of Birkin bags, a Chanel handbag, some Chloé sunglasses, and three Alexander McQueen scarves on my way through the accessories department. Then I filled one of the Birkin bags with every item in the Crème de la Mer range, plus three tubes of the £80 Elemis face cream that the sales assistant had earnestly recommended I use as hand cream last time I was in there (I had nodded politely, and then slowly walked away from her).

I am ashamed to say that the ritual of acquiring things I didn't really need cheered me up as much as it had in my pre-6DM life. While I was picking and choosing my way through items I could never previously afford I completely forgot my current situation – that the designer bags I now had would never be admired by anyone other than me, that my expensive face creams might slow my wrinkles, but no one would ever notice. I was worrying about looking good for a world that no longer existed.

I had no idea whether there would be anything still edible in the Food Halls but I shouldn't have worried; of course Harrods had a superior refrigeration and ventilation system.

I walked into the first of the huge rooms and took a deep breath, filling my lungs with the comforting smell of bread and cakes.

I smiled, once more transported from my current trauma to a happier time.

I grabbed a trolley and started to load up while stuffing my face with anything that didn't need to be cooked. Cakes, chocolates, pasta, fresh meats, cured meats, cheeses, fruits, vegetables, pastries, sausages, sauces, rice, cereals. The fresh bread was hard and stale but there was plenty of packaged stuff that was still good, so I threw armfuls into the trolley. I filled one trolley, and another, and a third.

I was manic and in a frenzy of food. I grabbed things to eat, took one bite, and then threw them away if I didn't like them. Sauces, juice, crumbs and chocolate smeared my face.

Food Halls ransacked, I moved on to the booze. Another two trolleys were filled with every conceivable variety of alcohol I could find. The most expensive bottle of champagne they stock? Why, the vintage Krug of course. I'll have five bottles of it. Vodka? Why not? Gin? Yes please. I opened bottles, took a swig, and discarded them immediately if they weren't to my taste. To begin with I put them back on the shelf, but then, holding a bottle worth £45 in my hand, I stopped, turned and threw it against the wall.

And, with that act of mindless violence, all of a sudden I realised I was angry.

In fact, I was furious.

I didn't know at what, or who with, but I was furious about something. I picked up random bottles and threw them into a pile on the floor, smashing them again and again until the floor was covered in liquid and the room stank of booze. Within minutes I had raged through half the stock on the walls and had a flash of being appalled at my wanton destruction. But that quickly passed to be replaced with more anger and bitterness. I didn't care! Who was going to stop me? No one else was here, I could do what I liked!

I tried to push over a whole display cabinet. It wouldn't budge, and I got angrier and angrier until I was yelling and shouting and sobbing, and then, just as suddenly as it had started, it was over.

I collapsed to the floor, exhausted and crying.

Of course I was angry.

I was angry at Harrods for having such robust displays, I was angry at 6DM, angry at the scientists for not finding a cure, angry at the government for not having a secret bunker to go to, angry at the stupid human body for being so easy to kill, angry at everyone for dying, angry at my parents, angry at James.

I was angry that I was alone. Angry that I was lonely and sad and scared and confused and useless and didn't know what to do or where to go.

But what I was most angry about was that I was pretty sure I would be lonely and sad and scared and confused and useless and wouldn't know what to do or where to go from now until the day I died.

It was Christmas Day and I was sitting in a pitch-black room, in a puddle of alcohol, in what were probably extremely flammable trousers.

I grabbed the nearest unbroken bottle, twisted the cap off and drank.

It was Scotch and burnt my mouth, but I didn't care.

I waited until I could feel the warmth of the Scotch permeating throughout my body and fuzzing my mind before I struggled to my feet and walked back out to the Range Rover.

I left the trolleys of food and booze where they were.

I drove slowly back to the Langham, swigging from my bottle. I didn't have anywhere else to go. At least it was beautiful there.

I was walking back into the hotel when I heard it.

Faint and far away but definitely something. It undulated through the streets, high-pitched and monotonous. An alarm maybe?

It stopped.

I strained my ears to hear it again, and back it came. Stop, start, stop, start.

I turned away from the hotel and began to walk towards the source of the noise.

It started again, louder this time, at a higher pitch.

Maybe it was a klaxon, something to call people closer?

Maybe it was someone else who had survived.

It had started to rain, hard, piercing droplets that were closer to ice shards than water. I didn't care; I like rain, and I had to know what was calling me.

Hotel, Scotch and Range Rover forgotten, I followed the sound of the noise.

I love walking in the rain.

I love the smell of fresh spring rain as it hits the ground early in the morning, I love the sound of rain as it lashes my window-pane in the deep of winter, the splash of rain as it whips up out of a puddle when a car rushes past too close to the pavement. I love walking in rain, listening to it pitter-patter onto the roof of my coat when I have pulled it up to create my own private house of protection from the outside world.

Rain washes away old dirt and old stains and makes new things grow.

I was standing in the rain the first time James told me he loved me.

————

Twelve years ago, despite my pain and panic, I had forced myself to board the plane to Thailand less than twenty-four hours after James had kissed me. Xav was bubbling with excitement at three months in his second favourite hedonistic tourist destination (Ibiza obviously being his first love), but I was a mess; torn between leaving my troubles behind and staying to embrace my future.

In the end I chose the easiest option and allowed myself to be practically carried onboard the plane by Xav's unbridled joy.

It was the last time I would successfully go through with a difficult decision for the next ten years.

I returned from Thailand with the obligatory woven bracelet, a new tattoo, and a new sense of calm.

My previous worries and panic attacks seemed to belong to another version of me. My time spent abroad, with a perma-stoned Xav and a bunch of middle-aged hippies with no life goals or plans to go home, had allowed me to create a new me, a me that didn't worry about her identity, future, or inability to write anything meaningful. The new me was relaxed and happy, ready to leave her anxiety in the past.

Once home I began working for *Shipping and Ports: Global*. A magazine for those in the shipping industry and those who were just 'enthusiasts'. It was incredibly male-dominated and they needed to up their female quota so were more than happy to employ someone who had a background in journalism, had travelled, and didn't 'write like a feminist' (that is an exact quote from the conversation I had with the editor when he rang to tell me I had got the job.)

I visited ports across the globe, reporting on the latest container and cargo ships, ferries and cruise ships. It was less glamorous, less well paid, and less exciting, but it meant I still got to travel and gave me a new-found love of ports, industrial estates, and huge Russian cargo ships with crews of twenty.

Within weeks I had settled into my new job and writing role, and I loved it. Really, really loved it.

I loved writing about things that were completely separate to me – about ships rather than feelings, facts rather than opinions. And, it turned out, I loved what I was writing about. I'd always liked the sea, but I'd never truly appreciated the huge ships, the massive ports, the industrial estates that surrounded them. The lone pubs with aged strippers shaking pint mugs for pound coins. The surly captains with their rum or whisky or vodka, offered in white tin mugs. The crew members who made fishing nets out of old cargo netting and then extended them on ropes hundreds of feet long to drag through the water. The huge engine rooms where ear defenders are a must and conversations are held in sign language. The fact that tankers no longer have a steering wheel, but that most crew members can still find their way via the stars. I was told stories of fifty-foot waves, onboard hookers, pirates and port police. I slept in hammocks and packing crates and ate whale and sea snake. I liked the crews and, once they had got over their disappointment that I wasn't going to sleep with them, they liked me. I became pen pals, of sorts, with many of them; I would receive filthy postcards from some far-flung port, with a scrawl of foreign language that I could never decipher, or a crude drawing of a penis on the back.

I had a battered duffle bag pre-packed with wet weather gear, thick jumpers, old jeans, and steel-toed boots. You can't drag a suitcase up six flights of steel stairs to the bridge of a tanker (as I soon learnt) and if you wear anything other than old, gender-neutral clothes you are likely to be mistaken for a visiting sex worker (as I also learnt). Plus, most of the ships are held together with grease, oil and dirt, so there's not much point in wearing anything you actually like.

I loved my job and I was good at it. Freed from the constraints of writing about anything meaningful or personal, the writer's block disappeared and articles that were filled with wit and charm were flying off my computer once more.

But it wasn't enough.

The 'new me' that had returned from my travels slowly disappeared as I realised I had returned to exactly the same place and the same life that I had been so keen to run away from previously. I was no closer to knowing who I was or what I wanted. I tried to start writing a new novel, but couldn't think of anything I wanted to write about. I just stared at the screen for hours as it remained blank. My mind felt empty. I felt empty.

Maybe this was why the middle-aged hippies never came back home. Because when you do, you just return to the same place, the same you as before.

I hadn't found a new me, I was still lost.

I tried not to think about James, the contentment I had felt with him, the safety and security he had represented.

I tried to concentrate on myself, to think about how I could make myself feel better.

I held out for about six months.

I had to see him. I mean, not to try to kiss him or be with him, just to see him. Just to check he was okay.

I pretended I had an interview near his office and asked if he wanted to meet for a quick drink after work.

He looked fine. Damn fine. Damn, damn fine.

He'd got a new job, not in creative as he had hoped, but he was head of advertising at his new place, so the money was much better.

He was living in a flat with a mate.

He had a new girlfriend.

It was nice. Two friends having a drink and chatting about their lives.

Really nice.

I was catching the train to Liverpool for an article on a new super tanker, so he walked me to Euston station and we hugged goodbye.

I waved him off and then walked to the end of the platform, stood in the rain, and wept angry, disappointed tears. Angry at myself because I still wanted him desperately, disappointed at him for not feeling the same way.

Resigned, I picked up my bag to get on the train and felt a tap on my shoulder.

He was there.

The rain fell onto my cheeks, mixing with my tears, and he wiped it all away as he held my face in his hands and kissed me again and again.

As the train guard blew the whistle James told me he was in love with me and wasn't going to let me get away again. I smiled all the way to Liverpool.

It was, and still is, the most romantic thing that has ever happened to me.

We moved in together three months later.

If my mum's heart had broken just a little when Xav casually announced to her that he was gay, and therefore not my one true love, it was mended once more when James and I announced we were moving in together so soon after rekindling our romance.

'Finally, here he is,' she must have thought. 'Here is her great romance. Here is her Hollywood happiness.'

But of course she had forgotten the sadness that the heroines of her beloved movies always go through.

The picture-perfect ending is never quite what it seems.

———

I followed the sound through the rain-soaked streets of London and finally reached the source of the alarm.

It wasn't a klaxon and it wasn't other survivors.

In fact, it wasn't an alarm at all and, if I had had any sense of self-preservation, I would have stopped as soon as I realised that. But I had clearly learnt nothing since seeing the overpass funeral pyre.

The noise was the monkey house at London Zoo.

Or, more specifically, it was a chimpanzee in the monkey house at London Zoo.

She was holding her dead baby in her arms.

The baby chimp looked as if it had starved to death.

All of the monkeys looked as if they were starving to death. They were thin, so very thin, but continuously moving; chattering and squealing, trying to pace the floor of their enclosure but falling, tripping and tumbling over constantly. Some of them made attempts to climb the ropes, but slid back down on sinewy arms. They were ripping bark from tree trunks and branches and gnawing it, spitting out the remnants. It was a macabre modern dance of madness and death.

'I'm so sorry,' I whispered to the mother chimp, placing a hand upon the glass.

The other chimpanzees in the enclosure stopped whatever they were doing and swivelled their heads. They rushed to me with a combined force I was sure would break the glass between us. They threw themselves at the glass, screaming and pummelling their fists, throwing their bodies against it. The noise and ferocity of it was terrifying. Their previous fragility was gone, they were fighting for their lives.

I backed away, horrified by their need.

Their efforts doubled. Many of them were bleeding, foaming at the mouth, crazy with hunger, thirst and fear.

Except for the one with the baby. She hadn't moved. Didn't even look up at me. She just continued wailing.

I turned and fled.

I moved through the zoo with the screams and cries of hundreds of caged animals ringing in my ears. Every animal was now alert to my presence, and it was as if they knew I was their last chance and final hope of survival. They screamed and roared and snorted and trumpeted and threw themselves against glass and wire and fences and stakes, and it was bedlam.

I screamed with them, put my hands over my ears, and ran.

I ran out of the zoo, through Regent's Park, past the open-air theatre, and out onto the A40. I ran down the middle of the street ignoring the abandoned and crashed cars, past Madame Tussauds, past Baker Street station, past Edgware Road, and then up through Sussex Gardens, where I slowed to a jog, a walk, and then finally collapsed into a sobbing, breathless heap.

I couldn't breathe, I couldn't stop crying, I ripped off my coat, and lay back on the pavement, letting the rain thrum down onto my face as I gasped for air and desperately tried to think of something, anything, other than the hundreds of animals I had just condemned to death. What could I have done? Found the keys to the cages? Opened the cages? Let them eat me?

I probably should have.

I couldn't do this any more, staying in the hotel, trying to ignore everything that was going on, trying not to cry, not to remember, not to give up, lie down, never move again.

'Someone please help me, please help me, please help me!' I screamed into the rain again and again.

The rain fell and the silence around me continued.

It was Christmas Day and I needed a miracle.

At that moment I didn't care what form it came in.

So I went to Xavier's house.

I have never done drugs.

It's not that I have anything against them, but I was pretty sheltered and lacking in friends to offer them to me when I was younger, and then, by the time I was old enough to be offered anything, I was best friends with Xav, and drugs were Xav's thing; so, by default, my thing was staying sober enough to make sure he didn't accidentally kill himself or anyone else when he was off his face.

Xav loved drugs. He bloody loved them.

He told me that a lot.

Of course, he didn't need to tell me; his constant consumption was proof enough of his unending romance with anything chemical.

I've never seen anyone so happy to have their appendix removed.

'Pharmaceuticals are the best!' he'd cackled as they wheeled him off for surgery.

Truth is, as with many other things in my life, the main reason I didn't take drugs was because I was scared. Scared of being out of control, of it making me even more mental, of the drugs reacting badly with the sleeping tablets I often took. I was scared of dying.

And, more than anything, I was scared I would like it, that it would be the one thing that made me feel better and would then be another crutch in my life without which I would be unable to function.

But that was before 6DM and this was after, and I think my body was currently incapable of producing serotonin or endorphins or whatever the hell is in charge of making you feel better about life.

So, I knew the risks, and I knew the dangers, and I didn't care.

I needed to escape myself, and I knew Xav was an expert in providing the means to do that.

Xavier lived in a five-storey mansion between Kensington High Street and the Royal Albert Hall. He had inherited the house from his dad. It was worth a fortune, and cost Xav a fortune to maintain. Luckily Xav's dad had also left him a massive inheritance, so he could well afford the upkeep.

Standing on Xav's doorstep in the rain I had a brief urge to turn and run; to pretend my best friend wasn't, in all likelihood, rotting away slowly inside the mansion.

But then, from the next-door property, I heard the unmistakeable wail of a caged animal. The tiny Pomeranian that had so irritated Xav with its constant barking and stinking pea-shaped faeces left regularly at the bottom of his steps. The Pomeranian was dying noisily.

No. No more misery today.

I entered the security code into the door lock and went into Xav's house.

All was quiet, white and peaceful inside. Xav liked clean lines, pristine floors, and furniture in hues of white and grey. He paid a premium to ensure the cleaners that visited three times a week guaranteed whatever hedonistic adventure had recently taken place in the mansion did not leave any permanent marks.

I sniffed the air and couldn't smell any telltale scents of decay: food or flesh. But I still needed to know.

I found him in his master suite on the fourth floor. A vast room that stretched across the whole house and contained a bed big enough to sleep six with no spooning needed. He was in the middle of the bed with a young, tanned Adonis on each side (twins?), gay porn playing on an endless loop on the 64-inch TV, a bottle of Dom clutched in his death grip, and a sandwich bag full of cocaine on the bedside table. All three of them were naked and draped over each other like some ancient bacchanalian scene.

For one brief flash I was sad. Xav had been sober and drug-free for over a year, and I knew that things must have been fucking awful for him to do this much coke and have a threesome with the Adonises.

But if the end of the human race didn't qualify as 'fucking awful', then what did?

I left them to it, but took the cocaine.

I'll be honest, having never taken cocaine before, it took me a while to get the hang of it. With every failed attempt to chop, line up, and snort it (I'd never done it, but had seen Xav do it enough times to know the correct terms at least), I had a very clear mental image of Xav's horrified face as I wasted clouds of premium cocaine by sneezing (cliché) and putting my still damp sleeves in the little piles of powder.

Finally, I successfully managed to snort a line up one nostril.

And then, because it is what I had always seen Xav do, I snorted one up the other.

It was pretty zingy and good and made everything speed up and made me forget almost instantly about the bad things and made me feel that maybe, just maybe, things would actually be all right and maybe, even though everyone was dead they weren't really dead because my love for them lived on and their love for me lived on too and as long as I was still loved then everything would be somehow be okay and wow, that's really deep and powerful thinking and I wish I had someone to tell it to in fact maybe if I had done this before I could have done it with Xav and I could have told him that I think I quite liked it and we could have gone dancing or to a party as I had lots of parties before where I hadn't done this and I can see why it would be good to have this at a party and how it might have been good to do it at a party with James because maybe we could have talked about things, like really talked about things and made things better or we could just have danced, yes, dancing would be good on this, maybe I should do some dancing or perhaps I should line some more up because I am not sure how often I should take it or maybe I should do some fun stuff first because it is Christmas Day, or at least I think it is still Christmas Day, it is getting pretty dark so yes, fun stuff and more coke or maybe more coke before fun stuff let me just think . . .

This went on for quite a while.

Finally, I decided it was time to go dancing. Luckily, I didn't have to go far.

Xav's house is essentially a five-storey adult playhouse. As well as his fourth-floor master suite there is a basement cinema and disco, a chef-quality kitchen (which he never used, but which did contain his most prized kitchen possession – a toasted sandwich maker), a huge sitting room complete with open fire and 80-inch plasma smart TV, two floors of guest bedrooms and bathrooms, and a roof terrace that had to be seen to be believed.

Dancing would make me feel better. It always did.

I've always loved to dance; twirling around with my mum in our kitchen when I was little. Old dance steps and routines that she had done when she was young or had learnt from the hundreds of musicals she watched. Then I graduated to school discos, where my dancing became a more self-conscious bopping from side to side than real movement. Then to clubs and parties with Xav where we would throw crazy shapes and moves safe in the knowledge that all the other dancers were too off their faces to care what we were doing. And then finally to nightclubs, where I danced with sophisticated women, wiggled my hips and learnt my movements could, and would, attract appreciative glances and comments.

I love to dance, but it's not the kind of thing you do on your own. I've always liked to have someone with me, someone else in the spotlight so that I don't feel people staring, someone who will take my hand and lead me if I forget my moves, someone to share the joy with.

But that was my old world.

This is the new world, and if I want to dance I am just going to have to learn how to do it by myself.

So I danced, alone.

———

James didn't like to dance.

That was the first surprising thing I found out about him. He'd sort of shuffle about at the side of the dance floor if forced, but otherwise preferred to stay at the bar. In fact, he wasn't actually that keen on music, he preferred Talk Sport. Also, the ginger flecks that I thought the sun had streaked into his hair were actually provided by Kirsty at Vidal Sassoon using bleach once a month, and the easy way he initiated conversation and seemed really interested in whatever you had to say was just a salesman technique he used to draw people in.

These are the sort of things you don't learn until after you have moved in with someone, especially when you make the decision to live together as quickly as we did.

But at the time I couldn't have cared less if things weren't quite as I thought; if James wasn't quite as I thought.

I had been scared and empty and directionless and now I was content and filled with love and had someone who was my map to future happiness.

It all seemed perfect; the meet-cute, the kiss, the moving in three months later to a flat where the only furniture we had was two garden chairs, a mattress, and the washing machine he had salvaged from his previous relationship. Spending weekends naked, eating heated-up pizza because we couldn't bear to leave the flat, me making him sandwiches for work and leaving love notes in the Tupperware, him surprising me at the station when I came back from assignments, three-hour baths, day-long drinking sessions, the time we got a whole club evacuated after we fell through the fire exit while snogging like teenagers.

I was happy. Really, really happy. I felt safe and calm and my heart was so full there was no time or room for worry or panic or thinking about my future.

Besides, it wasn't just my future any more. It was our future.

———

Xav's house was perfectly designed for me to live out my dancing dreams, he had a complete disco set-up, with decks and lighting system in his basement. He did some low-level DJing in his early twenties but was never reliable enough to make a proper living at it. So, when he 'retired', he moved his entire rig into his basement and set up his own mini club.

One of the reasons he failed as a DJ was because he couldn't resist dancing to his own records, so he'd never be back on the decks in time to mix in the next track. So, instead, he started to put together mixes on his Mac to play through the sound system.

He had mixes for everything: 60s, 70s, 90s, 00s (he refused to do 80s as he thought all music invented then was awful – we had many, many arguments about that). Disco, rap, funk, hip-hop, grunge, emo, reggae, chill-out, gabba, soul, Northern soul, grime, even classical.

I fired up his Mac, whizzed through his collections (I was doing everything so fast!) and chose an early 2000 dance mix.

I danced, and occasionally snorted more coke, throughout the mix's three-hour duration.

I danced on my own in an empty disco, with three dead men upstairs and thousands more rotting on the doorstep. The combination of the music, the sound system, the lights (and, of course, the drugs) meant that those 180 minutes were probably the last time I ever completely forgot where I was and what had happened.

I vaguely remember wondering if this was also the last time I would ever be completely happy.

'OF COURSE NOT!!' my drug-addled mind yelled at me. 'LOOK HOW MUCH FUN YOU ARE HAVING! THIS IS HOW LIFE WILL BE FROM NOW ON.'

After three hours of dancing I was exhausted, sweaty, and dying of thirst. I went to the kitchen and stuck my mouth under the cold tap, funnelling icy water straight into it. And then, because I now had a whole new rock 'n' roll persona, I grabbed a bottle of Dom Perignon from the booze fridge. I thought it was what the new me would probably drink in a hot tub.

Xav's hot tub is on his roof terrace: a lush, year-round jungle of foliage, with a bar, huge BBQ, sound system, comfy seating area, and hammocks hung from the leafy green ceiling. It really pissed his neighbours off mainly, I think, because Xav never invited them over to hang out there. It was one of my favourite places in the world.

It was freezing on the roof terrace, and the previous drizzle had turned to light flakes of snow drifting down from the black night sky. The hot tub was bubbling nicely, kept at an enticingly constant temperature of 100.5°F by Xav's extortionate electricity bill that he would now never have to pay again. I set a seven-hour chill mix on the sound system, put a couple of towels into the warming cupboard (also filled with huge fake fur blankets for snuggling), opened the bottle of champagne, stripped naked, and jumped in the tub.

I shuddered blissfully as the warm water enveloped me, and uttered a sigh of pure happiness. I chugged from the bottle of Dom and slipped back to bob on the surface of the tub. My body was exhausted after my three-hour dance session, my mind was blank after the administration of so much cocaine, and my emotions were dull from my horrific visit to the zoo. I was physically, emotionally, and mentally exhausted, and it felt great.

I lay in the bubbles, swigged from my bottle, stared up at the stars, and watched the snowflakes swirl around my head as the warm breeze from the tub lifted them back up to the sky.

By the time the bottle was finished, my racing heart had slowed to a steady pace, but my entire body was still buzzing with energy and my mind was both exhausted and wide awake. This wasn't good. I wanted to sleep. Then I remembered that Xav had prepared for all eventualities. I jumped out of the tub, wrapped myself in the now-warm towels, and went down to his bathroom. There were boxes of all kinds of pharmaceuticals – codeine, morphine, Tramadol, random yellow and red pills with no name, sleeping tablets, stuff for constipation and diarrhoea – a fully stocked mini chemist. I gulped down two sleeping tablets and went back onto the roof.

I wrapped myself in a couple of fur blankets and got into the closest hammock, setting myself to a gentle rock. As the sun slowly started to creep up over the buildings and the snowflakes danced happily around my head, I drifted off into a blissful, dreamless sleep.

Boxing Day

Hours later, when the sun was a dull ball high in the cloudy sky and my dreams were long forgotten, I peeled one of my eyelids open and wondered what fresh hell I had woken up in.

My head pounded, my body ached, my tongue was so dry I had to pry it off the roof of my mouth, and there was a disgusting metallic taste at the back of my throat.

I rolled (okay, fell) out of the hammock and rifled through the random boxes of meds I had brought up with me the night before and chucked on the floor.

I grabbed two of the only ones I really recognised (Tramadol), wrapped myself in dry furs, crawled to the bar to grab a can of Coke, took the tablets, and then climbed back into the hammock and waited for them to have some kind of effect.

It didn't take long.

Whether it was my already drug-addled system or the fact I was unused to narcotics, within fifteen minutes I was pain free, smiling gently, lying on my back and gazing beatifically at the sludge-like drizzle that was once more falling from the sky. The can of Coke was the most delicious thing I had ever tasted.

Effects of the Tramadol were arriving in rhythmic waves. If I tried to sit up, I felt a rush of unbalancing giddiness, so I stayed happily rocking in the hammock.

My mind couldn't hold a solid thought for more than a few moments and my body was rushing with waves of warm pleasure and it was all very, very enjoyable.

After about an hour, things had calmed enough for me to roll slowly from my hammock and warm up in Xav's vast rain-forest shower. I was still light-headed and smiling, so crept hand-over-hand down the stairs and raided Xav's spare ward-robe for clothes. Xav was reed thin, so none of his clothes would have got past my thighs; but luckily he kept a wardrobe full of outfits for those encounters that left his conquests with dirty, ripped or sometimes missing clothing items. I found some massive sweatpants and a flannel shirt, and moved with exag-gerated precision down the stairs again to raid Xav's kitchen for anything edible. As always, his fridge was empty, his freezer had nothing but ice cubes in, and his cupboards held only booze, mixers, maraschino cherries and protein bars, all of which I had for breakfast.

Every move I made felt slow and deliberate. My mind was working at half its normal speed and maybe an eighth of the speed it had been the previous night. My previous worries felt far away and inconsequential. I knew I might be the last person on earth, that my best friend was lying dead up three flights of stairs, that I had recently partaken in a particularly wild drug binge, and that I probably wasn't quite thinking straight, but it all seemed rather unimportant. The reaction of both my mind and body to such devastating circumstances was a resounding '*Meh*'.

My foremost thought was not about my circumstances but rather that I may have found the ideal crutch to help me survive in this desolate new world.

I wasn't sad any more. I was hungry and a bit bored.

I went out.

It was already getting late and I didn't want to go far, so I walked around the corner to the Royal Albert Hall.

I tried all of the entrance doors at the front, and the side doors, and the stage doors. They were all locked. I wanted to go in and look around.

The new medically-enhanced me was braver (and less in-hibited) than the me of the day before, so I broke in.

It was surprisingly easy.

I broke the glass of one of the front doors, cleared the shards away, and climbed through. It was gloomy inside but not dark, and when I flicked the light switches they responded accordingly. I wandered through the halls and corridors, exploring.

I went into the dressing rooms and looked at the signatures scrawled on the walls. I went down below the building into the storage areas and basement. I went to the backstage area and into the staff offices and cloakrooms. I sat in all the best seats. I climbed to the very top of the building and looked down at the tiny stage and chairs below its giant dome. I broke into a refreshment stand and ate the overpriced snacks. I went onto the stage and sang, marvelling at how good the acoustics were and how bad my singing was. I bowed and thanked the non-existent audience for their loud applause.

When I left, I closed the door nicely behind me and propped a framed poster from the wall into the gap where I had broken the window.

Then I walked up the road to Whole Foods to get something to eat that wasn't either protein powder or sugared cherries.

By the time I got back to Xav's, the effects of the Tramadol were beginning to fade and, as I opened the front door, I heard the Pomeranian whining once more.

I had two choices – tell myself that the last twenty-four hours had been a nice break from reality but now I needed to get a bloody grip and think about what I was going to do next, or . . . pop another Tramadol and worry about that all later.

I took the Tramadol with a nice glass of organic red, ignoring the warnings on the packet about mixing the drugs with alcohol.

Sitting at the kitchen table with my Whole Foods semi-healthy dinner, my red wine, and a new-found, chemically-induced enthusiasm for life, I thought about what I could do next.

Obviously, what I should have been doing was looking for other survivors. That was what I had promised myself I would do only twenty-four hours earlier. That was the sensible thing to do and what any other 'normal' person would have been doing at this point in their time as (potentially) the last human alive.

But I wasn't normal, and this wasn't normal behaviour for me.

For the first time since the outbreak of 6DM, and maybe for a long time before that even, I felt weirdly happy and content. I knew it wasn't real, I knew it was chemically induced, I knew it wouldn't and couldn't last. But I just didn't care. I was tired of being sad and lonely and scared, and if I wanted to replace human contact with drugs and ignore the plight of humanity, then that was up to me. There was literally no one to stop me.

So, I wrote a list of all the places in London that I wanted to visit.

I was quite selective.

I discounted anywhere too far away (Kew Gardens, Ally Pally, Wembley stadium), anywhere too 'secure' (MI5, Downing Street, Tower of London), anywhere that I would need to ride up or down in an elevator (the Shard, Sky Garden), anywhere outside or where something might be dying (all of the parks and the Aquarium) and shops, which were overwhelmingly dark and starting to become very smelly.

This left the Natural History Museum, Science Museum, National Gallery, Victoria and Albert Museum, British Library, British Museum, St Paul's, Houses of Parliament, and Tate Britain.

The last thing I wanted to do in any of these places was trigger a secret alarm and end up in some security cage or stuck in a barred room until I died of thirst. If I was going to die, I wanted it to be because I had planned it, not by accident, so I was going to be very, very careful.

December 27th 2023

I started my tourist attraction bucket-list the next day at the Natural History Museum. Surprisingly, someone had been there before me and one of the main entrance doors had been prised open.

Inside it was silent, peaceful and awe-inspiring.

The size of the building and the exhibits it contained left me, literally, open-mouthed. I had been to the museum before but to see it in complete silence, to experience it without being surrounded by hordes of chattering children; my jaw dropped, and I gaped at its grandeur.

I happily roamed the vast building for most of the day, losing track of time and, at one point, losing myself completely in the warren of rooms on the upper floors. I committed the cardinal sin and touched multiple exhibits, multiple times. I left the well-defined visitor path and wandered through the attractions themselves, trailing my hands over dinosaur models, onto cool, old bones and through soft warm fur.

The sun came out and shone through the windows, lighting up years of exploration and archaeology and discovery and, if I were to be the last person ever to see this amazing place, then I was definitely one of the most appreciative.

I discovered that multiple people had used the open entrance before me.

In the dinosaur exhibition I found a man with his arms wrapped around a young boy. They were lying in the corner of the room facing the dinosaurs. The boy had a small trickle of dried blood coming from his nose, but the man seemed perfectly preserved, like one of the models. The boy was nestled in his father's arms, his head laid comfortably on his chest, his eyes closed, his face peaceful. He might have been asleep. A final visit to a place they had both loved, a quick drink and vitamin pill and a cuddle that would last for ever. An ending filled with love.

In the hall housing the blue whale bones, three separate people had sat down knowing they would never stand up again.

I should have been horrified, sad and distraught. Maybe it was the Tramadol I had taken earlier, but instead of being appalled I was strangely comforted that, in the midst of all the horror of the outbreak, they had all thought to come here to die. Somewhere so beautiful, poignant and peaceful.

After the Natural History Museum, I visited one place from my list each day. Some of them were still open, some of them I broke into, and some of them had been broken into by others and I simply followed the already available route.

St Paul's, I walked into and then left immediately. It was like a vision of hell, or some zombie film, filled to the brim with corpses. The pews were full, so people had lain down in the aisles, up the stairs, even on the altar, to commit their final sin. Embarrassingly, it hadn't even occurred to me that this might have happened, that this famous and beautiful building would have been gifted as a place of peace to these people in their final hours.

The Houses of Parliament were completely empty. None of the politicians cared enough about the country at the end to choose it over their family, and who could blame them for that? I spent the day walking from one end of the building to the other, drinking tea in the restaurant, shouting in the debating chamber, looking into each of the private offices. I thought about defacing the offices of some of the worst MPs but didn't. What would be the point? They would never know, and no one else would either. I felt like 6DM and their inability to protect themselves from it, despite their nefarious natures, was punishment enough.

In the Science Museum I explored the rocket exhibition with

my grubby little hands, crawled inside the lunar module, sat in all the planes, trains and automobiles that I could, and marvelled at the wonder of it all. I tried out all the experiments, games, and hands-on exhibitions without queueing or waiting, and I played with all the toys in the gift shop and took a couple of chemistry sets with me to do at home.

I was equally hands-on at the Victoria and Albert and British Museums, opening cases and studying their contents wherever possible. Some of the exhibitions I left, knowing that once I opened the case to the twelfth-century scroll it would disintegrate to the elements in weeks; I was hungry for knowledge and experience, but not a total heathen. But I did break into some of the clothing exhibits, desperate to feel the material and weight of the garments. I tried on the Princess Diana dress, or at least I tried to try it on but couldn't get it past my thighs. I lay in a sarcophagus, but then got freaked out that it might close with me stuck inside.

I timed my Tramadol dosage so that I was in front of great works of art in the National and Tate galleries just after popping the pills, and I gazed up at their mastery while feeling the rush of chemicals to my brain and veins. I tried very hard to appreciate their beauty for a significant amount of time but, despite the drugs, I succumbed to boredom once the chemical rapture ended. I have always been obsessed with the feel of paintings, always wanted to run my fingers over their uneven surfaces and feel the texture of the paint and the history contained therein. So I did. I touched them, feeling the surface of the canvases, the bumps, the waxiness of the paint and, here and there to my delight, a paintbrush bristle stuck deep into the thick paint of a work of genius.

The British Library was another magnificent palace of knowledge and history, and the contents should have kept me interested for days. But they didn't. It was too sad to stay there long. Someone had Sellotaped a note to one of the front doors that read:

If you are reading this, please take care of these books they may be the only part of humanity we have left

Just one handwritten note. The last act of someone heading home to die.

I made sure all the windows and doors were closed before I left.

As the drugs in my veins increased, so did my recklessness. I went where I wanted and, despite my previous vow to avoid shops, I started to break into boutique ones that were still locked to take things I didn't need. I was a huge, flightless magpie, immensely attracted to shiny things. I threw the new things I collected into an ever-growing pile in one of Xav's spare rooms when I got home. I never looked at them again.

I marvelled at the way life had just . . . disappeared. Coffee shops still had tables outside, empty trains littered the tracks waiting for commuters who would never come, buses were parked everywhere, silent and still. Thousands of bikes were chained throughout the city, waiting to rust over the next hundred years.

I went to King's Cross and wandered across the concourse, up and down the platforms, and onto the tracks. I stood in the middle of the main departure hall and yelled my name, listening to it bounce around the huge empty space, filling the void with its noise. I realised no one else would ever yell my name again.

The walls of the station were lined with posters and photos, even hand-painted pictures of people, moments captured from another time. From a distance I thought these were missing person posters, but there were so many, hundreds and hundreds lining the whole front wall of King's Cross. It was only as I drew closer that I saw what they were.

There is no word to describe them, it was never invented. I suppose I would call them death notices. Pictures and words and poems and letters to those who have died. Like the wooden crosses in the graveyard, this was a testament to memory, to not wanting to forget. '*Please remember my little girl in your prayers*',

'For my Grandpa who lived till he was 93', 'For Kate, John and Billy, you were my life, wait for me'. So many, so much death, so much pain. It was so sad. Too sad.

I left quickly and took my next dose of Tramadol two hours early.

Late one afternoon, I walked to the middle of Waterloo Bridge and stood alternating between facing Westminster and facing the City. Nothing moved except the water beneath me. The whole of London was silent and still. I've never heard the Thames; its sound has always been obscured by the more immediate noises of London: traffic, roadworks, chatter, hubbub. The river is loud. It's a huge body of water forced through a channel at high speed, and it roars its way along; rushing, splashing, gurgling through.

The sun set, the night approached, and for a long while I stood mesmerised by the water tumbling beneath me and by how easy it would be just to fall down into it and be carried away to . . .

. . . nowhere.

I wouldn't go anywhere. I would sink. It would be cold and wet and I would drown under Waterloo Bridge.

I hate the cold.

I walked slowly home.

I settled into a comfortable routine.

I would visit a place of interest in the day, come home early afternoon, eat dinner, watch a movie, maybe have a dance, go in the hot tub, then fall asleep in the hammock.

All of this was accompanied by a pharmaceutical routine that allowed me to function, sleep, and experience a certain amount of happiness. I took Tramadol at set times during the day and sleeping pills at night. I tried to limit the amount of cocaine I was using to the odd sniff here and there when I was feeling particularly despondent because I found it was making me increasingly paranoid and jittery. Already, I was getting accustomed to my new regime. I no longer needed to sit down for an hour after taking Tramadol, it no longer caused a rush of warmth through my blood stream and, if I was late taking a dose, I found my hand would start to shake and my breath was harder to regulate until I popped the next pill.

I still got dressed each morning, combed my hair and put make-up on. I kept the cupboards of my home – as I now thought of it – filled with food and drink, and I made a cursory effort to keep it clean and tidy although it became a bit smelly and I did sometimes have trouble finding clean plates.

I thought I had an appropriate post-apocalyptic level of domesticity and routine and I was very happy in it. Ignoring my plight suited me just fine and, as long as I had the drugs and food and places to hang out, I think I would have bumbled along quite happily for the foreseeable future.

If the lights hadn't gone out.

———

It seems ridiculous to say that I couldn't change a lightbulb when I moved in with James but it is true. I suppose it's the sort of thing that happens when you are on your own and then you learn how to fix it by trial and error, but I'd never been on my own so it had never happened to me, and therefore I had never learnt.

After James and I moved in together and after many trips to Ikea to furnish our house with an assortment of lights, I finally learnt how to change an (Ikea) lightbulb.

But that is about all I learnt.

James liked to organise and sort things, and I was quite happy for him to continue with that. James found the first house we rented, took charge of setting up the utilities, scheduled the bills, did the DIY, found and booked our holidays – he even did most of our shopping and cooking. And I let him get on with it.

Without knowing quite how, I found myself living in his favourite part of London, watching his TV shows, hanging out with his friends, drinking his choice of red wine, and listening to hours upon hours of Talk Sport. By the end of the first month that we lived together I was no longer vegetarian; it was just too hard to settle for gnawing on a dried-up veggie sausage when James was gorging on chicken stuffed with lemon and coriander butter.

I was still struggling to write my next novel. My heart and life might have been full, but the pages remained blank. Time spent staring at my empty notebook now felt like time wasted, time I should have been spending with James.

It became harder and harder to leave and travel to far-flung ports or to spend uncontactable days in the middle of the Atlantic on the newest oil tanker. James missed me and I missed him. James was doing really well at work and, along with a new promotion, his social life was busy. He wanted me to be there for dinner parties with clients, he wanted to show me off. I wanted to be there for him, but turning up last-minute to work events still dressed in waterproofs and steel toe-capped boots was not the required look.

His face fell every time I told him I was going to be away for a few days, and I began to dread it when my editor called me into his office to tell me about the newest exciting liner I would be travelling with.

The final straw was the night I came back early from a trip away to find impromptu Friday after-work drinks being held in our flat. The laughter at my duffle bag and wet weather gear was good-natured and inclusive, but the comment that floated down the hallway to the bedroom after me didn't feel quite as well meant.

'I thought you said she was a proper journalist.'

I'd thought so too for a while.

In the end, my career change wasn't a difficult decision to make. We needed to earn more money if we were going to afford a deposit for a mortgage. We needed to attend more events together if James was going to continue to be promoted. We wanted to spend every night together, not be apart for a week every month.

I loved James, he was my future. Maybe now, writing was my past.

January 3rd 2024

The power, of course, cut out at night.

It was January 3rd 2024, three days into the brand new year. I'd spent New Year's Eve alone for the first time in my life.

I was sleeping in Xav's spare room (now my bedroom) as it was blizzarding outside, making the hammock an unenticing prospect. It was pretty late and I was just getting into bed when the bedroom light went out. I thought the bulb had gone but when the hallway lights wouldn't come on either I carefully felt my way downstairs to try to locate the fuse box. Not that I would have had a clue what to do with it.

As I reached the kitchen, Xav's intruder alarm went off. It is a noise I suspect they play over the tannoy in hell; less an alarm and more of a metallic cat screech, ear-shatteringly loud and piercing.

I panicked and ran full pelt from the kitchen straight into the stairs bannister, smacking my face into solid oak and dropping to the floor like a stone.

I came to, lying on the floor, with my face covered in dried blood. I was freezing cold, my head was pounding, and it hurt to breathe through my nose.

The alarm was still shrieking, adding to the agony in my brain, so I went to the hallway cupboard, where I knew the reset switch was, and banged my fist against it.

Blessed silence.

But now I could not only feel the thump, thump, thump of my pounding head but also hear the snuffling noise I was making with each hard-fought breath and it was seriously freaking me out. Too scared and in too much pain to look in the mirror, I crept back to my bedroom, took two Tramadol and two sleeping pills and passed out.

I awoke in darkness once more. The clock on the wall said it was 6 o'clock, but I had no idea whether that was 6 a.m. or 6 p.m.. I fumbled for my mobile phone, which told me it was 06:00.

I gingerly put my hands up to my face; my nose was still there but it felt misshapen and lumpy. I had a large bump under one eye and realised I was struggling to see out of it.

My face felt cold. My hand felt cold. In fact, I was still bloody freezing. The house was freezing, and when I tried the bedside light it still didn't work.

I got up and opened the curtains to let some street light in and it was only then that I fully understood what had happened.

There were no street lights or house lights or any other signs of electricity. As far as I could see out of the window all the lights were off.

The power had gone.

I was in shock. I went down to the kitchen to make a nice cup of tea and have a sit down to think. But then I realised I couldn't make tea any more.

Panic levels rising, I decided to Google 'lights going out' on my phone, but when I went to open the internet there was no Wi-Fi. I switched to 5G.

Nothing.

I hadn't checked anything on my phone in a couple of days and, whether because of the lack of electricity or purely by co-incidence, the internet had also stopped working.

No more internet meant no more daily checks of Facebook, Instagram or Twitter. No more reading old emails or flicking through photos on the cloud.

I burst into hysterical tears.

I wept for the internet and my last connection to my past. I wept for hot tea and hot showers and hot food and central heating and cold beer and TV and music and disco lights and hot tubs on the roof and all of the things that I could no longer have. I wept for the home that I had made for myself that had been easy and warm and cocooned from the horrors outside. I wept for the loss of my cosy post-apocalyptic life. I wept because I was frightened to go outside and face this new, dark world.

As I blubbed snottily over the kitchen counter I realised there was another reason for the growing bubble of panic inside my chest – I was about six hours late for my dose of Tramadol and, despite promising myself I wasn't reliant on it, my body was very strongly telling me that I was.

I dragged my painful and swollen face up the stairs to get my pills and got my first disgusting glimpse of the reality behind my façade of cosy domesticity.

The house was an absolute mess. Rubbish strewn across the floor, piles of rotting food left by my bed, wet towels discarded carelessly, clothes heaped onto every available surface, bottles smashed in the corner, stacked towers of filthy crockery and glasses balanced precariously on scratched, dirty furniture. My bedding was streaked with filth that I couldn't name. Food? Bodily fluids? My room stank.

Added to the horror of the house was my growing realisation at the horror of my situation. What the hell was I doing? I was cocooned in Xav's house enjoying a relaxing narcotic holiday. Why wasn't I looking for anyone else? I was merrily cruising the London tourist trail rather than trying to find out if other people were still alive. What if there were children? Babies? I should have been finding the last survivors of the human race, not lying in a hot tub. I had to get out, find people, do something.

Worst of all – maybe I'd left it too long? I might have missed my chance of finding anyone else alive. I might now really, truly be alone, and it would be entirely my own fault.

I rushed to the bathroom, swallowed down my normal Trams dosage with water from the tap, and then added an extra tablet for good measure.

I hadn't checked the TV since I'd arrived at Xav's to see whether the BBC broadcast was still running and if anybody had used it. It hadn't even crossed my mind that I should be the one that should go there and use it. Why hadn't I used it? My only chance to speak to the entire country at once, to see if there was actually anybody else still alive, and I had been having a fucking disco instead.

I had to go, I had to do something.

I had to get to the BBC building right now.

I didn't think I would be going back to Xav's house.

I look back on it now and think it must have been the drugs playing with my mind but, at the time, I genuinely thought there would still be people out there, that someone would call or come to the BBC when they saw me.

So, before I left the house, I went upstairs to say goodbye and thank you to Xav.

The heating that I had been using had accelerated the decomposition of the bodies dramatically and, even through my broken nose, the smell when I opened the bedroom door was almost enough to make me turn tail and leave.

But he had looked after me in his life, and in his death, and I had resolved to leave the drugs I had taken there with him. He might need them in the afterlife. I held my breath and crossed over to the bed, told Xav I loved him and kissed his stinking, rapidly blackening cheek, put the cocaine and Tramadol on his bedside table, waved a friendly goodbye to the Adonises, and left the room.

Then I went back in and took the Tramadol with me because I am a bad friend, a weak person, and had recently, I realised, become a drug addict.

January 4th 2024

It was snowing heavily so I didn't want to walk to Broadcasting House, but Xav doesn't own a car. Needs must and, as I learnt, stealing a car in this new world is incredibly easy.

I started a technique that day that I still use now. I simply went to the nearest road with plenty of cars parked on the street, broke into the easiest-looking house, found the car keys (almost always in a bowl in the hallway or in the kitchen or in a key safe on the wall), stood on the doorstep of the house and pressed the unlock button on the key. In the silence and dark of the new world the *clunk-click* of car doors opening and the flash of head-lights is like a homing signal.

So, break into house, find keys, use keys to find car, get in car, start engine, drive off; when car runs out of petrol simply repeat the process.

I say 'simply'. It took me an hour to pluck up the courage to break into a house, thirty minutes to realise that keys are mostly kept in the kitchen, and nearly an hour of trying the key in different car doors to work out I could just press the unlock button.

I am not a criminal mastermind.

Also, don't run out of petrol in the middle of nowhere at 3 a.m. when it is pouring with rain and you have no idea where you are. Trust me on that one.

I got to Broadcasting House four hours after leaving Xav's.

The power was still on.

I was worried that I wouldn't know where to go or what to do when I got to the building; but I needn't have been. I think the

BBC must have developed instructions for what to do in the event of a population-decimating apocalypse many years ago. They literally walked me through the entire thing from when I entered the doors to the building.

Printed signs welcomed me and showed me the way to go to the studio, encouraging me to take the stairs rather than the lift in case of power outages.

Once in the studio more signs told me what the equipment did, where to sit, how to put my lapel mike on, where to look, and even what to say.

It was all simple, straightforward, and made so that the most technophobic amongst us would find it easy.

It scared the shit out of me that someone had planned for this.

I realised I had better go and see what my face looked like, and maybe make use of some of the make-up that had been thoughtfully left for me, before sitting in front of the camera.

I followed the handy signs to the toilets and found a body slumped in one of the stalls.

It was the first time I had seen someone who looked like they had died as a result of 6DM rather than T600.

It wasn't pretty.

She was surrounded by her own shit and vomit and had bled from the eyeballs, nose, and ears. Her head was back, her mouth open as if her last act in life had been to scream, either in pain or maybe at the injustice of it all. I didn't recognise her as someone off the TV so maybe she had come here to broadcast before she became ill.

There was nothing I could do for her now. I left the ladies and followed the signs to the gents instead.

There was no one in there.

I looked at my face in the small mirror above the sink.

It was both worse and better than I had imagined.

My left eye, which had been closed and I had been unable to see out of, was a deep shade of purple but had started to open slightly and seemed to be healing already. My nose may have been broken, I'll never know, it was definitely about three times its normal size and flattened dramatically on one side.

The biggest shock though was my general appearance.

I hadn't properly looked in a mirror for about a fortnight. In that time I seemed to have aged five years. The eye that wasn't swollen shut was bloodshot and puffy. My face was bloated and flushed and spotty and had a weird sheen to it that did not look like a natural, healthy glow. Despite using incredibly expensive shampoo, my hair was a dry, messy, wild frizz-ball, and my fringe was already growing over my eyes.

I don't think I am overly vain, but I looked fucking awful and there was no way I was going on TV like this.

I used practically everything in the make-up bag and all the hair products I could find by hunting through the desks of now dead people. It took nearly an hour, but by the time I sat down in front of the camera I was reasonably sure that I looked like an ordinary woman who had suffered a terrible car crash, and not a crazy bag lady whose cat wouldn't even eat her.

I had looked at the suggested text to read in the handy notes left on the desk, but it was strangely stilted and impersonal (Hello. My name is — I am alive and at BBC Centre. If you too are alive, please call me on 0800 915 4650. Thank you). I also wasn't sure where the number they gave would go through to, so I decided to say my own message.

I practised off screen a few times and it sounded fine, but once in front of the camera I panicked and so ended up saying:

'Hi, I mean hello. How are you? Sorry about my face, I bumped into a bannister in the dark. Ha ha! No really, I did, this isn't from someone hitting me (awkward pause). Err, so, I am alive and am at the BBC Centre and am hoping that maybe there is someone else out there alive as well and that if there is you can come here and we can meet. I've been in London and it's fine here so far, but the power is starting to go out so I'd probably get in touch sooner rather than later if I was you. Sorry I'm rambling. So, I am here and I'm going to stay here and it would be great if you could come or give me a call on my mobile. I am on 07689 341244.

I'm going to leave a sign in front of the screen, so you'll have the number. Great. Oh, and Happy New Year. Ha ha. Okay. Sorry. Right, hopefully speak to you soon. Take care . . .'

Then I lost my momentum and sort of just wandered off to the side and then wandered apologetically back on and replaced myself with a big bit of cardboard with my phone number on it.

It was only after I had put the sign up that I realised I had forgotten to give my name.

I went in front of the camera and repeated my speech on the hour, every hour, for the next three days.

I stayed in the BBC Centre, just in case someone came or called. There was food in the vending machines and cafeteria, and plenty of magazines to read, plus there were sofas to sleep on in the dressing rooms of the big stars.

At first, I distracted myself by wandering the halls, looking at photos of famous people doing fabulous things and snooping in dressing rooms and offices; but after a while it got repetitive and who was around to care if I found haemorrhoid cream in the dressing room of a certain well-known newsreader, who was I going to tell? So, I read the magazines and tried to find a dose of Tramadol that made me look relaxed on camera but not zoned out, and also chilled me enough so that I didn't act on my increasing urge to go outside. I tried very hard to convince myself that I wasn't taking more and more Tramadol with less and less effect. But I was.

I was desperately missing James and my mum and dad. I had a permanent ache in my chest that no amount of Tramadol would take away. I couldn't sleep, didn't want to eat, and spent hours staring out of the window hoping and praying that someone would walk past.

By the fourth day, despite the drugs increase, I had gone from calm and friendly to pleading and crying. My time on camera was spent begging someone, anyone, to reply. Please, please, just call me or come here. Please.

I don't want to be alone any more.

By the afternoon of the fourth day I was running out of things to read, things to eat, and hope that anyone was ever going to contact me. I had also run out of Tramadol and was perilously close to full-on panic so I decided to risk going out to replenish my supplies.

It was raining again. The temperature outside had risen in the last two days and the difference in the decomposition rate of the bodies that surrounded me was smell-able (not sure that's a word – I can't look it up). I was sorry that my nose had healed enough for me to start to breathe properly through it again.

London fucking stank.

It smelt a bit like our bin used to smell when we put empty plastic meat trays in there without washing them, or like the food recycling bin after a week in the sun, but it actually smelt far worse than anything I had ever smelt before because I knew what it was. Thousands and thousands of human bodies slowly rotting.

I gagged and gently wrapped my scarf around my face to ward off the stench.

I scrambled into my car and shut the door, gasping happily in the familiar stink of a smoker's vehicle.

I drove the one hundred feet to the nearest chemist and dashed from the car, running through the open front door at full pelt. I skidded on something on the floor and slid on my arse across the room before coming to a sudden stop by banging into the payment desk.

I stood up slowly, yanked my scarf from my face and vomited the Mars Bar I had stuffed down earlier all over the floor of the shop.

Not that it mattered. The floor was already covered in all manner of bodily fluids and by-products. There was a group of bodies to the left of the counter and they had been leaking copiously for some time. It was like I had stepped into the money shot from the world's worst torture porn movie. God knows how they had got there, what they were doing there, or what had happened to make them so . . . runny.

I wasn't going to hang around to try to find out.

Gagging and crying, I slipped and slid from the shop, gasping from the smell and shock. Outside I collapsed to the pavement and wailed out loud to no one. My hands were covered in blood and fluids that no person should ever have to touch, and my clothes were smeared in the same.

I ripped off my clothing and stood naked in the rain trying to wash the physical and mental memory of what I had just encountered from me. I was freezing, but I didn't care. I screamed and screamed into the stinking London air and barely held onto my sanity.

It was only when I paused for breath that I heard someone screaming back.

At first, I thought that it was the chimpanzee again and that I had somehow stepped back into that hellish nightmare, but then I realised it was coming from multiple places and that it wasn't the same voice.

In fact, it wasn't a scream at all.

It was a bark, a wail, a screech, a caterwaul.

I thought back to Xav's neighbour's dog and realised in horror that the noise was the neighbourhood's beloved pets. There must be thousands all over London locked in houses waiting, in vain, for their owners to release them.

What were they drinking? Oh God, what were they *eating*??

That thought snapped me out of my reverie and back to my present naked state.

All my previous middle-class sensibilities and fears now forgotten, I smashed the window of the nearest clothes store, checked for occupants, and then quickly dried and dressed myself. I wrapped a clean scarf around my face, abandoned the car and, ignoring the smell and noise as best I could, jogged back to the BBC.

The power had finally gone out.

In the thirty minutes I had been away, the BBC had been plunged into darkness and any hope I had of contacting other survivors was over.

I sat on the floor.

The internet was gone, TV was gone, I could barely get a signal on my phone, and the landlines were dead. The power was going out rapidly, and food would soon start to go off.

I was scared. Scared of being alone, scared of living, and scared of dying.

All this fear and pain and hopelessness, and yet I still couldn't bring myself to take the T600.

I hated myself.

I hated London.

I couldn't stay there.

I didn't know what to do.

I wished Ginny was with me. Ginny would have known what to do. Ginny always knew what to do.

———

Genevieve Mabuto was the first, and only, real 'girlfriend' I ever had, and the only reason I survived my new office career.

After I left *Shipping and Ports: Global* it should have been nearly impossible for me to find a good job with my lack of office skills and experience. But I simply mentioned my unemployed status to Xav, who braved one of his rare chats with his dad, and a week later I was the executive assistant to the EMEA insurance director at Worldwide Insurance Solutions in the City.

I hated it.

It was obvious I'd never worked in a proper office before. I didn't have a clue what I was doing and everyone around me knew it.

They also knew that I had got the job through my connections and had jumped into a coveted position that had been due to go to someone else.

Hannah Chambers.

Hannah was the executive assistant to the HR director and the leader of the EA gang, and had wanted my role. She never forgave me for getting it.

Hannah was only working at the bank to earn enough money to pay for her flight to go and work with Ugandan refugees. She was pretty and kind and funny to everyone . . . except me. And everyone loved her . . . except me.

The first thing she said to me on my induction day when I turned up in my black trousers and white shirt was 'Catering's downstairs.'

The next day as I walked across the office wearing a similar outfit, she yelled, 'Have you even been home?'

By the end of my first week she was commenting on the frequency of my visits to the bathroom (where I was going to cry). And by the middle of the next week I had stopped drinking after my first cup of tea in the morning so that I only needed to go to the toilet at lunchtime and when I left work. And still she accompanied my every stroll past her desk with some cheery aside like 'Here comes the office's little ray of sunshine.'

Which tells you how fucking miserable I was because I normally am a little ray of fucking sunshine. Well, most of the time

On the Friday of my first week, Hannah walked through the open-plan office loudly declaring that it was 'The EA lunch. Let's go girls.' I grabbed my stuff and walked over to the lifts with everyone else. She waited until I tried to step into the lift and then said, 'Not you. You're not invited.' I thought she was joking, so tried to step forward. She sidestepped, blocking my path. 'You're. Not. Invited.'

As the door closed she gave a sarcastic wave and everyone laughed.

After that I was excluded from everything; lunches, EA meetings, after-work drinks, the 5k charity run. Hannah never missed an opportunity to laugh at me, point out something I'd done wrong, or try to mess my work up. God forbid anyone left a message for me with her – I'd never get it. Yet somehow no one picked her up on it, no one mentioned how horrible she was to me, everyone still loved her.

It was awful.

I should have done something, told someone, put in a complaint

– but I didn't. I slunk in and out of work for a month, and then I gave up.

I got in early on the day I was going to resign so that I could print my resignation letter off without anyone seeing it.

So, I was pretty annoyed when Ginny slapped my resignation letter down on my desk and said, 'You can't resign like that! And why are you resigning? You've got the easiest director here.'

I was resigning because I was completely miserable. Because I desperately missed my ships and my ports and writing about my ships and ports. Because I was being bullied. Because I hated being stuck in an office with women who knew how to dress well and do their make-up and hair correctly when I didn't. Because I didn't have any friends that were girls who could tell me how to do my hair and make-up correctly. Because I used to be a little ray of sunshine and now I wasn't.

I didn't tell Ginny this. I just looked down at my resignation letter and shrugged.

On it I had written:

'Please accept this letter as notice that I am resigning. Thank you and regards.'

Ginny looked at the letter, and then at me, and then she laughed.

'Come on, I'm taking you out.'

Ginny had started in the company as a temporary admin officer. She'd quickly ousted the existing admin manager and taken her place, becoming a permanent member of staff. She then decided she didn't like the title Admin Manager, and so had changed it to Office Manager. She'd accomplished all this in under six weeks.

On paper her role was junior to mine and all the rest of the EAs', but that wasn't how Ginny saw things. Nothing happened in the office without Ginny's knowledge and approval: stationery orders, working rotas, desk changes, sickness approvals, even leave had to be signed off by Ginny. She looked down at all the other admin staff and never deigned to be part of the EA lunches or socials. Within two years she would successfully transition to the EMEA sales team and would be, by far, their top sales person.

On the day I was due to resign, Ginny took me for a two-hour liquid lunch and got me so drunk that I fell asleep with my head on the desk at 4 p.m. and my resignation letter ended up in the recycling bin.

The next week I didn't get invited to the EA lunch again, but I didn't care, I was invited out by Ginny instead.

By the end of that month it was common knowledge in the office that Ginny had my back, and things improved dramatically.

Even Hannah was scared of Ginny.

When Ginny and I were having our, now regular, Friday lunchtime drink, Hannah sidled over to our table. 'We're having an EA meeting this afternoon. You should come along.' She gave her sweetest smile. 'No hard feelings.'

Ginny downed her drink and returned Hannah's smile with a charming one of her own. 'Fuck off Hannah, you total bitch,' she said sweetly.

Hannah never spoke to me again.

———

As much as I wanted her to be, Ginny wasn't with me now. I had to make a decision about my future, I didn't have any choice. The time had come to leave and go to . . .

I didn't have the ending to that sentence yet, but I couldn't live in Broadcasting House, and I didn't want to be in London any more. My love affair with the city was over. The only thing left here was death and memories I couldn't allow myself to think about.

I resolved to spend the next day before I left London stocking up on supplies (drugs) and releasing as many trapped animals as I could.

I soon realised it was mostly dogs that were trapped – people had obviously just let their cats out to fend for themselves, which made me wonder why I hadn't seen more.

In the first three houses I broke into, the dogs were either already dead or too weak to do anything other than cry out helplessly. I was too much of a coward to put them out of their misery so I spooned water into their mouths and left them with plenty of food and water and left the doors to the outside open.

It was heartbreaking.

The fourth that I broke into had a small terrier who bounded up to me, let me scratch him behind his ears, and then skipped happily out of the front door. He was perfectly happy and perfectly fed. How? My imagination immediately jumped to half-eaten corpses sitting in the front room, but this house didn't smell like someone was decaying inside it. I walked through to the kitchen and saw the answer to my question. Six enormous bags of dried dog food ripped open on the kitchen floor and every single bowl, cup, dish, saucepan and piece of Tupperware had been filled with water and distributed throughout the kitchen and front room. The mantelpiece was crowded with photos of an elderly couple walking, playing with, and holding the terrier. At the end they had attempted to provide for the one they loved the most.

I went to six other houses, two with a cat and dog that had nothing, two with dogs that had food and water left for them, and the last two where the dogs had obviously found their own source of food in the way that I most feared. These dogs raced straight out of the houses, snarling and yapping in a way that convinced me the pet-rescuing section of my life story was probably just about done.

The last pet I broke in to free was a golden retriever; bones showing through where his fur had fallen out from lack of nourishment. I thought he was dead at first, but when I got closer he lifted his head and attempted a big doggy smile that I returned in spite of myself. I realised it was the first time I had genuinely smiled in days. I spooned some water into him, and put water and food next to him and left. But as I approached the door I heard him whining behind me and turned to see him struggling, shakily, to his feet to follow me.

I didn't want him.

I wasn't here to start an animal shelter.

I knew then that my Good Samaritan work was over; this, like most things in my new world, was just too upsetting.

I drove back to the nearest residential area and swapped my sensible Golf for a Porsche. It took me nearly two hours to find the right house and the right keys to get the car, but Porsches had been James's favourite and I felt I owed it to him to leave London in style.

I went to the nearest supermarket and filled the boot of the car (which it took me a good ten minutes to work out was in the bonnet) with food and water.

Then, despite my previous protestations, I went back and got the golden retriever. I don't know why, maybe it was because he had made me smile. Maybe it was because I was so painfully lonely.

No amount of drugs could displace that.

I carried the bag of bones that was the dog to my car while all around us other creatures wailed and barked and screeched.

I put the dog on the passenger seat, got in, revved the engine loudly to drown the noise from outside, and left London for the final time.

I named the dog Lucky.

January 10th 2024

I didn't have a plan when I left London. I didn't know where I was going, had no idea what I should do next. I just wanted to get out, to get somewhere with no sounds, no smells, and no imprisoned animals to feel guilty about.

The roads out of the city were empty. Once more I saw a few crashes, a few abandoned cars, but no traffic and, thankfully, no corpses. Street and traffic lights still worked and I obeyed them out of habit.

I saw no plumes of smoke this time. I supposed that the constant snow and drizzle must have, at last, put out the fires.

I was still regularly seeing people out of the corner of my eye but, after climbing thirty-six flights of stairs on my last day in London to investigate what turned out to be battery-operated Christmas lights and a life-size cardboard cut-out of Elvis, I was getting far more picky about which of these ghostly figures I followed up on.

Although I very nearly did take Elvis with me.

Because it was the first motorway I saw signs for, I got on the M1 and headed north.

It was completely deserted. I saw maybe one abandoned car every hundred or so miles, but that was it.

It was satisfying to be on the move and leaving the city behind.

The Porsche only had a Bluetooth system so I couldn't play music, but the engine made a pleasing purr that reverberated through the car. It was like driving a giant kitten. The rain had stopped and it wasn't cold enough to be icy, so driving on the empty roads was easy. Lucky was curled up asleep in the passenger seat, snoring softly and filling the car with the smell of wet dog, which, under normal circumstances, would have been unpleasant, but was strangely comforting after the smells of the last few days.

In homage to James, I decided to open up the Porsche and see how fast she could go. I was zooming along at 105 mph when there was a frightening screech from the back wheels and I skidded across two lanes; which would almost certainly have meant certain death if the road had been as busy as usual.

I didn't want to risk crashing the car and bleeding slowly to death alone on the M1, so I reduced my speed to a sedate 60 mph.

I was continually distracted with the changing landscape that bordered the motorway. Already things were falling into disrepair. The rain and wind had caused mud and rockslides on banks bordering the road and, with no one to shore it up, initial damage that might have been quite small had grown rapidly. Building sites were a mess, with cranes tipped, tarpaulin flapping, and caravans overturned. In one place the bank at the side of the motorway had slid away and the entire hard shoulder was missing. I saw two bridges partially collapsed.

Perhaps more worrying was the lack of electricity in many towns and villages. I had expected it to happen in London where ambient usage was huge but thought that the smaller, less populated areas would be fine.

I was wrong.

There seemed to be no rhyme nor reason to the outage. Watford was dark, but Luton (much bigger) still had power. The next-door neighbour of a village that still had power would be without. I would drive through miles of motorway with no lights and then suddenly be floodlit in the most random of areas.

If I hadn't been so enthralled with the changing landscape and scenery I might have noticed the petrol gauge on the Porsche flashing.

I doubt it, though, as I didn't know where the petrol gauge was.

I do now.

Nothing dramatic happened, the car just stopped working.

One minute we were cruising along, the next, sliding sedately to a halt in the middle lane of the M1.

In the middle of the night.

In the middle of nowhere.

The dashboard said it was 3.24 a.m. and two degrees outside.

I knew that we were past Northampton, but had no idea how far past or how far it was to the nearest town or village. We were on a dark patch of motorway and I could see no lights as far as the horizon. It was pitch black and it was raining again.

For a while I sat and watched rain drizzle silently onto the windscreen. The car got cold quickly without the engine running, and I knew that I would freeze if I tried to wait for the sun to come up.

Lucky woke up, whined at either the cold or the dark, and shuffled across onto my lap. He (I didn't know how to confirm this but I was going to go with 'he' for now) was warm and comforting so I let him stay.

In less than five minutes he was shivering, and my feet were freezing, so I knew we'd have to leave the car.

I hadn't brought a map or a torch or shoes, apart from a pair of Ugg boots that were more slipper than boot. I had a waterproof jacket, but not trousers. I had twenty bottles of water and plenty of food, but nothing to carry them in except 10p supermarket plastic carrier bags.

I pulled a couple more jumpers on and pulled the jacket over the top. I wrapped each of my boots in plastic bags and put a couple of bottles of water and two Mars Bars in another to take with me. I had no hat, scarf or gloves, so I put the hood of my jacket up and pulled the strings so it was tight around my face.

I came very close to leaving Lucky in the car, but I was worried that he might freeze to death. I put a jumper on him, too, to cover up the bald patches, and hoped he'd be able to walk far enough to make it to wherever we were going.

Obviously, I had no idea where that was.

Outside it was much, much colder than it had been in London. The section of motorway that we were on was a flat plain, exposed on both sides, and the wind was racing across, driving relentless drizzle straight into my face.

Lucky whined loudly and I didn't blame him.

We started walking.

I decided to stick to the motorway as I had no way of knowing if there was anything nearby and I knew there would be a service station at some point. I just didn't know how far it would be.

We walked for about fifteen minutes before I realised I had left the Tramadol, my mobile phone and charger in the car.

I don't know why I still kept my mobile charged and on. I had no internet access, no one had called me and I had no one left to call, but I wasn't ready to give it up yet. I think I still had hope I might need it at some point. Plus, there was no way I was leaving without the bag of drugs.

So, we turned around and walked back to the car.

I am sure that, by this point, Lucky was regretting that he had come with me. He must have wished he'd taken his chances back in his house.

I have no idea how long or how far we walked.

It was the most miserable night of my life. At least when James had died I had been warm and dry.

I took the plastic bags off my feet pretty soon after we left the car; they filled with water, making walking difficult and completely negating their purpose. My 'waterproof' jacket started to leak across my shoulders and down my back. My hands and feet were soaked, frozen, and lumpen, so that I had to sort of stomp along like some post-apocalyptic ogre.

I have no idea how Lucky kept going for so long. He was so skinny and angular, could hardly walk, and had only eaten half a can of dog food before I put him in the car. I soon had to take the jumper off him as it was soaked through with rain and dragging along the ground. Still, mile after mile, he shambled along, his fur soaked through, highlighting his tiny, emaciated frame.

Lucky gave up just as the sky was beginning to lighten on the right-hand side of the motorway. One minute he was dragging along beside me, a ramshackle bag of bones and dripping fur; the next he was . . . gone. I thought at first he had run off but then I turned and looked back along the motorway and saw he had collapsed on the road behind me.

I left him.

I was freezing and in pain and tired and didn't even know if I was going to make it, so to take him with me would have been ridiculous.

I got about twelve steps before I turned around.

I'm selfish, not a total monster.

I heaved him up into my arms, his sopping wet fur drenching me even further, and began to shuffle forward.

The sun was all the way up (or as much as I could see through the clouds and drizzle) and I was counting to a hundred and then sitting down for good when I saw a 'Services – 1 m' sign in the distance.

My initial reaction was to put Lucky down and leave him on the road, get to the services, then get a car to come back and get him.

But, for once, I was completely honest with myself and admitted that if I left him here I wouldn't be coming back for him. He chose that moment (wisely) to open his eyes and try to lick my face, which he was pathetically unable to summon up the strength to do, and that only made it cuter.

I staggered off the motorway into the services complex with Lucky half thrown over my shoulder, my jacket and clothes soaked through and my Ugg boots a tattered mess dragging from my feet.

I have never been so happy to see a Days Inn Motel in my life.

The reception doors were open and the foyer was full of rain, rubbish and leaves, but they had electricity, which meant they might have heating and hot water.

I was grinning like an idiot.

The room doors were controlled by computer key card.

I stopped grinning.

I went to the first floor of rooms, put Lucky down, and tried each of the room doors. They were all locked.

In frustration I kicked the door of the nearest room as hard as I could.

It caved in with hardly any protest and swung back.

My mouth fell open. Either being the last person alive had given me super-powers or the security in the hotel was not good at all.

I couldn't give a shit which it was.

The room was mercilessly empty, with a big clean double bed, fresh towels, and a shower that spouted out sweet, scalding water.

I picked up Lucky and put him down in the bath at the end opposite the shower. Then I stripped and stepped creakily under the water, my aching muscles and bones crying out at being made to step up and over.

The last, however many, hours finally caught up with me as I stood in the boiling water and cried. Not tears of sadness but of joy at the simple euphoria of finally being warm and wet from water that was not freezing rain. I washed and shampooed myself and did the same for Lucky. He protested at first but after a while he couldn't deny the joy of warm water, and he rolled onto his back so I could gently soap his frighteningly thin, furry belly.

I patted him for the first time and he grinned back.

I dried us both in the huge white towels, put a couple of blankets on the floor for Lucky, and then climbed into the clean, warm bed with a sigh of happiness.

As I was drifting off to sleep I realised I hadn't taken my nightly 'medicine' but I was too warm and comfy to care.

A while later Lucky climbed awkwardly onto the bed and lay next to me.

I didn't push him off.

I was woken by Lucky licking my cheek. I was shivering and slimy with sweat.

I had turned the heating on full blast and the room was as hot as Hades, so I wasn't shivering because I was cold.

I had a brief moment of shock that I could be detoxing so quickly. But this was soon overridden by nausea, my pounding head, and the fact that my eye had developed a constant twitch.

I castigated myself for forgetting to take my pills yet again and vowed to be more regimented with my routine in the future. Then I popped my pills and lay back on the bed waiting for them to take effect.

I had a brief moment of clarity where I realised I should probably be more worried that it now seemed I was a fully-fledged drug addict than upset that I didn't have a strict enough drug-taking routine, but by the time the Tramadol were working their magic I was more concerned that I was now lying in soaking sheets and that I might imminently die of thirst and hunger.

My clothes were still drenched from the day before and the Days Inn doesn't stretch to bath robes, so I wrapped myself in a big blanket from the cupboard and ran barefoot across the car park to the food court, with Lucky shambling after me.

Thank you Watford Gap Services, you literally saved my life.

All the shops were open. I raided WHSmith, drinking three bottles of water and gorging on crisps and chocolate. I was worried about what to feed Lucky, but found some Dairylea Lunchables in the fridge that were still in date and he seemed happy with the ham from them.

Next, I kitted myself out with clean clothes from Cotton Traders. No knickers and only Crocs for shoes, but, after the day before, I wasn't planning on ever walking again and I reasoned that no one was alive to tell me off for going commando.

There were frozen burgers, baps and chips in McDonald's, and my mouth watered at the thought of them, but I had no idea how to work the cooking equipment so would most likely have burnt the place down trying to make my feast.

Further exploring uncovered a restaurant with a freezer-load of meals and a microwave. I ate mac 'n' cheese, lasagne, fish pie, and was just starting on a shepherd's pie when I was forced to admit defeat before I vomited. I put the pie on the floor and after some exploratory sniffing Lucky wolfed it down and whined at me until I got him another.

Clothed, dry, warm, and full, I wandered over to the huge windows that looked out across the car park and motorway.

It was getting dark again.

The motorway was empty and there were only five cars in the car park that I could see. Wind had blown rubbish and leaves and small branches around and one of the trees was half fallen and blocking the exit.

But it wasn't this that made it feel particularly post-apocalyptic.

It was the stillness.

I was in a place that was usually bright and inhabited 24/7, someone always awake, always moving.

The car park was still. The motorway was still. I was still, and even Lucky was lying still beside me.

Everything had stopped.

And it would never start again.

Ever.

My fight for survival was over. I felt a wave of depression washing over me.

Let's face it, no one ever wrote poetry about the Watford Gap Service Station when it was alive, fully functioning and inhabited, so I was hardly going to see the joy in it now that it was figura-tively dead.

I took Lucky back to the room and went straight to bed.

My sheets were still soaked, but I was too exhausted to change them so I just lay on top of the bed, wrapped myself in another blanket, and cried myself to sleep with a distressed Lucky whining along.

I woke early the next morning with a renewed sense of purpose.

I had charged my phone the day before and the clock told me it was 6am, so I had plenty of daylight ahead of me.

I knew what I had to do.

It felt like an icy hand was holding my heart, but I knew I was making the right decision.

I had to kill myself.

———————

I have felt that icy hand holding my heart before.

Just once.

James and I had been living together for about a year and, although we were still just about clinging onto the honeymoon period of our relationship, real life was already beginning to push its way into our happiness bubble.

James had been promoted at work, but his new job meant more hours, more stress, and fewer evenings at home with me. I had been in my new role for a few months but was beginning to wonder why I had agreed to take a job that meant I was home more when that time at home was increasingly spent by myself.

We'd had a couple of fights, nothing huge, just scraps about who should do the hoovering, whose turn it was to empty the dishwasher, who should go shopping after work now that James was coming home later. I soon found the answer to most of those questions was me.

That New Year's Eve we went to a fancy party organised by James's work, held in some posh restaurant with far-reaching views of the Thames and midnight fireworks. James had raised his eyebrows at my red, full-skirted 1950s cocktail dress, stating that most of the other women would be in little black numbers. I'd made an effort and thought I looked pretty, so was a bit disappointed he didn't even say I looked nice.

He was right. The room was full of tight, black dresses, a few sequins here and there, the odd jumpsuit. I was awkward, wanted to go home and change. James put his arm round my waist, said it was too late now, I could wear black next time.

I was soon distracted; free food, free booze, great music, it was a brilliant night. My red dress worries were forgotten.

Post-midnight, and the DJ was doing an excellent job, building the tempo, dropping in a few classics every now and again. Hardly anyone was on the dance floor. I was itching to dance; I was drunk, the music was good and I felt sorry for the DJ up there in his booth all alone with no one to appreciate him. Then he played Ten City 'That's the Way Love Is' and I was up and grabbing James's hand, dragging him onto the dance floor before he had time to protest.

For the first minute or so I was too drunk and happy to notice I was, unfortunately, the only one dancing. James was standing practically still, his face a stony mask of anger and shame. I stopped my joyous bopping abruptly to find a large majority of the room watching our unfolding dance floor drama.

Instantly sober, my heart plummeted. I grabbed James's unyielding hand and led him from the dance floor, smiling as though it had all been a merry joke.

I could feel the rage coming off of him in waves.

Back at the table he gripped the top of my arm slightly too hard.

'Don't ever fucking do that to me again.'

He stood up and went to the bar.

He didn't come back.

And that was when I first felt it. An icy hand holding my heart.

For the first time I realised this wasn't a given. We weren't set in stone. I could upset James. I could lose him.

I never danced with James again.

Not even on our wedding day.

———

So, icy hand on my heart or not, the decision was made.

If the only people left were the dead, then I would join them.

But, before I took that final step to end it all I first had to be completely sure, or as sure as it was possible to be, that I really was the last person alive.

So, I was going on a road trip.

I was going to drive to a remote part of Scotland and find a remote farmhouse and see if 6DM really had wiped out the rest of the human race.

If it had, I would kill myself.

While I was still sane enough to do it.

January 12th 2024

A strange sense of calm came over me as I breakfasted on mac 'n' cheese and planned my road trip.

My disastrous motorway breakdown had taught me a lesson. I wasn't going to get stuck like that again. If I was going to the wilds of Scotland I was going prepared. So, I needed to go shopping and Northampton was the closest place to do it, even if it did mean doubling back to get there.

As the sun started to rise, I went out to look at the vehicles in the car park.

I looked in the first HGV. There was a human-shaped mound covered with a blanket lying across the front seats. Lined up on the dashboard was a series of photos: a woman in her early forties smiling happily, three laughing kids on the beach, a family laughing on a picnic blanket, a school photo of the same three children. In front of each photo was a small bunch of (now dead) wild flowers. A simple display of love that made tears prickle in my eyes once more. I walked away quickly.

I decide to discount the rest of the HGVs – I wouldn't know how to drive them anyway.

I investigated the five cars instead.

Three of them were empty of occupants and keys.

The fourth had a very badly decomposing, extremely large man wedged into the front seat. There was blood and vomit on the windows and dashboard, and the smell was discernible even outside the car. I decided that moving him had to be a very, very last resort.

The fifth had a family in it.

Dad in the driver's seat with the mum in the back cuddling a toddler and an eight- or nine-year-old. They were all lightly purple, and the dad was starting to turn black around the edges, but none of them showed any signs that they were suffering from 6DM. They were just sitting there. No blankets or toys for the kids. Just like they had stopped for a wee and then thought, 'Fuck it, this is as good a place as any. Let's die here.'

With the kids.

At first, I was so shocked I just stood and stared.

Then I was angry. Really angry.

Here.

In the service station car park.

The Natural History Museum I can understand, but who the fuck drives their kids to a motorway service station to die? Maybe they were on their way to see someone? Maybe the car ran out of petrol and there was no more to fill it up with? But surely they could have got a room in the motel? Been in bed together, warm and cosy? And if he had petrol, why not drive elsewhere? A river? Even over the other side of the fucking car park to look at some trees.

The more I thought about it the angrier I got.

I stomped about the car park muttering to myself. I came back to the car and thumped my hands on the window. I tried to push and shake the car. I was filled with physical rage.

In the end I opened the car door and punched the dad in the face. He was on the verge of rotting and my fist pushed far deeper into his flesh than I like to think about after the event. I quickly shut the door again and staggered back, falling and landing on my arse.

I was breathing deeply and still muttering, my rage not yet completely spent.

Lucky, sitting a few paces back, whined.

I think he was beginning to realise I may not be the all-knowing rescuer that he thought I was.

I left the cars where they were. I couldn't face the fat man or the family.

I wandered to the petrol station, but there was nothing there.

There was, however, the beginnings of a building site next door where they had been doing groundwork for a building that would never now be built.

There was a small CAT digger with the keys in the ignition. It started first time and drove exactly like a car.

I put an extremely indignant Lucky into the digger bucket bit and we left the service station for Northampton at a roaring 5 mph.

Lucky was whining and shaking and I don't think he liked me very much at that point, but, for the first time in a very long while, I found I didn't particularly care what someone else thought of me.

————

When did I start caring so much what other people thought of me in my life before 6DM?

I want to say it was when James and I got together and especially after the New Year's Eve incident, but I don't think I can blame this one on James.

I know I wasn't that bothered when I was in my early twenties. No one was looking at me when I was working for the music paper – not when I was reporting on or interviewing bands far more exciting and glamorous than me. And of course there was no workplace dress-code at *Shipping and Ports: Global*.

Xav never cared what I looked like. Don't make the mistake of trying to stereotype him because he was gay. Xav was no more interested in hair and make-up than the average bloke (although he did have a rather unhealthy obsession with Tom Ford clothing and aftershave; and a rather unhealthy obsession with Tom Ford himself). My friendship with Xav was filled with dingy pubs or basement raves, music, gigging and festivals and five-hour debates about which was the best Springsteen album, but there were no makeovers or pillow fights.

I mean, I liked to look nice, wash my hair and put a pretty dress on, make an effort if we were going to a party. But I'd never had a blow-dry, had my nails done, got a spray tan, or gone to the MAC counter at Selfridges for a makeover. I think those are the sorts of things you do with friends who are girls, friends who have hair as long as yours.

But then I got a proper job in a proper office with proper women who owned more than one pair of high-heeled shoes. They looked amazing. I wanted to look amazing.

I wanted to look like the women in black at James's work events. I wanted to make James proud of me.

I was ripe, ready, and raring for a change. I wanted to become a woman.

Ginny was more than happy to help.

The ensuing makeover could have been ripped straight out of a 90s teen romcom with Ginny as my Fairy Godmother of style. She took me for a manicure ('you're not working on the docks any more'). She took me for a wax ('Jesus Christ, you can see that muff from space!'). She took me to a fancy salon that charged four times my normal hairdresser's price to cut and highlight my hair. It was worth the money.

Ginny was the first woman I properly went out to do 'girl-things' with. And it was brilliant and exhilarating and completely unlike anything I had done before. It was the new and exciting rush of moving in with James all over again, except this was better because this wasn't just a new relationship – this was a new me. A better me.

Ginny took me shopping and helped me choose new clothes, we had facials and got HD eyebrows. We went to cocktail bars and to nightclubs where the walls weren't sticky and people actually talked to each other rather than looking at the stage.

For the first time in my life I felt like a proper woman, and it was fun. Dressing up and doing my hair and make-up was fun, and being acknowledged for dressing up and doing my hair and make-up was fun.

Ginny was fun.

She was loud and adventurous and opinionated and, while I

increasingly craved the approval of others, Ginny couldn't care less what people thought of her. She was brave and bold enough for the two of us so, when I was with her, I could happily let her take charge, safe in the knowledge that we would always end up somewhere interesting and doing something exciting.

Plus, she really loved to dance.

For the first time in years, when Xav called, I was too busy to see him.

When we did finally meet, he stared at me.

'You look different.'

I smiled and tossed my newly highlighted hair.

'It doesn't suit you,' he said.

––––––––

It took three hours to get from the service station back to Northampton's residential area, and another hour to get a car and find the sort of store I needed.

I had never been to Go Outdoors before, but the name seemed to suggest that it might be what I was looking for.

The doors were open, but nothing had been taken, which wasn't surprising. Maybe if there had been more time, people might have thought about heading out to the wilds to escape 6DM, but there wasn't and they didn't.

For the record, Go Outdoors is a complete treasure trove for those looking to survive in the post-apocalyptic landscape. I highly recommend you pay it a visit if you ever need survivalist equipment to get by in this new world, which, of course, you won't.

The store was huge.

They had massive three-, four- and even five-section tents erected in the middle of the shop, and these were just a drop in the ocean of the camping and hiking equipment that they stocked. It had everything: clothes, tents, camping stuff, fishing stuff, skiing stuff, boots, rucksacks, bikes, a whole section full of things to do with horses, and everything you needed to furnish, attach, and pull a caravan.

Within an hour I had a whole new survivalist wardrobe, complete with cold weather clothing, wet weather clothing, thermal underwear (which I immediately put on), hiking boots, running shoes, warm boots, wellies, hats, scarves, gloves and goggles. I had water carriers, food tins, saucepans, three different types of lighter, a camping stove, sleeping bags, blankets, torches, a cool box, drinking bottles, and (optimistically) sun cream. I had a small rucksack, a big rucksack, and a first aid kit.

I'd collected enough equipment to fill a small van and by the time I had managed to stuff it all into the car only the driver's seat was empty. Lucky would have to perch on the sleeping bags I had stowed on the passenger seat.

The shop had no power and it was getting dark and very cold, so I decided to spend the night in one of the massive tents. I put sleeping bags on the floor and picked the warmest one I could find to lay on top of them and then covered that with the next warmest one. I made a nest out of sleeping bags next to my bed for Lucky.

I ate protein bars and Kendall Mint Cake for dinner, but Lucky turned his nose up at these culinary delights. I reasoned he'd not starve from missing one meal. Well, he'd not starve any more than he already had from missing one more meal. He looked at me reproachfully as I ate, and then wandered off in a huff.

I'd popped a couple of sleeping pills and was just drifting off in my sleeping bag bed when I heard Lucky growling and racing about on the other side of the store. I was warm, comfy and sleepy, so had decided to leave him to it when the growling turned to barking and then he went into a frenzy of growling and knocking things over before falling completely silent.

Reluctantly, and with growing concern, I climbed out of my cocoon. It was freezing. I jogged across the store in the direction of the noise.

Lucky had his back to me and was wagging his tail. Satisfied he was alive, I was about to head back to my warmth when he turned and gave me his big doggy grin.

I froze.

His mouth and nose were covered in blood. In front of him was a massive, bloody, dead rat. Half eaten.

Seeing me, Lucky picked the rat up, turned and dropped it at my feet.

I stared at the rat and then at him.

'No thanks, I've already eaten,' I said (or tried to say, I hadn't spoken in a few days so my voice was a little croaky).

He gave me a look that seemed to say, 'Your loss,' and went back to chewing on his rat.

I backed away slowly and tried to ignore the noisy crunching.

I woke up the next morning cold and stiff and vowing that I would never spend a night in a tent again.

Lucky was next to me, blood crusted about his mouth. I was torn between being disgusted and being relieved that he could provide for himself if he had to.

I didn't fancy protein bars for breakfast but luckily there was a massive Asda across the road from Go Outdoors. The doors were closed and much bigger than the flimsy ones I had broken through in London. I went back to Go Outdoors, found a mallet, and carefully started to smash through the outer door into Asda's enclosed foyer. I was going to smash through one of the windows, but was nervous about breaking such a huge pane of glass. As it was I ducked and ran away dramatically every time the mallet hit. It turned out it was safety glass, so broke into small chunks rather than huge jagged shards. I was almost disappointed.

First door successfully managed, I was just about to start on the inner door when Lucky whined.

I looked down at him and he whined again, staring through the door into the shop. I turned to see what he was staring at.

There was a single rat sitting just the other side of the door, peering through at us.

'Making friends with your next meal?'

I have no love for rats, but they don't freak me out the way they do some people. I was actually surprised that I hadn't seen more of them, now that there were no humans to chase them away.

I banged on the window to get rid of the rat.

It didn't move. In fact, it came closer and sniffed me through the crack in the doors.

'Cheeky little bugger,' I said, and banged harder.

Lucky whined once more so I turned to look at him again.

'Why don't you go in there and get it then?'

But he wasn't looking at me.

Twenty yards away, at the bottom of one of the massive glass windows in front of the tills there was a HUGE group of rats milling and scurrying about. Now that my attention had been drawn to them, I could hear a cacophony of chirps and squeaks through the glass. There must have been maybe two hundred of the squeaky fuckers, and some of them were big. Not big like a dog, but maybe the size of a small cat, so definitely not something you wanted crawling up your leg.

They seemed focussed on that one section of floor, running back and forth over a large lump, occasionally stopping with their tails in the air.

The rat at the door was still sniffing the air and now had his paws on the glass as if trying to push the doors open.

He let out a massive squeal.

The rats swivelled as one to face their compadre.

They paused for the briefest moment and then flooded towards the door where Lucky and I were standing, flowing over, and revealing for the first time, the mound with which they had been so preoccupied.

Whatever it had been it was now merely bone and gristle. It might have been one person or two, or maybe a group reduced to nothing more than leftovers.

There had been good times for these rats, but now their meal was coming to an end, and their eyes were on the next prize.

They were at the door in seconds, moving as a carpet of fur and tails. They went immediately onto their hind legs; scraping at the glass, checking for ways through. The majority centred on the crack between the doors and I swear I saw them get their little paws between and try to pry them open.

I backed off in disgust and horror.

Was this how the new world would be? Rats, who had discovered the joys of eating human flesh, hunting in packs that you'd never be able to avoid. Had the leftovers from their last meal even been dead before they started eating?

I tried not to, but I couldn't help but throw up my breakfast protein bar. The sight of my fresh regurgitated stomach contents seemed to excite the rats even more, and their scraping and squealing intensified – 'She's filled with good stuff lads! Let's get her while she's warm!'

Lucky was already halfway to the car, shivering, with his tail between his legs. I jogged over to join him.

'Let's go.'

He didn't need telling twice. Healthy sense of self-preservation that dog has.

I opened the car and hoisted Lucky onto the passenger seat and then squeezed into the driver's seat.

I was convinced that I could still hear the squealing and scrabbling of the rats. I purposely didn't look back as I locked the doors and started the car.

We drove slowly past Asda.

The rats weren't at the window.

Lucky barked and I turned to see the rats streaming from around the corner of the store.

They had come out through the back doors and were hunting us.

They were smart and resourceful. I was fucking petrified. I revved the engine and the wheels of the car screeched as I spun out of the car park. I looked in my rear-view mirror and swear I saw some of the rats give chase.

Lucky crawled onto my lap and, despite the fact it made driving hard, I let him. I needed the comfort of an animal that wasn't going to eat me. The thought of having slept the night in Go

Outdoors with the doors open and no protection was making me want to vomit again.

What might have happened if Lucky hadn't killed that rat? Was it a scout for the others? I patted Lucky again and again.

'Good boy, good boy, good boy.'

I drove around until I found the 'posh' part of town. I wanted a big rugged vehicle and, if possible, enough food to keep me going for a few days. I had decided I was going to avoid supermarkets from now on.

I came to a wide, well-maintained road that was lined with large houses set well back at the end of long driveways.

I decided this was the road for me.

The first two houses were occupied and, although I didn't see the corpses, I could smell them. I worked fast, now that I was aware that there may well be visitors other than me, and went straight to the kitchens where the inevitable key bowl or stand would be. The houses each had a Mercedes, one had a BMW, and the other an Audi, but neither was big enough for my needs. The third house had a good-sized minivan (no idea of the make) but it had less than a quarter tank of petrol when I started it up so I left it. No one was home in houses four, five, six and seven, but there were no cars either.

In the eighth house I hit the motherlode.

The house was the same size as the others on the street but looked older, grimier, and paint was peeling from the window frames. There were no cars parked outside, but there was a double garage, so I broke into the house to see if there were car keys. Inside, there was no discernible smell of rotting, but I knew that didn't mean there weren't dead people in there somewhere and I wasn't inclined to go hunting for bodies.

The house was bare and plain. Small sofa and TV, old-fashioned kitchen, well-worn carpet. Nothing like the opulence I had found in the other houses.

I found the fob for the automatic garage and opened it up.

I was initially disappointed with the Land Rover inside. It was an old model Defender, functional and sturdy, but definitely not the sexy SUV or American-style truck I had been hoping for. But as I looked closer even I, who have no car knowledge whatsoever, could see that it was well cared for. The back seats had been removed to make more space, it looked like it could handle a tough terrain, started first time, and had a full tank of diesel.

When I looked under the tarpaulin at the back of the garage I knew this was most definitely the truck for me. There were five large canisters filled with diesel. I didn't even have to open them to check; the smell once the tarpaulin was removed convinced me.

I thought I'd try the other side of the garage just to see if it held anything better, but the fob wouldn't open it.

Instead it had an electronic keypad protection system thing.

Now I was really intrigued. What the hell was in there?

I knew I had no chance of guessing the code, so my curiosity would have to go unanswered.

However, I thought I'd try the obvious before giving up.

1234#

Nothing.

Damn.

I kicked the garage door. It was much heavier than the other one and now I *really* wanted to see inside.

I yanked at it in frustration.

Turns out when electricity stops it either shuts electronic doors for ever or does the opposite. Luckily for me this had done the opposite.

The door swung up easily on well-oiled hinges.

The inside of the garage was so unexpected that for a moment I thought I was hallucinating.

I turned to look at Lucky, but he had chosen this moment to take a crap on the front lawn.

I turned back.

The walls were lined with shelves that were in turn stocked with row upon row of food and drink. Boxes of toiletries were stacked to the roof. Bags of unidentifiable equipment hung from the ceiling. Two massive chest freezers hummed in the corner, filled with frozen meats and vegetables. The other corner was taken up with books, DVDs, and CDs. One whole shelf was filled with something I didn't recognise at first, but now know to be fully automated phone chargers. Just plug it into your phone, wait five minutes, and bingo – fully charged.

The room was rammed with stuff, leaving just a narrow walkway to the back of the garage.

Where a door stood open and inviting.

It was, to my utter disbelief, some kind of underground bunker.

In the outskirts of Northampton, someone had been planning for the end of the world.

January 13th 2024

At first I was far too afraid to go into the bunker; what if the door shut and I was stuck in there?

I poked my head in, but could only see steps leading down.

I called out.

'Hello?'

My voice echoed into the brightly-lit passageway. No one replied. Obviously.

In the end curiosity won out again and I reasoned that there was: a) no one left to shut the door on me; b) bound to be a way to open the door from the inside unless they were planning to live down there forever; and c) if there *was* someone down there, they *probably* wouldn't want to murder me.

I still left a couple of heavy boxes propping the door open.

To be honest it was a bit disappointing.

Like the Defender, it was all substance over style.

The stairs came down into a central hall space and to the right was a large storeroom. On the other side of the hall was a small living space complete with sofa, table and chairs, TV, DVD player, and an old-fashioned music system. There was a small kitchen, then a bedroom with two sets of bunk beds and at the back a tiny toilet and shower. The water still worked, and there was air conditioning and power.

Still, an extremely depressing place to live out the apocalypse. Imagine sharing bunk beds in a bedroom with your parents for two years. Or longer.

They must have been planning to move all the stuff from the garage down into the storeroom.

But they never got the chance.

What happened? Did they get sick too quickly? Did they chicken out? Decide it was too depressing to lock themselves away for God knows how long? They weren't even in the house, so had they gone away and not managed to get back here? Imagine missing out on your life's work because you decided to take a quick last-minute trip to Spain and the PM randomly decided to close the borders while you were there? Imagine dying because of that.

At least this explained the austerity in the house. That's perhaps the most depressing thing. Living a lesser life so that you could live longer, and then dying before you ever got the chance.

I wanted to feel sorry for them, but my mind was filled with the memory of the steak I had seen in the freezer, the gas cooker in the house that still worked, the plain but comfy beds upstairs, and the front door that I could shut against small, furry intruders.

Steak, sleep, and security beats sadness every time in this new world.

I went back through the garage, filled my arms with food and drink from the store, called Lucky in from the garden, and went into the house.

I shut the front door.

Firmly.

With food, drink, books, and comfy beds in abundance I think I might have easily slipped into another state of lethargy in the house, except for one thing.

It was cold.

Really fucking cold.

In the house itself there was no central heating, no fireplace, no hot water, and no getting away from the fact it was the middle of winter and I was not used to a life without heat.

Of course, the heating worked in the bunker, but having to keep the door to the garage open meant it was only ever luke-warm at best, and even sitting wrapped in coats and blankets I was never fully cosy.

I tried to make myself shut the door. I played the argument over and over in my head. Why have a door that you couldn't open from the inside? I studied the door mechanism. It was a simple wheel that matched the one on the front and must therefore, surely, perform the same function. I tried it while the door was open and the locks moved in and out as they should.

If I could shut the door I would be toasty.

But, every time I moved to shut it I could feel panic rising in me, pushing past the drugs that had so efficiently kept it at bay in the last few weeks, and I knew that a full-blown panic attack would definitely be the end of sane old me.

I left the door open.

Plus, Lucky resolutely refused to come into the bunker. I tried treats, pleading, shouting, even carrying him in; he just ran straight back out again. He would not do it. If I was in the bunker, he was in the cold garage, and any time I spent down there was sound-tracked by his whining and accompanied by my guilt.

So, when I woke up on the fifth day to find the rain and clouds gone and bright sunlight at the window, I knew the time had come to leave on my expedition to find life . . . or death.

I ditched fifty per cent of the stuff I'd taken from Go Outdoors and replaced it with things from the bunker. Diesel, water, food, medicine, whatever I thought might come in handy. The back of the Defender was stuffed to the gills. I worried briefly about whether it was dangerous to take all the diesel, but then reasoned that I would rather die quickly in a fireball than slowly trapped in wreckage if we crashed.

This is how my mind now worked. I was changing to fit my new environment, just like I had changed to fit into my old one.

————

People don't change overnight, physically or emotionally.

I didn't wake up suddenly one morning in my late twenties and become a different person.

Instead, every day, there was a slight shift in me, so subtle that

I didn't even notice to begin with, a fraction of a fraction of a degree of something new, something not me; and by the time I did notice that things – that I – was changing, it was too late; I had already begun to forget the person I used to be.

It might have begun with my relationship with James, my new career on the corporate ladder, my friendship with Ginny, my increasing need for the approval of those around me, but there were a hundred things afterwards that added to it.

It was a gradual thing, the tiniest, smallest changes that aren't worth bothering about.

The physical changes that were part of my makeover needed maintenance; my haircut, nails, eyebrows, waxing, the new clothes needed a new diet and exercise regime to ensure I could fit into them. Small things, filling my life with a barrage of time-consuming rituals that helped me feel less empty.

I joined a gym and gave up carbs. I got rid of my wet weather gear and started shopping in Zara and Warehouse. I learnt how to do a cat's-eye flick. I wore heels instead of steel-toed boots. I started to drink wine and prosecco instead of beer and rum. I drank at the Chiltern Firehouse rather than the Carpenter's Arms. I genuinely knew someone called Orlando and I liked him.

I was promoted out of my EA position into one where I could use my writing skills and knowledge of the shipping industry to draft bids for large contracts of work insuring cruise liners and tankers. 'You've got a job writing again!' James grinned. I couldn't tell him it wasn't anywhere near the same, I couldn't crush his happiness. Instead I cried silently and secretly as I signed my new contract. My salary doubled, as did my working hours, and I no longer left the office at 5 p.m. on the dot to squeeze an hour of work on my second novel in before James got home.

It was all so subtle and slow that I didn't even notice I was morphing into someone else. And even if I had noticed, I am not sure I would have cared. I thought I was growing up, becoming the person that I needed to be, an adult.

I ignored the part of me that missed writing, that found herself scribbling paragraphs on scraps of paper while commuting to work. I ignored how, every time I read something great or saw an interview with an author I loved, I got a gnawing pang of jealousy in the pit of my stomach.

I was a grown-up now, in a grown-up relationship, with responsibilities. Grown-ups didn't chase wild dreams. I wasn't that person any more.

January 19th 2024

I'd been driving on the M1 for about two hours when I realised I didn't actually know how to get to Scotland.

I'd been for a weekend in Edinburgh before, but that had been by train. I'd never actually driven further north than Nottingham.

Damn you Google for making me rely on you and now no longer existing.

I pulled off at the first services I found and breathed a sigh of relief when I found an AA roadmap in the back corner of WHSmith.

I was then annoyed to realise I should have been on the M6 rather than the M1.

The M1 was the road north – everyone knew that. Stupid maps.

I picked Lairg as my destination. I had no idea what it was. Town? Village? Field? It was just past Inverness and I could drive most of the way there on the A9, and it seemed far enough away from any major towns to have a fighting chance at having missed the plague. I thought about going further, but wasn't sure how long the diesel would last, and I didn't want to get stuck in the middle of nowhere with no way of leaving apart from walking.

Amongst other, less useful things, some of the Russian sailors had taught me to sail. Only outboard motors and the rudiments of judging currents and which side to pass other boats on, I couldn't sail anything with proper sails; but, in theory, I could take a boat out to one of the small islands off the Scottish coast. But, I didn't know where I would get hold of a boat, wouldn't know where one of the islands was unless I could see it from the coast; plus, the weather had been awful and I didn't want to get stuck on one of the islands and slowly starve to death.

So Lairg it was. Remote enough to answer my question, but close enough to be safe.

Under normal circumstances, and especially given the lack of other traffic, I would probably have been able to do the journey from Northampton to Lairg in one day, two at the most. However, I was increasingly conscious that currently, if I was awake, I was high. Not London 'fall out of the hammock and have to crawl on the floor' high, but relaxed enough to not want, or be able to go, much above forty miles an hour. So, the normal one-day journey took nearly a week.

Plus, I wasn't in a particular hurry to find a reason to kill myself, so it was all self-preservation really.

I quickly developed a driving rhythm. Get up, eat, put diesel in the Defender from one of the canisters, drive, get hungry, pull over, let Lucky out, eat, get Lucky back in, drive, get tired, pull over at the next services, get sleeping bags and find somewhere to sleep, eat, sleep, repeat. To begin with I sometimes stopped if I saw a house with lights on or a car in an unexpected place. But I soon learnt that these incidences were much like the people I had 'seen' in London, and my impromptu diversions inevitably led to depressing scenes of death and decay or empty buildings that inexplicably still had power, so I stopped pulling over and began to drive past, saving myself the disappointment.

I was coming to the end of my fourth day of driving when I saw a glow on the horizon. I hadn't seen a town with working lights in two days and had thought that electricity must have been out all over by now.

I checked my map and realised the glow was most likely coming from Glasgow. My mind was immediately filled with possibilities. Maybe Glasgow had escaped the clutches of 6DM, maybe Glasgow was thriving, with electricity and gas and water and people. Maybe this was my sanctuary.

I drove recklessly towards Glasgow, unfounded hope filling my heart and making me push my foot heavily onto the accelerator.

Lucky was whining again.

I should have listened to him.

Glasgow was on fire.

Literally.

The whole place.

Or, at least, the whole place as far as I could see.

I must have stopped a good few miles from the outskirts but, as I stumbled from the car to stare at the city, the wind blew in my direction and smoke filled my lungs and stung my eyes.

The sheer size of the destruction made my mouth fall open in awe. It was incomprehensible and horrible and dreadful and disturbing and completely awe-inspiring in its magnitude.

How had it happened? It had been drizzling on and off for weeks; surely everything was too damp to burn?

I must have stood watching for at least fifteen minutes before Lucky's incessant whining distracted me.

I dragged my eyes away to snap a 'shut up' at him, but when I looked back I understood his vocal complaint.

The wind was blowing into my face and, while I hadn't noticed it while I was busy watching, when I looked away and then back again it was clear the fire was growing. Rapidly. Towards us.

Reluctantly I climbed back in the car.

We drove for nearly twenty minutes before we fully passed the flames. Lucky whined the whole time.

Driving got much tougher north of Glasgow. The scenery might have been gorgeous, but the road was treacherous; single-lane, winding, often sheer drops at the side. The temperature had dropped significantly and there were patches of visible – and invisible – ice.

I had been planning to spend the night in Aviemore, some-where I had actually heard of, but as I slipped and skidded my way up there it started to snow and I was scared of not being able to drive down in the morning, so I carried on and virtually slid down the other side of the mountain (okay hill, whatever).

We spent the night in a small and empty hotel outside of Inverness, and in the morning went into the town to do some shopping. We had somehow managed to eat most of the food and drink most of the water I had brought, despite raiding service stations and shops along the way. Clothes that I had got at Go Outdoors were already feeling too tight and now smelt of Glasgow smoke, so needed changing too.

I was extremely wary of trying a supermarket again, but didn't want to waste time raiding houses, so I found a Tesco superstore where the doors were already open and sent Lucky in.

I am brave and caring to the very last.

Lucky wandered out again ten minutes later still alive and sans rat or blood, so I reasoned it must be okay inside.

It was still the fastest shop I had ever done in my life.

More pertinent than the need to replenish food, water or clothing was my need to replenish my pharmaceuticals.

I had tried to cut back on Tramadol while driving, but the pay-off was that I needed more at the end of the day to take the edge off and allow myself to calm down enough to sleep. By the time dusk fell on each driving day I could feel the physical twitches begin as my brain became aware that it was free of narcotics, and if we hadn't found somewhere to stay by then, I would take the drugs anyway and drive at a hazy ten miles an hour until we stopped. I was down to my last six tablets.

I found a chemist on the outskirts of the city that had yet to be raided, but they only had three boxes of Tramadol – enough for about a week at my current rate of consumption – so I'd have to replenish again quite quickly.

As I walked back from the shop, I became aware that the street was rammed with parked cars. I'd had to leave the Defender in the middle of the road because all the parking spaces were taken, a fact that I hadn't registered at the time because I was getting used to driving and parking wherever took my fancy.

I wandered down the road trying to figure where everyone had been going.

I didn't have to walk far.

I turned the corner and there they were.

Perhaps a thousand, maybe more.

It must have been some kind of local football club or community centre. There was a long, low building on one side and they had erected a stage at the front of the space. There was no one on the stage (that I could see), just a huge digital clock (now blank) and a massive banner that read 'Together'.

And about a thousand dead bodies.

It must have been cold and stayed cold because they weren't visibly rotting; just blue-tinged and stiff. They lay where they had fallen or sat. Some had brought chairs to sit on, foldable camping chairs, garden chairs, dining chairs; three enterprising people had even dragged in a sofa. Some had brought blankets to sit or lie on, some were sitting on the grass, and some were propped against trees or fences. Some in families or groups, some in couples, some on their own. Some wrapped in duvets, some in thick winter coats, some in T-shirts, some dressed in dinner jackets and cocktail dresses. Young, middle-aged and old.

I didn't look too closely so I didn't know if any of them were sick.

Maybe it had been some religious thing. Maybe they were all Christian or Methodist or Baptist or Jewish or Muslim. Maybe there had just been too many of them for the local church, synagogue or mosque. Maybe they were members of the same school or community group or the Conservative Party.

But I like to think there was no 'old world' reason for these people to be here. It was just for people who didn't want to be on their own.

For people who, even in that very last moment, recognised their shared humanity and wanted to be together at the end.

God, I was lonely.

I was getting more and more used to the sight of death now. I think once you have watched your own husband die and then washed and dressed the bodies of your dead parents, the death of strangers doesn't affect you quite as much. I didn't feel sad when I saw dead people any more, it was the norm in my new world.

I vaguely wondered what would happen when the weather warmed up and they started rotting, but I knew that, one way or another, I wouldn't be there for that, so I didn't spend too much time worrying about it. I suppose I might have been losing my empathy.

Maybe the end of the world was turning me into a psychopath.

I might not have been scared at the sight of the dead bodies, but I realised I was scared *by* them. I was scared because they confirmed my worst fear.

Things didn't seem to be any different in Scotland.

I didn't make it to Lairg in the end.

I got lost and, without Google Maps or signs or anyone to ask, I drove around the Highlands in rising panic with no idea where I was.

The roads were icy and I was skidding all over them.

After a while I stopped looking for signs and just concentrated on keeping the Defender on the road and not in a ditch.

I couldn't remember if you were supposed to turn into or out of a skid and as a result I was just twisting the wheel from side to side.

Thank God neither James nor Xav were there to see. My extremely poor driving skills was probably the one thing they had ever agreed on and they would have had a field day with this.

———————

James was jealous of Xav. Who wouldn't be? Xav was rich, good-looking, lived in an amazing house and never worked. I was so used to it and to him, I never even thought about how weird or unfair it was any more, but for James it was infuriating that a simple act of birth had given Xav so much.

Xav thought James was boring.

When we did go out together they would get into niggly fights about who was going to pay for the round, or the pub being too dingy, or the music too loud. So when James suggested that I hang out with Xav on my own in future, I thought it would probably be easier all round.

James liked Ginny. Ginny was funny and smart and talkative and had charm to spare, so had James on her side within half an hour of meeting him. James liked hanging out with Ginny a lot.

Ginny actually didn't have much of an opinion about James, which was weird for someone who had an opinion about everything. 'He's just another middle-class white boy. They all look the same to me,' she'd said with a wink.

Xav and Ginny only met once.

It was at my thirtieth birthday party.

Ginny organised the whole thing for me as a surprise.

I hadn't thought about having a party. I didn't think I knew enough people for a decent sized party. I would probably only have invited James, Xav, Ginny, and my mum and dad – that's hardly a gathering, and definitely not a party.

This was something Ginny learnt as soon as she started to put together a guest list – I didn't really have any guests. But Ginny wasn't going to be defeated by my lack of a social circle, so she invited people from work, some of my old school friends, people from my Facebook account, some people she knew and I had met once or twice, and she got James to invite all his mates as well.

I knew something was going on because she was practically bubbling with excitement for the three days beforehand. She accidentally spilled the beans as we were getting ready beforehand at my house, which was a blessing as she also told me the dress I was wearing wasn't quite right, so I had time to change. As always, Ginny's enthusiasm was infectious and, by the time we had sorted my make-up and drunk a couple of glasses of prosecco, I was really excited at the idea of a party where I would be the guest of honour.

By the time we arrived at the bar where the party was being held there were 200 people all crammed in waiting to celebrate my big 3-0.

I knew maybe twenty-five of them.

My mum and dad came but only stayed about half an hour. It was very busy, very expensive, and the trendy DJ was very loud. 'They charged me £10 for a pint,' my dad shouted in my ear as he hugged me goodbye.

Then he gave me £50.

'You might need this to buy yourself a cocktail.'

Ginny did an amazing job introducing me to people I didn't know and dancing with me to all my favourite songs, which she had arranged for the DJ to play.

After the first couple of hours I just wanted to sit down for a bit. I wasn't used to being the centre of attention and it turns out it's pretty exhausting.

Xav rolled up about 10.30 p.m. looking petulant. James had forgotten to tell him about the surprise party; he'd gone to the original venue for the night and had only learnt where we were via Instagram.

I showed him the new Manolo Blahnik shoes James had bought me.

'Jesus, how do you walk in those things?' he shouted.

I couldn't. I'd had them on for one evening and nearly broken my ankle twice, but I wasn't about to admit that to him, so I just laughed wildly in the same way I had been laughing at everything for the past three hours.

'Are you drunk?' he yelled, confused.

It was at this point that Ginny walked over.

She stood square in front of Xav, crossed her arms, and looked him up and down, smirking.

'You must be the 'old' friend.'

Xav paused, very slowly crossed his arms, mirrored her expression, and then said, 'The 'best' friend.'

This is why I never introduced them. They could both be total bitches.

For a moment they just glared at each other.

Then Ginny looked pointedly at me.

'I thought you said he was good-looking?'

She grabbed my arm and dragged me and my wobbling ankles onto the dance floor.

An hour later the DJ halted the music and everyone sang happy birthday . . . to Ginny.

She dragged me up onto the DJ booth, made a joke out of it, and then made everyone sing it, again, to me.

It was one of the most excruciating moments of my life.

Xav grabbed me as I clambered down in my teetering heels. I hoped he was going to say something to make me feel better.

'Ha ha! You looked like a total fucking idiot. I'm leaving. The music's shit, and did you know that they're charging a tenner for a pint?'

He messaged me later.

'I hope Ginny enjoyed her party. What are we doing for your birthday again? Xx'

Bitch.

———

The weather outside of Inverness started to get worse at about 4 p.m., according to the clock on the dashboard. Light flurries of sleet, more irritating than worrying. By 4.30 p.m. the sleet had turned to snow, and the snow was coming at the Defender in flurries of huge, white petals, landing and almost immediately disappearing from the heat of the engine.

Maybe that's why I didn't notice my impending doom. Because nothing really touched the truck or me or Lucky. It was all in my periphery, all background noise to my intense concentration on living and thinking about my death at the same time.

My speed slowed from 15 mph to 10 mph to 5 mph and then to nothing. Visibility out of the front windscreen was so bad I don't think I even noticed I wasn't actually moving for the first couple of minutes.

My wheels were turning, but I wasn't going anywhere.

I looked out of the side window.

The snow was up to the bottom of my door.

For a few moments my brain refused to comprehend what my eyes were seeing.

Without even thinking, I turned to Lucky and said, 'What the hell? How has this just happened? What has happened? Jesus, where has all this snow come from? I mean . . . what?'

Then I stopped. Lucky was asleep. He opened his eyes, yawned, and looked as if to say, 'I am a dog. What do you want from me?' And then he went back to sleep.

It was the most I had spoken since I was at the BBC and it felt strange. Our normal conversation only went as far as, 'Here, Lucky', 'No, Lucky', and the old classic, 'We're leaving'.

I cleared my throat and tried again.

'I think we could be in a bit of trouble.'

Lucky didn't even bother to look up this time.

I turned the engine off and sat for a moment.

The snow was still falling thick and fast, and silently burying us.

We were on a high road with embankments falling away on either side. I peered out of the window to try to see what was beyond the road, but the snow obscured the view after six feet.

I opened the door and got out of the Defender and immediately regretted it. The snow was nearly up to my thigh. The wind blew snow in my face and without a coat on I was shaking with cold before I had shut the Defender door. But I was out now, so thought I'd better make the most of it. I waded to the edge of the road. It was like walking through freezing cold sand; at first it gave easily but, as the flakes gathered together, they formed a casing around me and I had to drag my legs as though I was wearing huge snow trousers.

I could see no more from the edge of the road than from inside the car, and when I turned back, I couldn't see the car any more and the channel I had made wading through the snow was filling up fast.

I struggled back to be greeted by Lucky's face pushed against the window. I opened the door and just had time to yell, 'Noooo!' into the wind before he launched himself out of the car and into my arms, pushing me back into three feet of snow and burying me in a cold, white icy death. I tried to shout at him again, but my mouth filled with snow and I had a brief, terrifying moment of thinking I would drown. But then he was off me and I was up and coughing and shaking and freezing. I turned to see that Lucky had almost fully disappeared into the snowdrift, so I grabbed him by the scruff of the neck and hauled him back into the car.

I scrambled in after him and shut the door.

I sat in the driver's seat and shivered and gasped for breath. I was covered in snow, soaked to the skin, and frozen.

So frozen that, for a moment, I thought I wasn't going to be able to move.

I was in full panic mode: mind blank, breathing difficult, heart racing.

And that's what saved me.

I panicked.

My heart raced and my temperature rose.

It didn't warm me completely, but it gave me enough impetus to turn the engine on and put the heaters up to full blast.

Five minutes later the car was warm and stank of wet dog.

I stripped off my wet clothes and wrapped myself in the sleeping bag that Lucky had been lying on.

I was confounded by the enormity of the problems I now faced. I needed to find dry clothes, but I hadn't bothered to keep any kind of system in the Defender and had just thrown things into the back when I was done with them. I wasn't even sure that I had any more clothes; I had been wearing the same ones (including underwear) for the last three days, and had left my previous clothes on whatever motel floor I had last dropped them onto.

I knew that my original Go Outdoors stash had included thermals and ski-wear, but couldn't remember if I still had them in the back. I needed food and drink in case we were really, really stuck, but again I couldn't remember how much was left. I needed to get the diesel in case the engine died. I needed to find a way of getting the car out of the snowdrift and then I needed to find a way of driving through three feet of snow.

I also needed a wee.

I couldn't hold onto a single one of these thoughts for more than a few seconds. My brain was clouded by a fog of fear and Tramadol.

But, as the engine warmed the car and my body temperature returned to normal, my fear subsided and I realised I was mentally and physically drained. Exhaustion washed over me in a heavy wave.

I needed to sleep. Once I had slept I would be able to think straight and work out a way to escape.

Through the haze and the blanket of impending sleep I tried to grasp the vague thread of an urgent thought that flitted across my brain; something about getting dressed and warm in case the engine failed. But, I was currently cosy, sleepy and content. When Lucky wriggled across the seat and laid his stinking damp head on my lap his reassuring warmth tipped the balance and, panic attack averted once more, I drifted off happily into the darkness.

January 25th 2024

I woke suddenly, roused by Lucky's barking.

For a moment I couldn't remember where I was and then I couldn't see where I was. The Defender had been plunged into darkness.

The engine was off and there was a strong smell of urine, which I feared I had provided.

It was cold.

I was cold.

I was really, really cold.

I knew I had to move fast before I got too frozen to do anything again, so I pushed through the seats into the back of the Defender and was immediately plunged into a pitch-black hell of sharp-edged boxes, falling tin cans, sloshing diesel canisters and non-descript plastic bags that could contain either useless pillows or essential thermals.

I should have worked my way around systematically, but instead threw things about like a mad woman. I grabbed anything vaguely soft and ripped into it, throwing anything that resembled clothing into the front seat at a still-barking Lucky. I threw potential food and water after the clothing, causing Lucky to retreat to the footwell. I narrowly avoided throwing a canister of diesel into the front when I mistook it for water.

Soon the front of the Defender was covered in a mountain of rubbish and I was starting to shake with cold. I ripped off my wet knickers and threw them to the back, climbed onto the front seat and laughed with glee to see that I had managed to find both thermal underwear and some puffy skiing trousers. I hadn't found a coat, so settled for layering three thermal tops and two jumpers. To finish off the outfit I put on two hats, a scarf, and some gloves.

I was so big I could hardly fit behind the wheel any more, but I was warm, so I was happy.

Lucky was still barking.

I coaxed him back up onto the seat and offered him a biscuit, but still he barked and whined, looking out of the windows.

'It's just night-time,' I scolded him. 'It'll get light soon, stop being silly.'

But then I looked out of the windows properly for the first time since waking.

The light wasn't right. It wasn't the pitch black of night, there were no snowflakes falling from the sky and no stars twinkling above me. It was a weird greyness, a darkness caused not by the absence of light but by the addition of something that was stopping the light getting through.

It wasn't night-time that was making it dark.

The Defender was buried in snow.

You know what?

I didn't panic.

I mean obviously I took a couple of deep breaths and my heart jumped with shock.

But I didn't go into full-on panic mode.

I didn't start gasping for air.

I didn't open the Defender's windows and claw at the snow, desperate to see the sky again.

I didn't scream and wail.

I pulled Lucky onto my lap and stroked him while breathing slowly and calmly.

In late 2010 I went to the Snowbombing Festival in Austria to review an up-and-coming indie rock trio. Having never been skiing, not really liking the snow or cold, and having never actually got around to seeing the band, my irreverent take was to spend the entire article talking about being buried alive in an avalanche.

I even did some lazy research on how to survive being buried in snow.

I'd read the wikiHow page, which came with pictures.

To be honest, compared to actually being buried in an avalanche, I was in no jeopardy at all.

I was warm and dry, I had plenty of oxygen, plenty of space to move about, food, water, clothing, and I knew which way was up.

The clock on the dash said it was 10.36, so it was theoretically light outside. I looked out of the windows to see if I could see daylight filtering through the snow. There was nothing. Just grey darkness.

The Defender had a sunroof, which was how I was planning to get out, but it was unhelpfully tinted so I couldn't see through. It was, however, manually operated, which meant I could open it and wouldn't have to try to smash my way out.

My plan was to open the sunroof and allow the snow to fall on to the front seats of the car and in doing so clear a space for me to crawl through and out. I scrabbled around in the footwell and found a random CD case that I would use as a shovel to dig the snow out of the way.

I was so intent on my escape that I almost forgot to think about what I was going to do when I did escape. I very nearly left without taking anything with me, which would have put me in a far more dangerous situation than I was currently in.

I also very nearly forgot about Lucky.

It took me an hour to gather everything I needed for my expedition. I took some food, spare clothes, thermal underwear, and gloves, a knife (no idea why), a torch, and all the phone batteries.

I stashed my bulging rucksack in the passenger footwell and slowly opened the sunroof, expecting a flurry of snow to fall into the Defender.

Nothing fell. It was literally ice.

I tried to scoop at it with my hands, but it was rock solid. In

the end I had to chip at it with the corner of the CD case. It took
for ever and was exhausting. After I had been chipping away for
an hour I'd only made a hole about a foot deep. My stomach began
to churn and I was wondering if maybe I should start panicking
just a little more when I stuck the CD case in and a huge chunk
of ice fell on us, followed by a flurry of snow that buried me and
Lucky, causing a frenzy of barking and coughing.

Then I looked up and saw the sky.

It turned out that the wind must have picked up overnight
because the Land Rover was buried in a snowdrift with snow
piled around and over it; but the surrounding snow level wasn't
much deeper than it had been the night before, maybe up to the
top of my thighs.

In the darkness of last night, I had seen nothing beyond the
road, but in the daylight I could see a smattering of houses gathered around a lake (loch?) across the fields. The closest looked
about half a mile away – an easy distance normally and surely a
manageable one through the snow.

I reached down, grabbed my filled rucksack and the empty
smaller one and coaxed Lucky onto the roof of the Land Rover.
He looked at the snow suspiciously and then, when I smiled at
him, he looked at me even more suspiciously. I petted him again.
'You have no idea what's coming.'

Have you ever tried to stuff a dog into a rucksack? I wouldn't
recommend it. Lucky ended up with his head and paws sticking
out of the top and the drawstring pulled tight around his torso
to keep him from wriggling out. It looked, and was, cruel. But
the alternative was him staying in the truck and either freezing
or starving to death, so cruelty won.

I clambered down off the Defender looking like a doubled-up
version of a foreign exchange student, with the rucksack of
essentials on my back and Lucky in his rucksack on my front.
They were both really fucking heavy and I struggled to stay
upright in the snow, stumbling first forward and then back as I
tried to get my balance.

Despite the effort it took to wade through it, I soon learnt the snow actually worked in my favour. If I waded slowly and gently, the snow supported my legs and helped to balance my heavy load.

I still wished I had done more leg work at the gym and bothered to learn how to engage my core.

I'm not going to write in detail about the walk to the cottage because I have no desire to relive it.

Ever.

I will say that by the time we got to the cottage it was nearly dark. That the walk there was the hardest thing I had ever done and made the walk up the M1 feel like a country stroll to the pub. I spent the whole walk petrified that I was going to fall forward onto my face and drown in the snow as I wouldn't have the strength to lift myself up again. Lucky whined and moaned so much I very nearly dropped his rucksack and left him, and the only reason I didn't was I didn't have the energy to lift my arms and take him off.

Five hundred yards from the cottage my legs simply wouldn't work any more and I thought I was going to tip forward and die face first in the snow, but Lucky chose that exact moment to start barking hysterically and, given the choice between staggering on or dying while listening to that racket, I chose the former. So, crying, cursing and vowing to never call Lucky a good boy again, I dragged myself the rest of the way.

When we got to the cottage, I dumped the rucksack and Lucky unceremoniously on the doorstep and tried the front door.

Locked.

I jogged around the house and found the back door.

Locked.

I had just struggled through hell to get there, so I wasn't going to let something as small as a locked door keep me from food and shelter. I found a small window that I thought I would be able to fit through and smashed it open.

I managed to hoist myself up onto the ledge and, too late, realised I should have put something over the broken glass as my clothes caught and ripped while I clambered through the window and fell in a heap onto the kitchen floor on the other side.

It was colder inside the cottage than outside.

I found a light switch and flicked it. Nothing. No gas came out of the cooker when I turned it on either.

I stumbled up the stairs and checked the bedrooms, but there was no one in them. I half slid back down and checked the front room, but it too was untenanted.

I checked the cupboards. Sugar, tea, and a few cans and other bits. The fridge was empty.

I started to panic. Where was the food?

I ran back upstairs. The beds had duvets and pillows on them, but no sheets or covers. The bathroom was bare – no toothbrushes, toothpaste, shower gel. No face creams or washes. I checked wardrobes and drawers and bookshelves and the airing cupboard. A few knick-knacks, a couple of spare duvets and pillows, but no photos or clothes or personal items. There were three books left in a bedside cabinet and that was it.

It was a holiday cottage.

A freezing, empty and lifeless holiday cottage.

My immediate reaction was to try somewhere else, but it was nearly dark, the snow had soaked through my waterproof trousers and my legs were freezing, the nearest house was maybe another half a mile away and, looking out of the window, I saw that it had started to blizzard again. I was physically exhausted and could barely walk through the house let alone drag myself through snow.

Leaving was not an option.

I had to stay put and I had to get warm. Now that I was cooling down after my epic battle to get there I was already shivering so badly that my body was twitching violently as if I were having a series of mini fits. Unless I could find some way to warm the cottage up, I was going to freeze to death.

The front room had an open fire with a huge stack of newspapers and a basket of logs to the side.

Even my limited knowledge of wood burning told me that a small basket of logs wasn't going to last long, so there had to be more somewhere. Or at least there did if I was going to survive the night.

I found the keys to the back door hanging on a nail by the door frame and opened it. The wind blew snow and hail in my face and took my breath away.

There was a storage cupboard just outside the back door, which was locked. I used the other key on the back-door key ring to open it.

It was filled with logs.

I believe I may have punched the air with joy.

Then I heard Lucky barking from the front and realised he was still stuck in the rucksack.

I don't know how long it took me to get the fire going.

I do know that it was fully dark, and Lucky was shivering as uncontrollably as I was, by the time I coaxed more than a few sparks from the logs.

I used up half the stack of newspaper by the fireplace and a good number of the smaller logs that, I soon learnt, burn a lot quicker and easier than the big ones. I was lucky that they had left four boxes of matches, as I used two boxes.

But I did it. I got the fire going because Lucky and I had not come all that way, been buried in a blizzard and trekked through three foot of snow for nothing.

I was determined that we would survive long enough to do what we had come to Scotland for. We would find people. Dead or alive.

———

It seems unlikely that I, someone who can panic at the sight of a long escalator, should have such a strong determined streak, but I do. When I make up my mind about something then that is it. I am all in. All the way.

And so it was with James and me. I was all the way in. Love, marriage, baby in the baby carriage.

I should probably have checked with him that he felt the same way.

But they never do have that moment in the romantic novel or movie do they? There's never a scene where the couple write To Do lists and check they match.

The first throes of love are too heady and exciting to be adult about your needs and expectations. Your needs and expectations at the beginning are sex, laughter, booze, more sex, maybe some food a few times a week, and then some sex again.

Then, if you make it through those first few months, 'I love you'.

And by then it's too late to go back and clarify exactly what it is you love and what you want.

You just have to hope that, by some miracle, you both want the same things at the same time.

I thought that if I made James happy then he would magically know how to make me happy in return, like in the movies, like how my parents were. So, I never explained to James what my expectations were, and therefore, can't blame him for not living up to them. He never knew that I thought moving in together so quickly would mean that we would get engaged, get married, and have kids at the same pace.

He couldn't have known that I needed these things to happen, and happen quickly, so that there wouldn't be space in my life or mind for me to dwell on the fact that maybe, just maybe I wasn't as happy as I had hoped, living my mum's romantic ideal.

But here I was, thirty-one years old, five years into a mature adult relationship, and no marriage or kids in sight. Not even an engagement ring.

We, like many others, were on the treadmill of life. Work, food, sleep, booze, going out, holidays, birthdays, Christmas, New Year. An endless wheel of endless small moments of joy and sadness that make up a life. A good life. A normal life. A safe life.

But I wanted more. I needed more. I needed proof that this

had been the right decision. I needed to be able to go to my mum and tell her I had done it, I had found the true love she had always wanted for me. I needed to wave my engagement ring at Xav and tell him he was wrong: James wasn't boring, he wasn't the wrong choice for me, he was right, we were right, and we were happy and we were going to be together for ever.

It was like a video game; do well at one level and then move to the next. I just needed to try harder, be better at my job, be thinner, be funnier, be a better girlfriend, make James happier.

Then I would level up to wife.

February 11th 2024

I have been at the cottage for seventeen days and I have written the entire contents of this diary, up to this point, in the last four.

The last two and a half months of my life.

I am writing this diary for the reasons I mentioned at the beginning – I do think someone should record the end of the world and, as potentially the only person left alive, the burden obviously falls to me.

I am using writing as a form of therapy because, for the first time since arriving at Xav's house, I am *drum roll please* drug-free.

And the crowd goes wild.

I am also writing this because, now that I am drug-free . . .

I
Am
So
Very
VERY!
Bored.

I spent the first two days in the cottage dealing with basic needs: warmth, food, water, somewhere to wee, somewhere to sleep. I also spent far too much time gazing out of the window at the nearest cottage, willing someone to appear at the window or for smoke to begin to rise from the chimney. Of course, they didn't and it didn't.

Apart from the conspicuous lack of signs of any other survivor, keeping warm was my biggest worry and took the most time. The first morning at the cottage the fire had gone out by the time I woke up. It was bone-chillingly freezing once more and I had to spend another miserable hour and nearly another box of matches getting the fire started again. For the next few days, every time the fire went out, I would be plunged into yet another clumsy-fingered, match- and wood-wasting fight for warmth until I eventually realised this couldn't go on and, through experimentation and a process of elimination, I learnt how to efficiently light the fire. I now have a pre-prepared supply of ripped-up newspaper, a collection of smaller twigs, and piles of small, medium, and large logs to feed my hungry fire god with. I am also proficient in coaxing fire back from the smallest ashy glow – it is infinitely preferable to starting from scratch. I try not to let the fire go out in the day and dread the mornings where there isn't even the smallest ember for me to blow back to life.

I have discovered that the other best way to keep warm is to stay dressed. All the time. I haven't changed my underwear or clothing in five days. I am pretty ripe. But it is too cold to wash anyway, so what's the point? Plus, I only brought three changes of clothes with me from the Defender, so everything I have has already been worn . . . for at least five days. I have had to ban Lucky from sleeping with me as I was beginning to smell of both sweat and dog, which is a very unpleasant combination. I have made him his own bed out of the log basket and a duvet and he seems pretty happy there. He is less happy that I still make him go out in the snow to wee and crap. I feel weirdly guilty that I don't go out and pick up his faeces, but then I reason that the only person who will step in it is me.

The final warmth lesson that I have learnt is to live in one room. On the first day I had the fire going for about six hours and it was still freezing. I couldn't work out why. Then I realised I had left the door to the living room open, and while I had made a cursory attempt to repair the kitchen window I broke using cardboard, it was still completely freezing in the kitchen and everywhere else in the house. So, I shut the living-room door and used a spare duvet to stop the draught coming in under it, stuffed newspaper in the window cracks, shut all the curtains, and within half an hour I was toasty warm. Now I go to the kitchen each morning for food and water and bring them back to the living room, and that is where I stay. All day. Every day. I live in constant gloom and, mostly, in one room. Poetry.

Apart from when I need to go to the toilet, which is a hell all of its own making.

I still have water in the taps, and the loo still flushes, but if I don't use it for four or five hours a thin layer of ice forms on the water at the bottom of the system. Normally my urine melts the ice (weirdly satisfying), but if I need to poo it's best to break the ice beforehand. All this was learnt by trial and error. I have learnt to hover over the toilet and, if I have to sit down, to warm the seat first. I left a significant amount of my skin on the seat before I learnt that trick. Also, being cold is not conducive to having a 'quick wee'; it seems that when you are literally freezing your arse off your bladder has the ability to retract in on itself and refuse to let go of its contents, no matter how badly you want it to.

To be honest, after the first couple of days of toilet visit trauma, I found a large mixing bowl in the kitchen, and now I just wee into that in the corner of the sitting room and throw it out of the window.

Every time I do it Lucky stares at me reproachfully.

I did an inventory of the food I had brought and that was in the cottage cupboards on the first day I was here. I had four tins of beans, two tins of soup, one tin of chopped tomatoes, two tins of sausages and spaghetti, two cans of beef stew, eight bags of crisps, three packets of biscuits, two packets of chocolate biscuits, one pack of tomato Cup A Soup, three cans of Pepsi, one box of tea bags, half a pack of sugar, one jar of black olives, three Mars bars and five tins of dog food. The cooker, kettle, and toaster don't work, but I found some old pans and an old tin kettle in the cupboards that I am using to cook and heat water over the fire with. There is actually a hook above the fire to hang the kettle on and, after the first few times that I burnt myself, I learnt to wait for the flames to die back and to always use an oven glove before attempting to get the kettle back off the hook.

The three cans of Pepsi, two of the bags of crisps, the Mars bars, and one of the packets of biscuits went into my tummy the morning that I arrived. This was before I thought about checking how much food there was. Once I had done my inventory and looked out of the kitchen window to confirm that going anywhere before the snow melted was going to be impossible, I started to ration my food. I have a cup of tea (no milk) and a biscuit for breakfast, half a can of something for lunch, and a Cup A Soup and the other half can for dinner, along with another two biscuits.

So far, I have fed Lucky all the dog food plus the two cans of stew and one of the cans of spaghetti and sausages. He whines a lot and is obviously hungry, but I am very, very resentful that I have to give him anything from my stash so he is definitely not getting more. Okay, I give him two biscuits at night, but that is it.

Even when I was still taking the drugs I was hungry, and now that I am off them I am absolutely starving. Constantly. I am leaving the tomatoes, kidney beans, and olives (or evil grapes as they were known when I was growing up) until last and if the worst comes to the worst I will be able to survive on the sugar for a few days. But I am not sure what will happen to Lucky; he can't hunt in the snow, and I don't think he'll eat olives, so at best he has two days of food left. I think I may have a week.

I sometimes dream of the three Mars bars.

I discovered I was running out of Tramadol on my third day at the cottage.

I had been so busy sorting things that I was happily popping pills as normal until I took the packet out of the box and realised to my horror that I only had twenty tablets left. I had been taking two (okay, sometimes three) roughly every four hours. That meant I had a maximum of three days left.

To begin with I wept and moaned to myself and paced the front room of the cottage muttering meaningless repetitions of 'Shit, what will I do, what will I do, I can't cope, shit, help me, someone help me.' Until I was verging on full-blown panic, had several misery-inducing visits to the toilet to shit valuable calories out as watery diarrhoea, and Lucky was whining and pacing with me in more distress than I was.

Not for the first, or last, time it was Lucky that saved me.

In an effort to stop me pacing and get me to pet him he manoeuvred himself in front of me and I fell over him, smacking my face on the stone floor. He went to lick my face and I swatted him away with the back of my hand, causing him to yelp and cower back into the corner.

I snapped out of my panic and started to weep. Lucky rushed over from his corner and licked away my tears. His complete lack of selfishness made me cry even more and I clung to his neck, soaking his fur with my tears until tears turned to sniffles, and half an hour later I had cried the worst of it out and was simply feeling sorry for myself.

I was stuck. The snow was still falling and was now halfway up to the windowsill. There was no way I was getting more drugs, so I either detoxed or took the twenty in one go and hoped that was enough to overdose.

I didn't think it was.

Plus, as I am sure you are starting to be aware, I am a massive fucking coward. I couldn't even take T600, let alone kill myself by overdosing.

I halved my dose each day in an effort to make the detox process less miserable.

It didn't work.

It was still bloody miserable.

Xav once told me that all detox stories are boring. He said

that they were the drug-takers' equivalent of the old vegan joke – How do you know if someone is vegan? They'll tell you. 'The basic premise of a detox story is that you were once having fun . . . and now you're not,' he said, 'and no one wants to hear the grim tale of how you went from one to the other, so just keep it to yourself.'

And if anyone should know about depressing detox stories then it is Xav.

––––––––

Xav was, is, and always will be, my best friend.

He was my confidant, sounding board, adviser, court jester and the one with whom I have shared the most fun in my entire life.

I loved him as much as and, at points, maybe even more than James.

However, he was not my rock. He was never my emotional support or the person I ran to when I needed help or strength.

He would have given it to me in an instant. But, unfortunately, I could never be sure that he would be around when I needed him.

It is probably understandable why I didn't go to my parents when I first started suffering from panic attacks and depression; I was embarrassed and scared and didn't know what they would think. For the record they would have been, and were when they eventually did find out, perfectly wonderful.

But, you are probably wondering, why didn't I run to Xav for help and support?

Xav wasn't there.

Xav was in rehab.

Xav was in rehab from the day before I received the first rejection letter for my novel until a week before we left for Thailand.

I could still have rung him and told him about my fragile mental health.

But I didn't.

Instead I rang him to see if he wanted to leave rehab and a week later go and spend three months in a place bursting with drugs.

Because, of course, it was always all about me.

Just one of many examples where I was too busy thinking about my needs to think about his.

We were as bad as each other.

Xav and I had much more in common than we ever truly admitted. He would always be an addict and I would always be a sufferer of panic attacks and depression. Neither of us would ever get the professional help required to deal with our issues in the long-term and therefore neither of us would ever be able to give the other the full amount of support they needed.

So, when mature, sensible, solid James appeared on the scene is it any wonder that I clung to him like the emotional rock he would prove to be?

Xav went to rehab three times. His first stint was when he was fifteen, at boarding school, and they realised he was drunk most days. The second was when he was twenty-five, and Rupert caught him smoking crack. The third was two days after I got married.

Rupert was dead by then, and it was my parents who drove him to rehab and checked him in.

It should have been me.

———

So, I am going to take Xav's advice and not repeat the misery of the ten days that it took me to get the Tramadol out of my system.

Suffice to say that the cottage was an efficient but not at all comfortable place to do it (I had extreme diarrhoea and left many layers of skin on the toilet seat). I was sick, my stomach was churning, I had stomach aches, bouts of shivering, headaches, muscle spasms and I was, and still am, sad, emotional and prone to outbursts of random tears and rage that cannot be entirely attributed to my lone survival of the apocalypse.

I found an ancient, three-quarters-full bottle of sherry in the front room cabinet and at the end of every day I successfully made it through I would take a massive gulp from the bottle. To begin with the taste made me grimace, but the fiery warmth that spread through my body and the very, very gentle buzz that calmed my brain was something I looked forward to all day. By day five I had even started to enjoy the taste.

I knew that I was coming out of the other side of my detox when, one night, I misjudged my gulp and spilled some of the sherry onto my arm. Lucky, not wanting to miss the chance of free vittles, rushed over to lick it off and his immediate grimace of revulsion at the taste made me laugh out loud. I knew then that I was going to be okay. Well, maybe not okay, but I was going to live.

I have now been completely Tramadol-free for twelve days. I still crave it, but I have no possible way to relapse at the moment so I am mostly able to ignore my cravings.

In fact, to my surprise, the cravings were not the worst thing about not being on drugs any more. The cravings I could handle and cope with.

No, the worst thing about being clean and sober was far, far more difficult to solve.

I was absolutely, completely and utterly dying of boredom.

Now that I had detoxed and had a routine for food and fire there wasn't anything else for me to do at the cottage.

Literally nothing.

I tried reading the old newspapers stacked by the fire, but most of them were too faded or mouldy. I normally masturbated two or three times a day, but could only do it when Lucky was asleep as it was too weird when he was watching me.

I tried playing games with Lucky, but I didn't have anything to throw for him other than small twigs ripped from the logs, and he tended to just sit down and chew them once he got them. Plus, it was hard to have a good game of fetch in a room ten foot square. I started to teach him tricks like giving me his paw and rolling over, but without the biscuits as a reward he was a pretty reluctant student.

Eight days after my last ever Tramadol I remembered the three books upstairs and bounded up to get them.

They were: *This Charming Man* by Marian Keyes, *Riders* by Jilly Cooper, and *Trump: The Art of the Deal* by Donald J. Trump.

Donald fucking Trump?! Jesus.

I read the Marian Keyes during the rest of that day, devouring it in a way that was wholly greedy, not bothering to try to pace myself. I stretched out *Riders* for as long as possible and read it over the next three days, rationing myself to a chapter an hour, or maybe two (three) at the most. I loved them both and vowed to read everything else the authors had written as soon as I left the cottage . . . if I left the cottage.

I promised myself I wouldn't read the Trump book.

On the morning of day thirteen I opened the front cover and started to read the Trump book.

I think I read the first three lines and got to the bit where he talks about deals being his art form before I yelled, 'FUCK YOU!', dramatically slammed the book shut, opened the sitting-room window, and threw it out. I spent a satisfying thirty minutes watching the blizzard bury it in snow.

Twenty minutes after that I was getting my boots on in the hall to go to retrieve Trump when I noticed the hallway table drawer. I opened it and to my utter joy found a visitor's book.

I bloody love a good visitor's book! All those different people, different opinions, different recommendations – it is normally the first thing I looked for when we visited a holiday home.

I pulled my boots off, went back into the sitting room, and settled on the sofa to read it.

There were three entries.

'Had a fab stay, thanks.' Ethel and Derek Jones, March 2023.

'Lovely cottage and brilliant views. Try the fish at The Old Trout Inn – absolutely delicious.' The Sanderson family, June 2023.

'The cottage was absolutely lovely and the setting is gorgeous. We very much enjoyed exploring the beautiful countryside. BUT, our stay was ruined when I found you had a book by Donald Trump in the cottage. I very nearly left immediately and checked into a hotel but my wife persuaded me to stay. I have, however, removed a random page and used it to wipe my ass. That is all that book will ever be good for.' Jed and Sarah Bookthwaite, Minnesota, United States of America.

Wow.

I flicked through the book. Jed had removed page forty-five.

I love you Jed, I hope you had a good and peaceful death.

It took me just two minutes to read the entire guest book, five minutes to find out which page of the Trump book Jed had wiped his arse with, and then thirty seconds to throw the book back out of the window.

I sighed and resigned myself to boredom once more.

But then I saw the pen attached to the back of the guest book and the two hundred fresh pages waiting to be filled.

I started to write.

Hi.

When I was fifteen I was in love with Keanu Reeves. Not a crush or a mere fancy, actual full-on love. I could see and feel his pain. I knew that people who thought him pretty but dumb just didn't know the real him. I genuinely believed that I would marry him some day and I would provide the light in his life that had been missing and he would provide the mature and constant love that my teenage heart craved.

I used to write a him a weekly letter, pouring out my love for him, my hatred of my small life and small achievements, my burning desire to write something great, the latest developments on my latest teenage literary tome, my desperate need for my life to begin in some way, in any way. I never sent the letters. They stacked up in my bedside cabinet over the course of about a year until my burning desire for Keanu faded into something more like the warm cherishment of a beloved family pet; someone you have known and loved for a very long time. Keanu was replaced by Steve who went to my college, someone whom I could love in flesh and blood but to whom I never once wrote.

It might seem weird that I never sent the letters. But sending them was never the point – writing them was. I wanted to write everything down, get it all out of me and then seal it safely in an envelope. I didn't care that no one would ever read them.

I don't care that no one will ever read this diary.

I just need to get this stuff out of me before the end.

Because I am still convinced that there has to be an end.

Sorry, there has been no change of heart.

In fact, being in the cottage has given me plenty of time to work out my plan for the end. I should probably capitalise that . . . The End.

I am going to go to Soho Farmhouse.

I am going to end my life in the place I spent one of my happiest ever weekends, in the world's most comfy bed, with an extensive choice of pillows and luxurious 600 thread-count linen sheets.

I almost can't wait.

You don't know Soho Farmhouse? Well, of course you don't. You are an ordinary person and not one of the chosen elite who get to experience the wonder of Soho House's members-only world of happiness.

Soho Farmhouse is one of the hotels owned by the Soho House members' club. They have hotels and clubs and meeting rooms dotted around the world that can only be used by members, or by those who are willing to pay an extortionate amount of money for twenty-four or forty-eight hours of temporary access to this joyous adults' playground.

I use the word 'hotel' loosely, as staying at Soho Farmhouse is more like staying in the luxury complex of a friend who owes you a massive favour and is going to make your stay the best couple of days of your life. James took me there for the weekend two weeks after he kissed me on the platform at Liverpool Street station.

I loved it.

I'll be honest, I didn't initially want to go; I was worried that we would stick out, that people would know I wasn't a celebrity, royalty, or actually even a Soho House member, and that they would treat me like a second-class citizen. But they either didn't know or, more likely, they didn't care.

We stayed in a studio cabin overlooking the river. I loved the massive bed, the Egyptian cotton sheets, the bath outside that we sat in during a storm and listened to the rain thrum on the wooden porch and the thunder rumble in the distance and then crash overhead. I loved the wood-burning stove that we lay naked in front of until dawn was breaking, talking about our future in a way that made me feel fully contented and happy for the first time in the longest while.

I loved the bikes that we rode around the grounds, laughing at the fact that neither of us could quite remember how to ride a bike and joking that the old adage most definitely wasn't true. I loved the grounds, the endless green fields and rows of lavender that perfumed the spring air and filled our lungs with a healthy flowery scent after the polluted stench of London.

I loved the farmhouse shop filled with items I couldn't afford, to use in a life that I would never live. I loved the restaurants with their false rustic charm and delicious homely food. I loved the staff who treated you like you might be a minor European royal, the author of the next hot new novel, or the lead in the next blockbuster British movie. I loved how they seemed to genuinely like their jobs and genuinely not hate serving me.

I loved that I was in a complete bubble. A bubble of love and of happiness and Egyptian cotton sheets.

By the end of the weekend I knew that I would love both James and Soho Farmhouse for ever.

I still feel that way. About Soho Farmhouse. I literally love it so much that I want to die there.

February 15th 2024

I have now been in the cottage for twenty-one days.

I completely over-estimated the number of days of food I had left. I finished the last of the sugar this morning and haven't had solid food for two days. Lucky hasn't eaten for nearly three days, as he completely refused the olives.

I am really, really hungry. My tummy rumbles constantly. I can't think about anything but food. I am already feeling weak, and dragging myself off the sofa to add wood to the fire is a huge effort. Lucky hasn't moved from his bed all day. I have been staring out of the window at the nearest cottage, but I am not sure I can make it, it seems very far away. And what if there isn't any food when I get there?

I could weep when I think about all the times I wasted or rejected food before. The times I didn't like the look of something or I only ate half of it.

There were times with James when I would reject whole meals because I was dieting or wasn't hungry or I was in a bad mood so would just pick at them. There were times I didn't eat just because James wasn't there to eat with me.

I was an idiot.

———

The time I think about most often was a random Saturday afternoon. James and I had been living together for six years, and we decided to go out for a few drinks.

It wasn't a special occasion, just a lazy Saturday of drinking. We grabbed a Chinese takeaway on the way home and stuck it in the oven while we had sloppy, drunken sex. Afterwards James fell asleep. At first I thought he would wake up, so I lay next to him, lovingly watching him.

An hour later my arm was numb and I knew he wasn't waking up that night.

But that left me without plans too. Did I eat the Chinese on my own? Did I wake him and tell him I was eating the Chinese? Did I leave the Chinese and eat something else? I was starving, but completely unable to make a decision for myself.

In the end I turned the oven off and climbed back into bed beside James with my tummy rumbling, and waited for sleep to come.

It took a very long time.

I should have eaten the food.

February 17th 2024

It is day twenty-three. My tummy hurts.

I am either going to the next cottage today or I am going to eat Lucky.

I went to the next cottage.

Lucky stared at me the whole time as I got dressed to go outside.

I tried to explain to him that this was actually better than the alternative plan of me eating him. He didn't understand.

When I went to leave, he tried to block the door. I was too weak to carry him, and the snow was now past my thighs so there was no way he could walk there himself but, obviously, he didn't understand any of this. I locked him in with the fire banked up with logs and an extra duvet in his basket.

I could hear his howls until I was halfway there.

With only an empty rucksack to carry, the walk was nowhere near as bad as it had been from the Defender, but I was very weak and hungry so it was extremely slow going. Once Lucky's howls had faded it was also completely and utterly silent. I stopped and listened. Nothing. Not only was there no human-made sound, there was no natural sound either. No birdsong, no rustling trees, no scurrying animals.

Complete silence.

I started to walk again and realised that the world might have been completely silent but I was a veritable cacophony of sound: the crunch of my boots in the snow, the swish of my waterproof trousers, the rustle of my rucksack, the trumpeting elephant snort of my breath as I gasped my way forward.

In fact, I was so busy listening to myself that when I heard the howling I assumed it was just Lucky again. But I was too far away to hear Lucky, so I stopped. This wasn't a Lucky howl. This was the sort of howl you hear in horror films just before something really bad happens. A bone-chilling howl. The howl of something that is going to eat you and enjoy doing so. Reluctantly I turned to look for the owner.

Wolves.

Five wolves standing on the ridge about one thousand yards away. I had no idea where they had come from. Did Scotland always have wolves? Had they escaped from somewhere?

The zoo-going, animal-loving part of me thought, 'Oooh, wolves! So cute!'. The part of me that didn't want to get eaten thought, 'Fuck. Run!'

I went with, 'Fuck. Run!' and part jogged/shuffled/staggered the last 200 yards to the cottage.

The wolves didn't move.

I didn't want to break a window, now that I knew I might not be top of the food chain, so I prayed that one of the doors was open. The back door was and, once I had shovelled snow away from it, I entered straight into the kitchen and didn't even bother going into the rest of the house. I immediately ransacked the cupboards, which were stuffed with food. I found a tin of corned beef, which I opened and ate in one go, and a tin of ham, which followed the corned beef. There were tins and packets and crisps and biscuits and a couple of cheap, obviously irradiated, Victoria sponge cakes that were still in date. I rammed things into my face and into the rucksack in maniacal glee.

Soon both the rucksack and my stomach were stuffed full and I was exhausted. I knew I needed to get back to Lucky, but I wasn't sure whether I should leave with the wolves there. I had seen wolves before at Woburn Safari Park, and those fuckers move. Even in the snow I was willing to bet they'd be down from that ridge and eating me within minutes if that was what they wanted to do. I couldn't see the ridge from the kitchen, so went into the front room to take a look out of the window.

And there she was.

The proof that I had come to remote rural Scotland for.

The glass of water, the empty T600 pack, a comfy chair – the last rites of 6DM. She was old, maybe late eighties, and frozen solid. She had a rug over her knees and a cat curled up in her lap. A perfect picture of domesticity if it hadn't been for the telltale signs of the sick bowl next to her and the thin trickle of blood coming from her nose.

I poked the cat with a stick to make sure it was really dead. It was.

When I finally looked out of the front window the wolves were gone, so I was charging back through the hallway to the kitchen to set off back to the cottage when I saw the dead woman's landline phone sitting on the hallway table.

Or rather I saw the answerphone message light flashing on the machine on her hallway table.

Maybe it was because it had been years since I'd seen a working answerphone, maybe it was because the flashing light surprised me, or maybe it was because I had some kind of premonition or sixth sense. Whatever.

I pressed play.

The metallic voice chimed out.

'*You have one new message. Message received December 14th at 4.39 p.m..*'

'*Doris, it's Susan . . . your sister.*'

A human voice.

It was the first time I had heard another person speak since I spoke to Tom Forrest about burying James.

I was so shocked I sat down on the floor and burst into tears.

'*I . . . I know we haven't spoken for a while. I wanted to see if you were okay. If you were sick yet? I'm not sick.*'

I stopped crying.

'*I was watching the ambulances going to the hospital at the end of our road. There were loads of them, but they've stopped now. I haven't seen any for over a week. I don't suppose that's good news. Jess rang and she's got it, and the kids. Jack went to see them a few days ago. He hasn't come back. I'm here alone. Well, the cat's here too I suppose. Anyway, I hope you're all right. Call if you can. Bye.'*

I played the message again. And again. And again.

The message was received on December 14th. James had been dead for nearly a week. Everyone had been dead for nearly a week.

Or so I thought.

I rifled through the table drawers.

Address book.

Susan.

Susan Palmers. 17 Collister Avenue, Easington, Banbury, OX15 6BN.

Telephone Number: 01295 657823

I picked up the phone. No dial tone.

My mobile was back at the cottage.

I ripped the page out of the book, grabbed my rucksack, and ran out.

The wolves returned to the ridge when I was about halfway back, but once more they just sat, stared, and howled.

I hardly noticed them.

I opened the door to the cottage and was immediately knocked flat by an ecstatic Lucky. He chuffed little barks of happiness and licked my face as I hugged and petted him and only moved away from me when I emptied two cans of corned beef and one of Spam into his bowl.

I grabbed my phone and dialled Susan Palmers' number. *Beep, beep, beep.*

Of course I had no signal.

Motherfuckers.

I sat on the floor and resisted the urge to hurl my phone at the wall.

Lucky came over to give me Spam-flavoured licks, and I hugged him and whispered into his ear.

'We're going to go to Banbury. We're going to find someone else.'

And then I laughed. Out loud. It was such a strange sound to my ears that I did it again, louder.

I don't think Lucky had ever heard me laugh that loudly before, because he skittered away and hid under the sink.

That night I was woken up by a sound I didn't recognise.

The wind was howling as normal, but something was also drumming rhythmically against the house.

Part of me wanted to see what it was, but a bigger part of me knew that I would be up in a couple of hours anyway and if I got up now I was bound to need a wee and that would be a whole load of hassle that could be avoided if I just went back to sleep . . .

By the time I woke the next morning the noise was gone and I had forgotten all about it, so I went about my morning ritual as normal. I put two more pairs of socks on and vowed to get slippers as soon as possible, stuck two jumpers back on and tried to ignore the stink coming off me, put more logs on the fire and got it burning strongly again, gathered all the dirty plates and cups from the night before and walked from my gloomy sitting room, through my gloomy hall, into my gloomy kitchen. I dumped the dirty plates and cups with the other dirty plates and cups (I rarely bothered to wash up), filled the kettle, got clean plates and cups, and took them back to the sitting room.

As normal Lucky whined and stared at my mixing bowl/potty and, as normal, I yawned and said a grumpy, 'No', so as normal we trudged back down the gloomy hallway and I opened the front door to let him out and HOLY MOTHER OF FUCK!

Green. Everywhere. Green.

The sky was still grey and threatening, but the snow was gone.

Completely gone. The sound I'd heard must have been rain, and it must have been coming down pretty hard, because now instead of snow I could see the loch and the houses on the shoreline and the mountains in the background and paths and roads and trees and grass and green, green, green.

I rushed out of the cottage without my boots on and stepped straight into a huge pile of Lucky's faeces.

Karma.

I didn't care. I ran around the side of the cottage and I could see the Defender. The fields to it were clear and the road was clear.

I could leave.

I could go and find Susan Palmers.

Soho Farmhouse would have to wait. I might have to put it off for ever.

I'm good at that, putting things off

———

It was James who finally persuaded me to get help.

I had been putting it off for years, thinking I was doing a good job of hiding my panic and depression.

I wasn't.

James and I had been together for seven years. We'd bought our flat, had birthdays and Christmases together and with our families. James was the advertising director at his company now and had his own office and executive assistant. I'd been promoted three times. Ginny had moved jobs and just met someone called Alex who she was spending increasing amounts of time with. Xav had remodelled his roof and was slowly turning his house into the premier party venue of West London.

I'd had a thousand small moments of joy that added up to a life well, and happily, lived.

On the whole.

Once experienced, panic attacks and depression never truly leave you; even if they aren't physically there, the memory is, like an imprint in concrete.

I'd had good days and bad days. Whole months without one panic attack and then weeks where I found it hard to step outside the flat and most definitely could not get on the underground or into the lift at work. I'd had days filled with sunshine and days where I lay in bed pretending to have a migraine but really blanketed in a cover of fog that would not lift. I'd had days that were exactly how I wanted them to be and then days where I had no idea what I was doing or why I was doing it. Days where I felt whole and days where I could feel tiny pieces of myself floating away, pieces that would be lost for ever.

I thought my problems had been successfully hidden behind my façade of migraines and adorable quirks ('It's a lovely day! Let's walk instead of getting the underground').

James knew though, of course he knew. He loved me.

It was nothing that he said.

In our whole relationship we never once talked openly about my panic attacks or depression. I never wanted to admit to them.

Instead, James came home one day with a can of squirty cream, the stuff that comes straight out of the nozzle.

'It lasts for ever,' he said, putting it in the fridge. 'Let's keep it and then when you are having a bad day you can just take the can out and squirt it straight into your mouth like this,' he demonstrated, 'and then I'll know you're having a shit time without you even having to tell me.'

It was a joke. But the love and flash of concern in his eyes was enough to tell me he knew. He knew I struggled. Every time I was sad and lay in bed all day, every time I sat next to him on the sofa twitching while pretending to watch TV, every time I convinced him to take the bus or clutched his hand too tightly on the escalator, he knew. He knew, and it hurt him too.

So, I went to my GP.

It was surprisingly easy and he didn't commit me.

Six weeks later I had my first therapy session. I sat down, the therapist said, 'So why are you here?'

And I burst into tears.

I didn't manage to talk, I just cried for the entire forty-five-minute session.

At the end the therapist told me he needed to see me again

so was going to make me an urgent referral for a twelve-session course.

When I left, I felt lighter. I was taking control and getting the help that I needed. I would see him every week and I would get better.

My appointment letter arrived five weeks later. Twelve sessions, one a month: the first one would be in nine weeks' time.

I cried again.

London was expensive. Even for middle-class, white-collar, no-children millennials like James and me, London was expensive.

I could have had private therapy sessions for £50 a pop – £200 a month. I thought it was too much.

I could have asked James, he would have said go for it. I could have asked my parents, who would have paid for it straight away and not even asked what it was for.

But I didn't ask anyone.

I was too scared what they might think of me.

———

Before I left the cottage I tried to reason with myself, tried to be cautious and methodical in packing up my things, taking stuff that might help on the journey, not rushing off straight away.

But, of course, that didn't happen.

I raced back inside the cottage, stripped off my shitty socks and pulled others on, rammed my boots onto my feet, threw a random assortment of clothes and other items into my rucksack, wrestled into another jumper, slammed my hat on my head, yelled to Lucky, 'We're leaving,' and was out the door and across the fields in five minutes.

Of course I was back at the cottage ten minutes later to get the Defender's keys and this diary.

I did actually pause when I saw the tangle of duvets on the sofa.

I had done all right.

I had found shelter, kept myself warm, found food and water, detoxed from drugs, and I had survived. In fact, I had kept myself and Lucky alive.

I allowed myself the briefest moment of pride and then I bounced out through the door once more to go and meet my fellow survivor.

Lucky was even keener to leave the cottage than I, and was standing by the Defender whining to be let in by the time I got there.

As I turned the ignition key I had a brief moment of paralysing fear that the Defender might not start but, trusty as always, she roared into life first time with a rush of blue smoke from the exhaust.

Those folks at Land Rover know how to make a good vehicle. If anyone ever does read this diary I want you to know that I thoroughly endorse Land Rovers as my vehicle of choice – apocalypse or no apocalypse.

I left the engine running, dived into the back and grabbed a can of Pepsi and a Snickers bar just as I realised I still didn't have a clue where we were.

I decided to drive down to the village and look for some sort of road sign.

Something or things were rotting in the back of the Defender, but I wasn't going to waste precious driving time cleaning it out, so I wound down the window of the cab to let some air in and heard a long, loud howl. Lucky dived into the footwell of the front seat and cowered there, shaking. As he did so, other howls joined the first, and Lucky whined softly. I wondered then if there had been another reason why Lucky did not like going outside of the cottage for a crap and for his rush from the cottage to the Defender.

There were eight wolves standing outside our cottage looking up at us.

I decided not to go back to the village and to stick to the road instead.

I drove for about two hours before seeing a sign for Inverness, which, it turned out, was only forty miles away, so we were back there by early afternoon.

My first instinct was to stop at a pharmacy and refill my prescription (that I had prescribed and written for myself), and I was actually taking the packets off the shelf before I stopped to think if it was really a good idea. I'd been free of Tramadol for about three weeks, and was doing okay, I didn't even really crave it that much any more, but was OBSESSED with chocolate in a way that couldn't be fully attributed to my near-starvation experience.

Also, I never realised how much I appreciated being able to have an easy and simple shit until I became constantly constipated from the Tramadol. There is a sweet happiness in a visit to the toilet that doesn't involve half an hour of straining and sweating and pleading with God to produce one tiny nugget of poo. These days I am in and out in three minutes with a smile on my face.

So, I thought, maybe I don't need to take any. Maybe I am stronger than that.

Also, it probably wouldn't set the right tone to meet my fellow survivor while high as a kite.

I took just one packet with me for emergencies.

We were leaving Inverness when Lucky gave a sharp bark. I slammed on my brakes and just avoided running over a large black dog racing out from an alley. The dog stopped and stared as if it had never seen a car before in its life. Then it nonchalantly loped on in the direction it had been going. As I watched it go, another dog exited the alley and followed, then another and another. It became a steady stream, all heading in the same direction; mostly in ones or twos, but every now and then in a bigger group.

The sun had melted the leftover snow and bathed the buildings in a rosy glow. The weather was positively spring-like. Things were starting to heat up and I realised that the bodies in the town gathering would soon be starting to defrost. And rot. And smell.

My stomach flipped as I registered that the dogs were all heading in the direction of the town gathering. There must have been at least thirty that crossed over the road in front of me, and God knows how many others from elsewhere.

I beeped my horn at the stragglers still wandering across the road and, when they ignored me, drove slowly forward.

And, as the sun started to set, I drove faster, putting as many miles between me and Inverness as possible.

I have always loved driving long distances on empty roads (hardly ever possible before) and now the road was all mine and the distance was huge.

However, driving post-apocalypse takes some getting used to. For a start, despite the fact there are no other cars on the road, that doesn't mean I don't look out for them. I still obey the Highway Code: stopping at (working) traffic lights, using my indicators, checking no one is coming around corners, going the right way at roundabouts. It is hard just to forget the rules that have shaped your driving technique for years.

I am both far too relaxed and also hyper-aware when I am driving; with no one else on the road it is very easy to lapse into a sort of dream-like state where you drive on instinct and don't take notice of anything around you. When this happens, I've found I can easily drive straight off the road without even noticing until I feel the change in terrain. As a result, I try to stay very aware of where I am, what is going on around me, what speed I am doing, where my next junction is, what signs are coming up.

I have stopped driving at night unless it is absolutely necessary because, I have discovered, I don't like the dark. Without electricity and without street lights it is very, very dark at night. I have driven in dark and remote places before 6DM, but I don't remember it being as dark as this. Maybe it is because it is winter, there is a lot of cloud cover and therefore very little starlight. Maybe it is psychological; I am alone, the night is dark and full of terror, and I am scared. The darkness extends endlessly in all directions beyond my headlights and my fear and loneliness extends with it. Endlessly and in all directions.

My saddest post-apocalyptic driving discovery of all though is that I cannot shake the feeling that someone else is going to drive over the horizon at some point. It feels like when I used to drive on motorways late at night and for the briefest of moments I would be the only car that could be seen in any direction and I would pretend I was the last person on earth (ha ha). Now I am potentially the last person on earth, but I still keep expecting to see headlights come over the brow of the hill.

Of course, they don't.

Even without driving at night, my desperation to reach Susan Palmers plus the lack of drugs in my system meant I did the previously week-long journey to Scotland in two days this time. I kept up a steady 70 mph on the motorway, which was what the Defender would do comfortably without starting to rattle.

Despite my excitement, I still forced myself to drive through Liverpool and Manchester, which were intact but devoid of signs of life. I had to check that there was definitely no one hiding in these huge conurbations, so found a high point in each city and pressed the Defender's horn intermittently for a couple of hours. No one came.

Once past Manchester my excitement began to verge on panic. Just to hear another person talk, to hold someone's hand, to smile and be smiled back at. I unknowingly drove faster every time I thought about it and had to slam the brakes on as the Defender started to shake in protest.

When I am not excited, I am worried. I worry that Susan Palmers may not have had enough food or water to survive since she rang her sister or that her cat has died and she was so lonely that she has already killed herself and all I find is a corpse.

I worry that Susan Palmers had 6DM all along and just didn't know it when she rang.

Susan Palmers is now my new, and only, reason to live.

I haven't thought about what I will actually do if Susan Palmers is dead.

I imagine that would send me spiralling into a depression without end.

————

I think everyone experiences depression differently. One person's 'bad day' is another's 'crawl under the duvet for a week'. For me, if my panic attacks turned the dial on my energy, emotions, and digestive system up to 11, then depression turned that dial down to −11.

It always felt like a blanket of inertia had been placed over me emotionally and physically. Given the choice I wouldn't have left my bed. Whereas normal me would get up, go out, look about and smile, depressed me would haul herself out of bed, struggle out the door, look at the floor the whole time, and forget how to smile. I could easily stare at a wall for an hour, with my own level of emotion perfectly mimicking its blank façade.

Sometimes I cried, sometimes I didn't. Often I continued with my life as normal, forcing myself to go to work, get tea, chat to people at lunchtime. All through the blanket of fog that lay upon me.

I should have paid for the therapy sessions, but I didn't, and things got worse.

Just like with the onset of my major panic attacks, there was no huge reason for my breakdown. I got on the bus home from work one day and when my stop came I found that I couldn't get off.

The fog was just too heavy for me to stand.

I couldn't get off in the bus station either.

In the end they called the police.

I cried.

The police were kind.

I was too sad to go back to James, so I went home.

My mum didn't ask me anything, didn't say anything, just wrapped me in her arms and held me as I cried and cried and cried.

She never asked why.

She just knew I needed her.

I didn't tell her why. I couldn't tell her why, because I didn't know.

I had everything I ever wanted. I was safe and secure. I had James, a great job, a lovely flat, money. Surely this was the perfect life? Every magazine, every advert, every television programme told me that I was living a good life, a life that I should be happy with.

I should be happy.

I should be happy.

I should be happy.

But I wasn't.

I stayed at home for nine days.

My mum fed me tea and chicken soup and stroked my hair as I slept for hours and hours.

She let James in to see me on day eight, when it became clear I wasn't going to tell her what was wrong.

He sat on the side of the bed and cried with me.

He loved me. He'd make things better. My life would be better. I would be better.

He asked me to marry him.

I hadn't changed my pyjamas in a week, my hair hadn't been washed in a fortnight, my skin was blotched from crying, and he asked me to marry him.

How romantic.

I laughed.

Not because I was happy, but because I suddenly saw how ridiculous it all was.

Me – chasing my romantic fantasy, determined to have this idealised life of happiness, and now I was engaged.

And depressed.

Maybe I should have said no, should have finally been honest with him and said, 'I have no idea who I am or what I am doing any more.' Maybe he would have said he didn't either.

Maybe things would have been different if I had been honest. Maybe not.

Instead, I told him I loved him too.

It was true, I loved him. James was my life. I didn't know who I was without him any more.

Without James where would I go? How would I manage? What would I have? Who would I be?

I wouldn't manage, I couldn't manage. I would be nothing and have no one.

James loved me and wanted to marry me. I had got what I wanted.

I would get married and have a family.

That would be enough.

We would both be happy with that.

February 24th 2024

I had no idea how to find Susan Palmers without Google Maps but I wasn't going to let that stop me from reaching my very own talking Wilson. I followed signs for Easington and then for the hospital and then methodically drove from street to street.

It took two and a half days to find the right one.

I've always had a really good sense of smell – that's why I smelt number 17 before I saw it.

Collister Avenue was lined with parked cars, so I had abandoned the Defender at the top of the street and was racing down it trying to spy the house numbers with Lucky yapping at my heels.

It was a smell that stopped me, not the numbers.

There was actually no discernible smell of decay in the suburbs – even for someone with a nose as sensitive as mine. Most houses had doors and windows shut, so there was very little room for the stench of putrefaction to escape.

This smell was new and made me stop.

It wasn't a nice smell, but it was something familiar that I hadn't smelt out in the open for some time.

I was trying to work it out when Lucky went into a complete frenzy of barking and raced up and down the footpath of the nearest house.

So I turned to look . . .

I didn't see her at first.

Instead, the first thing I saw was the doorstep and pathway, laden with piles of shit.

That was the smell.

Shit.

But not dog shit, that was what had been confusing me; I was used to the smell of dog shit now.

This was human shit.

That was when I looked at the window.

For a moment my brain refused to acknowledge what I was seeing. I thought it must be a statue or a tailor's dummy or a huge doll.

But it wasn't.

It was Susan Palmers.

My instant impulse was to charge through the front door and hug her.

I lurched towards the door, dodging piles of shit and yelling, 'Susan Palmers! You're alive! You're alive!!'

She began to bang furiously on the window and pointed at her front door.

I halted for a moment, hand outstretched for the doorknob.

She banged again, more furiously.

I stopped, looked at the door, took a step back.

KEEP OUT. I HAVE A GUN AND
I WILL FUCKING SHOOT YOU.

Thick, black and painted on the door.

Oh.

It really took the wind out of my sails.

I didn't know what to do.

My brain couldn't think past having the full-on heart-wrenching, happy-tear bawling, hug-fest that I had spent the last 450 miles and three months dreaming about.

But that obviously wasn't happening.

I picked my way back through the shit to stand in front of the window.

I couldn't see her very well as she'd covered the windows in clingfilm. I'd have guessed she was maybe in her seventies, wild hair greying, pale skin sagging. She was thin, very, very thin and when I looked closely it looked like her hair could have been falling out.

'Hello.'

It seemed as good a place as any to start.

'*Herroinhurgosmolof*'

No idea what she was saying.

I cleared my throat and tried again.

Lucky rubbed against my leg. I looked down at him.

'This is Lucky.'

'*Infckstrgogmesfd*'

It was no good, the window was muffling everything, I couldn't hear her.

I had an idea.

I rushed down the path and she started to bang furiously again. I turned to tell her I'd be back, realised it wouldn't be worth it, and so hurried on.

Susan Palmers banged furiously the whole time.

I picked a random house across the street, held my breath, and barged through the front door.

It was, miracle of miracles, empty.

I found what I needed and went back.

I held up the piece of paper I had written on in marker pen.

Hello

She stared at my sign for a moment and then disappeared.

A couple of minutes later she was back. She had her own sign.

> Don't come in I will shoot you

Not the most welcoming or warmest start to what might be the last friendship on earth.

Also, I was not entirely sure she actually had a gun. I was tempted to ask 'show me your gun then,' but was still hopeful we could be friends, so was composing something when she held her sign back up.

> I'm starving get me food

My first impulse was to be sarcastic and write '. . . get me food PLEASE'. Instead I wrote . . .

How? I can't come in

Get gloves and boiler suit and face mask and put them on then get food and water DON'T TOUCH ANYTHING WITHOUT THE GLOVES ON bring it back to me. And I need statins from the hospital pharmacy. I have high cholestrol. And I want some gin.

I burst out laughing.

She was serious.

She propped the sign up against the window and moved away.

I waited by the window for her to come back.

She came back.

Go now

What could I do? Say no?

I felt like my brain was going to explode.

I wasn't the last person on earth! Susan Palmers was alive! It was a fucking, beautiful miracle!

Not a perfect miracle of course, because she seemed a bit, well, a bit of a bitch actually.

If I'm being completely honest.

Maybe she was just one of those people it took some time to get to know. That was fine, we had all the time in the world.

I spent the rest of the day getting what she wanted. It wasn't easy, as the DIY stores were out of town so I had to drive around until I found one that had gloves and a boiler suit, and then I had to find a supermarket, check for rats, and get stuff as fast as humanly possible.

I went to three chemists looking for her statins. None of them had any in. It looked like she was right and it would have to be the hospital.

I went to the hospital.

The doors to A&E were closed. I stood far back from them, thinking about what I was going to do. I was wearing the boiler suit, so was physically protected from anything . . . mushy . . . that might be in there.

I walked slowly towards the door and paused again.

Twice I walked forward slightly, genuinely intent on entering the hospital, twice I backed off at the last minute.

It was no good. I couldn't do it. I couldn't go in after my last experience at A&E. She would have to do without her statins for now.

I reasoned with myself that it would be too ironic and cruel for her to survive 6DM but then die from high cholesterol. Not even a vengeful God would do that, surely?

The sun was starting to set as I got back to Susan Palmers.

She was not happy.

> WHERE HAVE YOU BEEN????
> YOU'VE BEEN GONE AGES

I felt a little guilty as I imagined how I would have felt if someone had taken ages to bring me food when I was starving. I shrugged an apology.

I had found a new kitchen message board in the supermarket to write on, so scrawled . . .

Sorry — no statins

I thought I saw her sigh.

> Put the boiler suit and face mask on again

I diligently obeyed.

> Stay there

She disappeared, and five minutes later I heard bolts and locks being opened on the front door. She came back to the window wearing a homemade boiler suit of black bin liners that literally covered her from head to foot apart from two tiny eyeholes. She had welding goggles on over her eyes. It was the stuff of nightmares.

'*hmmmpf vrn strpk cren*'

I couldn't understand a word she was saying with all the bin liners over her face. I shrugged. She indicated that I should bring everything in and leave it on the floor by waving her arms wildly.

I picked up the bags full of food and two litres of gin I had got, and carried them through the front door and into a small hallway.

Even with the face mask on the stench was unbearable and made me gag. For the first time since leaving the cottage in Scotland, Lucky left my side and stayed outside. He's not daft.

Turned out that she did have a gun.

Slumped in the corner with an unmistakeable large red (or once red) stain across his chest was a rotting corpse. He was still ripe.

I dropped the food and gin, shattering one of the bottles, and staggered back down the path, slipping and sliding in human shit along the way.

I didn't stop at the gate. I didn't stop on the street.

I called Lucky to me, and I left.

I walked to the end of the road and threw up.

I didn't go back that day.

I wasn't even sure I was going to go back.

Not a bloody please or thank you all day, and now this?

I finally find someone else alive, and she's a murderer.

She has a gun and she shot someone. Who's to say she won't shoot me?

I don't want to die.

At least not by being shot by Susan fucking Palmers.

February 26th 2024

Who was I kidding?

This is what I had wanted, what I had dreamt of ever since London.

Someone else alive.

And so what if Susan was a murderer? What was the worst that could happen? She shoots me. I'd literally been planning to kill myself anyway, maybe she'd save me the bother.

I was never going to just walk away.

I wasn't alone any more, and I would just have to make it work with her, even if she was rude.

Not the worst thing in the world.

Loneliness. That's worst thing in the world.

————

When the Coronavirus happened in 2020 Xav quarantined alone.

In the eight years that James and I had been together, Xav and I had gone from seeing each other every couple of days to snatching a few hours every couple of weeks and maybe a proper night out once a month.

When we did meet we could no longer discuss the most important parts of our lives freely; he couldn't understand my relationship with James, and I couldn't understand his continued narcotic obsession.

He no longer came for Sunday lunch at my parents'; I took James with me instead.

Xav was still my best friend, but we were no longer an integral part of each other's lives. The best parts of our friendship lived in the past now, mixed up in the memories of our younger, braver and easier selves.

Xav's dad died three weeks before lockdown. The funeral had been filled with Rupert's banking colleagues and little-known relatives hoping to be remembered in his will. Xav had smiled, shaken hands, and patted shoulders, but he looked grey and tired and old. He wasn't even high.

I was worried about him.

Going against James's wishes for once, I had stayed at Xav's for two nights following the funeral, and for those two days it was like old times. Xav smoked nothing stronger than cannabis and we danced to our favourite records, watched our favourite films, and talked until late into the night, successfully avoiding the taboo subjects of our respective most significant others.

But on the third night he threw a huge party, snorted a massive amount of cocaine, and declared himself now to be one of the richest men in London.

I left without saying goodbye.

Lockdown started about two weeks later, and he was alone.

We spoke every day during the first week. He said he was fine, he had food, booze, drugs, and the best party palace in London, how could he possibly be unhappy.

I only spoke to him twice during the next month. Each time he was short and hurried, said he was going for his daily walk or was busy cooking himself some food.

Xav never cooked.

In the middle of week five he rang me, crying. He was lonely. So, so lonely. So lonely, it was like a physical pain.

I was the only person who spoke to him, the only person who cared. He had no one else now his dad was dead. Rupert had left everything to him, so the distant family members who had attended the funeral had crawled back disappointedly to wherever they came from. Even his drug dealer wasn't picking up the phone.

He hadn't touched another person in five weeks, did I have any idea how horrible that was?

I do now.

I begged James to let him come and quarantine with us. Begged him. James said no. It wasn't allowed. Plus, Xav and he didn't get on, and Xav would be crawling the walls in our small one-bed flat within hours.

I knew James was right; he and I were having trouble enough getting along in such a small space while working from home, fielding constant calls from my mum and Ginny about wedding planning, and only going out once a day for exercise. Plus James and I had recently decided to start trying for a baby, so we were taking advantage of us both being at home and having a lot of sex. A LOT of sex.

I told James I'd go to Xav's.

No.

James was very firm.

I should have insisted that I go and see Xav, insisted that I help him in some way, but I was scared; scared of the virus, scared of going against the rules, scared of giving James something else to worry about when he was already worried about his job, his family, the economy . . .

Telling Xav I couldn't help him was horrible.

I didn't hear from Xav for nearly three weeks. Every time I called his home or mobile I got his answerphone.

Then, one day, on a regular catch-up call with my mum, I heard Xav in the background.

I couldn't understand it. How could I be hearing him? How was he there?

It turned out that although he hadn't been coming to Sunday lunch with me any more, he'd still been seeing my parents at least once a week. Probably more than I saw them. He had been for lunch or dinner, sometimes he would stay over.

So, when he rang my mum, crying, she had immediately dispatched my dad to go and fetch him and bring him back to quarantine with them.

I was absolutely fucking livid.

I refused to talk to him on the phone, but on the day lockdown lifted I was at my parents' by 7 a.m. so that he didn't have time to sneak back home.

I had never shouted at Xav. I did that day.

'THEY COULD HAVE FUCKING DIED, YOU SELFISH ARSEHOLE.'

He tried to explain, tried to tell me he was sorry. I wasn't having any of it.

I didn't speak to him again until my wedding day.

I understand why he did it now.

———

Susan Palmers was ready with a new sign as soon as I walked into her garden the next morning.

> He tried to get in and hurt me

I just stood there.

> Don't leave again

I didn't move.

> Thanks for the stuff

It was the best I was going to get.

I cleared the front path of her faeces and hosed it down. I never did ask her what happened to her toilet that meant she had to throw her shit out of the window. Maybe she just did it as a deterrent.

Once the faeces was finally gone, I got a garden chair, sat in the front garden, and we talked, as much as you can talk without,

well, actually talking. Susan wouldn't come outside, and I sure
as shit wasn't going back in.

I've been to Scotland. I met your sister.

She's alive???

Whoops.

**No. Sorry. She's dead. Sorry. I heard your answerphone
message and that's how I found you.**

Pause.

Its all right. We haven't spoken in 7 years. Shes crazy.

Oh.

I'm so glad I found you

Pause.

I had to eat my cat

Pause.

And next door's cat

I told her more about me.

I used to live in London. My husband died there.

And I learnt more about her.

So? All my family is dead. And everyone on this
street. And everyone in town. Everyone's dead.
We're the only two here now

Rude and blunt.

I bet it was them muslims that did it

Rude, blunt, and racist.

We should have let Trump do what he wanted to them

Rude, blunt, racist, and stupid.

> I saw two planes in the sky yesterday. It's the goverment seeing if we are alive.

Rude, blunt, racist, stupid, and possibly insane.

> I want to get out of here.

Rude, racist, stupid, possibly insane, and potentially my new life partner.

Six days later, full of the food and gin I had got her and revelling in having someone to spout her crazy theories to, she was positively ebullient.

And very keen to get out into the world.

I, on the other hand, was growing more reluctant to grant her freedom.

Having spent more time with her, I wasn't sure she was that stable – mentally or physically. What if she ate me?

Also, in all the peace and quiet of life as it was now, I had forgotten how fucking annoying it is when someone talks on and on about, well, nothing. And I couldn't even hear her! What on earth was it going to be like if she got out and could just rabbit on constantly with no barrier between us?

But she did make me feel better about myself and how I had handled the end of the world – at least I had managed to come this far without shooting someone or going completely insane.

Also, I was hardly going to leave her in her house to starve to death and, if I was completely honest, she had single-handedly stopped me from killing myself.

I reasoned that any companionship was better than no companionship.

So, I devised a plan.

I would get her a proper hazmat suit from somewhere, and then I could at least move her to a slightly nicer location while we sorted out what to do long-term.

Preferably somewhere that didn't have a corpse in the front hallway.

It took me two days to get the hazmat suit.

I had to find an army base, break into the army base, realise that there were no hazmat suits at that army base, so then go to an RAF base, realise that the only hazmat suit had a body in it already, drag that body out, vomit many times, have a freezing night's sleep in the back of the Defender, get up, not bother with breakfast, hose the hazmat suit down (inside and out), vomit again, and then wait for the hazmat suit to dry.

I was running low on diesel, so was bloody delighted to find that the RAF base had working fuel pumps, so I spent another couple of hours filling canisters and packing them into the back of the Defender.

It was pitch black by the time I was finished and, with no lighting, I couldn't see my way out of the base so was forced to remove all the canisters I had worked so hard to pack away and then spend another cold and uncomfortable night in the back, cuddling Lucky for warmth.

March 7th 2024

She had a new sign ready for me as soon as I arrived back.

FUCK YOU

Her mouth was spewing words I couldn't hear, but I knew they weren't friendly. When she paused mid flow to cough, blood splattered onto the clingfilmed window.

She was sick.

6DM sick.

Was it me? Was it the food? The gin? Something in the air that I'd let in?

Who knows.

I felt awful.

All that time alone. Eating all her food, her cat, her neighbour's cat. Posting her shit through the front door or throwing it out of the window for weeks on end. Finally thinking that it had all been worth it, that she was saved.

Compared to her existence I had been living the life of Riley. Freedom, food, drink, drugs, travel – like something from a *Sunday Times* supplement.

I can get you T600

I could faintly hear her shouting something profane.

I wondered if she was always this way. If she was always this horrible and mean and cruel and, well, lacking in basic humanity. Maybe she used to be nice and sweet and someone's grandma, with dishes of toffees scattered about her house.

Maybe not. I'm not sure my grandma even knew the word 'cunt'.

I went to get her T600 and nearly didn't return to Collister Avenue.

But, I felt giving her the T600 was probably the least I could do, seeing as it was highly likely I had also given her the 6DM.

you bring that fucking stuff in the house I'll shoot you

She didn't want the T600.

It took another four days for her to die.

I was convinced she was going to shoot me through the window – so I moved my chair back across the street so that I could still see her but was, hopefully, out of range of the gun.

I sat there each day and went to the house across the road to sleep at night. Lucky sat by me and whined every time Susan Palmers appeared.

When she had the energy she banged on the window and held up signs calling me a variety of colourful names normally involving the words 'fuck', 'cunt', 'shithole', and my personal favourite 'fucking killer bitch'.

The one thing that puzzled me even more than why Susan Palmers hadn't shot me, was why she hadn't come outside after she had got 6DM.

She could have died in the fresh air, or even carried out one of the painful murder scenarios she had dreamt up for me.

I nearly asked her once, but it was one of those very rare situations where I allowed my brain to catch up with my mouth and as I put my chalk to the blackboard I thought, 'Hold on, is this a good idea?'

I put the chalk firmly back on the grass.

By day three I was feeling far less sorry for her and increasingly sorry for me. The last person left alive with me was so MEAN. It was very obvious now that she would never have been a fun life partner and would probably have killed me the first chance she got. But, although I knew I was better off with her dead, the prospect of being on my own again filled me with despair.

I also couldn't deny the reality of what the death of Susan Palmers meant – that even if I did find another survivor, as soon as I spoke to them or tried to help them in any way they would, in all likelihood, die. Susan Palmers had succumbed to 6DM within a week of my food delivery – so the chances were that the same thing would happen again if I met anyone else.

Susan Palmers had put the final nail in the coffin that I had filled with my hope of meeting any other survivor.

I was responsible for killing Susan Palmers, and eventually, without even leaving her house, she would be responsible for killing me.

March 11th 2024

On the morning of the fourth day of my Susan Palmers death vigil I woke up to the sound of dogs barking. Lucky was asleep beside me as usual and he jumped up and bounded to the window.

Across the street in front of Susan Palmers' house was a gathering of maybe twenty dogs. Dogs of all shapes, sizes, and breeds, jumping up and down and barking in a frenzy. Whether they had been called there by Susan Palmers' recently decaying flesh or my fresh scent I wasn't sure, but I was glad I had shut the front door of the house I was staying in firmly the night before.

After discovering they couldn't get into Susan Palmers' house, the dogs calmed down and broke apart. A couple of them wandered across the street and started sniffing at the footpath to the house I was in. I clutched Lucky to me, half for comfort and half to keep him quiet. I was unsure of what being discovered by this pack would mean for us both. But soon, the larger members of the pack started trotting down the road in search of their next adventure, or dinner. The rest followed in twos or threes and, fifteen minutes after I had heard the first bark, the street was empty again.

Susan Palmers had left me one final note.

Your a killer fucking cunt. I hope you die in agony

Imagine spending four days dying from 6DM and saving all your hate up for one final message only to have it ruined by bad grammar.

Poor Susan Palmers.

———

This was not the first time I'd been called a cunt.

James's best friend thought I was a cunt. 'A stuck-up cunt' to be precise.

He, Matthew, was the friend that James was living with before we moved in together and, when I came downstairs after spending my first night at James's flat, he was making a cup of tea in the kitchen and his exact words were . . .

'Yeah, she's quite fit, but a bit of a stuck-up cunt don't you think?'

Matthew pretended he was talking about Kate Middleton, but we all knew he was talking about me.

He made me a cup of tea. I didn't drink it.

James continued to be best friends with Matthew. He was the only one of James's friends that I refused to hang out with. I couldn't really complain though, my best friend thought James was boring; so we agreed that James wouldn't have to see Xav and I wouldn't have to see Matthew.

Until James chose Matthew to be his Best Man at our wedding.

Surprisingly, it wasn't the fact that James had insisted on having someone who thought I was a stuck-up cunt as his Best Man that made me cry on our wedding day.

Despite everything I was doing that day to stave off panic attacks, depression and any other unwanted emotion, it turned out that all it took was a song.

The Carpenters.

The bloody Carpenters, and 'We've Only Just Begun'.

On a radio in the background as I was having my hair done.

All that stuff about starting out in life together and so many roads to choose and working together each day.

It was written for couples like my mum and dad. Couples who married when they were still at the beginning of their lives together and were still filled with hope and excitement for the journey to come.

It wasn't written for couples like James and me, who had already completed a large chunk of their journey.

My reality was the complete opposite to the one Karen Carpenter sang so sweetly about.

I had wanted James to ask me to marry him because he couldn't imagine life without me, not because we'd been together eight years so it was about time. I wanted to get married when we were still taking a leap of faith that it would work out, when we didn't know each other's bowel movement schedule, when we were still having sex because we JUST HAD TO, rather than when it matched my ovulation cycle.

I wanted a Karen Carpenter wedding and, as much as I told myself I was lucky to be getting married at all, the heart wants what the heart wants.

So, I started to cry.

I cried when my mum and Ginny, assuming that the emotion was all too much, rushed over and mopped up my fragile lady tears before they smudged my newly applied mascara.

I cried when my dad met me at the top of the aisle and walked me down with the proudest look on his face that I have ever seen.

I cried when James turned back to look at me and mouthed, 'You look beautiful.'

I cried the most when Matthew turned around and beamed at me as I walked down the aisle. I cried because I knew he still thought I was a stuck-up cunt, but James was his best friend and Matthew loved James, and James loved me; so if James wanted to marry me then Matthew was going to darn well support him in his endeavours.

It was during my dad's beautiful, heartfelt and loving speech that I stopped crying and started bawling because, there, surrounded by beaming faces I realised that all anyone in the room wanted was for me to be happy.

But I just wasn't.

It was Xav who finally stopped me crying.

But not in a good way.

I was sitting at the edge of the dance floor watching everyone I loved having the time of their lives to '(I've Had) The Time of My Life', when Xav appeared.

I hadn't spoken to Xav in seven months. He hadn't said he was coming to the wedding.

He was thin and crumpled. His hair was too long and his normally alabaster clear skin was a fester of spots and cold sores. I knew he was high before he even spoke to me, I could tell by the way he jerked his left shoulder every now and again, the way he tugged at the front of his hair.

'What are you doing?' he demanded.

'You're high.'

He shrugged and tugged his hair again. It looked as if it might be falling out.

'I said, what are you doing?' He almost shouted it this time.

I wasn't going to make a scene so through clenched teeth answered, 'I'm just having a break. I'll get back up in a minute.'

'No,' he snapped, 'I mean what the fuck are you doing?'

He wasn't just high, he was angry. High and rambling and angry.

'What is this?' He gestured to the huge wedding venue and heaving dance floor. 'You always told me you wanted a registry office wedding and just a dinner afterwards. And this?' he said, yanking a handful of my sweetheart-necked, tulle-skirted, full-length princess wedding dress. 'This isn't the dress you showed me. You wanted a short one.'

I shrugged.

'I've seen you miserable before, and I've seen you faking it. Doing your "everything's fine" smile.' He grabbed the corners of my mouth and pushed them up. It hurt. I pulled my face away. 'But this faking it on your WEDDING DAY. I mean, what the fuck? Why? Why all this? I don't understand you any more. I don't know who you are!'

I didn't know what to say. He was right. This wasn't the wedding I had dreamt of. It wasn't the wedding I wanted. It was the wedding my mum and Ginny and James had dreamt of and wanted for me.

The perfect wedding.

But I wasn't going to admit that to Xav. Not now.

I was tired and hungry and my wedding dress was digging into my hips.

But I had stopped crying.

I wasn't sad any more. I was angry.

And Xav was there. So I went for him. Full throttle.

'You don't understand me any more? You don't know me? I'll tell you why you don't know me, because I have changed, I've got myself a proper life and you can't understand that! Look at the state of you! You have money but you have NOTHING else. You didn't even have anyone who wanted to be with you during quarantine.'

He backed off from me as if I had hit him.

I wasn't finished.

'Some of us don't want to spend our lives pretending we're still twenty-one, some of us want to grow the fuck up! We want jobs and husbands and babies and real friends that aren't off their faces all the time. Some of us just want to try and be FUCKING NORMAL.'

His face was blank. His voice emotionless.

'Well, congratulations, because finally, you really fucking are.'

He turned and stumbled from the room, cannoning off tables and chairs on his way out.

I should have gone after him, but I didn't.

My mum told me they drove him to rehab two days later when James and I were on our honeymoon.

———

I didn't ask myself why I was going into the house to see Susan Palmers' dead body. I just knew I was going to.

It never crossed my mind to bury her.

I wasn't sure what I was going to find in the house, so was wearing the hazmat suit and had the helmet on, but I didn't use the oxygen tank as I had no idea how to work it and couldn't be bothered to try and find out.

I should have used the oxygen tank.

Susan Palmers was slumped in one of the sofa chairs. She was very, very thin and her eyes were wide open and stared straight at me. She had bled profusely from her nose, and the front of her filthy shirt was encrusted with a torrent of black, congealing blood. My skin crawled and I quickly threw a blanket over her. I could feel her dead eyes following me from underneath it.

The house was in complete squalor. Food, clothes, empty glasses, books, newspapers, scrawled notes and bits of paper, blankets and pillows on a filthy mattress all stiff with dirt and sweat. One corner was filled with plastic bags of human faeces. The kitchen held a pile of small animal bones that were picked clean and white. Many of the books had pages missing or had bites out of them. Everything was filthy, covered in a layer of grime and dust; the accumulation of nearly four months of dead skin.

Except for the bookcase.

All the books were on the floor and the bookcase was filled with photos in photo frames. Each framed photo was polished and gleaming. Placed in an exact spot. Each one captured a moment of happiness. Susan Palmers on her wedding day, shy smile and lace-capped veil. A man (her husband?) beaming with pride while holding a new-born baby as she smiles up at him, exhausted but happy. Children's birthday parties, Christmas, family holidays. Later pictures taken in a garden with grandchildren. Hers? Probably. In each photo she smiled. Carefree, relaxed, a woman content and happy with the people that she loved.

6DM must have started rotting her heart months ago.

On the mantelpiece was a graduation photo of a young man in gown and cap with his arm around Susan Palmers. He was smiling at the camera and she was beaming up at him, face filled with love and pride. In front of the photo was a small Dictaphone tape with the name 'George' on it.

The Dictaphone player was on the dining-room table.

I shut the door as I left the house, not wanting any of the smell and horror inside to be able to escape. I took the hazmat suit off, sat in my lawn chair, and listened to the tape.

Hi George darling, it's Nana. You know I'm not very good with my writing so I thought I would record this instead. You remember how gramps and I used to do this for you when you were at university? I wonder if you ever listened to them? Probably not. Don't suppose it matters now. And I know that you can't listen to this either, but I wanted to explain. I wanted to say sorry . . . sorry that I shot you. It wasn't because I don't love you! I love you very much. And your sister and your mum. And I know you think you were doing the right thing coming to get me, but I'm not sick. I'm really not. Your gramps went out at the beginning and didn't come back, so I haven't seen anyone else to catch it from and I'm not sick and I don't want to get sick. I want to live George. I've never thought about not being here before, about dying, but now that it is all around me, I don't want to. I don't want to die. So when you came into the house and then into the hallway even though I told you not to, well, I couldn't let you come any further. You'd have made me sick. You understand George, don't you? You were dying anyway and I know what your mum said about everyone getting ill in the end, but maybe I'll be okay. I'm so sorry, but I had to think fast and my brain has been a bit fuzzy since I shot your gramps and I couldn't think straight and I didn't want you to come in and you were dying anyway. But it wasn't because I don't love you. I love you very much. I just don't want to die. Your gramps did come back. He's in the back garden. I love him and I love you. I'm sorry.

When I went around the side of the house, I discovered a pile of fuzzy bones in the back garden. I assumed it was Gramps.

Susan Palmers really did want to live.

No wonder she hated me so much.

After listening to the tape, I went into the house across the road, got into bed, and stayed there.

I didn't cry. I think my tear ducts may finally have dried up or gone on a well-deserved holiday. I just lay in bed doing nothing. I occasionally stared out of the window, at nothing.

Lucky was worried about me. He lay with my hand on his head and if I moved it at any point he nudged my hand gently until it was back in place. He followed me to the toilet, to the kitchen, and lay next to me on the bed, climbing back on if I pushed him off. He brought me his ball to throw for him, but I just didn't have the energy.

I wanted to tell Lucky that Susan Palmers was dead. Everyone was dead. And now the fog had come and this time it might not go away.

I wanted to tell him I was afraid I may never get out of bed again and that this was it. No trip to Soho Farmhouse, no glamorous death in Egyptian cotton sheets. I would just slowly fade away in a heap of nothing until I was a pile of dust like the ones that had gathered in Susan Palmers' house.

I wanted to tell him to leave while he still could, that I couldn't be there for him any more, that I couldn't be there for anyone. I was done.

But I knew he wouldn't understand.

One of the drawbacks of having a dog for my best, and only, friend.

March 14th 2024

I got out of bed. Eventually.

I gave up on getting to Soho Farmhouse. I could barely make it across the room, let alone complete the long list of things that would need to happen for me to get to my suicide location of choice.

My new, very vague, plan was to drive to the first pharmacy I saw and grab some T600 before I lost my nerve. Then I was going to find a random hotel and spend a couple of days getting so ridiculously drunk that I either took the T600 in a drunken, maudlin moment or fell asleep and then woke up with a hangover to rival the one I had at the end of the (old) world so that I would want to take the T600 just to put myself out of my misery.

It wasn't a particularly good plan.

But it was good enough.

I found a Boots in the centre of Banbury with boxes of T600 just inside the door. I grabbed a packet and then didn't quite make it out of the shop before throwing up all over myself.

My tummy had been dodgy since a week before Susan Palmers died, and my random projectile vomiting had been happening on a regular basis. Neither Lucky nor I were a fan of it.

The nearest hotel to Boots was called Whatley Hall. It was no Soho Farmhouse, but it was big and had some lovely airy bedrooms, and lots of space. It was also clean, free from decomposing bodies and, miraculously, had electricity, central heating, and hot water. I went in the bathroom of the first room I could get into and showered three times before the smell of vomit faded.

I have spent the past three days throwing up for most of the morning and feeling sick for the rest of the time. The only thing I can face eating is peanut butter or Mini Cheddars. My stomach is churning and my head spins when I move too fast.

Maybe I am sick, maybe 6DM has mutated and this is how it is going to start, and end, for me. Maybe I am experiencing extreme physical symptoms of depression. Or maybe my body, like my mind, has just had enough and is finally giving up.

Prisoners kept in solitary confinement for long periods of time say (or did say) that the key to surviving with your sanity intact is to create a strict routine and stick to it. People who were in isolation alone in 2020 said the same – routine, routine, routine.

I have no routine now.

I'd had a routine when I left London because I had somewhere I wanted to go. I'd had a routine at the cottage because I was detoxing. I even had a routine when I left the cottage because I had Susan Palmers to get to and then look after.

But now Susan Palmers is dead and I have all but given up on the idea of dying at Soho Farmhouse, so I have nowhere to go and nothing to do.

I am just here. In Banbury. Alone.

I will always be alone.

I miss my family and friends. Every day. At some point in every 24-hour period I think of them and the ache in my chest returns; sometimes for a few minutes and sometimes for hours. I think of this as my penance for surviving.

There will be no end to the self-isolation I am in. There will be no vaccine developed. No lifting of quarantine laws, no celebrations at being able to see loved ones again, at being able to embrace freely once more.

This will never end.

I don't want to live like this any more, bouncing from place to place, chasing a dream that I now know isn't, and will never be, real.

I think I'm ready to go.

———

I was chasing a dream before the end of the world as well.

It is the same dream now as it was then; I want someone to be here, someone who will love and take care of me. Someone who will make it all better.

Ginny had that.

Ginny found all that and more – and she wasn't even looking for it. She'd been perfectly happy by herself.

Lucky cow.

Ginny met Alex in a bar. She wasn't interested in him, she was chatting to his better-looking, taller friend. But, in the great romantic tradition, he made her laugh. Alex made her laugh so much she can't quite remember agreeing to go out with him, but she did. A lot.

Soon, Ginny was no longer calling me up for Friday night drinks, she was calling me to see if James and I wanted to go to dinner at 'ours'.

They were one of those sickening couples that you want to hate but just can't. She was smart and beautiful and ambitious, he was kind and funny and adored her. I wanted to be annoyed by them, wanted to find their adoration of each other irritating, but it was impossible. Just being with them made you feel happier, bathing in their golden glow gave you a summery sheen that helped gloss over the cracks in your own life. James and I laughed, lovingly teased each other, and held hands more when we were with Ginny and Alex. Their joy made us joyful.

They moved in together and married in a timeframe that should have felt quick but just felt natural. 'We've Only Just Begun' could have been their theme tune, and Karen Carpenter would have been proud.

I was happy for them.

Until Ginny told me they were trying for a baby.

James and I were trying for a baby.

A baby was our next thing.

A baby would make everything better.

It had been over a year since James and I started trying for a baby.

James and I weren't trying for a baby any more, we were struggling for a baby.

———

I said that I don't have anyone who loves me and makes things better in this new world.

But that is a lie.

I do have someone.

I have Lucky.

I love Lucky.

Lucky is the thing that has made me happiest and brought me the only real joy I have known in this empty world.

Let's be honest, without Lucky I would probably have killed myself weeks ago.

He is happy and healthy now, my constant companion with his big, doggy grin permanently plastered to his face. He sleeps on my bed at night and wakes with me in the morning. He sits on my lap when I cry and licks away tears from my cheeks with his stinking, rough tongue. He is often the only reason I get out of bed. My heart lifts when I see him, and his warmth, weight and smell calm me whenever he is near. He has shown me more love than I have received from some of my human relationships, and I would be lost without him.

If this were a movie or a novel, then Lucky would be enough to save me. I would realise that I didn't need human interaction or love because I had Lucky and his love would be sufficient.

But this isn't a movie. I ache for human contact. Every time I hear my own voice it shocks me. No one has said my name for over three months. Is it still my name any more? Do I still exist? I could be anyone. Am I even still me?

I am definitely not the same person I believed I was before. I am a murderer, a bully, a thief, a burglar, a former drug addict. I am weak and I am scared and I am tired all the time.

I feel like I've been lying about who I really am for years.

I can't lie any more.

I don't think I really like the person I have become, but then I wasn't particularly keen on the person that I was before 6DM either.

And at least I am honest about who I am now.

I love Lucky, but he isn't enough to save me.

Tomorrow is March 17th.

March 17th is my birthday.

It feels like a good day to die.

March 17th 2024

Happy birthday to me.

For the first time since Susan Palmers died I actually managed to wake up and get out of bed in the morning on March 17th because I had big plans for my last day alive.

I was going to shave my legs.

For the last three months my lifestyle has been an extreme mix of feast or famine and I have in no way taken care of myself. I am bloated and slovenly and sluggish. I wear what is comfy and warm and not what is attractive or fashionable. I burp and fart loudly and at will – often startling Lucky, to my strange delight. My face is pale and puffy and spotty, and my hair is shocking. I haven't seen my real hair colour in over ten years, and now that I can, it turns out that it is mostly mousey and grey. My fringe was in my eyes and I had been pinning it back, but a couple of days ago I finally snapped and used some kitchen scissors to cut it. So now I am puffy, spotty, grey and have the haircut of a village idiot.

It feels like the least I can do before I die is have a bath, shave my legs, and apply a bit of deodorant.

It was only after I had bathed, exfoliated, shaved, waxed, plucked, washed and moisturised that I realised how ridiculously needless my efforts were. There was no one left to appreciate my smooth skin, my artfully plucked eyebrows. What was I doing? Adhering to social norms to the very end is what. Primping and preening and prettying like the good middle-class girl I was always destined to be. Even here, at the end of my life, I was doing what I had been taught. Why? No one would notice or care.

Except maybe Lucky before he inevitably eats me.

My plan had been to get riotously drunk but it is already late afternoon and I am still sober. Not for any noble or selfless reason. I have just been too nauseous in the past few days to want to drink any kind of alcohol.

However, I am bravely sipping a glass of gin because I am definitely going to need some Dutch courage. Turns out, it's not as easy as you might think, killing yourself.

Because that is, of course, what is happening here. I am not sick. I might be mentally a bit unstable, but there is nothing physically wrong with me. I am perfectly fit and healthy if you discount the random vomiting, tiredness, bloating, and spots.

There is no physical reason for me to die. I am killing myself because there is also no physical reason for me to live. I am killing myself because it is the easy option for me. Easier than having to live in this new world.

Except, as I say, it is not as easy as I thought it would be.

The physical act of swallowing something that will end your life is a tough thing to make yourself do. Every time I think about it, I start to panic and feel sick. I am pretty sure it's not a good idea to throw up immediately after you have taken T600.

I made the mistake of reading the information leaflet that came with the T600. The first line is '*THIS MEDICINE WILL KILL YOU*'. Which was not unexpected. What is unexpected is the number of unwanted side effects that can happen. Migraines, blood clots, paralysis, fainting, fits, sudden inability to breathe. Sudden inability to breathe? I thought I was going to drift into a nice sleep, not fight for my last breath. I suppose if I were suffering from 6DM, these side effects would seem like a walk in the park. I am sure most people didn't even bother to read the leaflet. But I have. And it is frightening.

The worst part is the bit about children. Specifically, the line that says '*Do not try to resuscitate or prolong your child's life once you have administered T600. Your child will fall asleep as their organs shut down. Do not try to wake them.*' I hope very few parents read that section.

It was still only early evening when I had finished my bath and leaflet reading and it somehow felt too early to kill myself.

Death feels like the act of night, not late afternoon.

I had only managed a few sips of gin, so decided to take a wander around the hotel, drink more, and try to calm my thundering heart.

I walked down to the staff locker room, which is my favourite place in the hotel, and immersed myself in my favourite human-contact-starved act – rifling through the belongings of the hotel employees, devouring their lives like my very own soap opera. I had been in there many times already, soaking up the details of other people's mini dramas, and I knew all their secrets – who kept new underwear in their locker, who had an autograph book with hundreds of signatures in it, who kept three different mobile phones for his two girlfriends and one wife. I found out that Sophie had been trying for a baby for a year and that she was due to be fertile again at the beginning of November. She had three different brands of pregnancy test in her locker already. I discovered that George's wife had left him, and he'd kept the 'Dear John' letter she sent him. Emily had credit card bills from six different companies, all over £10k, all overdue. She was probably quite thankful for 6DM.

Eager for more snooping and more knowledge on this, my final day, I headed to the duty manager's office and was surprised to find the door locked. If there are two things that I have learnt in my post 6DM life, it is that one: a locked door normally hides something of extreme interest, and two: locked doors are easier to open than you think. One big shoulder shove and I was in.

And immediately I regretted it.

There was nothing life-changing in the duty manager's office. No mass of dead bodies, no lone crusader barricaded in to the last, no secret science laboratory working on a cure.

The room was decorated to welcome the duty manager back to work, or maybe just back in for a visit to work.

Deflated balloons, banners, and bows. All manner of pink decorations congratulating him or her on their new arrival.

A baby girl.

Born before 6DM? Most probably. A room decorated to

welcome someone who never came back, to congratulate them on a baby that no one got to see.

Maybe that's why the room was locked – people can only take so much sadness.

My stomach lurched and tears pricked suddenly at my eyes. A baby girl. A long awaited, much anticipated bundle of joy to love.

I know what it is like to want that, to long to hold a baby in your arms. To think you have that opportunity and then to have it cruelly snatched away.

I stumbled backwards, tripped over Lucky, and landed on the floor. I kicked the door to the room shut with my foot.

I walked slowly down the corridor with Lucky by my side.

I wish I could write that someone came just at that point. That I heard footsteps downstairs or a car driving down the street outside. That it was the army, the Red Cross, another lone survivor who wasn't going to die as soon as they met me.

But no one came.

The only noise was the slap of my bare feet and the soft tap of Lucky's paws on the floor.

I took Lucky to the kitchen and opened all the edible food that I could find: biscuits, crackers, frozen meat, big blocks of cheese, catering sized cans of beans and tomatoes. I wasn't sure how long it would last, but it was better than nothing. I filled all available bowls with water and left them on the floor. Then I remembered that he mostly drinks from the toilet.

I got myself a glass of water.

I wandered through the building opening doors and lifting toilet seats to give Lucky access to wherever he might be most comfortable.

I took the water back to a new room with a fresh bed and fresh sheets.

I put it on the bedside table with the T600.

I sat on the floor with Lucky and stroked him and whispered over and over what a good boy he was.

When he was asleep, I picked him up as gently as I could and took him out into the corridor. He woke up as I put him down on the floor and immediately tried to get back in the room with me.

I locked him out.

He howled.

I cried despite promising myself I wouldn't.

I opened the window so that I could hear and smell the rain that had inevitably begun to fall.

I am in bed, propped up on the clean, white pillows.

The T600 and glass of water are beside me.

It is time.

I am clean and dry and warm and comfortable and tired and sad and lonely and done with surviving in this world on my own.

I am not going to write some kind of dramatic final sentence or deathbed confession. I have done things I am not proud of and things that I would never have thought myself capable of – both good and bad.

I hope someone finds this journal. And if you also find a shaggy golden retriever at the same time, he likes to be tickled behind his left ear, and his favourite food is biscuits. Tell him I love him and, if there is an afterlife, I will be missing him in it.

If there is one message that I leave then it is this: I survived, but I never had a life.

It is time.

Then, as I was lying there, listening to the rain fall, smelling the sweet dampness coming in through the window and lifting the T600 to my mouth, I remembered.

In that briefest, tiny moment between life and death it was my sense of smell that saved me.

It was a smell that I remembered, or rather a smell that I had forgotten to remember, that saved my life.

———

Like I have said before, smell has always been my most evocative sense.

When I was young and my dad was working late I used to sleep with one of the boxes that his aftershave bottles came in. I cut eyeholes in the box and drew a smiley mouth on the front, but obviously that wasn't the thing that comforted me (it actually looked terrifying). It was the smell.

I can smell when rain is due, when snow is coming, and when the seasons are about to change. I can smell a certain scent and instantly be transported back to yesterday, last week, last month, or five years ago. Like the smell of school, or a certain pub I went into when I was younger. I used to be able to identify different parts of London from their smell, Hyde Park Corner with the mixture of exhaust fumes and greenery, Covent Garden with baking cookies and beer, the Southbank with river water and ice cream sellers.

Smells can make me happy, sad, and scared. They can comfort me or send me spiralling into depression.

Before I left my mum and dad's for the last time I took a T-shirt from each of their drawers and sealed it in one of the thousands of Ziploc bags my mum kept handy for emergency situations. When I am having a really bad day, I open one of the bags and bury my face into it, drugging myself in the memory of when I was young and loved and protected.

After over two years of trying for a baby with James, I could smell when my period was about to start.

I did everything right. I tracked my cycle, exercised, ate healthily, stopped drinking, took vitamins, we had sex according to a strict schedule, in the missionary position, with my hips on a pillow, and I lay that way for at least ten minutes after; trying not to move while precious sperm slowly leaked out of me. I read all the books, joined all the support groups, did all the research, and bought all the recommended fertility aids.

James did everything right, too. He exercised, ate healthily, stopped drinking so much, started wearing loose cotton boxer shorts, took vitamins, refrained from wanking in between my regimented sex sessions. He held my hand when we went to see doctors and consultants, held me close when I cried after every negative pregnancy test.

I tried to stay positive, tried not to get sucked down by the endless waiting, the endless cycles of temperature testing, sex, and then waiting again. I tried not to let James see how disappointed I was, that once more life was filled with dissatisfaction; but every now and then I would catch him watching me, and his face would look resigned. Resigned to the fact I was unhappy again.

I should have stopped, should have just relaxed for a while, taken a break. But I couldn't; I was determined.

And every month I'd go to the toilet, have a wee, and just know I was about to get my period.

I would smell the blood on its way. James thought this was disgusting and ridiculous and impossible.

But I was always right.

————

I hadn't smelt my period on its way since 6DM.

I hadn't had a period since James died.

I put the T600 and glass of water back onto the bedside table, opened the door, and was knocked over by a near-deranged Lucky charging into my arms. He was shaking and whining in fear and distress.

I was crying and stroked him again and again, trying to soothe the pain from him.

'I'm sorry,' I whispered. 'I'll never leave you again. I promise.'

Then I went to get something from Sophie's locker.

I came back to my room and drank the glass of water on my bedside table for a completely different reason to the one I had originally poured it for.

Then I went into the bathroom, had the most important wee, and took the most important test of my life.

Then I waited for the longest three minutes of my life.

Then I looked at the results.

Then I drank another glass of water, did another wee, and took another test.

Then I did it again.

After checking the results of the third test I was convinced.

I am pregnant.

March 18th 2024

I was in shock, so the first thing I wanted after finding out I was pregnant was a massive alcoholic drink.

I actually went as far as to walk down to the bar and get myself a glass before I realised that drinking alcohol was no longer allowed.

I settled for a milk-less, joyless cup of tea instead, while feeling guilty about the several sips of gin I had drunk the previous day.

Then I remembered that it wasn't just alcohol that I had subjected my foetus to. Cocaine, Tramadol, sleeping tablets. I think I had taken morphine a couple of times by mistake.

I started to panic about the effect this might have had on the baby. I know that you get a free pass up to about six weeks because Ginny told me that, until then, the baby is pretty much just a bunch of cells. I'm not confident this is true, but I'm clinging to it.

I haven't had sex for nearly three months now, so I am one hundred per cent past the six-week point.

I definitely wasn't detoxed from Tramadol by six weeks. Had I hurt my baby? How did I find out?

For the thousandth time I cursed Google for no longer being around.

In the end I settled for re-reading the information leaflet in the emergency packet of Tramadol that I still had. It said not to use when breastfeeding and not to take without speaking to a doctor or pharmacist if you are pregnant, but it didn't say it would kill my baby.

I decided to believe it.

I was struggling to remember when my last period was.

It must have been about a week or so before I last had sex, but I couldn't remember. At the time I was convinced I was infertile, so I was no longer recording my fertility cycle. I have no idea when I actually conceived the baby.

If I'm honest, I don't even know who the father is.

It was all Harry Boyle's fault.

———

Harry Boyle is not the name of the romantic lead in a Hollywood movie. Harry Boyle is the bloke that comes and fixes your washing machine.

The Harry Boyle I knew was one of our clients at the insurance company and was a total arse.

Harry Boyle was rude and brusque and impatient. He swore constantly and treated everyone like his subordinate, often demanding that people move out of a chair he wanted or go get his coffee, no matter how senior they were. He was a nightmare client and, despite the fact I was now head of new business for EMEA, it took him five months to even bother speaking to me, other than to ask if I could 'pop downstairs and grab him a sandwich'.

As far as I was concerned, the longer he ignored me the better.

But then, after two years of trying to get pregnant and at the point where I was exhausted by it all and ready to give up, James and I were finally offered IVF by the wonderful, amazing NHS.

One round, one shot, one chance at happiness and joy.

I started the IVF injections, and my hormones and diplomacy skills went to shit.

We were in the middle of a client meeting with Harry Boyle. It was a Friday night and we had been in the meeting for three hours. Everyone knew he was just keeping us there because he could. He was the client: he could do whatever he wanted.

Finally, at 7.16 p.m., our meek and mild new business director plucked up the courage to suggest that we table the discussion for the night and pick it up again on Monday morning.

For once, Harry seemed to be reasonable and agreed that everyone could go home.

And then come back on Saturday morning.

I was tired, hot, hormonal, and perilously close to missing the time for my next injection.

'No,' I said. Okay, I may have yelled it rather than said it.

The room fell silent.

'What?' He turned and gave me the full power of his glowering stare.

'No. We're not coming back in tomorrow. We're all tired and we all deserve the weekend off, and this can wait until Monday morning. You don't need to sort this tomorrow, you are just making everyone come in because you're being a total shit . . . and it's "pardon", not "what".'

I didn't wait around to be yelled at or fired.

I did what all sensible and mature women do in times of crisis. I hid in the toilet.

My colleague Sarah found me there.

'Fucking hell.'

'Shit. Did he go mental? Am I fired?'

'He laughed and said we can pick it up on Monday.'

'Oh.'

'Maybe he'll stop being such an arsehole now.'

'Doubt it.'

'You going to hide in here all night?'

I nodded.

Sarah smiled.

'Probably for the best.'

I hoped he'd be gone by the time I slunk back into the meeting room to get my stuff, but he was still in there, chatting to the sales director, with his back to me.

He was ridiculously tall, with a mass of dark curly hair that he never seemed to get cut. His clothes were expensive and fitted him beautifully. I knew that other people in the office thought he was good-looking but, for me, his horrible personality and shitty attitude cancelled out any good looks that might have been lurking behind his perma-scowl.

He turned and caught me staring.

For a moment he glared.

Then he flipped me the bird and smiled.

Caught completely off guard, I burst out laughing.

I blamed the hormones.

————

You would think that finding out I was pregnant would change everything.

That I would have a new-found lust for life, be galvanised into action, start planning straight away for the future of my baby and me.

It didn't and I didn't.

I've wanted to have a baby for many, many years but that was the old me in the old world where I had a husband and a home and hot water and midwives and doctors.

I have none of that here.

I have done the sums the best I can and I think I am roughly about sixteen and a half weeks pregnant. Maybe seventeen weeks. That means I will give birth in early September.

In around five months.

If I am going to have the baby, I need to stop surviving and start living the life I have so far not been able to build in this empty new world.

I need to start eating proper food, drinking two litres of water a day, taking pregnancy vitamins.

I need to find somewhere proper to live. Somewhere I can have a routine. Somewhere I can give birth. Somewhere warm and safe and comfy.

It seems like a lot to do and I don't know if I can do it. I've never given birth, never had to plan for anything, never had to take responsibility for someone else. I've never even had a pet.

Five months to find and make a home. And a baby. In me. By myself.

I don't think I want to. Not on my own. I don't know how. I don't think I can.

Dictaphone Recording (Tape 1 / Recording 1)
(Transcribed)

(Woman's voice speaks into Dictaphone.)
Hello? Hello? I need to check this thing is working.
It's me. Is this working?
(Dictaphone is turned on and off.)
It's working. I can hear myself. I . . . I, sorry —
this isn't about me speaking, this isn't . . . I mean
I just need to . . .

(Pause.)

My phone is dying. Every time I switch it on it
takes longer to work and this morning there was
nothing on the front screen. Just . . . blank. I've
turned it off and on again and it's back but it's so
faint, I can hardly see it. I'm going to lose
everything, all my photos and texts and messages
and . . . everything.

(Crying.)
(Deep breath.)

I've managed to access my voicemails and I don't
want to lose this, I can't lose this, I have to save
it.
It's my mum, my last message from Mum . . .

(Brief pause. Rustling)

Computer Voice: 'You have one saved message'
Beeeeep
Hello sweetheart. It's Mum.

(Pause.)

So, it turns out that the cold I thought your dad
had was actually 6DM and I'm afraid I've got it now.
We're . . . not great.

(Coughing.)

We didn't tell you earlier because we didn't want
you to worry. I know the trains aren't running and
you hate driving and so please don't try and come to
see us. Anyway, there won't be much point now. Your
dad and I are going to take T600 in a bit because,
well, it's time we think. Your dad never was very
good at being ill was he?

(Forced laugh.)

I just wanted to call you first to hear your voice
and to tell you how very, very much we love you and
how happy you made us and how you are the absolute
best thing we ever did with our lives and we will
miss you so, so much.

*(Pause, muffled sobbing, male voice
in the background says something.
She takes a deep breath.)*

Your dad's saying I promised I wouldn't cry. Daddy
is also saying he loves you very much and would tell
you himself but I am hogging the phone as always!

(Half laugh, half sob, deep breath.)

Your dad's right, I shouldn't cry, because we have
been the luckiest people in the world to have you.
You have been everything we ever wanted. You are
strong and loving and kind and we are so proud of
you and... and... I wish we could have been with
you at the end. I hope you are okay and not in pain
and that you and James are together. Don't worry
about us, we are fine, we just want you to be okay,
we love you so...

Beeeep

Phone message cuts off.

End of recording.

March 18th 2024

That was the final time I ever heard from my mum.

She called as I was sitting in the bar when I had gone out during James's sickness. I was talking to someone else when she rang so didn't notice the call. I listened to the message after the other person left.

I should have gone to them there and then. I should have found a way, stolen a car, forced someone to drive me to them.

I should at least have called back.

But I knew that speaking to my dying mother would push me over the edge.

The entire fragile world that I had built, with me at the centre, was imploding. I was soon going to be alone, completely physically and emotionally alone for the first time in my life; and seeing or speaking to my parents at that point would have made that terrible future too real for me to cope with.

I wasn't the person she had thought I was, I wasn't strong or loving or kind.

I didn't go to see them and I didn't call her back. I was scared and selfish to the end.

And I still am.

I don't think I will make a good mother.

I wasn't a good mother to my first baby.

I lost my first baby.

———

The IVF worked. I was six weeks pregnant and glowing with happiness and hormones.

The scan should have been a formality.

But there was no heartbeat.

The lovely lady who was doing the scan spent precious NHS minutes searching, but I knew from her face that it was a waste of time.

It hadn't even crossed my mind that this might happen, that I could be pregnant but not pregnant at the same time.

The cells hadn't developed into a baby. They were just cells. And soon my body would acknowledge them for the invaders they were, and reject them.

And I would smell my period on its way once more.

James told people I had lost the baby.

'Lost the baby' – such a ridiculous phrase. Like I left it at the cheese counter in Asda. Like it was my fault. Like I was careless with its life.

I wasn't careless. I hadn't lost it. It had moved out of its own accord.

James tried to comfort me, tried to make me feel better. We could keep trying, pay to go private, he was happy to do that, he said. But we had been together nine years now and I knew him – I knew when he was lying.

He brought me tea and hot water bottles and went shopping for sanitary towels when I couldn't face leaving the house to get them for myself.

He had no idea what he was buying and came back with Tena lady pads for bladder incontinence. The bleeding was so heavy I wore them.

I examined every blood clot I passed for signs it was a small part of my baby. There were none. It was just blood.

We were never alone, there was a constant stream of visitors – my mum and dad, James's mum and dad, even a few of James's friends came to drink tea and offer sympathy.

I stayed in our bedroom.

Ginny came round and was the one person whom I allowed to come upstairs into my room of pain. She held my hand as I cried. She was pregnant with Radley, but didn't tell me and successfully hid her happiness while listening to my endless litany of loss.

Xav didn't come. He had been out of rehab for nearly three months and my mum told me he was doing really well, seeing a therapist and going to NA meetings regularly. Xav had tried to contact me when he was in rehab. As part of the rehab journey I was someone he needed to say sorry to. He wanted me to come to joint therapy sessions. I had said I was too busy making a baby to be part of his drama.

Now I was too busy losing a baby for him to be part of mine.

I cried and I slept and I stared out of the window, and ten days passed and I woke up one morning and realised it was all over.

My physical and imagined future was over.

No pregnancy, no baby, no plans for the next day, week, year, or decade.

I was just me again.

I was a blank shape. A now-empty blank shape lying in a space on our bed. Doing and feeling nothing.

Early April 2024

I spent another two weeks at the hotel.

Well, I think it was two weeks, but I am not entirely sure as my phone died completely the day after I recorded Mum's voicemail onto the Dictaphone.

Without my phone to remind me of the date I lost track of the days pretty quickly and allowed myself to drift from one day to the next doing the barest minimum to survive.

I was still suffering from morning sickness and, following the loss of my phone and all the memories it contained, I felt like I was grieving for the dead all over again. And this time I had no drink or drugs to dampen the pain.

But then, one random morning, I was in the hotel kitchen, standing at the sink drinking a glass of water when something amazing happened.

I felt my baby move for the first time.

Wriggling in my tummy.

A small flutter that I thought was indigestion at first but, when I took another gulp of the icy water and felt the fluttering again, I thought maybe, just maybe.

So I did it again. And again.

Until I was sure the baby was half drowned.

'That's woken you up, hasn't it!' I laughed.

I laughed with my baby.

Something was in there. Someone was in there. Starting to wriggle around.

Physical confirmation that he or she existed, that he or she was alive. For the first time I truly understood that this was no longer about me. Or at least it was no longer just about me.

The baby couldn't fend for itself. It couldn't drink from the toilet or catch a rat if it was hungry.

If I died the baby died, and if I gave up the baby gave up.

And just like that I realised I didn't want to give up. Not any more.

It was time to go, time to find a home for my baby and me.

I needed a proper plan this time. A plan for a life.

Mid April 2024

Unfortunately, the new, enthusiastic, focussed me was just as scatterbrained and unorganised as the old, suicidal me.

In my excitement to leave the hotel I once more forgot to check that I had everything I needed.

So, when I pulled over on the A43 to fill the Defender with diesel and found that I had forgotten to bring a funnel to do it with, it immediately took the wind out of my newly billowing sails and I saw it as a sign that I was only ever going to be a badly prepared and unfit mother.

I had at least had the luck to run out of diesel smack bang in the middle of suburbia. Funnel central. So I grabbed my rucksack and Lucky, and set off towards the nearest house-lined street.

The first thing I noticed was the rubbish. Lots and lots of rubbish. Rubbish flying in the wind, tumbling along the gutters, stuck in trees and in fences and bushes, and whirling in mini cyclones at the corners of buildings. At first, I couldn't work out where it was all coming from, but then I noticed the ripped and battered black bin bags that were also lying or flying about. It must have been bin day just before or during 6DM and, good citizens that they were, the residents must have put their bins out as normal.

Except this time no one came to collect them.

The bags weren't intact, so something must have ripped them open. I walked a bit faster, imagining giant rats or feral dogs roaming the streets but, turning a corner, I came upon the most obvious culprit.

The street was covered in shit. Not dog or fox shit. Bird shit.

Cars, pavements, lamp posts, houses; all covered in splatters of white, runny, bird shit.

Staring sideways at me through its beady yellow eye was a giant seagull.

Easily the size of a small dog, it sat in the middle of the pavement laconically pecking at . . . something vaguely white and rotten. I didn't dwell too much on what it might be.

I walked slowly towards the bird. It continued to eat. I moved forward again, and this time it turned its head to look at me. I stopped walking immediately. Its evil yellow eyes stared. I stared back. It blinked. I took a slow step sideways. It could have the pavement if it wanted. The seagull cocked its head to one side, blinked again, opened its sharp, hooked beak, and let out a loud, barking yell.

The yell was immediately returned by a hidden multitude of other harsh, rasping barks, and I jumped at the loud cacophony of noise. Lucky growled and charged towards the seagull, which, rather than take flight, stood its ground, reached forward, and pecked Lucky on the nose. Lucky yelped and raced back to hide behind my legs. I, meanwhile, was more interested in where the collective cries had come from and, looking up, I saw that the roofs of the houses were lined with seagulls, all bobbing their heads up and down and now, it seemed, crying out in support of their compadre who had bitten Lucky.

I have never seen the movie *The Birds*, but I had seen enough clips from it to know the damage that could be done by average-sized crows, let alone these dog-sized, evil-looking rejects from some low-budget horror movie. One by one the roof dwellers took flight, filling the air with flapping wings and cawing cries. I tried to tell myself that my stomach-cramping fear was unfounded, that they were simply putting on a display and I should just move smoothly to another street; but when the first one dived down and tried to peck Lucky's tail, I ran.

I pounded down the street, rucksack banging against my back, but, turning the corner, saw that the next road was also lined with houses and roofs decorated with seagulls. Lucky changed tactic for me by racing up the path of the nearest house. I followed, building up speed to force the door open with my shoulder. At the last minute I decided to try the door handle and, when it opened straight away, I went tumbling straight down the hall head over heels. Lucky followed, careening into me, and I quickly rolled over and crawled on my hands and knees to the front door to slam it shut, just as the first seagulls were landing on the porch and looking inquisitively in at us.

'What the hell was that?!' I yelled at Lucky. Both of us sat, panting and staring at each other.

Then I threw up onto the hallway floor.

It was the smell.

The smell of decaying human flesh.

I wiped my face and put my sleeve over my nose and mouth, which didn't help one bit. I ran into the kitchen, opened the window, and stuck my head out, sucking in air from outside. A seagull flew down and landed in the back garden. I pulled my head back in, pulled the window to, and breathed through the little gap.

I couldn't think straight; both my brain and body were screaming that I had to get away from the stench. Yet, at the same time, although it was wrong and twisted and unexplainable, I had to see what was causing the smell. I grabbed a tea towel, took two huge gulps of fresh air, wrapped the tea towel around my mouth and nose, and went into the front room.

The decor and their clothing told me they were old, but I wouldn't have known that just from looking at them. There wasn't enough left of them to be able to see. They were sitting together in the middle of the sofa and they were rotten. Their clothes were still pretty much intact, but their faces were covered in maggots and sort of caved in where their cheeks should have been. Their clothing shook and wriggled with the movement of whatever burrowed unseen beneath it. Their scalps and hair writhed with maggots, and thin white slivers of skull were visible in places. Fat lazy flies buzzed about the room, alternatively landing on the bodies and on a bowl of rotting fruit by the window. A veritable smorgasbord.

I threw up again, into the tea towel, smearing sick all over my face. I stumbled out of the room, up the stairs, and locked myself in the bathroom. I opened the window wide, not caring if a seagull flew in and pecked me to death at that point. Lucky scratched and whined at the door and I let him in. I washed my face, threw the tea towel out of the window, sat down on the toilet, picked up Lucky and hugged him to me.

Outside the seagulls cried and swooped at my abandoned tea towel.

I sat on the toilet until it started to get dark outside. After a while Lucky clambered off me and curled up on the floor to sleep. I hugged my knees to my chest as it got colder in the bathroom, reluctant to close the window and let the smell permeate the room again.

I didn't know what to do. I was desperately thirsty, but the water coming out of the tap was a rusty brown colour so I didn't think it wise to drink any, and my rucksack with my drinks in it was downstairs. The skin on my scalp was crawling and I became very conscious of my breathing and started to breathe more deeply and struggle to take in all the air I needed. My heart had begun to beat faster. I couldn't seem to sit still any more, instead twitching every few seconds and having to stretch and un-stretch my legs. All symptoms of an encroaching panic attack that would be manageable for about fifteen minutes before transforming into God knows what; a wild and uncontrollable desire to flee out into the deadly street most probably.

Five minutes later I stood up and forced my brain to come up with a plan before I lost all ability to think rationally.

First, I raided the medicine cabinet and found a pot of Vicks VapoRub, which I administered liberally to my nose.

The seagulls had quietened over the past hour and I looked out of the window hoping against hope that they had moved on. No such luck. Most were back on the rooftops, a few milled about on the road. I thought some of them might be sleeping, so I threw a shampoo bottle through the window to see what would happen. Every single head snapped to attention as the bottle hit the pavement.

With the Vicks smeared on my nose, and a J Cloth wrapped about my face for extra protection, I charged noisily down the stairs, grabbed the rucksack, and ran back upstairs to the toilet.

I wasn't hungry, but I chugged down two cans of Fanta, resulting in profuse burping from me and many looks of incredulity from Lucky.

By now it was pitch black outside and the seagulls were still and silent.

My heart was racing, I was sweaty, breathless, and had started to hum a tuneless song to myself.

At the bottom of my rucksack was my 'only in a desperate case of life and death' emergency Tramadol.

I looked at them for a long time.

And then I took them out and held them in my hand for even longer.

Eventually I put them back in my rucksack.

I reasoned that if Lucky and I were going to make a run for it, then we should do it at night.

I stuck my head out of the window to see which was the best way to run.

Then something caught my eye.

A cat. Dark and sinuous, padding noiselessly down the street, half hidden in the shadows.

My instinct was to yell a warning and my mouth opened, ready to shout. But I snapped it shut again and looked up to the roofs.

Nothing. The birds were still and silent.

Then, achingly slowly, one lone head turned in the direction of the cat.

A moment later, as if by some silent signal, all heads lining the houses opposite swivelled in the same direction. Yellow eyes like the headlights of a car stared down into the night.

I didn't want to watch, but I couldn't tear my eyes away.

They launched as one, a flurry of wings and cacophony of harsh barking cries. The cat was frozen in shock for the briefest of moments, and then they were upon it. It didn't even have time to try to flee. They surrounded it in a frenzy of crying and ripping and squealing. They pulled the cat apart and then fought over the largest bits, tearing at the carcass and nipping at each other. I realised that this might be why I hadn't seen more stray cats.

In the melee, one of the birds took a particularly vicious bite to the throat and fell to the ground. They were on it before it had a chance to stand, adding cannibalism to the night's menu.

I felt bile rising in my throat and ducked back through the bathroom window, slamming it shut behind me.

I sat heavily onto the toilet and Lucky jumped up onto my lap, shaking and whimpering. We both jumped as something thudded onto the closed window behind us. There was a terrifying sound of glass cracking.

I grabbed Lucky and ran into the nearest bedroom, slamming the door and racing to the window to pull the curtains shut. I cowered in the corner of the room and burst into tears.

I didn't think I would sleep, but I did, waking as the sun was rising, with the sour taste of fear in my mouth.

Lucky and I spent the day in the bedroom, where I alternated between trying to focus on a plan to get us out of the house and wallowing in misery that I was going to die in a 1950s terrace in a suburb, at the mercy of murderous seagulls.

Late in the afternoon as the sun was setting I finally made up my mind and made a promise to myself. I was better than this. I hadn't survived this long just to die of hunger in a room with a chintz bedspread.

I was going to live.

I was going to live and have my baby and make a life for myself.

I crept back into the bathroom with my heart racing and Lucky whimpering softly behind me. The window was cracked, but still intact. My rucksack was where I had left it.

I took my emergency Tramadol out of my rucksack and flushed each tablet down the toilet.

I forced myself to think. There must be something I could do, some way out of the house, some way to get away, something they would be scared of . . .

I reapplied my Vicks, silently left the bathroom, and raided the bedrooms for something I could use to distract the birds. I was looking for anything noisy, a gun (long shot, I know), a flare gun, a wind-up radio, a tambourine; anything that could make sound.

There was nothing.

Reluctantly I resigned myself to the fact I would have to go back downstairs, so I applied more Vicks and made my heart-pounding way back down. I was just about to give up when, at the very back of the cupboard under the stairs, I hit the jackpot. An old box of fireworks.

I took the fireworks upstairs, along with the car keys I had found hanging by the back door.

I went into the bathroom, carefully opened the window, leant out as quietly as I could, and pressed the door open button on the car key.

Nothing.

I leant out further and pressed again. This time there was a joyful *clunk-click* and a flash of lights from a car down the street on the right. The seagulls snapped to attention once more. Bastards.

I studied the fireworks. I wasn't sure what to do. I couldn't let them off from the window and I couldn't go outside to put them properly in the garden. I decided the best thing to do was throw the box the opposite way to the car and then throw a lit firework into the box to light the rest. It is what you are always cautioned never to do when you are younger, so it was bound to work.

I waited until it was fully dark, the seagulls were silent and the night perfectly still, and then I leaned precariously out of the bedroom window and threw the box of fireworks into the neighbour's garden. It landed upright, which was good, but some of the fireworks bounced out of it, which was bad.

I had chosen two 'fountain' fireworks to light and throw into the box, so I loosened the fuses and got them ready. I decided I would have a better chance if I was downstairs already when I threw them, so I put on my rucksack and coaxed Lucky back downstairs.

I opened the front door gently and slowly, freezing stock still when it emitted a troubled squeak. I peeked out. The birds were still and quiet, completely unaware of the great plan afoot. I took the matches from my pocket and struck one to light the first firework. It wouldn't light. I tried again and once more, nothing. The birds were starting to move, behind me Lucky whined softly. I dropped the first firework and grabbed the second. Again, nothing happened. Panic rising, I tried once again, and this time the wick sparked and flared to life. At the same time, I felt one hundred beady seagull eyes swivel in my direction; I chucked the firework at the box and slammed the door shut.

A cacophony of cawing and crying began outside as the seagulls registered my movement. I waited for the bang and hiss of the fireworks. Nothing. Sweat dripped down my back. Still nothing. Suddenly, there was a noise like a bomb going off, followed by the familiar *whhhheeeeeeeee* of a rocket.

I flung open the door and was running down the path in an instant.

But Lucky was not with me.

In my joy at forming a viable plan I had forgotten to factor in what Lucky's reaction would be to the fireworks. He raced back through the house and cowered in the kitchen. I yelled to him from the path, but my voice couldn't be heard and he wouldn't have listened even if it could.

The fireworks were going crazy now and a rocket whizzed past, a foot from my face.

I couldn't leave him, not here.

I stormed back into the house, the smell of sulphur now replacing that of flesh, and ran into the kitchen. Lucky was shaking with fear and struggled like crazy when I tried to pick him up. I was in no mood to coax, so grabbed him in a bear hug and ran, dragging him out of the front door.

A fountain of sparks exploded just as we were jogging down the garden path, showering us both, causing Lucky to literally shit himself in fear and setting my hair on fire. I didn't stop. I stumbled off the path and onto the street with my hair smouldering.

I couldn't remember which car it was. In the dark I couldn't see the colour or make and I hadn't thought to count how many away it was. The keys were, stupidly, in my pocket and I struggled to shift a wriggling Lucky and get them out. Behind us the fireworks had started to ebb off and I became acutely aware of all the seagulls circling above.

I had just managed to get the keys out and was searching for the unlocking button when something swooped down at us. I dropped the keys and nearly dropped Lucky. I bent for the keys and it swooped again. This time I got the keys but did drop Lucky, who charged off up the road. I pressed the right button and saw a flash two cars down. I stood up and raced to the car, yanking the door open as another seagull swooped at me. As the seagull tried to peck at my still flaming hair, a rocket came out of nowhere and hit it full force, flinging it to the ground. I jumped into the car and slammed the door shut as the rocket exploded, firing sparks and seagull all over the windows.

For a brief moment I sat in absolute shock, staring at the remains of the exploded gull, then I realised my hair was still smoking, so I frantically patted at it until I was sure it was out.

Next moment something heavy hit the car door causing the entire vehicle to shake.

'What now?!' I thought.

Then I heard frantic barking and pushed the door open without even looking. Lucky scrambled into the car, smearing mud and dog shit all over me and the seats. I yanked the door shut and then he was on my lap covering me in more shit and licking my face.

Despite the smell and the spit and the shit, I let him.

Something thumped the car again and we looked through the front windscreen. A seagull sat on the bonnet staring in at us.

Lucky and I looked at each other, then I put the key in the ignition and started the engine.

Some of the seagulls were still on the road as we drove away; I tried to hit each and every one of them.

The car, Lucky, and I were all covered in mud and shit, but compared to the stink and mess of the house it was weirdly bearable, so I didn't stop to change cars.

Dawn was breaking as we left the residential area and drove through an industrial estate nearby. There was a waste dump on the estate, one of those huge landfill sites where everything that can't be recycled goes. I stopped the car beside it and gawped. The entire site was covered in seagulls, there must have been thousands. The ground undulated with them and the sky was filled with their cries. Even inside the car with the windows shut, the noise was deafening.

I realised that I might not be at the top of the food chain any more.

I didn't go back to get the Defender straight away. I found a hotel and took eleven cold showers before I was sure both Lucky and I were shit-free. Then I sat in another hotel room with the door firmly locked, and panicked for the next two days.

But I had made a promise to myself – I was going to live and have my baby and make a life for us – and to fulfil that promise we needed the Defender, and we needed a home.

Luckily, in a different lifetime, James had already found one for us.

———

Two weeks after the NHS scan, when all the leftover baby was out of my body, James made me take a shower and then forced me to eat chicken soup while he went to borrow a car from a friend.

I didn't want to go anywhere, but he said we needed to get out of town for a bit.

James was incredibly busy at work, still trying to re-build the business after the mess that lockdown had left. I should have recognised the sacrifice he was making to try to help me, to try to help us.

I should have seen the week away for what it was – a desperate attempt to reconnect us as a couple – to give us an opportunity to come together in grief rather than have it drive us apart.

I didn't see that. I couldn't see anything beyond my own pain.

James had rented an 'eco-home'.

It was more like a fancy hut.

On the edge of a small woodland in the middle of a nature reserve, with a rushing stream running past, yards from the front door, and a well-tended fruit and vegetable patch and fancy polytunnel filled with huge tomato plants, berries and beans to the side from which we were allowed to eat anything we liked.

Made from dried mud bricks, with a thatched roof, solar panels, a reed-bed sanitation system, water that somehow came directly from an ancient well - I don't know how it worked, I'm not a plumber. The hut had a wood burner that heated the whole place and boiled the giant tin kettle, well, I say 'the whole place', but it was only one room. A large square room with a kitchen in one corner, a sitting area, and then a 'bedroom' on the mezzanine level at the back of the cabin.

The guest book said that the solar panels would generate about five hours of electricity a day so please do remember to switch things off when not in use. What things? There was no TV, no phone signal, no Wi-Fi, an ancient radio, and an outside shower.

It was a modern-day Hobbit House.

I was appalled.

I wanted warm, soft luxury to wrap myself in, not hemp and hardship.

It was cold and dark and smelt of wet wood when we arrived. I wrapped myself in a thick, scratchy blanket and lay silently on the bed. James got straight to work making things homely and quickly lit the wood burner, put the kettle on, christened the composting toilet, and almost burst with delight when he discovered the clay oven for cooking just outside the door.

I'd never known him to be the 'back to nature' type, but it seemed that he had found his happy place. He smiled for the first time since the scan, and hummed happily to himself as he bustled about.

On the third morning I left the Hobbit House for the first time. It was early, James was still asleep, and the sun was just peeking through the woodland. I'd spent another sleepless night staring at the ceiling and couldn't take watching James slumber contentedly for one more minute, so I pulled a coat on over my nightie and went outside barefoot.

It was freezing. And breathtaking. One of those mornings that is filled with promise of the beauty that is to come. Everything sparkled, the trees were filled with buds bursting with new leaves, the birds sang, the forest floor rustled, it smelt fresh and green and healthy.

I was alone. For the first time since the scan I was truly alone, and I just wanted to get rid of the pain inside me.

I took a deep breath in, filled my lungs with the morning air, opened my mouth and screamed.

No, not screamed, yelled. A primeval, guttural display of the pain and anger that I felt. My first display of emotion that wasn't crying, right up from my now empty belly, vomiting out of me and into the world.

It felt amazing. How often do you get to yell at the top of your lungs? Really let rip and channel all your pain and anger into noise? I highly recommend it.

The forest fell silent. In wonder? In fear? Who knew?

James came running from the Hobbit House, still half asleep, petrified of finding his wife ripped in two by some forest monster.

I continued yelling until he grabbed and shook me, terrified that I had finally lost it.

'What?! What are you doing?!' he yelled.

I was a mad woman, consumed by pain and grief and anger.
I wrestled out of his arms.

'Get off me! Leave me alone!'

'Just stop it! Talk to me . . .'

'I don't want to talk to you, I don't want to talk to anyone,
you don't understand, you can't understand . . .'

'I can't understand if you won't let me, if you won't talk to
me about it. Please. What is it? What is wrong with you?'

What was wrong with me? Where would I start?

I couldn't tell him that I was filled with pain and rage and fear
and longing and loss. Longing and loss for something that had never
been mine in the first place. I couldn't tell him I was scared that
maybe it wasn't just the baby that I had lost, that maybe it was also
our last chance at happiness. I couldn't tell him that I didn't know
what to do now, I didn't know what the next rung of the ladder
was, didn't know how to make him happy, how to make me happy.

So I just shrugged.

James took a deep breath, stepped back away from me and
stared at the floor.

'Look. We shouldn't have come here. It was a bad choice.
You're not happy.'

He looked up.

'I don't think you're happy anywhere any more. I don't think
you're happy with me. I . . . I just don't know how much longer
we can keep trying at this . . .'

And even though he was talking about me and my happiness
I knew that, really, he was talking about himself.

I had lost the baby and, despite all of my efforts, I was losing
James.

I reached forward to take his hand but he moved further away
and turned back towards the Hobbit House.

'It's fine. I'm just tired.'

And, in that instant, I knew he was right.

He was tired. Tired of me.

We left the Hobbit House that afternoon and went home.

Late April 2024

Even though the last time I had been there had been steeped in misery, I knew that the Hobbit House would be the perfect place to wait to have my baby. It was pretty much self-sufficient, away from any potential places that rats or seagulls might gather, and was small enough for me to manage on my own.

So, given all the recent drama with the birds, it would be nice to be able to say that I gathered everything I needed, came straight to the Hobbit House, settled in and have been living quietly and easily for the last four months, gestating my child in peaceful harmony with the new world.

But that's not what happened.

For a start I had completely forgotten where the Hobbit House was.

I hadn't been paying much attention when James drove me there. I knew it was between King's Lynn and the Norfolk coast, but I didn't know quite where. It turns out that that's a pretty big area and driving around hoping that I would see a sign for it didn't actually work very well.

I couldn't find it.

But I did find a rose-covered cottage like something from a Jane Austen novel. It had running water, an open fire, an AGA, a rocking chair in the front room and, mercifully, no rotting bodies upstairs or down.

It was perfect.

I drove to the nearest shopping outlet, checked for rats, and then went to town. I got everything. Food, fresh bedding, pillows, duvets, blankets, towels, cleaning products, clothing, toiletries, dog treats and about twenty new balls for Lucky, books,

magazines, CDs, batteries and battery-operated CD and DVD
players. As it had been Christmas time when 6DM hit, the shops
were full of decorations and battery-powered fairy lights so I
took armfuls to decorate and light the cottage with. The Defender
was so rammed with stuff that I had to drive with Lucky sitting
on my lap, which, now that my belly was definitely starting to
protrude, neither of us particularly enjoyed.

I spent the afternoon and next day unloading and pottering
about the cottage, and then I sat on a chair in the front garden
in the weak April sunshine and felt a small wave of contentment
wash over me. I felt like this was somewhere I could settle for a
while.

Unfortunately, I was wrong.

The following morning the toilet stopped flushing, and by the
afternoon there was no water coming from the taps.

I must have just been using what was left in the tanks.

Fucking idiot.

I wasn't ready to give up on my cottage dream just yet and so
I drove to King's Lynn and went to the central library.

It took me roughly ten minutes of research to learn that the
cottage would never again have running water and that if I wanted
to live there I would have to drink bottled water and either dig
a medieval Glastonbury-style, hole-in-the-ground, faeces-
dumping-trench or turn a nearby field into a field of shit and do
my business there each day.

Neither sounded particularly appealing or practical and both
made me feel like I would be turning into a countrified version
of Susan Palmers.

I sat in a library armchair to sulk and, as always happens
when I am stationary for more than a few seconds, Lucky
appeared and dropped one of his new balls in my lap for me
to throw for him.

I threw it, half-heartedly, and it bounced away with surprising
speed on the wooden floor. Lucky went skidding after it, barrelled

into a stand full of leaflets by the reception desk, and colourful pamphlets flew in all directions.

'Lucky!' I scolded, getting out of my chair to clear them up. He gave me a doggy grin.

I actually bent down to clear them before I realised that no one else was ever going to come here, so what the hell was I doing?

And then I saw it.

Escape the stress of modern life. Enjoy our environmentally-friendly, no impact, organic ecosphere.

It was a leaflet left by the Hobbit House hippies.

The beautiful Hobbit House hippies.

Turns out the house was only a couple of miles away.

Before I left the library I took every novel by Marian Keyes and Jilly Cooper that they had.

So, back to the rose-covered cottage I went, back into the Defender went all my precious new things, back on my lap went Lucky, and off to the Hobbit House we drove.

The Hobbit House was still there, sitting squat in the middle of the clearing, in the middle of the woodland with the river bubbling along beside it.

I stopped the car for a moment and sat staring. This was not a place of happy memories. It was a place of endings, the end of my last pregnancy, the beginning of the end for me and James. I am not particularly superstitious, but I did wonder if this was actually a good idea.

Lucky, it turns out, is not superstitious at all or given to moments of contemplation because while I was having mine, he decided to bark continuously and scratch at the door to be let out.

I decided that the fact he was keen was as good a sign as any.

I got out of the Defender, walked decisively forward, and pulled on the front door to the Hobbit House. It wasn't locked and, when the stomach-churning smell of rotten flesh greeted me, my immediate thought was that someone had actually chosen this dark hole as their final resting place. Lucky, who had been ready to rush in and explore, backed up swiftly and sat down with an 'I ain't going in there' look on his face. I was inclined to agree with him but our immediate options were limited so I had to make sure that this definitely wasn't one of them.

It was a badger.

It was dead in the corner, rotting and covered in maggots.

I wrapped a scarf around my face, grabbed a handy big stick from the woods to scoop the carcass up with, and set about removing it.

Badgers are surprisingly huge and heavy.

In the end I had to put gloves on and manhandle it into a bin bag and then drag it outside.

After the badger was gone, I used my new cleaning products to scrub away the remnants (you should be thankful I am not expanding on that description), and then disinfected and scrubbed the entire floor.

Throughout, Lucky stared at me with such blatant disgust that I got fed up with him and purposefully threw his latest ball into the stream. He went and got it and then came back and shook his wet fur all over me and my clean floor.

He was getting a bit cheeky, that dog.

Despite all my cleaning, the room still stank of dead badger and, not for the first time, I cursed my amazing sense of smell.

———

It was Harry Boyle's smell that made me first notice him again.

I'd all but forgotten that Harry Boyle existed in the month that I had been off work after the miscarriage; but eventually I had to go back to work. I couldn't keep sitting at home on the sofa crying, especially now that James and I had an unspoken agreement that we wouldn't be in the same room as each other for more than five minutes at a time unless entirely unavoidable.

Neither of us had mentioned the fight in the woods since we got back from the Hobbit House. I was in complete emotional turmoil and desperate for James to comfort or love me, but he was cool and distant, and his controlled facade froze my heart. I should have reached out to him, apologised, begged him to love me again, but my voice was paralysed by the fear of rejection. At night we lay beside each other in bed, careful not to touch accidentally, and both of us made excuses to be out of the house as much as possible. Going back to work was one of those excuses.

The office lift was going up and the blanket fog of my depression was descending when Harry Boyle got in on the fourth floor.

'You look like shit.'

I stared up at his scowling face and burst into tears.

He tutted, muttered something like 'fucking women', and then pulled me into him and wrapped his arms around me while I cried mascara streaks into his incredibly white, well-ironed shirt.

And then it happened.

I smelt him for the first time.

Not his deodorant or hair product or expensive aftershave.

Him.

It wasn't anything he had artificially put on, it was his sweat, his scent, his musk, the smell that made him, him.

It was fresh and new and it wasn't James or anything that reminded me of James or of the sad little life I was currently living.

Harry smelt of money and privilege and excitement and unexplored possibilities.

Harry smelt of escape.

Early May 2024

It took about ten days for the rotten badger stench to fully disappear from the Hobbit House and during that time Lucky and I slept in the Defender. By the time the stench had gone, my tummy was a medium, round, hard football that made it extremely uncomfortable to sleep anywhere other than a proper bed, so I was very happy to finally 'move in'.

I used the time to clean, organise, and furnish our new home. The wood burner still worked but the clay oven outside had a huge crack in it and didn't heat up properly no matter how much wood I put in. I got new bedding and towels and cushions, and everything for the kitchen, and rugs for the floor, and paintings for the walls.

The reed-bed sanitation system still functioned, and the toilet had a very healthy flush (God knows what I will do if it ever breaks). Water gushed from the well-fed taps but there was no hot water, and the solar shower didn't work, so I relied on the kettle for hot water. I also discovered that there was only about an hour of electricity a day, nowhere near the five that the guest book promised, so I broke into the storage hut that the solar panels were linked into to see if I could find out why.

The lying hippy bastards were hooked up to the national grid.

There was an electricity meter in the hut and cables running underground. The solar panels obviously only provided about an hour a day, and the rest was from Eastern Electric. So much for a good electricity supply. But an hour a day was better than no hours, and at least it meant I wasn't entirely dependent on candles at night.

The walls of the storage hut were lined with racks containing all manner of gardening equipment and tools, and there were three huge bags full of firewood. It wasn't the 'sustainable, foraged wood' that had been advertised. It was from the local garden centre.

The Hobbit House was now rather lovely. It was filled with bright cushions and rugs and strung with Christmas fairy lights, and I'd manhandled the rocking chair from the cottage into the Defender and brought it here to place in front of the wood burner.

So, when it poured with rain on the first night we slept inside our new home, I sat in the rocking chair in front of my wood burner with Lucky snoring at my feet and began to learn to knit clothes and blankets for my baby.

I had jumped my first hurdle. I had provided a home for my growing family.

And in that moment, on that rainy night, by the fire, I allowed myself the smallest glimmer of hope. I started to believe that I could really do this. I had managed to come this far. I could give birth to my baby and raise him or her in the deserted landscape amongst the remnants of the world that once was.

I could work hard and survive in this world. I was determined that I could, and would, make a life here for me and my baby.

As if to show solidarity, the baby gave my tummy a resounding kick. I smiled. I could do this.

———

In another life, one that seemed so far away now, I had been determined with Harry Boyle.

Determined that I wasn't going to throw my decade-long love with James away just because Harry smelt nice.

I was a better person than that.

At least I thought I was a better person than that.

I started to smell Harry everywhere: when he was in the office, after he had been in the office, when he was walking up the corridor, if he had just come out of the lift. I could tell if he had been speaking to someone or used a certain cup or glass. I used to follow his smell from room to room. I craved it. I had no idea what 'his' smell was, and it nearly drove me insane. I went to Selfridges and demanded to sniff every man's aftershave. I smelt hair products, face products, deodorant. Nothing had that same scent.

I was addicted to it and I couldn't get it anywhere except from him.

Without even realising it I began to worry less about making James happy and more about my clothing, hair and make-up on the days I knew Harry was going to be in the office.

I began to overlook his rudeness, the scowling, and the swearing, and instead saw the intelligence, how he treated everyone in the team the same regardless of rank, the way he inspired confidence and made people work harder. I liked the tall solidity of him, the way you couldn't help but notice when he entered a room, the way he used his hands to gesture as he talked.

I started going to all of the meetings that I knew he was going to attend, and then I noticed he was watching me in those meetings.

And still, nothing happened. I continued to convince myself that nothing would happen.

But, of course, it did.

The day I first kissed Harry was a beautiful spring day.

A day that was fresh and new and filled with possibilities. I had woken up sprawled in a shaft of bright spring sunshine and my heart had been filled with hope. I decided to ask James to go for dinner, decided to be brave, break our impasse and offer him my heart once more. It was spring, things grew again in spring, maybe that could include us.

But, walking into the kitchen, I found that James had escaped the flat early to go to the gym before work. He'd left a note saying he was staying out for dinner. The sun disappeared behind a cloud and I cried in the shower.

I wanted to escape too, but where would I go?

By the time I had finished with my third meeting of the day the sun was once more high and bright in the sky. People were shedding winter cardigans, leaving them draped over the backs of chairs and taking their sandwiches to the park to allow the noon sun to gently roast their white wintery skin.

Harry leant over my chair.

'It's too sunny to be inside. Let's run away.'

We got on the River Bus down the Thames. Filled with commuters and excitable tourists standing up top in the sunshine, pointing out famous sights and the odd fancy hotel that they mistook for a famous sight. It was noisy and busy.

We didn't speak.

I leant over the guardrail and stared down into the foaming river, rushing on its way, so sure of the journey ahead. The sun was warm on my neck and the light-dappled water was hypnotising. I felt calm and drugged. I had no choice but to be carried along. Anything that happened now was out of my control.

The boat hit a current and rocked side to side. Harry, standing behind, grabbed the guardrail either side of me. I could smell him, feel his weight, reassuring and solid.

I turned in his arms and squinted up at him. He scowled down as he brushed my windswept hair from my face.

'I'm a bit of a mess,' I said.

He gave a short bark of laughter.

'Yes, you really fucking are,' he said.

Then he kissed me.

Late May 2024

Despite my previous bold, brave statement of hard work, determination and survival, I didn't actually do anything for most of May.

The weather was very warm so I would wake up, roll out of my bed, put the kettle on, grab some cereal and the least disgusting non-dairy alternative to milk that I could find, make tea, grab a book, and then move out to one of the sunloungers in the garden and lie there until my stomach told me it was lunchtime. Only then would I struggle off my sunlounger, curse my lack of bread, dairy products and processed meat, and heat something from a can for lunch. Then it was back to the sunlounger to alternately nap and read until I felt it was time for dinner.

I was too lazy to try to cook anything more elaborate than the contents of a can. I had resigned myself to a life without fresh fruit and veg or bread or dairy and, in my lethargic state, anything more involved than opening a can of beans and heating them in a pan seemed too much like hard work.

I did wash, but the camping shower I had got from Go Outdoors (in what seemed like a different lifetime) was literally a clear plastic bag hung on a peg. The bag held five litres of water, which sounds a lot, but definitely isn't when you are trying to get the soap off the lower part of your body, which you can no longer easily see. It was also rubbish for washing my hair, which was constantly knotted and sweaty and smelly, so one day I just grabbed my kitchen scissors and cut it off. Not just my pony tail, the whole lot. Cut and trimmed up the back of my neck. It felt short and spiky and amazing and, from what I could see in the tiny bathroom mirror that the Hobbit House had, looked pretty cool too.

I couldn't stand anything tight around my tummy and I had forgotten (or superstitiously refused) to get any maternity clothes, so most of my clothes – barring a kaftan, dressing gown and couple of huge jumpers – were too small for my growing belly. Mostly I didn't even bother with clothes any more, just wandered around in a pair of huge granny knickers that I threw away and replaced with new ones when they started to smell bad.

There were only two things that I paid attention to and did rigorously without fail.

One was clean my teeth. I brushed and flossed and tooth-picked and mouth-washed and cleaned those enamel jewels until they sparkled. I had never paid much attention to my teeth before. I saw my dentist every six months, had a couple of fillings every other year, and just bumbled through life taking them for granted. But, ever since 6DM, I have taken the best, the most expert, the most excellent care of my teeth. I remember seeing a segment on the news about NHS dentist waiting times and how some people had resorted to pulling their own teeth out rather than wait six months to see a dentist. They interviewed one of these self-torture victims and she had the thousand-yard-stare and sorrow-filled brow of someone who has experienced a pain that no human should go through. She had been beaten by the contents of her own mouth, her will to live had been taken out along with her teeth. *That* is the image I see every time I flirt with the notion of missing my cleaning session, and it is that image that always makes me haul my rapidly expanding, pregnant arse off the sunlounger/sofa/bed/rocking chair and into the bathroom for a damn good scrubbing.

The other thing I do without fail is apply sunscreen. Not some crappy cheap stuff either. I have the five-star UV rating, super strong, could practically visit the surface of the sun, takes seventeen minutes to fully rub in, best sunscreen that money can buy. There are illnesses that I can't do anything about: brain haemorrhage, heart attack, appendicitis, most of the cancers, sepsis. But skin cancer I can and will guard against. I haven't got this far to just allow myself to be fried like a little bit of bacon by the sun's almighty glare.

Such was my lethargy during the first part of May that I didn't even really play with Lucky that much. He, like me, seemed content to sit, sleep, and eat most of the time. Sometimes he'd disappear into the woods for a few hours and I'd hear him barking and scurrying around as he chased squirrels. I didn't worry if he disappeared, he always came back. I brought him a variety of dry and canned dog food, and he wolfed them all down. I made him take dog vitamins, which he hated, but he took them and then stared woefully at me for ten minutes after. He sat on my feet when I was in the rocking chair, lolled by my side when I was on the sunlounger, and slept on my bed at night. He continued to be my funny, furry, loving life partner. I just hoped he didn't get jealous and eat the baby when it arrived.

And that was it, that is what happened for most of May. Nothing much really.

I still wasn't sure I was capable of making my life any better than this all by myself.

———

If you'd asked me ten minutes before Harry kissed me if I was capable of having an affair then I would have said no.

At that point I had no idea what I was or would be capable of.

Kissing Harry on the River Bus with the sun shining down and the Thames roaring in my ears was all-encompassing, all sensation and exhilaration, there was no room for thought or reason. But, as soon as we stopped and I pulled back and looked into dark brown eyes so different to the blue I was used to seeing, reality came crashing back in.

I was hit by such a wave of guilt I nearly fell over. I think Harry thought I was overwhelmed by the kiss and performing an old-fashioned swoon. He caught me, but I wriggled away.

This wasn't one of the mid-meeting daydreams I'd had about kissing Harry.

This was real.

I was an adulteress.

Five hours later I sat at the kitchen table in my flat. Our flat. The flat I shared with my husband.

I was halfway through a bottle of gin, in the midst of a giant panic attack, and stricken with shame.

I had to tell James. I had to tell him everything. I had been bad, I had done an awful thing, but I wouldn't do it again. I would make more of an effort, I would be happy, we could be happy.

I just needed James to tell me he still loved me, that he was still with me, that he would still take care of me, that he would make everything better.

It was another two hours before James got home.

I sat in darkness in the kitchen, and he stopped in the hallway when he saw me. The hallway light left his face in shadow, but I could tell by the way his shoulders slumped that he was still tired of this, tired of us.

Tired of me.

I couldn't do it.

I didn't know if it was the gin, my panic, or his dejection, but the words wouldn't form. I couldn't tell him.

Instead, I walked to the fridge and took out the can of whipped cream that he had periodically replaced, but which I had never used.

I took the lid off, shook it, and then squirted half the can straight into my mouth.

The fridge light lit my face, which pleaded with him to understand, pleaded with him to remember.

He didn't move from the hallway, so I never knew what his expression was, but when he spoke his voice was filled with sadness.

'I think that stuff's out of date.'

Then he went into the bedroom to get changed.

I was too late.

———

As I said, I'd been pretty lazy while at the Hobbit House. I was still waiting for someone else to come and take over, someone else to do all the hard work.

I hadn't really cleaned, I hadn't tidied. I had picked up after myself just enough to keep the Hobbit House pleasant and liveable and not let it slip into the fetid state of Xav's house.

Without the convenience of weekly recycling and refuse trucks I had had to find somewhere else to dump my rubbish, so I had been putting it into the electricity storeroom with the vague plan of getting rid of it somehow once every six months (preferably without having to visit a dump).

So, it was something of a surprise when I opened the storeroom door one evening to throw my bag of rubbish in, to find that I couldn't.

In a month I had managed to fill the storeroom with forty-two black bin bags full of rubbish. Forty-two. Admittedly, around twenty of those were from when I had first cleared the Hobbit House out and got rid of anything old or mouldy or not country-cottage enough for my liking. But still, that's nearly a bag of rubbish a day.

And the smell . . . for a moment I thought my morning sickness had returned, but then I realised it was just my involuntary reaction to being presented with the smell of death all over again.

I had forgotten that I had put the badger in there.

Without the use of the recycling bin that was normally in my kitchen I had also thrown my leftover food, scraps and unwashed empty tins, Lucky's leftover food, scraps and unwashed empty tins, and the occasional stray dog turd into the bin liners.

It stank.

I loaded the Defender with the rubbish, drove into King's Lynn, and avoided having to visit the local dump by finding a random house on a random road with a door that opened and dumping my rubbish inside, shutting the door firmly after me when I was finished.

I had to do something. I had to find a way to live that didn't create so many leftovers.

I went back to the Hobbit House and, for the first time since I had arrived there, walked around the side and looked at the polytunnel and fruit and vegetable patch to see if there was any sort of composting area. If my mum could fit one in her little suburban garden, surely the hippies could fit one in here.

You'd have thought I would have walked around to look at the vegetable patch before, seeing as I was having desperate pregnancy cravings for anything green. But I hadn't. Maybe baby brain is a real thing.

There was no compost area that I could see, and the vegetable patch was a complete mess. Weeds and plants and unidentifiable green things all over the place. Things climbing up stakes, things growing over the sides of the borders, things pushing through netting. The polytunnel was worse; I could hardly see inside because it was so overgrown and the plastic sheeting was dripping with moisture in the afternoon heat. A less lazy part of me remembered the summers spent in the garden with my mum, and how disappointed she would be with me for letting things get so bad, so I bent over and half-heartedly pulled one of the larger weeds out.

It came up easily.

And on the end of the weed was a carrot.

A tiny, underdeveloped, twisted carrot. But a carrot, nonetheless.

I was so shocked I sat down on the ground with a bump.

And then I ate it.

I didn't even brush the dirt off properly, I ate half carrot, half mud.

And then I pulled up the weed next to it, found a carrot on the end, and ate that too.

And the next, and the next, and the next.

I went back into the Hobbit House and rummaged in the weekend bag that I had managed to keep with me for the last six months.

They were still in there, my mum's gardening gloves.

I took them out and was assailed by the pungent earthy, green smell that washed over me from them. Tears pricked at my eyes but, rather than cry, I smiled as I pulled them on.

Mum would have loved it here.

I spent the rest of the day rampaging through the fruit and veg patch and polytunnel like a mad woman.

The polytunnel was so verdent I could hardly get through the door and, once inside, couldn't tell one plant from the next. Plants had grown into each other, over each other and through each other, all struggling upwards towards the light. I slashed and struggled through grabbing whatever I could.

Outside I found carrots, potatoes, some tiny cabbages, plums and gooseberries. In the polytunnel were green beans growing up sticks, what I thought were tiny cucumbers, but now know are courgettes, lettuce, rhubarb, some actual cucumbers, a row of half-grown leeks, onions, a couple of big pots of tomatoes, and to my utter joy, three rows of raspberries and a patch of strawberries. Most of them still had some growing to do but, be still my rumbling tummy, some were ready to eat straight away.

I gathered everything that was ripe, and far more of the non-ripe things than I should have, and spent the rest of the day in a fresh, vitamin-fuelled daze. I ate most things raw and threw the rest into a pot and made it into a strange vegetable soup. Lucky came back from one of his woodland rampages to find me drooling tomato juice from my mouth and slopping a ladle of soup into a clean bowl for him.

He did not share my enthusiasm. He wouldn't even go near it.

And I am not ashamed to say I took it right back out of his bowl and ate it myself.

By the end of the day my tummy was so extended with fruit

and vegetable gas that the baby was doing somersaults trying to find a comfortable place to float, and I was walking around burping and farting.

Lucky refused to sleep on the bed that night and instead slept by the front door as if poised to escape, should one of my cabbage-fuelled farts burn the place down.

I really tested the reed-bed toilet the next day.

My vegetable patch/polytunnel discovery galvanised me into action. It would have made my mum incredibly proud that I was finally getting to put her gardening training to use on something bigger than a pot plant.

However, while my pruning skills might have been just about okay, I soon learnt I had little to no knowledge of fruit and veg growing and had no idea how to take care of the polytunnel or anything in it. I needed guidance and I needed tools. I drove to the nearest garden centre.

Or, at least, I started driving to the nearest garden centre but was sidetracked by a pick-your-own raspberry farm that, when I went to pick my own, also had strawberries and cherries. I collected seven punnets full. Then on my way back I saw a place advertising runner beans. Worth a shot, I thought. Two hours and three bags of runner beans later the sun was setting and I was heading home, garden centre visit-less.

My brush with near-starvation in Scotland was still fresh in my mind and I had already started to half-heartedly stockpile canned goods for when winter arrived. I realised that my veg patch and visit to the pick-your-own farm had given me the opportunity to stockpile fresh food also. But once back at the Hobbit House I saw I had a problem: the world's smallest fridge and therefore the world's smallest freezer section. I needed another way to preserve the bundles of fresh stuff I now found myself with.

So, back to King's Lynn Library I went for books on preserving and pickling, plus armfuls on gardening, growing your own fruit and vegetables, and how to recognise what to eat and what is poisonous (very, very well used by me). Then it was off to Wilko's for every pickling jar they had, plus sterilising tablets, vinegar for pickling, and sugar for jam.

The library was a goldmine of information about the local area and stocked an abundance of leaflets recommending pick-your-own places and even a lavender farm. For the next two days I did a tour of the surrounding area and got more raspberries and strawberries, plums, rhubarb, broccoli, cucumbers, runner beans, potatoes, and some random lettuces and leaves. I was too early in the season for most of them but, as long as they were ripe enough to eat, I didn't care if they were small, into my bags they went.

It took three days to can and jam everything I had collected. I canned most of the raspberries, strawberries and plums and made jam with the leftovers. I pickled the cucumbers, but have absolutely no idea what they will taste like – I guess if I start starving to death I won't care. I lined the shelves of the store-room with my jars, and then put the onions and potatoes in hessian sacks in the darkest part of the storeroom and hoped for the best.

I hope the potatoes don't rot. If the chap in *The Martian* can last on them for two years, then so can I.

Two years is a long time to eat nothing but potatoes.

Ten years is a long time to be with just one person.

After that amount of time you know everything about them; their smell, taste, jokes, moods, fears, dreams, hopes.

Nothing about me was new for James. Nothing was exciting.

I was new and I was exciting for Harry Boyle.

Harry knew almost nothing about me.

Harry knew I was the EMEA new business lead, that I lived in London, and that I was married.

That was it.

Harry might have made a joke about me being a bit of a mess, but he didn't know that was true, not really.

Harry knew nothing of my past, nothing of my panic attacks, depression, miscarriage. Harry didn't know Xav or Ginny or my mum and dad.

Harry didn't know I preferred baths to showers, that I liked to sleep on the right of the bed, that my feet always seemed to be cold.

James knew me. James knew everything about me, and I hadn't made James happy.

But I could make Harry happy.

When I was with Harry it was like the last ten years were erased. It was like I was erased. I could be who I wanted to be. I could start over.

And this time I was going to do it right.

I invented someone new. A new me.

I was funny and erudite and knowledgeable and smart. A raconteur with a raft of wonderful and detailed experiences stolen from the memories of pretty much everyone I knew. Very few of those stories were real, but all of them provided the colourful experiences of a life that Harry believed I had been lucky enough to live.

I presented Harry with an amalgamation of people and personalities. I was literally the perfect woman. I had no weaknesses, no faults, only charming quirks and eccentricities.

I glittered with life and vitality. For the first time, I looked rich and successful and was part of a rich, successful couple.

Harry took me to the best restaurants, bars and places in town. I went to the Ritz, the Dorchester, Soho House, the Mondrian. I marvelled and delighted at them and I was marvellous and delightful in them.

I didn't include anything in my new persona that might have given the game away, that might have alluded to my real life. I didn't talk about my failing marriage, the all-consuming level of guilt I felt, the almost constant level of panic I now found myself living with.

I didn't tell Harry how exhausted I was: exhausted by the

subterfuge, exhausted by the huge amount of work it took to keep looking good and being good for him, exhausted by lying to my husband, family, and friends.

Exhausted by the effort of trying to be someone different, someone perfect, someone who didn't exist.

Again.

Mid June 2024

I finally got to the local garden centre to get my gardening supplies about a week after I had meant to go.

It was the first time I had been in a shop for at least a month and it was suddenly jarring to find myself back in the real world. The old world. I realised that in this world it would for ever be Christmas, for ever be decorated with tinsel and lights to celebrate a holiday that no longer existed. Would I still celebrate Christmas? I wasn't sure.

I heard the noise when I was packing seeds and tools into the Defender.

My new world is far from quiet. Sure, there is no traffic or machinery or human chatter, but there is a constant background hum, chirp, whistle and rustle from a hundred thousand mini beasts that are going about their daily business in close proximity to me. But that is all just background noise. Anything new always comes as a shock, whether it is the clatter of a pan falling on the floor or the squeal of some small animal that Lucky has pounced on in the woods.

This sound wasn't frightening, it was familiar.

It was a cluck.

And then a squawk.

My heart jumped, and I spun around.

A high fence separated me from my quarry.

I sprinted over, pulled myself up onto my tiptoes, and peeked across.

They were scrawny and scarred and had lost half their feathers, but they were alive.

They were chickens.

Lucky came streaking in from the side like a bullet of pure fur, power, and hunger.

'YOU BLOODY DARE!' I roared.

He skidded to a sudden dusty halt that would have been funny under any other circumstances. But this was not funny. I could tell he wanted the chickens just as much as I did. He looked up and, I swear, pretended not to see me. He wriggled his belly close to the ground and started to snake forward.

'LUCKY!' I shrieked it this time, determined to assert my power, even if only the top of my head was visible to him.

The chickens were going batshit crazy at the sudden presence of a hungry dog and a screaming human. They were running all over the place, and I was afraid they'd drop dead from fear.

I lowered my voice and used my 'do not mess with me' tone.

'Lucky, you come back here, right NOW!' and, thank all the gods in heaven, he did.

I heaved a sigh of relief, dropped to my knees, and hugged him. He was too heavy for me to pick up now (Lucky had put on quite a bit of weight during our few weeks of rest) so I lured him into the Defender with a handful of biscuits and ignored his howls when I locked him in there.

Then I went back and looked at my scrawny chickens. Three were white and one was brown. There were fourteen massive sacks of seed stretched from one end of the fence to the other. The bags were empty, but must have kept them going until now.

I knew nothing about chickens except that they get eaten by foxes and, if you wanted them to lay eggs, you needed to have a cockerel nearby. There was no cockerel in with them, so these chickens were destined to be my dinner.

My mouth began to water. Chicken! Roasted, baked or fried. Chicken! No idea how to kill, pluck or prepare them, but who cared? Chicken!

I was so lost in my reverie of meat that I almost didn't hear the sound that took away my chicken-based fantasy.

Then I stopped.

It was quiet, it was weak, it was far away, but it was unmistakeable. A cockerel's crow.

He was sitting in the doorway of a shed at the end of the next field. When I appeared, he raced across the field towards me with such enthusiasm that I completely forgot our comparative sizes, shat myself, and ran away, slamming the gate to the field behind me to shut him in.

He just walked under the gate of course.

I went back to the library.

Chickens are very sociable creatures and like company and humans.

I read this in my chicken book, but had also learnt it first-hand by the time the chickens moved into the ugly but usable chicken pen I had built a week later.

While I got their new home ready for them I visited them every day at the garden centre to feed them and change their water. They would crowd around me clucking and chirping and within three days they would let me pick them up and stroke them. By the end of the week I was very glad I hadn't eaten them.

They laid their first egg two weeks after moving into their new home. I don't think I can ever adequately describe the pure joy I felt holding that warm, speckled egg in my hand. My brain said that I should keep it, that it was symbolic, that it meant I was becoming adapted to, and successful in, this new world.

My tummy said, 'Fuck that!'

I ate it boiled and dipped in salt and pepper. It was truly delicious.

I named the chickens Hetty, Netty, Letty and Betty and the cockerel was Simon.

I nearly named the cockerel Xav, because of his friendliness, neediness, strutting about, and obvious beauty – even with half his feathers missing you could tell he was a looker. But I decided it would be too sad to be reminded of my former best friend every day.

————

I don't want to be reminded of my best friend every day because he wasn't my best friend at the end, or at least I wasn't his best friend. I didn't deserve to be.

I wasn't a good friend to Xav or Ginny in the last six months before 6DM.

I saw very little of either of them during that time, but told myself I had every excuse not to.

Ginny was heavily pregnant. We still spoke regularly on the phone and messaged pretty much every day, but whenever I saw her in person, saw her now huge belly, it just reminded me how empty I was; an emptiness that even Harry couldn't fill.

She was, of course, incredibly sweet about it and didn't even mention my conspicuous absence at her baby shower.

I didn't deserve her sweetness.

Xav was more difficult to avoid and ignore. He had yet to relapse after his last visit to rehab and was making heroic attempts to repair our friendship. I don't know whether I was cruel to him because I thought he deserved it, or because it made it easier for me not to see him.

But I was cruel to him, very cruel.

It wasn't that I ignored him or refused to see him, I saw him quite regularly. But I kept him at a distance. I kept him out of my life, out of my family, refused to allow my mum and dad to invite him for Christmas or birthdays. When we met I would only talk about work, the news, movies, bands; nothing serious, nothing deep, nothing about me. I refused to let him back in. I wouldn't forgive him.

I think my refusal to love Xav again broke him. I was his family, and I rejected him. He was quieter now, smaller almost. He didn't laugh with me any more, didn't tell me about his latest conquest or a funny story from his gym. He asked me earnest questions, tried to needle information out of me, tried to hold my hand. All the while his eyes pleaded with me to forgive him, to let him back into my heart.

I didn't.

I hate myself for that.

James never knew I was seeing Xav and Ginny less.

James thought I saw them at least a couple of times a week, and some weeks even more.

That was the time I spent with Harry.

I used my best friends as cover for my affair.

I pretended I was going to therapy sessions with Xav to try to make our friendship work again. I wasn't.

I pretended I had gone to Ginny's baby shower. I hadn't.

Instead I spent the afternoon getting drunk with Harry.

James thought I was being brave and strong and a good friend.

It turned out James didn't know me that well after all.

July 2024

By the middle of July, now that I had a burgeoning smallholding, my days of lazing around were over.

Every day started just after dawn when I heard Simon crowing.

I'd built Simon a special 'man-shed' and chicken run (a large rabbit hutch with some chicken wire attached), but he was incredibly adept at getting out of it so in the end I just let him run free. Some mornings he would crow from quite far away and I could ignore him for a while. Most mornings he sat right outside the door and whenever it was too hot to close the door overnight, he would walk right into the Hobbit House and yell from below the bed.

Once I was up, Simon would strut about the house and butt his head against my leg until I gave him something to eat to keep him quiet. Chickens will eat pretty much anything, so they got a lot of my leftovers. (I am hoping I might find a stray pig at some point so that I can feed my leftover crap to that too.)

I am reluctantly grateful for the agony I went through learning to light a fire in Scotland as it now means I can get a fire going in the wood burner and have the kettle suspended over it within ten minutes of getting out of bed. I would then get dressed (mostly just in knickers and a huge garden-centre Christmas T-shirt) and go out to check on the girls. Their feathers were growing back and they had managed to put on a surprising amount of weight in the month that I had had them. They too wanted a bit of love and attention, so I normally sat with them while they had their breakfast and they pecked and I patted. I liked that they needed me.

Most mornings Lucky would still be snoring when I got back

inside after feeding the girls, as he is lazy and surprisingly adept at ignoring the noise made by Simon. Like a mother trying to rouse her sleeping teenager, I would clatter about until he deigned to get out of bed and eat the breakfast I had made for him. If it wasn't raining I ate my breakfast outside – either cereal or a tortilla with jam.

I had finally worked out how to make my own bread. At the beginning of June I discovered the naan aisle in the supermarket had packs that were still in date, so I ripped them open with my teeth, sat down on the floor, and chomped my way through two bags. Utter, utter joy. Then I realised I had been thinking purely traditionally with my limited choice of bread products and actually weren't there ones that didn't need to be baked in an oven? Back to the library I went. One week, and lots of experimentation later, I had learnt that I was able to make a very tasty tortilla, a pretty good batbout (a sort of Moroccan puffy bread), a passable pitta bread, and a slightly doughy naan. There are others that I could make – cornbread and oven-top scones for example – but these all need butter and milk, so are off my menu for now. But I am not complaining! I am very happy to have any bread choice at all.

In fact, I am pretty happy with my diet in general now. Don't get me wrong, I still massively miss meat and dairy, but, along with the bread, I also made another discovery in June, which is always my next morning job after the chickens: fishing.

The stream at the back of the Hobbit House positively teems with small to medium sized fish. We'd had a load of rain at the end of June and the river was practically breaching the bank. The sun had returned a couple of days later and I was sitting dangling my hot and swollen feet in the river, when a fish jumped right out and landed on the grass by my side.

Somehow I resisted my natural reaction, which was to jump up screaming, and instead I grabbed it by the tail and smashed its head on the stones next to me. Blood flew everywhere and it lay limp.

Then, before I could be consumed by further guilt, I took it back to the house, cut its head off, cut it in half and fried it in a pan.

I ate the lot, bones and all. I had no idea what type of fish it was and it was only after I had eaten it that I stopped to worry it might not be a type of fish one should eat. But, when I woke up the next morning and was still alive, I jumped straight in the Defender, drove to the garden centre and got netting.

Thank you shipping crewmen for teaching me the rudiments of net fishing.

It took a few attempts to rig a good netting system. In the end I made a sort of bag out of the netting that gapes widely at one end. I tether this to a stake, stick some tortilla in the back, float it in the water overnight, and hope for the best. It's not ideal and isn't always successful. Some mornings there is nothing in it, some mornings anything in it is too small to eat and, if it rains overnight, I normally come out to find the bag has slipped the tether and floated off, sometimes never to be found.

I hardly flinch at all when I kill them now. I have two large stones at the side of the river. I lay them on one and bash their heads in with the other. When I am done, I wash the blood off the stones. They are pretty small, so it takes three or four to make a good meal. But if I have had a particularly good haul – five or more fish – I will try to preserve the extra. I am experimenting with salting them and putting them in the storage cupboard. I am not sure if it will work, but the storage cupboard is yet to start stinking of rotting fish, so I am hopeful.

Once I have checked the fishing net, I head for the fruit and veg patch and polytunnel. I am finding it more and more difficult to do any significant digging or weeding, so I tend to just collect the ripe stuff and pull out a few weeds here and there. I am eating mainly fresh things at the moment and saving the tins for winter. Rice, pasta, flour, oils, tins, and lots of gravy and mixes are all still in date and, I should imagine, will pretty much last for ever, but everything else is either out of date or running low on time. Milk, butter, cheese, yoghurts, meats, processed meats were all done months ago. Chocolate, biscuits, crisps, cakes, packaged breads, nuts, cereals, drinks and even coffee and tea are either past their sell-by date or getting close.

However, I am discovering that rules on food consumption are pretty fluid in the new world. For example, potato-based crisps are stale and disgusting, but something maize-based like Wotsits or tortillas are normally fine – maybe a bit chewy, but definitely still edible. The same goes for biscuits. Anything covered in chocolate is probably bad, but your average digestive or short-bread? Still totally yummy. As long as it doesn't smell bad, I take a nibble and see. My parameters for what is, and isn't, edible have widened considerably. A carrot that I would previously have deemed too ugly or blemished or even wonky to eat goes in the pot along with the rest of them. Skin and all. I am too hungry to waste anything.

By the time I am done with my fruit and veg the sun is normally high in the sky and I am sweating and knackered. So, if I can be bothered, I treat myself to a dip in the river, which is icy cold to begin with and then refreshing after five minutes. I will normally be dive-bombed by Lucky as soon as he realises where I am, and then Simon might wander over and strut at the edge chattering away.

One happy family.

Lunch is leftovers or whatever is easy, as by now I am seriously flagging. I stuff it down and then fall asleep.

I don't know how long I sleep for or when I wake up because I don't have a clock or phone any more. These days I wake with Simon and go to sleep when it is dark or I am tired.

I spend the rest of the afternoon doing whatever is most urgent. I inventory food or preserve surplus fruit and veg, I collect twigs and fallen branches for kindling, I attempt maintenance on the Defender using one of the many books on car mechanics that I now have, I wash my clothes in the stream using eco washing powder, I sow seeds in the polytunnel, I cumbersomely climb a ladder and try to patch small holes in the thatched roof of the Hobbit House where rain has started to drip through, I clean out the chicken hutches and repair their wire run, I check and reattach my fishing nets, I do any number of the many, many things that always seem to need to be done just to survive.

When the light starts to get dusky I re-bait the fishing nets, feed the girls again, and try to chase Simon into his chicken hutch – knowing full well that he'll be out of it the moment my back is turned.

Some nights I go back into my house, make a lovely supper of fish, potatoes and vegetables, followed by pudding of stewed fruit. I watch a DVD or read by the fire, then brush my teeth, wash my face, apply moisturiser, change into a clean nightie, and go to bed. Some nights I eat a bag of crisps and go to bed in a dirty pair of knickers.

I have started to dream again.

I hadn't dreamt for years before 6DM, at least, not dreams that I could remember the following morning.

But now I have started to dream again. Bright, vivid, physical dreams that seem so real that when I wake up I am disappointed to find them not true. I dream that I am sitting in my rocking chair breastfeeding my baby. That my baby is learning to crawl on the grass by the stream. That my baby is rolling a ball for Lucky. That my baby is sleeping gently in my arms as I sing to it all the songs that have ever been, or will ever be, written or remembered on this earth.

I never see the face of my baby, just the form, the weight, the smell of him or her.

I am trying not to see this as a bad omen.

August 2024

It is the middle of summer and I have a growing tummy and a growing family.

Life is now almost idyllic – especially in comparison to the things I have written about before.

No more struggles with sadness or addiction or suicide; I seem to be contented, busy, and productive.

Which I am.

Mostly.

I am busy because I have no choice. Keeping the chickens, managing the veg patch, fishing, looking after the Hobbit House, preserving food for the future – this all takes a lot of work and I am now getting very, very large, so I do everything very slowly.

But, often, I will find myself wondering if I am 'making busy' to distract myself from the fact that, despite being pregnant, nothing has changed.

I am still alone.

I have my idyllic setting and my little pseudo-family and we bumble through each day in a happy muddle, but I still fall asleep each evening without speaking to another person.

Or do I?

Because, each night, as I drift to sleep I trace my hands over my ever-growing belly and whisper to the person growing inside. I tell them of my life before and of the people I loved, my friends, my family, the world that we lived in. It soothes and gratifies me that I can now do this without crying, that I can speak of the legacy left by those I loved with deep emotion but not necessarily deep sorrow.

I whisper secrets that I don't even allow myself to fully hope, secrets and dreams for our future. That my baby will arrive safely and that we will, eventually, find other survivors. That we are not the only ones left.

I whisper how I owe my baby my life so, in return, I will give them theirs too and I will do everything to make sure it is a happy one.

When waves of sadness threaten to envelop me, which they still do, I lie on my back by the river and stare up at the cloud-less, plane-less blue sky and feel my baby kick at my enquiring hands and I know, I know that this is about so much more than just me now.

And yet, despite my ever-growing love for the person inside me, I am not preparing for the arrival of my baby in any way.

I have done and collected nothing. No Moses basket, no clothes, no nappies, no wipes, no bottles, no pram, no toys, nothing to bathe it with, feed it with, burp it with. I haven't read any books, I haven't watched any DVDs, and I definitely haven't listened to anything about birth or babies.

When I was trying to get pregnant in my life before, I didn't watch or read anything about birth and babies out of superstition. So, I have never seen *One Born Every Minute* or watched *Call the Midwife*. The closest I have been to any kind of birthing manual is the scene where Katherine Heigl gives birth in *Knocked Up*, and I watched that about fifteen years ago and all I can remember is a lot of screaming. Not particularly educational.

Ginny had a Caesarean with Radley, and her only comment on the procedure was that she was glad she had lots of drugs and make sure you drink lots of water after because you do not want to get constipated. She did not elaborate on why and I was too polite to ask.

I have not yet put any thought into where and how I am going to have the baby. I mean, I obviously can't go to the hospital, so I am planning to have the baby in the Hobbit House, but I will surely need supplies other than towels and hot water to do so.

But where do I get the supplies from? I am not going to chance going to the hospital to get them, so will a GP surgery have them? And what supplies do I need exactly?

I have made important changes to my life and the person I am. I have taken responsibility for me, my baby, and my animals. I have found us a home and food and water and safety. I am slowly accepting my past and believing that I can have a future. But the chaos and uncertainty of giving birth and having a tiny baby in this world without anything I recognise as normal in it? I am not sure I can.

It still feels like it is too much to think about.

It feels like it is something that I will think about tomorrow . . . or the next day.

I may have decided I would ignore the impending birth of my baby for a while, but my baby had other ideas.

I didn't feel any pain or any lessening of movement or cramps. It was an ordinary morning and I had woken up in an ordinary way and gone for a wee before going out to feed the girls.

There was blood in my knickers.

Just a smear.

A smear of bright, red blood.

I was almost too scared to wipe between my legs. Too scared to find out if something was really wrong.

There was another smear on the tissue when I did finally wipe.

I went straight to the sink and drank a glass of cold water – my now trusted technique to get the baby to kick. I felt a lazy bump to one side of my belly and almost cried with relief.

I went back and lay in bed for, what I thought, was about an hour.

I shouted at Lucky when he tried to jump up on the bed with me.

There was another smear when I next went to the loo, and another an hour(ish) later.

I drank more water and got more kicks, but my heart was still beating out of my chest.

I was nine months pregnant, I was so close, please Lord, don't take this from me now.

With the amount of water I had drunk the baby was now wriggling around, kicking and jabbing me in my tummy and back. I have never been so happy to feel that movement.

The bleeding had stopped by the time evening came, but I stayed in bed the next day as well, just to be sure.

When I eventually got out of bed I moved slowly and carefully and sat down to perform chores where I could.

It was a wakeup call.

This was happening.

I was having a baby.

I might die giving birth to the baby. I might die after I had given birth to the baby. But the baby was coming, and ignoring that fact would not stop labour from happening.

I went baby shopping.

I'm not going to bore you with the details of the crazy amount of stuff I collected but, having put it off for so long, I definitely went over the top and got far too much stuff.

I have had to wrestle the mattress from the mezzanine down onto the lower floor (the stairs to the mezzanine were getting to be a bit of a squeeze anyway) and have stored all the stuff I got on the mezzanine level.

It just about fits.

The most surprising thing about my shopping trip wasn't the huge amount of random crap that I brought home and will never use, it was me.

I haven't seen myself in a full-length mirror for, well, as long as I can remember.

I haven't seen myself pregnant.

I am huge.

I was wearing a 'funny' man's Christmas shirt that I got from the garden centre in size XXXL. The buttons at the front were straining. As usual I hadn't bothered with trousers.

I stripped the shirt off, fascinated by the sight of my hugely extended belly. The skin on it looks like it could rip apart at any moment, it is stretched to capacity, bulging and ready to burst. When the baby moves you can see it from the outside; my stomach ripples, disconcertingly similar to the scene in *Alien*.

In contrast, the rest of me is thin. Much thinner than I have ever been. Not skinny, just minus the extraneous fat layer that my beloved processed food had always bestowed upon my bones. And, despite my judicious application of sunscreen, I am tanned. Very deeply tanned. I am also hairy. I no longer bother to shave anywhere, so my armpit hair is luxuriously long and silky. My leg hair seems to have stalled at about two centimetres long and is more like a blond fur that coats my legs.

The short, tufty, home-cut hair on my head is a strange mix of mousey with grey and blond streaking. I move closer to the mirror. My face is covered in freckles and there are white bleached laughter lines at the corners of my eyes. My eyes are clear and bright and happy.

I look happy.

Maybe I am happy.

Nothing about how I look says that I am the last person alive on earth, that I am about to give birth to a baby alone, in the backwoods of Norfolk.

If I didn't know me, I would say I was a happy, contented person.

I think maybe, finally, I am becoming a happy and contented person.

———

There have been moments before when I thought I was happy and contented. When James and I first got together, when we moved in, got married, when I was pregnant last time.

There was even a point when I thought I might be happy and contented with Harry, that he would be the one who could make my life complete.

But then Ginny gave birth and three weeks later I met Radley for the first time.

Ginny was on maternity leave, so met me for lunch during the week. It was just the two of us and Radley.

It was a beautiful late summer day and we sat outside in the shade.

When Ginny arrived she was a crazy fireball of contradictions; three weeks post-birth she was exhausted and joyful, teary, and filled with wonder, slumped and shuffling after her Caesarean, but walking on air. She had no make-up on, her hair hadn't been styled in weeks, her nails were ragged, and breast milk had leaked through her bra onto her dress, but she looked fucking radiant.

I had freshly blow-dried hair, perfect nails, a full face of make-up and was wearing a new Zara dress in readiness for seeing Harry later; I felt grey and haggard next to her.

She appeared in a flurry of pram and bags and baby. Radley was crying.

'She needs feeding but I'll wet myself if I don't go for a wee. Here, hold her for a sec.'

And, shoving a bawling bundle of blankets at me, she was gone.

I looked down.

A tiny, angry face with eyes screwed shut in pure rage peeped from the blankets. The noise was horrendous, and faces were beginning to turn my way.

I didn't know what to do. I shushed Radley, jiggled her, awkwardly tried putting her on my shoulder. The noise increased.

In desperation I stuck the knuckle of my forefinger into her screeching mouth the way I had seen people do on TV. The effect was instant.

She shut up and sucked on my finger.

Her entire body relaxed, face uncrumpling, legs stopped kicking. Then she opened her tiny, scrunched eyes and looked at me.

Deep, dark brown pools stared up, and she saw me.

She really saw me.

I held my breath, expecting another scream.

Instead, she smiled. Some might say it was gas, but I know it was a smile.

And, just like that, I knew I would never be happy and contented with Harry.

I was pretending again, pretending to Harry, pretending to be the person he wanted to try and make him happy. Even worse, I was pretending to myself. I wasn't happy, this wasn't me, I wasn't . . .

'Hey!'

I was yanked from my thoughts back into the real world. I looked up.

It was James. He was smiling down at me.

For the first time in weeks.

'Hi. Wow. Er, what are you doing here? I thought you were working?'

He wasn't smiling at me. He was smiling at Radley.

'My meeting was cancelled and I obviously haven't met the little one yet so I thought I'd pop down and see if you were still here. She's gorgeous.'

Laughter. Ginny was back. She reached for Radley.

'She really is! Here, have a hold.'

Ginny passed Radley over. James had three nephews, so was far more experienced in holding newborns than I. He took her and immediately started that side-to-side rocking people who know how to comfort babies do instinctively.

'Nice moves.' Ginny smiled.

She turned to me.

'You didn't do too bad for your first time either.'

Shit.

I'd told James that I had already been to see Ginny and Radley when I went out with Harry the previous week.

James paused in his rocking.

'I thought you said you saw her last week?'

My mind was blank. I looked at Ginny, eyes wide with panic.

Radley started to cry again and Ginny reached calmly for her.

'She did! But Radley was fast asleep and I don't like to disturb her when she's sleeping 'cause it doesn't happen often.'

She laughed, James laughed, I tried to stop my heart from beating out of my chest.

'Right, I'll get some drinks.'

James went to the bar and Ginny started breastfeeding.

She looked at me.

'Someone else?'

I gave the briefest of nods, not trusting myself to say anything in case everything came blurting out.

'You're not happy with James.'

It was a statement not a question.

She looked down at Radley, and then up at me steadily.

'Sometimes it doesn't matter who else you're with, if you're not happy with yourself.'

She held my gaze until I felt tears pricking at my eyes and I had to look down at my hands.

I tried to make a joke of it.

'When did you get all wise?'

Ginny smiled down at Radley again.

'They come with a handbook.'

She reached across the table and held my hand.

Then James came back with the drinks.

I was not a happy or contented person then and I am not a happy or contented person now.

I am fucked.

I have just finished reading:

Better Birth: The Ultimate Guide to Childbirth from Home Births to Hospitals

The Positive Birth Book: A New Approach to Pregnancy, Birth and the Early Weeks

Your Baby, Your Birth: Hypnobirthing Skills For Every Birth

Gentle Birth, Gentle Mothering: The Wisdom and Science of Gentle Choices in Pregnancy, Birth and Parenting

Your Pregnancy Week by Week: What to Expect from Conception to Birth

Happy Birth Day: How to Have the Best Possible Pregnancy and Birth

and I am completely and utterly fucked.

This is not me. I am not gentle or nurturing or relaxed or positive.

I cry and panic and find new situations very unsettling.

I do not cope well with blood. I spent two days in bed for a 'smear of blood' last week. If I have a heavy period I have been known to feel faint.

I am not good at planning nor, on the other hand, am I willing to go with the flow. I nearly had a panic attack three days ago because I thought I'd run out of salt.

I am not able to cope with pain on my own. I sprained my ankle once and couldn't walk for a week – James had to carry me to the bathroom for the first two days.

I am not calm and measured. I spent the first month after 6DM getting high rather than looking for survivors.

I DO NOT WANT TO GIVE BIRTH DRUG-FREE! I was drunk and/or high for the first three months that this baby was in me, and I think it only fair that I should get to be in the same state when it leaves.

Do you know what an episiotomy is? If you don't, then take my advice and don't ever bother finding out.

I know what an episiotomy is. I know that they are often necessary if the baby's head is stuck. I have all the graphic and gory details about something that is normally performed by a trained professional after they have administered drugs to stop the pain of performing the episiotomy on their labouring victim.

I don't have a trained professional. I don't have pain-numbing drugs. I don't even have a sharp knife to perform the episiotomy with if I need one.

I may very well have to cut the fleshy bit between my vagina and my anus using a butter knife while I am high on nothing stronger than paracetamol.

I don't even know if I am allowed to take paracetamol.

I feel like the lead in an American high school abstinence PSA; I had sex and now I have to face the consequences, which will be ripping my vagina in two without painkillers.

No. Sorry. Not doing it.

The baby will just have to stay in me.

————

The abstinence PSA would have been very proud of me because I didn't have sex with Harry. Not for the whole time we were seeing each other.

I wanted to. There were multiple times when I really, really wanted to. We often ended up in bed together doing 'everything but', and I knew that a lawyer would find very little difference between his fingers being inside me and his penis.

But there was a difference to me.

Every time I thought of having sex with Harry I thought about having sex with James at Soho Farmhouse.

I thought about how it wasn't just sex with James at Soho Farmhouse. It was a physical and emotional act, something so all-encompassing that I felt like my mind, heart and body orgasmed all at the same time. I had learnt that there was a difference between normal sex and sex with someone you loved; they could both end in orgasm, but only one of them ended in total satisfaction.

With Harry it would just be normal sex. I didn't love him.

Harry never forced me. Not once. He never made me feel uncomfortable or that I owed him in some way for all the places he took me, the money he spent on me.

I told myself that he was probably getting it elsewhere so didn't care that much.

But now I think it was because he was actually a nice person and willing to wait until the time was right for both of us.

Just one of the many ways that Harry Boyle turned out to be a much nicer person than me.

Meeting Radley was the beginning of the end of my relationship with Harry.

A tiny baby.

A tiny baby that just knew, by instinct, that she could be who she liked and do what she wanted and the world would still revolve around her. She wasn't going to pretend. If she was sad she would cry, if she was hungry she would scream until she got fed, when she was tired she would sleep, and when she was happy she would smile. She made it all seem so simple.

By the time the first 6DM victim was sneezing in Andover, I had been seeing Harry for nearly six months, and the cracks in my carefully curated new version of me were beginning to show.

The physical effort of continuing to be Harry's ideal was exhausting. I let things slide. I no longer had weekly waxes and blow-dries. No longer carefully reapplied lipstick for every meeting we would be in together, no longer carried lacy thongs in my handbag to change out of my comfy M&S panties into when we met after work.

I was mentally shattered with hiding who I really was. I wanted to talk about something real, about my envy of Ginny, how desperately I missed and wanted to make up with Xav, how my mum was getting older and I was no closer to finding the happiness she so longed for me to have. I wanted to be honest about why I didn't want to go for drinks on the 52nd floor of the Shard, why I preferred to walk everywhere rather than get on the underground.

But I couldn't do that, I couldn't be honest with Harry. I couldn't tell him that everything he knew about me was a lie.

I couldn't tell Harry that when I was with him I was once more moulding myself into the person I thought I needed to be to ensure someone else's happiness and not my own. That I was so desperate for him to love me that I'd changed myself into the person I thought he would want.

I couldn't tell him that I'd wasted the last ten years doing exactly the same thing with James.

A three-week-old baby might be able to be honest, but I wasn't.

Dictaphone Recording (Tape 1 / Recording 2)
(Transcribed)

> *(The same woman's voice again, speaking*
> *into the Dictaphone.)*

Hello? Hello? I need to check this thing is still
working. It's me. Is this working?

> *(Dictaphone is turned on and off.)*

It's still working.

> *(Sobs.)*

I . . . I need to speak to someone.
I'm scared.
I wish there was someone to talk to.
I need help.
I just want to talk to someone. I just need someone
to tell me it's going to be okay.
I'm so alone.

> *(Sound of crying for some time.)*

Something terrible has happened.

Recording ends.

Late August 2024

My baby was due in two or three weeks.

Having read the birthing books I now knew that I needed to go to the hospital and get things for the birth, but every time I thought about writing a list of what I might need, I would start to feel sick and sweaty and I suddenly found myself with something much more urgent to do.

I am not stupid, I realised that I was not panicking about writing a list.

I was panicking about the hospital.

I hadn't been near one since my failed attempt to get Susan Palmers' statins (I hadn't thought about Susan Palmers in weeks.)

I only stood by the doors then.

The idea of actually having to enter the building and see the chaos and mess and tragedy within made my skin crawl.

I hadn't seen a dead body for nearly four months. What would they look like now? What would they smell like? What would 1,000 of them that have been sealed inside a hospital for nine months smell like?

I didn't want to find out. So I kept busy with other things.

I was nesting.

The Hobbit House gleamed. I had washed everything inside it, swept the floor a hundred times, cleaned the windows and kitchen, scrubbed the toilet, tidied and ordered all my baby items, bottled, canned, salted and stacked enough food to last for months.

The polytunnel and fruit and vegetable patch had been picked and pruned and weeded and seeded. I had stockpiled wood and tinder for the fire. I made extra fishing nets and refined my fishing system. I had salted and stored over two hundred fish. The chickens shone with health and happiness. All their feathers had grown back and they were fat and happy in their new home. They each laid an egg a day and rushed to greet me morning and night. Simon had settled into following me around for most of the day, chuntering at me and occasionally stopping to peck at and chase Lucky.

Everything and everyone was ready for the baby's arrival. Except me.

It was a Sunday.

Sundays are my official days of rest.

I do, eat, watch, and read what I want on Sundays.

We were having what the BBC would once have termed a heatwave. It had been hot since the beginning of June and hadn't rained for twenty-six days. I had to water the polytunnel and vegetable patch with a bucket from the river, which was hard work and boring. The water level in the river had dropped considerably, and I was only catching fish every third or fourth day (although I was not too worried about this as, in addition to my salted fish, I had 106 cans of tuna, 67 cans of sardines, and 24 cans of salmon in the storage hut).

The worst thing about the heatwave was that the Hobbit House got unbearably hot within a couple of hours of waking up. I stopped using the wood burner to boil the kettle and used the firepit outside instead, but I was still forced out of the house mid-morning until late afternoon by the heat.

On this Sunday I had got out of bed to feed the chickens, got tea and biscuits, and then climbed back on to the bed to watch *Gilmore Girls* on DVD until the Hobbit House got so hot that I was lying in a slick of my own sweat.

I moved outside and lay in the shade on an ancient sunlounger, which just about managed my weight, and devoured one of the trashy magazines that I now limited myself to only reading on a Sunday. Lucky splashed in the river, came over to shake water all over me, and then charged into the woods to crash about in the shade for the rest of the day. Simon strutted around outside of the chicken run to show the girls just what they were missing. They ignored him.

I was very, very horny. All the time. Another by-product of late-stage pregnancy I have discovered, which is annoying, because masturbating is not that easy when you can barely reach your clitoris because of your enormous belly. I had already masturbated that morning, but was ready to go again. I am perfectly happy to wander around naked now, but am still not comfortable with wanking in the open air where the animals can see. So, I dragged myself back into the Hobbit House for a sweaty ten minutes of self-love. I am desperate for some porn or a vibrator to liven my frequent masturbatory sessions, but the garden centre didn't stock such items (they should have – I bet they would have made a fortune.)

Itch scratched, I was then hungry. Hungry but lazy. So lunch was crisps, more biscuits, raspberries in syrup, and some chocolate that had gone white at the edges but still tasted okay.

I ate on my sunlounger, threw my rubbish on the ground, and then settled down for a well-earned nap.

I thought it was Lucky, back from the woods, and waking me up to play with him.

He snuffled at my face and growled slightly.

I swatted him away and shifted position.

Lucky didn't smell right.

Lucky has stinky dog breath but otherwise he smells of grass and woodsmoke and sunshine.

Whatever had sniffed me smelt of blood and river water and pain.

The wood didn't sound right.

The wood was quiet. I couldn't hear Lucky crashing about, I couldn't hear the constant birdsong that came from the trees. The girls in the chicken run were quiet, no clucking, no chuntering at Simon's egomaniac display.

Simon wasn't chattering.

Simon was squealing. High-pitched, distressed screeches of pain or fear or anger.

I opened my eyes.

I couldn't move. I just stared at it.

I don't know what it was.

I'm not a dog expert.

It was big, the size of a Shetland pony. It had a huge head with massive, teeth-filled jaws, but its body was sinewy, sleek, and run with muscle.

It didn't look like any dog that I recognised. It might have been a dog once, someone's family pet or warehouse guard dog. That past life was now long gone.

It was panting. I didn't know whether from exertion or excitement or both.

It loomed over me, surrounding me in a fog of foul, wet breath.

Half of me thought that maybe I was stuck inside one of my all-too-realistic dreams. That this beast had to be a figment of my imagination.

Almost in slow motion a fat globule of spit fell from one of its fangs onto my cheek.

This snapped me from my shock.

I lurched awkwardly to the other side of the sunlounger and rolled onto the grass, landing on all fours.

I snapped up to look at it again.

It crouched, tensing, ready to pounce.

One of its eyes was missing. Not sealed shut, just . . . missing. A deep blood- and pus-filled cavity that seemed to watch me more than its functioning eye.

I was stuck.

The river was behind me, and my path to the safety of the Hobbit House was blocked by the beast.

Simon was going crazy by the chicken run, and the beast snapped its head around and barked at him. It was a horrific, rough, throaty roar that ripped through our peaceful sanctuary and silenced Simon instantly.

The beast turned back to me, the growl still rippling through its throat. I couldn't help the whimper that escaped me.

I looked for a weapon, a refuge, anything.

The baby was doing somersaults in my tummy, alerted to the danger by the adrenaline that now raced through my body.

The beast pounced on top of the sunlounger and roared once more.

Lunch was served.

I staggered back towards the river. I would have to take my chances splashing through and hope that by some miracle I could outrun it.

The beast crouched again. I could see the muscles that rippled along its entire body as it readied itself to pounce.

I wrapped my arms around my belly. I was crying. Not like this. Not like this.

It leapt. I stumbled backwards and fell over with a yell.

I was bringing my arms up to shield my face when a golden streak hurled itself through the air, slamming into the side of the beast and knocking it off course.

Dark and golden fur tumbled across the grass and the air was filled with a cacophony of barks and snarls and shrieks and my sobbing.

I ran.

I didn't know what else to do and, even now, I don't think there was anything else I could have done.

So, I ran.

I charged into the Hobbit House, slamming the door behind me.

I raced into the kitchen and grabbed the biggest knife I could find, ready to defend myself and my baby to the death.

I stood panting and weeping for ten minutes before I calmed down enough to realise that there were no longer sounds of fighting from outside.

In fact, the fighting had moved on almost as soon as I had raced into the Hobbit House. The beast had chased Lucky into the woods. The beast was gone.

The beast was gone.

And so was Lucky.

I didn't go out to look for him until dark.

I should have.

But I didn't.

There is no excuse.

I was just scared.

The night was hot and sweaty, but I still dressed in the toughest clothes I could find – thick waterproof trousers, a heavy wax jacket that I couldn't zip up, thick gardening gloves, and a bicycle helmet that I didn't remember getting.

I attached a head torch to my bicycle helmet, armed myself with my knife, a dustbin lid and a mallet, and went into the woods.

It was pitch black and silent.

The silence scared me.

By now, I was used to the natural noises of my new Hobbit House world.

During the day, thousands of bugs crawling through the grass or buzzing in the air, a chorus of birdsong, the occasional crashing of something big in the woods, the chattering and scampering of cheeky squirrels that were now bold enough to run into my kitchen to see what they could steal. At night the hooting of owls, constant rustling of small things moving in bushes, bats swooshing and swooping in and out of the trees, rutting foxes and hedgehogs squealing, deer that often stepped delicately out of the woods to nibble on chicken feed that had spilled on the grass.

There was none of that.

There was only me panting and crashing about.

'Lucky!'

My voice was cacophonous. A huge, booming noise in the vast, dark silence.

I tried again, quieter.

'Lucky . . .'

Nothing.

I didn't want to go further into the woods. I was scared I'd get lost. It was too dark to see further than my light and I was already disorientated even though I was only about ten feet in.

But, Lucky had saved my life. Again.

I plunged further in, whispering his name.

Forty paces in, my foot sank into something soft, slightly warm, squelching and horrific.

I opened my mouth to scream, and threw up.

I didn't want to look down, but had to, my foot was still inside whatever I had stumbled onto.

Please don't be Lucky.

It was the beast.

It was dead, and something bigger than the beast itself had already eaten most of one side of it.

This time I screamed.

And then started to hyperventilate.

There was something living in the woods, next to my home, that was big enough to sit down and eat half of this hulking monster.

I felt bile rising in my throat once more.

I completely forgot about Lucky, I just knew I had to get out of the woods as fast as possible.

I didn't know where I was. My sense of direction had got mixed up in the horror of what I had found, and now I didn't know where I was.

I spun around in circles trying to see the way out, light from my head torch dancing crazily on the tree trunks.

Then I heard a whimper.

I knew immediately it was Lucky.

He was about ten feet further in. His golden fur had been turned to dark rust by the dried blood that matted it together. One of his ears was torn in half. His beautiful face had deep scratches down it. The beast, or something worse, had ripped a series of deep welts in his side that were oozing dark black blood onto the forest floor.

His breathing was shallow and his eyes glazed with approaching death.

I burst into tears, fell to my knees, and awkwardly hugged him to me.

There was nothing I could do.

We were lost.

Lucky was going to die there in my arms as we waited for the sun to come up.

Then I heard the rustling.

Something was coming. Fast.

I reached for my knife and shifted Lucky so that I had some chance of defending us.

Simon came charging out of the bushes chuntering and chattering, livid at having been left behind while I went on my adventure.

Obviously, he didn't show us the way home – this isn't the Famous fucking Five. But he did show me which direction I had come from, and, after ten minutes of staggering that way with Lucky in my arms, I saw the familiar glow of the Hobbit House just peeking through the trees.

I laid Lucky on the kitchen table and wept continuously as I tried in vain to clean him up. The blood on his face and ear had already crusted over and the wounds were pink and neat. But the deep welts in his side were still oozing and were an angry dark red colour. They smelt bad. I cleaned them as best I could using disinfectant like my mum used to do for me when I grazed my knee. I didn't know if I should put anything else onto the welts, so I just kept wiping the fresh blood away as it oozed through.

I was covered in blood and mud and had the guts of the Beast still clinging to one of my feet, but I didn't even notice.

Lucky, my true love and trusted best friend, was dying.

By morning the blood coming from Lucky's wounds was mixed with pus, and he no longer opened his eyes when I petted him and crooned his name. His breathing was short and shallow and coming in fits and starts.

I had stopped crying. Now I just felt sick and tired and I wanted to crawl into bed and stay there for ever.

It had never even crossed my mind that something might happen to Lucky. But, now that it looked inevitable, I realised I might not be able to go on. I literally wouldn't be able to function. I would simply crawl into bed and let nature take its course. Baby or no baby.

My bed looked so inviting.

I could move Lucky over to lie next to me in comfort as he slipped away and then I could wait to join him.

Like I almost had with James.

No.

James was inevitable. Lucky wasn't.

The Defender was very low on diesel, so I went to the storage cupboard to get more.

There was none.

I had wasted all my diesel on trips to the garden centre. Many, many trips to the garden centre.

There was less than a quarter of a tank. Maybe enough for one trip into town.

Not enough to go to the vets to get stuff for Lucky and then go back to the hospital for me.

**Dictaphone Recording (Tape 1 / Recording 3)
(Transcribed)**

I am at the hospital. In the car park. I don't have
enough diesel to go to the vets as well so I'm going
to get things for Lucky here.
I don't even know if he is still alive.
            (Sound of crying and sniffling.)
I don't know what I can do to help him.
I need to be quick but I'm too scared to go in.
I don't want to do this.
I don't want to do it alone so, so... I have the
Dictaphone around my neck.
                    (Sobs.)
So that I have someone to talk to.
            (Half laughs, half sobs.)
I'm a fucking idiot.
  (Sobbing, deep breathing, rustling and movement.
            Voice comes back but is muffled)
I'm wearing the hazmat suit. It's so tight, the baby
is very unhappy.
            (Half laughs, half sobs.)
I don't know why. Maybe it will help with the smell.
Maybe I am scared of catching something. Honestly,
it feels like armour and it feels like protection
and maybe it will make me feel a bit less scared.
I have to do this. I have to do this...
      *(Two-minute time gap in which there is heavy
            breathing and rustling.)*
I'm at the main doors to the reception area. It's
dark inside, there're no lights on so I can't see
in. The doors aren't automatic any more so I am
going to... have to... force them...

                    (Loud grunts of exertion.)

Jesus Christ.

Oh God.

Oh fuck, oh fuck, oh fuck.

 (Heavy breathing, retching, incoherent muttering.)

Don't throw up in the hood, don't throw up in the
hood. . .

                    (Heavy breathing, groaning.)

There's . . .

Oh God . . .

                         (Groaning.)

Deep breaths. Deep breaths.

                     (Deep, slow breathing.)

There are. . .bodies everywhere.

        They're . . .(clears throat). . . moving.

They're moving because there's, I don't know what
they are . . . beetles? Bugs? Something. There's something all over them. And in them. They are, well,
they are living in them.

There's thousands of them. The bugs, not the
bodies.

The bodies don't look human any more. They are
puddles of brown goo or brown husks or vague mounds
on the floor.

Except for the ones that are still on the chairs.
The ones on the chairs still have . . .

        (coughs and voice becomes higher pitched)

. . . they still have faces. Some of them still have
faces. And hair. And bugs free-flowing in and out of
their rib cages.

        (Hysterical laughter which turns into sobs.)

I have to get out of here.

        *(Four-minute time gap in which there is heavy
                breathing and rustling.)*

Why don't hospitals ever have maps that are easy to
fucking read?

*(Three-minute time gap in which there is heavy
breathing and rustling.)*

I'm at the maternity ward.

I don't want to go in.

I don't want to see this. It isn't fair. Why? Why do
I have to do this? I don't want to.

(Sobs. Deep breath. Sobs again.)

For fuck's sake just get it over and done with.

(Door creaks open.)

Oh.

(Deep breath. Voice breaks as she speaks.)

They are all in bed.

There are no bugs here. I don't know if that's
because it is sealed off or because they just
haven't bothered coming up here yet.

The covers and blankets are still intact. They look
like mummies.

There are . . . there are no babies in the cribs.

They all have their babies with them.

They held them at the end.

(Pause.)

I really want to hold my baby.

*(Crying and movement. Doors open and shut. Rustling
and banging.)*

Shit.

I don't know what I need. I am just grabbing
everything. Scalpel, gauze, plasters, tape, what I
think are needles and threads. I don't know if
there's anything else I need for the baby. I've
got . . . blankets . . . are these forceps? I won't be
able to use them so what's the point . . . nasal aspirator, I'll take that . . .

(More rustling and banging.)

Shit, there's no medicine. I'm going to have to find
the pharmacy.

(Something heavy clangs onto the floor.)

Fuck.

The gas and air bottle is too heavy to carry.

> *(Door opens and closes. Quiet. Only heavy breathing.)*

I'm so sorry. I hope you're with your babies now.

> *(Sobs. Sounds of running and fast breathing. Four-minute gap)*

Why is the pharmacy always in the bloody basement?

> *(Door bangs.)*

Shit. It's been raided.

> *(Fast breathing and sounds of frantic rummaging. Rattling of pill bottles thrown to the floor.)*

Yes! Oh, thank God. Thank you! Thank you! Got them.

> *(More rattling of pill bottles, then sound of a zip being pulled. Door opening and shutting. Feet running. Panting. Door creaks open.)*

> *(Sudden silence.)*

> *(Whispering.)*

Shit. Rats.

> *(Quiet movement and rapid, short breathing.)*

They're right by the exit. About, maybe, thirty of them.

Shit. Shit. Where did they come from?

Oh fuck.

> *(Whispering.)*

They're coming towards me.

> *(Something creaks and bangs.)*

I don't know if they've seen me. I'm on a trolley bed above them.

> *(Shallow breathing. Faint squealing and scampering.)*

> *(Sigh of relief.)*

They've gone.

> *(Creaking and movement.)*

> *(Then . . . scampering. Squealing.)*

Get off me!

Ow! Get off! GET OFF!

Ow!

I'll stamp on you I will, I'll kill all of you!

(Heavy breathing, loud rustling, squealing, cries of pain, running.)

Oh fuck, oh fuck, oh fuck. Someone help!

(Loud squealing and rustling.)

(Something falls heavily and clatters across the floor.)

Get off me!

(Groaning. Squealing. Rustling.)

(Running feet.)

(Creak of a door opening and banging shut.)

They bit me, they BIT me!

I'm out but they bit me! Christ, they would have eaten me!

They attacked me! How did they know? How did they know what I was?

(Running.)

I'm out, I got it and I'm out.

(Very loud rustling. Deep breathing, sobbing. Voice is no longer muffled.)

I want to go home.

Recording ends.

August 2024

When I got back Lucky was still alive. Barely. His side was oozing thick pus and smelt like the dead corpses from five months ago.

I dissolved antibiotics and pain relief tablets in water and spooned it into his mouth, massaging his throat to make it go down like I had seen vets do on TV.

I cleaned his welts again and sprayed antiseptic on them.

Then I sewed the deep gashes shut.

He woke halfway through for a few minutes and tried to bite me, but was too weak. So, instead, he howled pitifully until I howled along with him. Then he passed out again.

I only had to stop sewing twice to vomit, which I think was pretty good going.

I used a running stitch.

I had no idea what I was doing.

After I had finished I showered outside and the water ran deep burgundy red.

I carefully moved Lucky from the kitchen table onto my mattress and lay down next to him.

I was more tired than I have ever been in my life.

As I closed my eyes to sleep I realised that, if Lucky was dead when I woke up, I probably wouldn't leave the mattress again.

September 2024

I wrote my last diary entry two weeks ago.

Lucky is still alive.

I don't know how long I slept after sewing Lucky back together. It was dark when I got up and seemed a very long time before the sun rose again.

Literally and metaphorically.

After that sleep I found the alarm clock (yes, I have one, I want to be able to time my contractions . . . if they ever bloody well start) and I set it to ring every four hours.

For the next five days I dutifully gave Lucky antibiotics and water every four hours, and cleaned and creamed his wounds three times a day.

At first, I thought it wasn't making any difference and he would die anyway. He slept the whole time, his breathing was shallow and ragged, and the gashes in his side still stank and wept copious amounts of pus.

But, on day four, he opened his eyes and his side didn't smell quite so bad.

By day six he could lift his head enough to sideways drink from his bowl so that I no longer needed to spoon water into his mouth. On day eight he started to eat again, and on day ten I carried him out to sit in the shade by the river. He mustered enough energy to bark at Simon, and I knew he was going to live.

It is now day fifteen, and we have got into a routine of me carrying him out to the river and then bringing him food and water all day. He is still worryingly skinny and weak, so I am letting him eat whatever he wants. So far that mainly seems to be corned beef and tins of beef stew. If I open a can and he doesn't want it, I eat the rest for my dinner. I'm not proud.

Three times a day I carry him to the edge of the woods and leave him for a bit to do his 'business'. Then I carry him back to the river and clean up whatever 'business' he has left.

He is not daft, and I am beginning to suspect that he is starting to fake his level of weakness. This afternoon when I left him by the woods I could have sworn I saw him streaking back to his blanket when I was coming to get him. He hadn't done his ordinary afternoon crap nearby so I think he had done that elsewhere. When I picked him up he gave me his most innocent doggy grin and licked my face.

He's definitely milking it.

And I couldn't care less.

He can milk it from here until eternity if he likes. I am just so happy he is better. I can't stop smiling and hugging and kissing him. He has stopped smelling of rot and is beginning to smell of grass and sunshine again, and I am astounded by how comforting that smell now is to me – and appalled by how much I took it for granted before. The first time he managed to lift his head up and give me a doggy grin after he started to get better, I thought my heart would burst with happiness.

I would carry him to the ends of the earth, fetch his food and water until I die, and clean up his crap until my arms fall off.

He is my family.

———————

The last time I saw my family, my other family, was November 2nd 2023.

My mum and dad had their traditional fireworks party in the back garden. 6DM was racing across America and, even though there hadn't been an official announcement yet, people were naturally social distancing. But everyone loves fireworks and, as the party was outside, it was pretty busy in my parents' back garden.

Everyone at the party would be dead in a little over a month.

Ginny and Alex had popped in to show Radley off to my mum and dad and Ginny generously allowed my mum a cuddle, but I could tell she was already nervous of letting anyone other than herself or Alex hold her. They left the party straight after. In my wildest dreams I would never have thought that the next time I would see Ginny would be the final time I would ever see her and that she would tell me to buy a gun.

Xav hadn't come to the party. My mum and dad had invited him, but he had said he was busy.

I hadn't seen Xav in about a month and had been hoping he would be at my mum and dad's. I wanted to make up with him, to beg him to forgive me. I had lost James, was in the process of losing Harry, and had realised I was dangerously close to losing Xav if I didn't stop being such an idiot.

He was, and always would be, my best friend.

I should have called him, but I was worried I would be too late. That he, like James, would have given up on me.

I was too scared to call and find out.

I hadn't seen Harry in a fortnight as he was busy fighting the economic impact that 6DM was already having on his company; so I hadn't had a chance to talk to him, a chance to end things.

That's a lie.

I could have seen him. I was avoiding him so that I wouldn't have the chance to talk to him or end things.

The only positive was that, during the fortnight where I hadn't seen Harry, James and I had reached a weird equilibrium. We'd both been at home more, so had tentatively started to talk, have dinner together, sit next to each other on the sofa to watch TV. The day before he had laughed at a crap joke I had made. Not a forced laugh, a real bubble of merriment escaping out of him.

It was nearing the end of the party. My mum and dad had put music on and a few scattered people were dancing.

'Let's Stay Together' by Al Green came on and people coupled off.

It was one of my mum and dad's favourite songs and I was watching them laughing in each other's arms in the middle of the lawn. My dad couldn't dance for shit so my mum basically had to pull him around, stopping him from tripping over their feet.

But they didn't care. They were laughing with each other, blowing puffs of frosty breath into the air, pretending they were smoking. After all this time they were still in love, still each other's favourite person, still naturally, and without any effort at all, making each other happy.

I didn't have to look to know who it was when I felt someone reach for my hand.

The hand that held mine had been doing so for over ten years.

James was watching my parents too. He turned and smiled at me.

I looked at our hands, our fingers intertwined like so much of our lives were.

I pulled him gently towards the other dancers.

He paused and then tugged his hand softly and carefully out of mine.

'I'm just going to get a drink.'

He kissed me on the forehead and went into the kitchen.

And then I knew. I knew he loved me, I knew he would never leave me, and I knew I would never leave him.

But, together, neither of us would ever truly be happy.

So, I walked to the middle of the grass in my parents' back garden, and I danced.

I danced on my own to one of the greatest love songs of all time.

No one stared, no one pointed at me, no one cared.

But I cared.

I was dancing and I was happy.

On my own.

At the end of the song I looked up and saw my mum and dad staring at me. They held their hands out for me to join them, but I shook my head.

I grinned at them.

I like to think they knew then that I was going to be okay.

I lay in bed the next morning for a long time after James had gotten up.

I couldn't think how to say what I needed him to hear.

I knew it started with something about how me being unhappy wasn't his fault, about how it wasn't anyone else's fault but mine. I wanted to tell him that I hadn't taken the time to fully form 'me' before I became part of 'us', that I needed to learn to love myself as much as I loved him, I needed to start dancing on my own more. I wanted to tell him something wise about loving yourself before you can love anyone else, like Ginny had told me. It all made sense in my brain, but would probably have fallen from my mouth in a jumble of words and lost meaning.

In the end, when I eventually got out of bed, I didn't tell him anything.

Because when I went into the kitchen to sit down and talk to James, he told me the PM had collapsed the Channel Tunnel.

Then he took my hand and held it tight.

I didn't pull away.

September 21st 2024

By my calculations, I am now somewhere between six and twenty-four days over the date when I should have given birth.

What shall I moan about first?

The rain.

It started raining at dusk four days ago and, after fifty-four days without rain, I was ecstatic. No more watering the vegetable patch! More fish! Green grass! I went outside and danced around, literally naked, in the rain.

I fell asleep to the magical sound of it thundering on the roof of the Hobbit House.

And I woke up to the sound of it still thundering on the roof of the Hobbit House.

By that afternoon the vegetable patch was thoroughly soaked, Simon had taken up permanent residence in my doorway to hide from it, and the thundering on the roof was becoming a form of Chinese water torture.

Three days in and the vegetable patch is flooded and water has leaked into the polytunnel and started to flood that as well, Simon has now moved into the kitchen area, the roof of the Hobbit House has a leak in one corner, and I can hear ominous dripping in three other places.

The river is lapping at the top of the bank so I have had to move the chickens into the Defender in case their chicken run is flooded. The Defender is actually abandoned halfway up the drive because that is where it finally ran out of diesel after my trip to the hospital and, barring diesel gushing miraculously forth from the ground, that is where it will stay for eternity.

Lucky is still thin, but otherwise displays all the excitement and new-found energy of a six-year-old after a bout of illness. He keeps running out into the rain to play and then bounding back into the Hobbit House and shaking muddy, dog-stinky water all over the furniture I have just cleaned. I still love and appreciate him very much, but am thinking of putting him in the Defender too.

My nesting has gone to shit because there is mud all over the floor of my home and dog-water splatters on the walls, ceiling, and furnishings.

The baby feels as if it is trying to push its way out of the top of my vagina, I am so huge that there is no place I can comfortably sit, and I HAVE BACKACHE. In fact not backache, back-agony. It doesn't matter though because I am so anxious about 'not being in labour when I should be in labour but being happy that I am not in labour because I am scared to be in labour and not sure I can survive labour' that I am constantly pacing around the tiny Hobbit House because, of course, I can't go outside BECAUSE IT IS RAINING!

And my other question is – if it's raining, how can it still be so fucking hot?

I need to calm down.

Fuck it. I'm having a beer.

September 22nd 2024

I don't know if it was the beer, but last night I slept, properly slept, for the first time since after Lucky was attacked.

I slept and I had an incredibly vivid dream.

I dreamt I heard an aeroplane outside.

Not unusual. When I first was alone, I used to imagine I heard them all the time. I was constantly scanning the sky or jumping out of bed to look out of the window. Of course, there was never anything there.

In my dream I was so convinced there was a plane that I got out of bed, put wellies and a coat on, and went out in the rain to look.

The dream felt so real. I could feel myself hauling my huge tummy out of bed, struggling into my boots, pulling on my too-tight raincoat.

And when I went outside I saw it. I saw the lights of the plane getting higher and higher into the sky, flashing and blinking red. I stood and watched until I couldn't see them any more.

When I woke up this morning my pillow was wet and my boots and raincoat were by the front door. Wet.

But, I don't have time to think about the potential significance of that now.

It is still raining and the river breached the bank last night. Water is now edging towards the doorstep to my home.

I am trying to move things off the mezzanine so that there is space for me, Lucky, and, I suppose, Simon to move up there if we have to.

It's not ideal, but I can't leave.

I don't know where we would go and, without the Defender, we have no way of leaving anyway. We'll just have to stay here and wait for the rain to stop.

I am weirdly calm.

The river is rising, we are about to be flooded, and my tummy has been tightening all day.

I'm pretty sure I am in labour.

September 23rd 2024

I wrote my last entry late last night and the sun is now just coming up so I am setting my alarm clock to say it is 5 a.m. I need to know the time so I can monitor how things are going, and 5 a.m. seems as good a time as any to start.

I am definitely in labour. My back pain has ramped up a notch, and the tightening in my tummy is now starting to become painful. And regular. It feels like the cramps you get from a bad stomach bug.

Oh, and my waters have broken. All over the floor of the Hobbit House. Someone should warn you how much of that stuff there is because it is everywhere. Everywhere. I'll be honest, seeing as it looks like the ground floor of my house is about to be flooded I haven't really bothered clearing it up that much. I am starting to feel a bit knackered so am prioritising what needs to be done.

I have been out in the rain already and given the girls about three days' worth of food just in case this goes on for a long time. The water is a long way from the Defender so they should be fine until I can get to them again.

I have organised the mezzanine and laid out all my labour equipment. Weirdly, considering my baby shopping and visit to the hospital, there isn't as much as I thought there was. Blankets, nappies and clothes for the baby, towels, bottles of water, energy bars, some paracetamol (turns out it is fine to take), three hot water bottles, a couple of buckets in case I can't get down to the toilet, books, my CD player. I've got the scalpel and the nasal aspirator. Not sure what exactly I am going to use either of them for, but better to be safe than sorry.

I haven't managed to get the mattress up here, so I am going to have to give birth on the floor. I have made a sort of nest out of blankets and towels that is pretty comfy and I imagine that, when the time comes, the lack of a comfy mattress will be the least of my problems. Lucky is eyeing my nest up enviously.

I'd brought a huge tub back from the garden centre and had been planning to fill it with hot water and sit in it like a mini bath to help with the early pain, but I can't fit it inside the Hobbit House and I am not sitting in it in the rain, so that's out.

I'm already exhausted, but am panicking too much to sleep, or even sit, so I have been pacing the floor because all the books say that is good for helping things move along. Obviously, it's not a huge space that I am pacing in, so I have managed to go back and forth 622 times so far. I am going to see if I can get to 1,000, and then I am going to try to sleep again.

I didn't sleep.

I've just been for a wee and something massive fell out of my vagina. I was both panicked and elated and thought maybe I had just given birth and experienced the easiest labour ever. No such luck. It was a huge blood clot. Literally the size of my fist. The fact that I nearly vomited when I saw it doesn't bode well for when things get messier.

I am in a lot of pain now. The tightening in my tummy is very strong and when it happens I have to stop whatever I am doing and sit down. I have timed it on my alarm clock and it is happening every six minutes.

I have taken two paracetamol as is recommended.

It has done fuck all.

All the books say that I need to measure my cervix.

Not just my vagina. My cervix. I need to stick my fingers up myself and feel about to see how big the opening is. God, just writing that makes me want to throw up.

You'd think with the amount I have been wanking lately I'd be totally fine with having a good old rummage.

I am not.

My alarm clock says it is now 08.16.

I have been sick and have diarrhoea.

I don't know if that is part of labour or just because I am panicking so badly.

I want to pace, but there is now an inch of water on the ground floor and so Lucky, Simon and I are cooped up on the mezzanine.

Lucky is anxious. He knows that something is wrong with me and keeps nuzzling in for cuddles and reassurance and then wriggling out of my arms when a contraction grips me and I squeeze him too hard. Simon is anxious because he doesn't like the water. He paces at the edge of the mezzanine like an expectant father. I would laugh at him if I had the energy.

I've tried sleeping, reading, humming, meditating (sort of), and listening to music, but nothing is distracting me from the pain.

I need to do something else to pass the time and I need to tell the end of my story. In case something happens.

In case I die.

I need to write about the last night.

———

When I walked out of work for the very last time, I went straight to the pub with my work colleagues. As soon as we sat down, I called James. He was already on his way to his sister's to see her and his nephews and said he might meet up with me later but would probably just go home. He sounded depressed. I asked if he wanted me to come home and was hugely relieved when he said no. I was, understandably, starting to panic and, for the first time, I thought having him with me might actually make it worse.

Following the destruction of the Channel Tunnel and the insane few weeks that had followed there had been an unspoken agreement between us that we would act like the past few months had never happened. We were united once more in our fear of this new unknown terror.

But, as much as I tried, I couldn't help but be angry and

disappointed that the end of the world had cheated me out of my chance at a new beginning. How ironic that now, after all this time, James needed me as much as I needed him.

I rang Ginny while downing my second glass of wine. There was no answer. I hoped this meant she was out of range, hidden with Alex and Radley in some mythical northern fortress.

Harry texted continuously, asking where I was, asking if we could meet. I ignored him.

By the end of my third glass of wine, I was lonely.

My workmates were perfectly nice people, but there was really only one person I wanted to spend 'last night' (as people had christened it) with.

I didn't know where Xav was and even if I did he probably wouldn't have wanted to come and spend the last night with me. And I wouldn't have blamed him.

Despite everything that was happening, I still hadn't called Xav. I was still too scared of what he might say.

But now it really was the end of the world.

Fuck the end of the world, fuck the past and fuck my fear.

I rang Xav.

He didn't answer.

I persuaded my workmates to move on to my favourite bar. It was heaving. Everywhere was heaving.

I stood in the corner alone, closed my eyes, and remembered.

This had been the first bar Xav had taken me to after he had rescued me from my non-blind date. Nearly twenty years ago we had stood here and I had drunk half a pint of snake-bite and black and listened to this crazily exotic creature explain the best way to get served if you were underage. I had taken all his advice, gone to the bar . . . and been thrown out.

Xav had changed my life and, for a while, he had been my life.

I had to see him before the world ended.

I opened my eyes, searching for the easiest way to push through the throng of people in front of me.

And then I saw it. An unmistakeable flash of angelic blond hair.

I pushed through the crowd and we met in the middle.

He pointed to my wine.

'They served you this time then?'

I laughed and then burst into tears.

We both cried. We both tried to say sorry. We both agreed it was too late to waste time on apologising.

We both knew we were going to die.

I begged him to come and stay with me, he told me he'd rather die of 6DM than be bored to death by James. I told him to go to my parents' then, I was happy for him to go this time.

He shook his head.

'Not this time. This time's different. They deserve to just have each other to worry about at the end, not me as well.'

My eyes welled with tears again.

'I don't want you to be alone.'

He took my hand.

'Sweetheart, I won't be alone.' He glanced over to a group of blokes who were standing in the other corner, openly admiring him.

Xav had never been keen on being the last one at any party, and the end of the world would be no different. He wasn't going to stay at the bar until it closed, wasn't going to wait patiently for the end of the world, he was going to meet the end of the world head on.

He decided to throw an impromptu 'End of Days' party at his house. He wanted me to go to his party, spend one last night with him there.

Unlike Xav, I was almost always the last one at all of the parties we went to, including his.

I was the one who found people's coats, ordered Ubers, kicked people out when they wouldn't leave.

I was the one left in charge, the one who cleared up afterwards, tidying away other people's forgotten leftovers and memories.

I didn't want to be the last one at his party this time. It would be too sad.

I shook my head, not trusting myself to speak without crying again.

Xav touched his hand gently to my cheek and stood up. I gripped his hand.

'Don't go!'

He smiled the sweetest smile.

'I love you.'

He pulled me to him, enveloped me in a hug that smelt of Tom Ford, cigarettes and a thousand memories, and whispered in my ear.

'You're stronger than you think. Try to remember that.'

He was wrong.

I wasn't strong at all.

As soon as he walked away I texted Harry back.

We were at a club and I was dancing when Harry arrived.

He walked straight onto the dance floor and started dancing with us. No stopping for a drink, no lurking at the bar, no bopping by the fringes of the floor; straight in and on it.

He was awful. Really, truly a terrible dancer. Worse than my dad.

I stopped and stared.

He didn't even notice for a while, he was just happy. Happy dancing.

When he saw me he stopped, held his hand out for me to take, and then pulled me to him.

He span me around, and there, on the dance floor, in front of everyone we worked with and everyone we had spent months hiding our affair from, I kissed him.

Maybe if I hadn't just said a final goodbye to my best friend, who I had wasted months not talking to, maybe if Harry hadn't been such an awful dancer, maybe if I hadn't been looking for a distraction from my encroaching panic attack, maybe if it hadn't been the end of the world . . .

Maybe then I wouldn't have chosen that moment to finally have sex with Harry.

But all of that was happening, so I did.

I kissed Harry on the dance floor and then dragged him into the disabled toilets and we fucked against the wall.

It wasn't great.

Not his fault – if you can have an orgasm in a disabled toilet on the last night of the world while trying to ward off a massive panic attack and struggling not to let your knickers fall onto the filthy floor – then you are a better woman than I.

Harry didn't have the same problem.

He is potential Daddy number one.

After the disabled toilet interlude I went back to the dance floor and spent the next hour dancing and drinking the tequila shots that were frequently offered to me.

Harry kept trying to get me to stop dancing and start talking, and I kept ignoring him.

Finally, he picked me up and carried me off the dance floor. I was in hysterics. The hero was carrying me off into the sunset! Here we go Mum – end of the world, and I did it! I was the heroine in my own romantic movie!

Harry put me down.

'Let's get out of here.'

I was drunk and laughing.

'I don't want to.'

'I want to be with you. I want to be with you at the end. I love you.'

I laughed again. Uproariously.

Not the reaction you want when you have just told someone you love them.

'You don't love me! You don't even know me. Come and dance!'

I grabbed his hand and tried to yank him back to the dance floor, but he pulled me to him.

'I do know you. I just want to be with you.'

I stopped laughing.

'Well, that's not what I want.'

'What do you want then?'

I didn't think, I just snapped back . . .

'I just want to be left alone.'

It was a drunkenly impulsive comment.

But the moment it was out of my mouth I knew it was true

I had never been alone, never stood by myself and handled things for myself. I had left it up to other people in my life to make things better for me – my mum and dad, Xav, James, Ginny, and even Harry.

I'd used them all as an excuse never to become who I really wanted to be.

That was what I should have said to James, that's what I should have told him.

But James wasn't there, Harry was.

So it was Harry who looked at me with eyes full of confusion.

'I'm sorry, I have to go,' I mumbled, pulling away from him and rushing out of the club.

I didn't know where I was going, didn't know what I was going to do. I only knew that I had to have some space to think, to work out what this revelation meant.

But, as I stepped outside the club I was pulled into a cab by well-meaning workmates intent on one last hurrah, given a bottle of vodka to swig from, and laughingly persuaded to go to the lap dancing club 'just for one'.

My previous resolve, the urgency I had felt and the very epiphany that I had just experienced, slipped away into the drunken haze of the night.

When I woke in bed late the next morning I really didn't remember the night before.

But two days later, when my head had stopped pounding, and my vision cleared enough to read the sixty-two texts that Harry had sent me, my memory began to come back.

Of course, it was Harry I met in my favourite bar after my fateful visit to the hospital when James was sick.

Harry was clearly ill too, but only just – in the first part of 6DM where it only feels like a cold. I didn't tell him what was going to come next.

I thought he was going to ask to be with me at the end again, but he didn't.

He had something else to tell me.

He coughed, took a large swig of whisky and coughed again.

'I know you better than you think. I know you used to write. I read your stuff when you were with the music paper.'

This was news to me. I'd never met anyone who had recognised me from my previous career.

'It was good. I liked it and I liked you. I didn't recognise you at first, in the office, you seemed so different. I was going to say something, but I didn't think you'd want to be reminded. Cool music journalist to, well, this.'

Thanks.

'But I watched you. I watched you at work, and it was still there. The way you talk to people and are with people and the way you write, even just updates. They're funny. That's why I wanted to be with you, to get to know you better. I wanted the woman who called me a shit, who cried in the lift and who leant on me.'

I think this is the point where I started to cry.

'But you weren't her with me. You were different. You weren't the person I had thought you were, you weren't the one I really wanted to be with. I saw flashes of her, but it felt like you were pretending to be someone else. Like you don't even like who you really are, which is fucking ridiculous.'

He coughed again, and this time his hands had flecks of blood on them when he took them away from his mouth.

'So, you're right. I don't know you, I never got the chance. You never let me. And I tried. I really fucking tried. And if you'd just let me be with you and not some fucking pretend version, then I think I would have really liked you . . . and maybe you might have liked you as well. But, I suppose, neither of us will ever know now.'

He kissed me on the forehead and left.
I never heard from him again.

I went back to James, cared for him, had sex with him (potential
Daddy number two) and then watched him die.
Then I began my new life. On my own.
Last one at the party.
The final party this time.
It turns out both Xav and Harry were right.
The real me is stronger than I thought.
And I like her.

———————

I hurt.

Not just my tummy. All of me hurts. I can't even explain what
it feels like because it doesn't feel like anything I have ever experienced before.

When a contraction happens now, I can't think or move. My
body is frozen in a rigor mortis of pain that means I can only
groan incomprehensibly until it passes. It drives all rational
thought from me and I would do anything to stop it. Anything.

I have no idea how other women summon the energy or
wherewithal to scream; I can barely manage to breathe.

I know it sounds like I am being dramatic, but if you've never
felt it you don't know what it is like so SHUT THE FUCK UP.

I wish there was someone here I could shout at.
Or hold the hand of.
Or kill.

The contractions are coming every three minutes. I don't have
time to relax in between as the books say I should, I don't have
time to start breathing properly again before the next one comes,
I don't have time to think.

I can't have a baby like this.
I can't write any more.
I can't hold the pen properly.

Dictaphone Recording (Tape 2 / Recording 1)
(Transcribed)

(Heavy breathing and rhythmic panting.)
The... contractions are now two minutes apart.
They're so painful. I don't think I can cope much
more. I am so tired.

(Sobs.)
So, I have two minutes to talk, to do this, while I
still can talk.
Oh God, not yet...

(Long, low groan, panting, crying,
deep breath.)
It... it is still raining.
The water is deep. I don't know how deep. Nothing is
floating yet, but I think it would be up to my
ankles. I don't know what will happen if it doesn't
stop soon.
Why is this happening?
Is this God? Maybe 6DM was sent by God. Maybe he
wanted everyone to die but I didn't, and so now he
is sending other things to kill me. Did he trap me
in the snow? Did he send the beast to eat me, but
Lucky saved me? Is Lucky my angel? How will Lucky
save me from the flood?
Oh God, that's insane. Am I finally going insane? Is
this it?
What if my baby isn't immune? What if my baby isn't
immune to 6DM and gets it and dies as soon as it is
born? What if this has all been for nothing?
Oh God, another one...

(Deep, prolonged groaning, crying and panting.)

Oh God, oh God, how much more? I can't do it. I can't
do it.

I'm so tired. I'm so alone.

I want my mum. Please, I really want my mum.

　　　　　　　　(Sobbing and crying.)

Okay . . . okay.

　　　　　(Deep breaths, inhaling and exhaling.
　　　　　　There is a long pause.)

So, this is for you little one. This is your
message.

I love you. I haven't said that before I don't
think, and I should have, because I do, I really do.
I love you.

I don't care if you are a boy or a girl. I will love
you. I don't care if you are straight or gay or
happy or sad or good or naughty or quiet or loud.
You never need have to try and make me happy, or
pretend to be better or different or who you think I
want you to be. I will always love you just the way
you are. And it doesn't matter that I don't know who
your dad is and it doesn't matter that your dad
isn't here. We can be happy. I will make a life for
both of us that we will both be happy in, I promise.
I love you.

Please come out of me.

　　　　　　　　　(Sobs.)

Recording ends.

INSERT: ITEM #6294/2

Dictaphone Recording (Tape 2 / Recording 2)
(Transcribed)

(Panting and crying.)
It's been two hours. I've been pushing for two
hours. I thought it would have been over by now.
It hurts so much, it hurts so much.
(Panting and groaning.)
I'm scared. I don't want to do this on my own. I want
my mum. I miss her so much. Please help me...
(Groaning.)
I have to push, I have to push ...
I can't DO THIS!
Help me someone please, help me...
(Panting and breathing. Movement.
Sobs. Groans.)
Okay, okay, right, I'm kneeling up, which is good. I
am trying to breathe right and panting lots so
that's also good.
(More panting.)
But I am pushing and nothing is happening. My baby
is not here. I can't see anything because my tummy
is massive.
I'm going to have to feel for my baby. I can't leave
it there, I can't not know, I have to just do it.
Okay. Fuck.
This is... Christ it's a mess down there... Jesus,
is that blood? Should there be that much blood??
Okay... feeling... now... ha!
I can feel it!

My baby, I can feel its head! It's just inside! It's
here! It's here!
I can do this! I can do this!

Recording ends.

Dictaphone Recording (Tape 2 / Recording 3)
(Transcribed)

(Hysterical sobbing.)
It's stuck, my baby's stuck.
The head is just at the opening, but I've been
pushing for fifteen minutes and it's not moving.
It's stuck.
I can't get it out. I can't get a hold on the head.
I've tried to get it but I can't, it's too slippery.
(Sobs.)
I'm so tired.
I think my baby is dead.
(Weeping and movement.)
I have to cut myself. I don't have a choice. I can't
do anything else. I have to cut myself and hope the
baby comes out and that I don't cut the head.
(Clattering and movement. Panting.)
I can't see what I am doing. I don't know how to do
this... I just have to hope...please God, if there
is anyone anywhere please help me to save my baby,
please let me...
(Screams.)
It hurts, it hurts so bad. I don't know if I'm doing
it right. I can't see... I can't feel if...
(Screams.)
Oh fuck, I'm tearing... it's tearing me...
(Yells of pain. Grunts of exertion.)
Oh God, oh God, the head's out. The head's out! I
can feel it! I can feel the head!
I need to wait for the next contraction... come
on... come on...
(Pants and grunts.)

Got to . . . get . . . the shoulders . . . out! They're
out! The shoulders are out! Oh God, it's coming! My
baby is coming . . .
It's out.

> *(Hysterical sobbing and laughter.)*

It's a girl! I've got a little girl!

> *(Movement, panting, more movement.)*

She's not crying.
She should be crying. Please cry! I can't remember
what to do if she's not crying.
She's not the right colour. She should be turning
pink. Why is she still blue?
Please cry!
She's not breathing.
She's not breathing!

> *(Frantic sounds of movement, a dog barking, three
> loud slaps.)*
>
> *(A tiny cough. A baby cries weakly.)*
>
> *(Laughing and sobbing.)*

That's it! That's my good girl!

> *(Laughter and kisses and movement.)*
>
> *(Baby cries louder.)*
>
> *(Some time passes.)*
>
> *(When she speaks again the voice is weaker.)*

That's it.
She's breathing and she's pink and she's beautiful!
She's beautiful.
And we are lying together in our nest. Yes we are!
Aren't we little one!
She's beautiful and perfect and tiny. And shhh,
shhhh, it's okay my sweet love. Mummy's here. I'm
here to take care of you. I love you. It's okay.

> *(Baby gurgles and hiccups.)*

Hello! Hello, my darling. Welcome to our world.

> *(Pause. Groaning and deep breaths.)*

I think . . . ooh . . . okay . . . that's fine . . . that's

just the placenta . . . that's supposed to happen.
It's fine . . . I'll be fine . . . that's fine. Let's
just rest for a bit . . .

(Pause.)

Grace . . . your name is Grace . . .

(Baby coos and makes clucking baby noises.)

That's a good girl . . . here . . . you want to feed?
Let's try feeding you . . .

(Noises of baby suckling.)

There we go my darling . . . such a good girl . . .
That's a lot of blood . . . not sure how much is
normal . . . I should have read more about what
happens after. Mummy isn't very good at planning!

(Very weak laughter.)

You're hungry. That's it.

Look Lucky!

She's here!

Our darling Grace is here.

(Deep breathing.)

We did it.

I did it.

I'm just . . . really . . .

I don't know, all that blood . . .

I feel a bit . . . I think I'm just tired . . .

. . . we're fine, you feed and then we can get up and
think about moving if this rain doesn't stop . . .

. . . it's getting quite high . . . I need to clean this
blood up . . .

. . . you're fine, fine . . .

. . . so much blood . . . I'm just tired . . . I'm
fine . . . just tired . . .

. . . I'm just going to close my eyes . . . just for a
moment . . .

. . . just a little sleep for Mummy and . . .

. . . then I'll clean up the blood . . .

. . . just a few minutes and . . .

```
. . . then . . .
. . . we'll get up . . .
        (Rain continues to drum on the roof.)
                (Dog starts to bark.)
                (Baby starts crying.)
        (These noises continue for 4.38 minutes.)
```

Recording ends.

Catalogue number: UK6294

Item(s): One handwritten diary, two 30-minute Philips LFH0005 mini-cassettes, eleven child's drawings.

(Original diary and mini-cassettes transcribed by Ms Bethany Clift – April 2042)

Date of discovery/location/finder: 26 May 2041/The Seaview Café, Marine Parade, Dover, United Kingdom/ Corporal Timothy Jones (C23967)

Details: Diary and tapes found on table in café.

No other items found on site.

History team found and excavated location of 'Hobbit House' in Norfolk. Land Rover Defender abandoned in driveway. Three graves at back of house contained chicken and dog bones. No other bodies or bones found at location.

House was in significant state of disrepair having been empty for many years. Contained clothing and items from one female adult and one female child (up to age 6). Walls covered with crayon drawings depicting house, river and various animals. These drawings were added to the catalogue.

It is not known how the diary and tapes travelled from Norfolk to Dover.

Sixteen people were rescued alive from Great Britain between 2025 and 2027. No children were rescued, and no adult matched the description of the diary author.

The author's name and the current status of her, and the child (Grace), are unknown.

Acknowledgements

My thanks must go firstly to my amazing agency, Jonathan Clowes and especially to my incredible agent, Cara Lee Simpson, who has literally made my dreams come true. Not only is Cara a brilliant agent, she is also an insightful reader, gives excellent advice, answers my endless questions, calms my every panicked outburst and is an all-round lovely human being. I am incredibly lucky that she is my agent and I cannot thank her enough for all she has done, and continues to do, for me.

Secondly, to my wonderful editor, Kimberley Atkins, who has made the entire editing experience (which I was dreading) a complete joy. Kim has helped me to improve my book beyond my wildest expectations and made me a far better writer in the process. She is kind, patient and bloody brilliant at her job and, like the Land Rover in my novel, I highly, highly recommend her to anyone looking for a fantastic editor. My thanks also to the entire team at Hodder who have been amazing from the start. They have all been so enthusiastic about my book, worked so hard to make it a success and given me the most stunning cover and brilliant marketing campaign. I am forever in their debt.

To my Mum and Dad – thank you for all your love, support, childcare, ideas, gentle but insistent nudging in the right direction and for believing that I would get to where I was going some day, even if I took the roundabout route. I can only apologise that the first book ever dedicated to you both starts with the words 'Fuck You'. Please forgive me, I love you both beyond words.

To my brother and sister, Amanda and Ben, for always supporting me in my adventures even as they were undertaking their own. To have siblings that I can forever count on to be there in both good and bad times is a blessing that I cherish – plus you are both always willing to head down the pub to celebrate or commiserate at a moment's notice which is also a blessing and one that is most under-rated.

Thanks also to my extended family – Alison, Richard and all the Handfords and Robinsons who have been nothing but supportive and lovely throughout. I am so lucky to have family ties with, and be married into, such a brilliant group of people.

To my friends who have listened to me go on and on about my book and not once told me shut up – or at least not to my face. And, in particular to Amanda (again) and to Claire Williams who read the submitted version of the novel and gave hugely valuable feedback and support at a time when I was having a major wobble. Thank you.

To my NHS colleagues who do such incredible and difficult jobs day in, day out and yet still found time to listen to me, advise me and support me and who, mostly, managed to successfully hide their shock when they learnt I had actually secured a publishing deal. I am proud of our NHS, proud to say I worked for the NHS and proud to say I was your colleague. In particular I would like to thank Jo Franklin who has been a relentless supporter of my career, in all its many facets, since she first met me. Jo – your constant belief in me has helped me through my many moments of self-doubt, so thank you for everything.

And last, but most definitely not least, to my family. Sam and Tilly – you have no idea what my book is about and will most definitely not be reading it until you are at least eighteen. But, when you do finally read it, I would like you to know how much I love you and how much it helped that you just accepted that Mummy was writing as the reason why I couldn't do any of the thousands of things you asked in the last couple of years. Also – always be the person you want to be and never give up on your dreams – no matter what Daddy and I say!

Pete – I don't have space to write about all the things you have given or done for me that I am thankful for – I tried but Hodder refused to make the book 100 pages longer. You are my love, my light, my rock and my happiness. You support me in everything I do, love me just the way I am and always dance just because you want to. I am not a good enough writer to express as eloquently and expansively as I would like how much I love you but I will keep trying and, maybe by the time I write the acknowledgements for my tenth book, I will have managed it. I love you.

Finally(!) book acknowledgements are hard to write because they are set in stone. They are not like Oscar acceptance speeches where they are played once and then mostly forgotten about, if I have forgotten to thank someone here then these pages exist as a constant reminder. So – if it is you that I have forgotten then I can only apologise. Feel free to let me know the next time I see you and I will definitely include you in the next ones.

Thanks for reading. I hope you enjoyed the novel.

Beth xx

This book was created by
Hodder & Stoughton

Founded in 1868 by two young men who saw that the rise in literacy would break cultural barriers, the Hodder story is one of visionary publishing and globe-trotting talent-spotting, campaigning journalism and popular understanding, men of influence and pioneering women.

For over 150 years, we have been publishing household names and undiscovered gems, and today we continue to give our readers books that sweep you away or leave you looking at the world with new eyes.

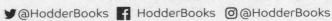

Follow us on our adventures in books . . .
🐦 @HodderBooks   f HodderBooks   📷 @HodderBooks

HODDER &
STOUGHTON